# Casual

# Encounter

## Complete Series

### By M.S. Parker

This book is a work of fiction. The names, characters, places and incidents are products of the writer's imagination or have been used fictitiously and are not to be construed as real. Any resemblance to persons, living or dead, actual events, locales or organizations is entirely coincidental.

Copyright © 2015 Belmonte Publishing LLC
Published by Belmonte Publishing LLC

All rights reserved. Without limiting the rights under copyright reserved above, no part of this publication may be reproduced, stored in or introduced into a retrieval system, or transmitted, in any form, or by any means (electronic, mechanical, photocopying, recording, or otherwise) without the prior written permission of the copyright owner.

The author acknowledges the trademarked status and trademark owners of various products referenced in this work of fiction, which have been used without permission. The publication/use of these trademarks is not authorized, associated with, or sponsored by the trademark owners.

ISBN-13: 978-1511544757
ISBN-10: 1511544759

# Table of Contents

Casual Encounter Vol. 1 ............................................................ 1
Chapter 1 ................................................................................... 1
Chapter 2 ................................................................................... 9
Chapter 3 ................................................................................. 18
Chapter 4 ................................................................................. 25
Chapter 5 ................................................................................. 36
Chapter 6 ................................................................................. 46
Chapter 8 ................................................................................. 64
Chapter 9 ................................................................................. 83
Chapter 10 ............................................................................... 86
Casual Encounter Vol. 2 .......................................................... 90
Chapter 1 ................................................................................. 90
Chapter 2 ................................................................................. 95
Chapter 3 ............................................................................... 101
Chapter 4 ............................................................................... 109
Chapter 5 ............................................................................... 121
Chapter 6 ............................................................................... 131
Chapter 7 ............................................................................... 147
Chapter 8 ............................................................................... 161
Chapter 9 ............................................................................... 179
Chapter 10 ............................................................................. 183

**Casual Encounter Vol. 3** .................................................. 186
Chapter 1 ................................................................................ 186
Chapter 2 ................................................................................ 190
Chapter 3 ................................................................................ 199
Chapter 4 ................................................................................ 207
Chapter 5 ................................................................................ 215
Chapter 6 ................................................................................ 223
Chapter 7 ................................................................................ 233
Chapter 8 ................................................................................ 243
Chapter 9 ................................................................................ 253
Chapter 10 .............................................................................. 261
**Casual Encounter Vol. 4** .................................................. 270
Chapter 1 ................................................................................ 270
Chapter 2 ................................................................................ 279
Chapter 3 ................................................................................ 291
Chapter 4 ................................................................................ 298
Chapter 5 ................................................................................ 303
Chapter 6 ................................................................................ 312
Chapter 7 ................................................................................ 319
Chapter 8 ................................................................................ 330
Chapter 9 ................................................................................ 335
Chapter 10 .............................................................................. 343
**Casual Encounter Vol. 5** .................................................. 352
Chapter 1 ................................................................................ 352

| | |
|---|---|
| Chapter 2 | 365 |
| Chapter 3 | 373 |
| Chapter 4 | 380 |
| Chapter 5 | 385 |
| Chapter 6 | 395 |
| Chapter 7 | 401 |
| Chapter 8 | 410 |
| Chapter 9 | 419 |
| Chapter 10 | 434 |
| Chapter 11 | 437 |
| Other book series from M. S. Parker | 443 |
| Acknowledgement | 444 |
| About The Author | 445 |

# Casual Encounter Vol. 1

# Chapter 1

## *Aubree*

Everything was perfect.

My wedding dress was the most beautiful thing I'd ever seen. I'd fallen in love with it the moment I'd first seen it at the bridal store and everyone said it was made for me. The only one, of course, who hadn't given an opinion was Ronald, but everyone assured me that he'd love me in it.

As I stood at the back of the church, watching my bridesmaids make the slow walk up the aisle, their royal purple dresses shimmering, I hoped everyone was right. I wanted today to be the most special day of my life. I was marrying the man I loved and I'd remember this day forever.

Then came the wedding march and my dad gave me a supportive smile. We started down the aisle and the audience stood. All eyes were on me, but... no one was smiling. In fact, the expression on every face – my friends, my family, my co-workers – was one of pity. I didn't understand. What was wrong?

I was halfway toward the front when I looked up. My bridesmaids were all there, lined up in order. My two closest friends, my sister-in-law and my cousin. Their face held pity as well. I looked to my right. The groomsmen were all there, including my brother, but I didn't see Ronald anywhere.

My heart began to pound as my father and I kept walking. Where was Ronald? Why wasn't anyone stopping the music and looking for him? Why was the priest just standing there, a solemn expression on his face?

Suddenly, the pressure on my arm was gone. I looked to my right but my father had disappeared. A glance to my left and found him sitting with my mother now and they were both looking expectantly at the priest. I turned toward the old man as well.

"Dearly beloved," he intoned in a flat voice. "We are gathered her to witness the humiliation of Bree Gamble as her fiancé Ronald Peterman has chosen to desert her on their wedding day..."

I jerked awake, a protest on my lips and breathed a sigh of relief as I flopped back down onto my pillows. My pulse was racing and there was a thin sheen of sweat on my skin despite the air conditioning in my tiny bedroom.

It was a dream. A nightmare. Sort of.

I turned my head and in the dim early morning light, made out the stack of presents sitting in the corner of my room. Their unopened paper and untouched ribbons reminded me that it was a nightmare based on reality. While the events hadn't played out the same way, the 'humiliation of Bree Gamble' had occurred.

I rolled away from the gifts and punched my pillow a few times, wishing it was Ronald's face instead. He and I had dated for five years, then been engaged for nearly two. Everything had been perfect – until *that* day. I'd been standing in front of the mirror, waiting for my maid of honor to come and tell me it was time. Instead, she'd come into the bridal room looking both pissed and upset in equal measure. Ronald had left... with our wedding coordinator.

Over the past week, I learned that the two of them had slept together one night when Ronald had volunteered to go over the seating arrangements because I'd been sick. Now, they were living together in the apartment we'd picked out, leaving me to figure out the best way to return all of the gifts we'd never opened.

I closed my eyes for a moment, wishing I could block out my memories as easily as I could the gray light. The pain was still fresh, but I supposed that was normal. It had just happened last weekend. This past week, I'd intended to be on my honeymoon, but instead, I'd given the tickets to my parents, hoping the Caribbean cruise would make up at least some of the cost of the wedding. I hadn't gone crazy with it, but I was the only girl, so my parents had been more than happy to pay for the wedding of my dreams.

I barked a harsh laugh. For the past nine nights, I'd been learning the hard way that there was a difference between a day-dream wedding and an actual dream wedding. I sat up and raked a hand through my short, cocoa-colored curls. I was still getting used to that. My hair had been down to the middle of my back last week, but on Wednesday, tired of moping around the house and avoiding phone calls, I'd decided I wanted to make a change. I'd gone into a stylist and gotten my hair cropped shorter than it had ever been before. Even I didn't recognize me sometimes.

I glanced at the clock. Five minutes until my alarm was scheduled to go off so no point in laying back down. I climbed out of bed. Other than that one little foray to the salon, today is the first day I ventured outside my apartment since my non-wedding. I hadn't even gone to the teachers' meeting on Friday.

Headmaster Norris had already given me permission to miss the meeting for my honeymoon, so she was willing to give me time off for my bittermoon as well. She'd been pretty sympathetic and it hadn't taken much to convince her I was having a hard time pulling myself together. That wasn't entirely true. I wasn't falling apart. Sure, I'd spent pretty much the entire week in my pajamas, sitting on the couch binge watching television shows online, but I wasn't breaking down in tears or drowning my sorrows in alcohol. Double chocolate fudge ice cream worked just as well.

I was actually looking forward to getting back to work, getting my mind off of things. One of the reasons I'd been thrilled to get hired at Legacy Academy last year had been their rigorous academic standards. Their students were among the brightest in all of Chicago. Keeping lesson plans that would engage, interest and challenge students whose IQs were in the gifted to genius ranges was quite a challenge.

The one thing I wasn't looking forward to, however, would be the questions from students and staff as to why the diamond ring they'd gushed over hadn't been joined by a wedding band, but had, rather, disappeared. Only a couple of the other teachers at Legacy had been invited to the wedding, but I was hoping they'd at least told the faculty what had happened. I didn't want to spend the entire first day having to repeat that story.

Almost unconsciously, my thumb rubbed against the inside of my ring finger. In the two years I'd worn it, I'd gotten in the habit of playing with my engagement ring. Ever since I'd taken it off and mailed it back to Ronald, I'd found myself behaving as if it was still there.

My phone buzzed as I finished laying out my clothes. I glanced at the name before swiping the screen to read the full message. I'd gotten a text apology from Ronald a few days ago and ever since then, I felt a knot of dread inside me whenever my phone alerted me to a text.

This one, however, was from my best friend, Adelle Merriman-Dane. She and I had grown up next door to each other in one of Chicago's middle class suburbs and we'd been inseparable almost from moment one. Our birthdays were even only two weeks apart, with me being the older one. We'd been through a lot together. My mom's breast cancer, her father's heart-attack. Her marriage at twenty-two and then being widowed just six months later. Everything had just brought us closer together. She'd been the one to tell me about Ronald leaving and the one who'd held me while I cried, telling me I'd feel better in time.

I read through her text, the tension inside me easing when I saw that it wasn't more bad news.

Hey sweetie, wishing you luck on your first day back. Don't let the little hellions get to you. Don't forget dinner at L20. You, me and Mindy are getting our wine on Friday night!

I managed a faint smile as I sent back a quick thank you and five emoji shaped bottles of wine. Adelle and I had made Friday dinners a thing since we were in college, though those had usually consisted of pizza in our dorm room. When she'd married a dot-com billionaire, we'd started going through the finer restaurants in Chicago. By the time I met Mindy at Legacy while we were both student teaching three years ago, Adelle and I had regular reservations at L2O, a beautiful seafood restaurant with amazing service and even better food. Adding one more to our table hadn't been difficult.

I climbed into the shower and thought about how nice it would be to drown my sorrows in some expensive wine. It had taken me a while to get used to Adelle paying for our Friday nights out, but once she'd shown me the extent of the fortune her late husband had left her, I hadn't let it bother me. I'd do the same for her if the situation was reversed.

I dressed automatically, but when I looked in the mirror to apply my make-up, I did a double take. My skin had always had a golden touch to it and it got even darker if I tanned, but now I looked practically pale. The circles under my eyes were purple, almost the same shade as my violet irises, and I looked at least ten years older than twenty-five. I scowled at my reflection and then got to work. By the time I finished, I didn't look completely like my old self, but I was at least presentable.

I took a deep breath and looked myself square in the eye. I could do this. So what if my entire adult life so far had been as Ronald's other half. I'd moved into my own apartment after I'd signed my contract at Legacy. Granted it was in Washington Park, but it was still my own place. I could stand on my own two feet.

I kept telling myself that as I headed out the door, determined to have a good first day.

# Chapter 2

If the whole wedding thing hadn't been an issue, the first two weeks back to work would've been great. I had amazing students. A few who were going to be a handful, but only because they were so smart. No complaints about the curriculum or reading lists from either students or parents. After the first day of fielding questions, everyone basically ignored what had happened, which suited me just fine.

Even all of this, however, wasn't enough to lift my depression. My determination that I would be okay was getting harder to stick to. It seemed like everywhere I went, I was seeing happy couples and wedding announcements. They were all over TV too. Worse, I hadn't considered this as a possibility when I'd been planning my reading lists for this year. I always re-read the books with my students, which meant I'd spent the last two weeks dealing with Romeo, Mr. Darcy and Heathcliff. At least my seniors were reading *Paradise Lost*, no romance in that one. Though I had to admit, by comparison to

Ronald, even Satan was looking pretty good at the moment.

Now, as I was making my way through L20 to the table where Adelle and Mindy were already sitting, I wondered what they'd say if I ordered something stronger than wine. I didn't even know if they served that kind of alcohol here, but I was seriously considering finding out. To top it all off, as I walked by the table closest to where I'd be sitting, the man dropped down on one knee and his girlfriend squealed. It took all of my willpower not to tackle the happy couple or, at the very least, scream at the girl to 'run'.

"Here," Adelle handed me a glass of wine before I'd even taken a seat. She glanced at the kissing couple and rolled her eyes. "His timing sucks."

I shrugged and took a gulp of the wine, barely registering anything beyond the buzz as it hit my empty stomach. "He'll screw her over soon enough. They all do."

Mindy winced and I wondered if I'd spoken loud enough for the couple to hear. Oh well. Harsh truth. The girl would learn sooner or later. I took another drink of my wine.

"So, Mindy, did you have any more problems with Frank?" Adelle asked, not so subtly changing the subject.

I forced myself to pay attention as Mindy caught us up on her latest incident with her nosy old neighbor who'd taken to lurking outside her apartment door so he could hear everything going on inside. About ten months ago, he'd found out that she was bisexual, and now, her every move was cause for complaint.

Mindy narrowed her eyes and tossed her strawberry-blond curls over her shoulder. She was the smallest of the three of us, the very definition of petite, but when she got riled, she wasn't someone to mess with. "He told the building super that I was violating some sort of ethics code of conduct by having both men and women spend the night."

As my friends began to debate the merits of taking legal action against the creepy old man, I let myself zone out. I didn't want to think about anything or anyone. Nice, quiet darkness; that sounded good. I snapped out of it for a few minutes when the waitress took our orders and chatted a bit, but once she was gone, I was back to letting everything just slide by. I thought too much anyway. Not doing it would be good for me.

I wasn't even aware that I'd been eating until Adelle's impatient voice interrupted my non-thoughts. "Sorry, what was that?"

She gave me a stern look. "I was saying that you're being quieter than usual and I was wondering how you were doing." She glanced at Mindy who shared a concerned expression. "But I guess that answers my question."

"I'm fine," I snapped then sighed, instantly regretting how I sounded. "Look, it's just going to take a while, okay. Ronald and I were together for seven years. It's not that easy to get over someone like that."

Adelle's face tightened slightly, not enough that anyone else would've noticed, but I did. I reached across the table and put my hand on hers. "I'm sorry. I wasn't thinking."

"It's okay." Adelle smiled. "Morgan's been gone for over two years."

I squeezed her hand before releasing it. Even Mindy didn't know how much Morgan's death had devastated Adelle. My best friend sat here now in designer clothes, her long chestnut brown waves styled by someone who made more a year than I did, and I knew she'd trade it all for just one more day with her husband. He'd been the love of her life and she missed him terribly. She'd dated in the years since his death, but never anything remotely serious.

"You know what you need," Adelle said. "You need to get back on the horse."

I laughed.

"I'm serious," she said. "If there's one thing I learned from losing Morgan, it's to live life to the fullest, and that means moving on. The best way to do that is to get back in the saddle."

"You're really enjoying these horse metaphors, aren't you?" I drained my glass. "Need I remind you that, before I started dating Ronald when I was eighteen, I'd had a total of two boyfriends and one of those was Timmy Gardener in the sixth grade. We held hands on the haunted hayride and that was a big deal." I poked at my food. "I've never even slept with someone other than Ronald."

"All the more reason for you to get back out there," Adelle said. She grinned, her crystal blue eyes lighting up in a way I knew was trouble. I wasn't going to like what she was about to suggest, but that wouldn't stop her from suggesting it. "I know the perfect way to get things started. You need to fuck someone."

I was glad I didn't have anything else to drink because I probably would've spit it out. "I'm not going to hook up with some random guy."

She shook her head, giving me her 'no shit' stare. "Of course not. You're far too conservative for that."

I opened my mouth to protest, then snapped it shut again. She was right. Out of the three of us, I was definitely the most... conservative. Growing up, Adelle used to tease me about being innocent and naïve. I was a bit more worldly wise than I had been back then, but I was still far from adventurous, especially when it came to sex.

"There's this guy. Absolutely gorgeous and hung like a fucking horse." A gasp from one of the other tables said Adelle wasn't being as quiet as she thought. She grinned and kept going. "He's perfect."

I shook my head. "I don't think so."

"Come on, Bree. Why not?"

"Reason number one: I'm not ready to date." I held up a finger before she could offer any sort of argument against that. "And reason number two: I know what kind of guys you like."

"What's that supposed to mean?"

Mindy and I exchanged glances.

"You do tend to gravitate towards a certain...type," Mindy said tactfully.

"And what type is that?" Adelle asked.

"Flaky," I supplied. Adelle glared at me. "Ninety percent of the guys I've seen you date were either hipsters who were right at home in a coffeehouse poetry read or frat guys with more brawn than brains. Basically, whoever you think is going to be good in bed."

"That's not true."

I sighed. "One name, Adelle. Tad Boffer."

"What was wrong with Tad?"

"He was a twenty-one year-old poet who wrote about meat," I said.

She grinned at me. "But you should've seen what he was packing."

I groaned. "Seriously, Adelle?" I shook my head again. "And you wonder why I don't trust your taste in men most of the time."

"How about this?" Mindy interrupted.

I turned toward Mindy, hoping Adelle would take the hint and not press the issue.

"There's a guy from my building who would be absolutely perfect for you," Mindy said. "He's cute. White blond hair, sea-green eyes." She fanned herself to try to break the tension with a laugh. "Over six feet and muscles... oh my."

I chuckled and she looked relieved.

"Seriously, Bree," she said. "He's a great guy. When I met him, my first thought was that if you hadn't been with that creep, Ronald, I would've introduced the two of you. He's so your type."

It was funny she said that since I didn't even know what my type was. I didn't ask though. I didn't want to give Adelle another reason to suggest I try new things.

"I'm not sure," I said. I didn't want to hurt Mindy's feelings, especially since she'd saved me from having to tell Adelle no, but I didn't think this was a good idea. "It's only been two weeks."

"Drinks," Mindy said. She glanced at Adelle. "I'm not saying sleep with him. Just meet him for drinks tomorrow night."

My eyes narrowed suspiciously. "Why's he free on a Saturday night at short notice, if he's so great?"

Mindy flushed. "I may have told him that I had someone I wanted him to meet."

"Mindy!"

"I didn't make any promises," she quickly said. "I didn't tell him anything for sure, but I wanted to make sure he was available if the opportunity came up."

I scowled at her but she just looked at me, hope filling her eyes. I sighed, one drink couldn't hurt. Plus, it appeared I didn't really have much of a choice, not unless I wanted to make Mindy look bad to this guy. I closed my eyes for a moment. Maybe it wouldn't be so bad, I told myself. It might be nice to have a civilized conversation over drinks. Get to know someone. Laugh, flirt a little. I opened my eyes and saw Mindy watching me anxiously.

I nodded. "All right," I said. "Drinks tomorrow night at O'Mallys. I'm taking a cab so I can get plastered if this guy's a 'just my type' prick."

"Deal," she said, beaming. "I'll go call him right now and tell him the good news."

I glanced at Adelle as Mindy pulled out her phone.

"I still think you need a good lay more than a date," Adelle said.

I shook my head. Casual sex just wasn't my thing. I'd never tried, but I didn't think I could do 'no strings.' Even with a fling, there'd have to be some sort of connection. I was just wired that way.

# Chapter 3

What had I been thinking? Agreeing to go on a blind date with this guy from Mindy's apartment building had to be one of the dumbest things I'd ever done. It was impulsive, rash and completely out of character. Then again, I reasoned, considering the way my life had gone this past month, maybe doing something against my natural instincts was exactly what I needed right now. If taking my time, thinking things through nice and slow when it came to my relationship with Ronald had led me to this point, maybe it was time to reconsider the way I looked at things.

Not that I was desperate or crazy enough to go with Adelle's suggestion of hiring a hooker. No, a blind date was as adventurous as I was going to get.

If I could figure out what to wear.

How pathetic was that? I'm twenty-five years-old and had no idea what I should wear on a first date. It wasn't surprising, really. After all, it had been seven years since I'd last had one.

Damn it, why did everything remind me of Ronald!

I'd been a college freshman at the University of Illinois when I'd met him, a teacher's assistant for my general psychology course. He'd asked me out after just a couple weeks and that had been that. We'd kept it quiet until the end of the semester, but we'd been a couple from that point until the day he'd walked out before our wedding. And it hadn't been like our first date had been anything I'd really needed to dress up for. We'd had a picnic on the quad with peanut butter and jelly sandwiches, a thermos of Ramon noodles, some Saltines and two slightly warm beers we'd had to sneak and pour into red plastic cups. I'd found out later that Ronald had cleaned out his cupboards and fridge for the meal. His roommate had been pissed. At the time, it had seemed romantic.

I shook my head, trying to banish the memories. I didn't want to think about Ronald or anything we'd done together. The problem with that line of thinking was that if I disregarded that part of my life, there wasn't much in the past seven years I could think about then. He was there through all of it, intricately woven into almost every memory.

A knock at my door startled me.

"Cavalry's here!"

I sighed in relief as I heard Mindy's muffled voice. I hurried down the hall and through my tiny living room. When I threw open the door, she grinned at me, most likely because I was still wearing my ratty cotton robe with dancing bananas. She and Adelle had constantly told me to get rid of it and buy something sleek and sexy. I refused. My banana robe was comforting, and during times like this, I needed as much comfort as I could get.

"Oh, sweetie, I knew you'd need some help, but I had no idea it'd be this bad." She gestured at my robe, rolled her eyes and then headed straight for my bedroom.

I was so glad to see her that I couldn't even pretend to be annoyed. I just followed her into the bedroom, ready for whatever advice she could give me.

"Did you realize it's been almost a decade since you've gone on a date with someone? Like a real getting-to-know-you date?" She put her hands on her hips as she looked at the clothes strewn across my bed. "Things have changed."

"No, Mindy," I said sarcastically. "I thought it was still the custom to bring a chaperone to make sure that we kept a respectable distance for each other as we took an evening stroll home from the barn-raising."

She rolled her eyes again. "Always with the sarcasm, Bree." She gave me a sideways look. "You know, it's a good thing your students can't hear how you talk outside the classroom."

I picked up a pillow, threw it at her and whined, "Just help me figure out what to wear."

She laughed as she caught the pillow and then tossed it back onto the bed. I was glad it was her and not Adelle who'd come over. I loved my best friend to death and we'd both grown up in working class families, but she sometimes forgot that I wasn't in the same financial situation as she was now that we were grown.

Case in point, my entire apartment was smaller than the first floor of her townhouse. And my clothing selection was much more limited, even though it usually filled my tiny closet to overflowing. Most of my clothes were for work, new ones bought over the last year with the belief that finances would soon be a little less restrictive. Ronald and I had worked hard on our budget so that we could afford a place in a nicer neighborhood, but I'd managed to figure out how I'd have enough for a couple new outfits for school, ones that made me look more like a teacher and less like a student. Now, I had clothes I probably could've done without and the same crappy apartment I'd had for the past year instead of the cute little place Ronald and his new girlfriend, Sami, were renting in Lincoln Park.

"Bree?" Mindy nudged my arm. "Where'd you go?"

I blinked and gave her a tight smile. "Nowhere good." I gestured toward the bed. "Let's find me something to wear and you can tell me all about how dating's changed since the Dark Ages."

I didn't think relaxation was going to be an option, but I at least calmed down a bit as Mindy started going through my entire wardrobe. I could almost pretend she was helping me get dressed for a girls' night out. She wore the same weary expression now that she did then, clearly telling me without saying a word that my fashion sense was horribly lacking. Not that I dressed like a bag lady or anything like that. No, her problem with my clothes was that I tended to dress simply, nothing bold or outrageous. I was the kind of person who could wear pretty much anything in my closet to work while Mindy had to choose carefully so she didn't end up in an outfit that showed far too much cleavage for a high school math teacher.

"When we get our Christmas bonus this year, you and I are going shopping," she said as she reached the halfway point. "If you're getting back into the game, you have to dress the part."

I didn't tell her that I didn't want to get back in the game. I didn't want games at all. In his apology text, Ronald had said that he never meant to hurt me, that it wasn't something he planned... blah, blah, blah. It was all the same shit that I'd heard a million times in movies, and I'd always wondered who those assholes thought they were fooling saying it. Ronald and Sami might not have been having some year-long affair – hell, they might not have even been looking at each other for more than a month – but it had been a game nonetheless. A short one, but one I had lost.

"No," Mindy said firmly. "None of that."

"None of what?" I asked.

"No thinking about your asshole ex tonight. No comparing my guy to him." Mindy put her hands on her hips. For someone so tiny, she could be kind of scary. It was probably what made her a good teacher. "Tonight's about moving past Ronald and getting the attention you deserve." She picked up a top and a skirt. "Put these on."

I stared at her; she had to be kidding.

"These were a Halloween costume from college," I protested. I'd been a sophomore and Adelle had helped me pick out the clothes. I'd lost my virginity that night, and I'd never worn the outfit again. I wasn't even entirely sure why I'd kept it, then almost laughed at myself with that thought. I knew exactly why I kept it, sentimental fool that I was.

"And they're the only thing in your closet that doesn't make you look like a schoolteacher." She folded her arms and gave me her best 'don't argue with me' look.

"But I *am* a schoolteacher," I retorted, earning another eye roll from my friend. Despite my comment, however, I slipped off my robe and started to dress. I'd already chosen a pair of white lace panties and bra, but that was because I didn't really have much of an option. The only lingerie I had that was truly fancy was what I'd bought for my honeymoon, and that wasn't something I was prepared to wear just yet, especially not on a first date with a stranger.

"That's better," Mindy said as she looked me over with a critical eye.

I looked at myself in the mirror. I was still the same size I had been when I was nineteen and that was a good thing. I didn't think I'd have been able to fit in this outfit if I'd put on any weight. The skirt was tight black leather that hit me mid-thigh, just barely long enough that I didn't look trampy. The shirt looked more like a camisole than something I should wear in public. Thin straps, clinging material and short enough that if I raise my arms too high, I'll be showing off a strip of golden flesh. The skirt was black, the shirt a deep, rich purple that made my eyes look darker than usual. In a detached sort of way, I knew I looked good, but there was a difference between knowing it and *knowing* it.

Mindy reached up and teased my curls back into place. "I still can't believe you cut off your hair."

I frowned. "I needed a change."

She wrapped her arms around me and put her cheek on my shoulder. "I know you did, and that's why it's so important you do this. You deserve to have it all, Bree."

I didn't say anything, but I let her hug me. I knew she meant well, but moving on wasn't going to be as easy as my friends seemed to think it should be. It wasn't like some casual encounter was going to mend my broken heart. I wasn't going to find a Prince Charming to erase seven years with love at first sight. I believed in real love, but I just wasn't sure it applied to me anymore.

# Chapter 4

I stood in the doorway and scanned the crowd at O'Mallys, searching for my date. Mindy had given me a basic physical description, but I didn't have a picture or anything like that.

"Bree?"

I turned my head toward a man sitting at the bar, waving at me. I made my way through the crowd to the empty seat next to the man I assumed was Steven.

"Steven Danforth." He held out a hand and I shook it. "You look even more beautiful in person." He grinned, a dimple creasing one tanned cheek. "Mindy showed me a picture of you so I'd know what you looked like."

As I took a seat next to him, I wondered what picture she'd used.

"So you and Mindy went to Myrtle Beach for spring break last year?"

I groaned. I knew what picture she'd used and I was going to kill her. Adelle had paid for the three of us to spend a week at a beach house last year. The three of us had been on a private beach half the time, which meant I was fine wearing the skimpy bikini Adelle had bought, insisting I start on my wedding tan. I generally avoided having my picture taken, but it had been vacation, so I'd given in and taken a few. All three of us had framed pictures from that week and Mindy's were of the two of us in our bikinis.

I nodded. "A friend of ours rented a beach house." A wave of relief washed over me as the bartender approached. I really needed something to take the edge off. I ordered a Sea Breeze. I was a bit of a lightweight when it came to drinks, so I wanted something I could sip on all night rather than down in one gulp.

"I'll take another Irish Car Bomb," Steven said with another easy smile. As the bartender left to get our drinks, Steven angled himself toward me so it was obvious the two of us were here together. "You and Mindy work together?"

"I teach English." I tried to cross my legs and discovered that my skirt was too tight to do that. I had to settle for crossing just my ankles.

"If you'd been my English teacher, I might've actually done my own homework." His eyes sparkled, telling me he was joking. He leaned forward slightly so that our knees were touching. "Seriously though, how in the world do your students concentrate with someone as gorgeous as you teaching them?"

I blushed. His compliments might've been on the clichéd side, but they were the first ones I'd gotten in what felt like a long time. Ronald and I had been in one of those long-term couple ruts where compliments were few and far between, so having someone tell me how beautiful he thought I was, no matter how cheesy the line, was nice. Still, the attention made me squirm.

"What do you do?" I asked, almost blurting out the question to shift things away from me.

He looked pleased that I asked, but didn't answer until he downed his entire drink in one go. Wow. Definitely not a lightweight. I sipped at my Sea Breeze, taking it slow. My nerves, however, kept me coming back for more as Steven began to talk.

"I'm an advertising executive at Harman and Foreman." He paused to speak to the bartender, "Bourbon this time. Neat." He glanced at me. "And another Sea Breeze for the lady."

I started to say that I didn't need another one, but then I glanced down and saw that my drink was already half gone. Apparently I'd been drinking more than I'd realized.

"Anyway," he continued. "I started at the agency right out of college – Columbia, with honors – and got a promotion within six months." His eyes ran down the full length of my body and then back again.

As I finished my drink, I let his words wash over me. It seemed that once I'd gotten the pump primed, he wasn't about to slow or stop. He told me all about how his company relied on him because he was the best at what he did. As our conversation shifted from his work to his hobbies, I got the impression that he was the best at everything he did – at least, according to him. A champion swimmer. Good enough to be a ski instructor. Better surfer than half those assholes who got all the attention in Hawaii.

If it hadn't been for the fact that I was halfway through my second Sea Breeze, I would've yawned and told him I was too tired to stay out any later, never-mind the fact that it was only eight o'clock. Instead, I decided to enjoy the free alcohol and let him drone on and on about what I was quickly beginning to understand was his favorite subject: himself.

"What do you think about that?"

I suddenly realized that he was asking me a question. I gave him my best charming smile and hoped he'd repeat what he was talking about so I didn't have to look like a complete idiot and ask.

"I mean, I know most women don't like hockey, but I think if you saw me play, you'd feel differently."

I resisted the urge to roll my eyes and it was harder than I thought. I needed to slow down on the drinks or I wouldn't be able to stop myself from blurting out whatever I was thinking. I tended to have impulse issues when I got drunk.

"I actually do like hockey," I said. At least I wasn't slurring my words yet. "My brother played when we were kids."

"Does he play now?" Steven asked. "Maybe he could go a little one-on-one with me so you could see my skills. I never disappoint when it comes to physical prowess." He wiggled his eyebrows suggestively and I almost laughed.

I finished my drink and set the glass on the counter. I frowned. When had I gotten a third one? I could've sworn I'd only had two, but there were three little stir stick things on the bar next to me. Another Sea Breeze had magically appeared. I knew it wasn't a good idea, especially since I hadn't eaten anything since my salad at lunch, but it was beckoning me, telling me that if I drank it, the last of the fuzzy hurt I was feeling would go away. I scowled at the glass as if it were personally responsible for the fact that I was pretty sure I was in for a hell of a hangover tomorrow.

"Are you okay?" The question should've been concerned, but it sounded more like Steven was annoyed that I'd interrupted what I was sure had been a fascinating story about something amazing he excelled at.

"I have to use the restroom," I announced. I slid off of my stool, preparing to make a confident exit, only to find that I wasn't exactly in the best shape to stand.

Everything tilted as a wave of dizziness washed over me. I put out my hand to steady myself and heard breaking glass as I knocked my newest drink to the floor. Okay, I was more drunk than I'd thought. Was it possible I'd had more than three drinks? I thought hard as I worked to get my feet underneath me, but I wasn't doing so well at multi-tasking at the moment.

Steven stood and wrapped his arms around me, pulling me into a standing position. I managed to get my feet to stay and waited for him to let me go. He didn't. If anything, he held me more tightly so I had to crane my neck to look up at him. He smelled like some kind of aftershave, and while I was sure it was probably a good scent most of the time, at the moment, it was a bit overwhelming.

"I think I better take you home." He chuckled and I felt the vibration against my palms.

I started to shake my head and then decided that probably wasn't a good idea; I was dizzy enough. With my luck, I'd completely lose my balance or throw up. Possibly both.

"Or maybe I should take you back to my place." He cupped the side of my face and his touch was enough to jar me out of a completely drunken stupor.

I jerked back, barely catching myself. "I don't think that's a good idea." My eyes caught something behind his half-empty glass of bourbon. More of those little stir sticks, and I was pretty sure his drinks hadn't come with them. Had he intentionally been getting me drunk?

Before I could confront him about my suspicions, he'd closed the short distance between us and was reaching for my wrist.

"I think you're in no condition to decide what's best for you." He grinned again, but there was something darker about that smile than there had been earlier. "Let's go."

I glanced toward the bartender, but he was at the other end of the bar, thoroughly engrossed in a conversation. I didn't know what to do. I wasn't exactly sure how much danger I was in. Maybe he wanted me to go with him because he was going to take me to Mindy's since they lived in the same building. Something in my gut said I was being naïve... well, stupid actually. But would it be an overreaction if I screamed? I didn't want to go with him, but I didn't want to be the girl who freaked out on a blind date.

My alcohol-soaked brain couldn't process the information quickly enough and Steven managed to pull me several steps before I began to struggle. Well, it was more like I yanked my arm but got absolutely nowhere.

"Let me go." I tried to make my voice as firm as possible. "I'll take a cab home."

"I think it's better you come with me." Steven's fingers tightened around my wrist.

Before I could decide if now was a good time to scream, a tall, broad body inserted itself between Steven and me, forcing him to let me go.

"I believe the lady said she wanted to take a cab." A deep voice rumbled.

I rubbed my wrist as I looked up at my white knight. I was tall, over five-ten in heels, but this man towered over me. He had to be at least six-five, six-six, and solid muscle from the looks of him. Blue-black curls that had that 'just fucked' tousled look that I'd always secretly loved.

"Fuck off," Steven snarled. "This isn't any of your business."

The stranger looked down at me and I found myself staring into a pair of intelligent dark gray eyes. "Miss, do you want your date here to take you home or would you prefer I called you a cab?"

I opened my mouth to answer, but never got the chance to get a word out because Steven grabbed the man's arm and attempted to turn him around. I saw those gray eyes darken and then he was moving himself, gracefully sidestepping as Steven attempted to throw a punch. Somehow, the stranger managed to keep me behind him, out of harm's way, as Steven cursed, stumbled, and then tried again.

This time, when the stranger moved, he gave Steven a little push that sent my date slamming into the bar with enough force to make him slump to the ground. He wasn't unconscious, but he didn't look like he was going to be getting up anytime soon.

My mysterious savior turned back to me and gave me a hard smile. "Some people don't understand the proper way to treat a lady." He held out his hand. "Let me help you get home safely."

Common sense said that it'd be just as crazy to go with this stranger as it would've been to go with Steven, but I could barely think clearly. I needed home and bed. I nodded and slid my hand into his. Warmth spread through my palm and fingers from where they touched him and I wondered if he felt the same way. Probably not. He was probably holding my hand to lead me through the bar and make sure I didn't pass out or something like that.

He flagged down a cab with ease, then surprised me by sliding into the back seat with me. He looked at me expectantly, and then asked, "Address?"

"Oh, right." I flushed and rattled off my address.

The stranger leaned forward to speak to the cabbie, but I didn't listen. I was concentrating on not blacking out or throwing up, which took more concentration than one would think. When the stranger settled back in his seat, I found myself staring at him, focusing on using my eyes to trace his strong jawline and high cheekbones. He was a perfect balance between pretty and masculine, the kind of guy that pretty much every straight woman or gay man would find at least moderately attractive. Not that I could figure out why anyone would think this man was anything less than smoking hot.

He looked down at me then and I saw the corners of his mouth twitching. Apparently, he found the fact that I was staring at him to be funny. I probably should've been insulted by that, but I couldn't do anything except wonder what his lips would feel like against mine. Against my throat. My breasts. My pussy throbbed at the thought of that sinfully delicious mouth tasting it.

"We're here." He opened the cab door and a gust of wind snapped me from my fantasy.

I scowled and climbed out of the cab, taking his hand again so I didn't fall. I looked up at my apartment and was struck with the sudden desire to ask my rescuer if he wanted to come up so I could properly thank him.

"Are you okay to get up there all right?" His expression was one of concern.

"I'll be fine." My head was still blurry, but clear enough to know what the smart thing to do was. Certain lower regions of my body disagreed, but I didn't let them make the decisions. "Thank you for your help tonight."

"It was my pleasure, Miss." He bent over the hand he was still holding and pressed his lips against the back of it.

Well, shit. How was I supposed to not react to that?

Knowing I'd blame it on the alcohol tomorrow, I threw my arms around my mystery man's neck and pulled his head down so that I could kiss him. I saw a moment of surprise and felt his body tense for a moment before his arms slid around my waist and he leaned into the kiss. His mouth softened, then he took control, changing what would have been a sloppy, drunken kiss to something else.

His tongue parted my lips, twisting and curling around mine, drawing it into his mouth. When he sucked on it, I moaned and his hands flexed against my back, burning through the thin material of my shirt. His fingers brushed against the bare skin exposed at the base of my back and a part of me wished he'd take further liberties and explore. While his hands remained where they were, his tongue delved back into my mouth, thoroughly possessing every inch of me.

Then, he was stepping back and my head was spinning for a whole new reason. Something bright passed across his eyes, then disappeared behind the polite compassion I'd seen before.

"Have a good night, Miss." He gave me a half-smile. "And pleasant dreams."

He waited until I was safely inside the building before he got back into the cab, but the cab didn't pull away until after I looked out the window of my apartment. How sweet! He'd waited to make sure I'd gotten inside safely. I sighed and smiled. If I had any luck, I'd have very pleasant dreams indeed.

# Chapter 5

If I dreamt of my hot savior, I didn't remember. I did, however, remember with annoying clarity the events of the previous night. It seemed that I'd had enough alcohol to behave like an idiot and to have a massive, splitting headache, but not enough to make my memory too hazy. That sucked. If I had to suffer through the indignity of knowing I'd nearly fallen in the bar, been the cause of a fight and had then thrown myself at a total stranger, shouldn't I have at least gotten a reprieve on the hangover?

I groaned as I forced one eye open. My curtains were drawn so the only light in the bedroom was my alarm clock, which was currently telling me that I'd slept at least three hours past my normal weekend wake up time of nine o'clock. It was times like this that I was glad I lived alone. There would be no one to shame me into attempting to function at the moment.

I crawled out of bed and headed the few steps across the hall to my bathroom, pausing every second step or so to wait until everything stopped spinning before moving on. I downed a couple painkillers, drank a few wary sips of water and then slowly made my way back to bed. As I crawled under the covers, I noticed I'd managed to shower and put on pajamas last night, which was more than I'd expected. Granted, the pajamas were on backwards, but at least I was clothed.

I debated the merits of fixing my pajamas but fell back asleep before I could make a decision. When I woke up again, the clock said it was a little past two. I knew I should probably eat something, but the idea of food didn't seem like a good thing at the moment. Based on my very few previous experiences with being hung over, I knew I'd probably feel up to something later tonight, but even the thought of eating right now was enough to make me gag. I'd made it through this whole thing without throwing up and I fully intended to keep it that way.

I closed my eyes and tried to go back to sleep. Mindy would want a report of how things had gone, but I really didn't want to get into that right now. All I wanted was to sleep the rest of the weekend away and then bury myself in work come Monday.

No, I realized, that wasn't the only thing I wanted. A pair of dark gray eyes danced behind my closed lids and they were quickly followed by those lips. I made a sound and pulled my blanket up against my face. That mouth. I could still feel it against mine, the way his lips had moved, how his tongue had explored every inch of my mouth.

I'd kissed exactly five people in my entire life. Ronald, of course, but there had been four others.

Jason Keller had given me my first kiss when I was eight and he'd been the older man at ten. I'd played Spin the Bottle the summer between eighth and ninth grade and my former boyfriend Timmy had stolen a kiss then. He'd moved away a few weeks later. My junior year of high school, I'd gone to a party and gotten drunk for the first time. Apparently, Adelle and I had kissed during a game of Truth and Dare. I wasn't sure that counted since I had little more than a fuzzy impression of it. And then there'd been Vincent Ryan, my high school crush, who'd given me a kiss after senior prom.

Not a single kiss had even come close to the one I'd had with my knight in shining armor. I tried telling myself it was just because I really didn't have any good comparisons. After all, aside from Ronald, the other kisses had been when I was young and inexperienced. I snorted at the thought of myself as experienced now, then winced at the pain in my head.

Youth had nothing to do with it. Ronald was an adult and I'd loved kissing him. He'd made me shiver with delight, but I'd never felt my knees turn to jelly when we'd kissed. It had been like that in bed too, I admitted for the first time. I didn't have anyone else to compare him to, but I knew there hadn't been the same kind of fire between us that other people had. Sure, I enjoyed having sex with him and he'd been a fairly considerate lover, but I'd never dreamed about him. Fantasized about him. I'd never felt the need to touch myself because I couldn't stop thinking about his hands on my body.

Not like the hands I'd had on me last night.

"Fuck," I mumbled.

I knew it probably wasn't a good idea, but I couldn't stop myself thinking about him. From the first moment I'd looked into his eyes, I'd felt desire heating me up. Then we'd kissed and it had been like fireworks or lightning or something else that had a burst of energy and light so strong that it was dangerous. I'd wanted to feel his hands on my bare skin. Running up my back. Cupping my breasts. His fingers between my legs, touching me.

I sighed and flopped onto my back. The sudden movement wasn't a good idea, but it at least broke my train of thought for a moment. I closed my eyes and tried to fall back asleep, but my savior came creeping back in, bringing with him vague fantasies of his body and mine, writhing together in pleasure.

I grabbed an extra pillow and pressed it against my face, letting out a cry of frustration. I had thin walls and the last thing I needed was one of my neighbors thinking I was in trouble and calling the cops.

Why couldn't I stop thinking about him? I wanted to sleep away my hangover, forget about that disaster of a date and move on, but every time I tried to clear my mind enough to drift off, he came popping back in. What was it about him? Sure, he was hot, but so were a lot of people. I mean, Mr. Finkle, the biology teacher, had a certain bookish hotness to him, but he wasn't the one plaguing my thoughts. And it wasn't my ex-fiancé either.

I caught my breath as I realized I'd passed a milestone. For the past two weeks, every thought of Ronald had brought with it pain and longing. Every time I'd used the words 'ex' and 'former,' it had been like a part of me being ripped out. Just now, when I'd thought about him, however, there'd only been a twinge and a pang of regret. Something had changed. Halle-fuckin-luiah.

Had it been my decision to go on the blind date, signaling that I was trying to move on? That was possible, I supposed, but even when things had been going well at the beginning with Steven, I hadn't been able to truly see myself with someone other than Ronald. Was it possible that it had been my white knight? The fact that he'd rescued me, protected me? He'd done what Ronald had promised to do. And then there'd been the desire I'd felt for him, something so strong that I couldn't entirely blame it on the alcohol.

That, I knew, had been the moment I'd first realized I could be with someone else. Without even telling me his name, the stranger had not only rescued me from Steven, but had started to free me from my past.

I groaned in frustration. It so wasn't fair.

My phone rang, the sound cutting through my head in a burst of bright, musical pain. I grabbed for it, not even bothering to look at the caller ID before answering.

"Hey there!" Mindy's bubbly voice came from the other end. "I got tired of waiting for a report on how last night went. I'm hoping this means it went well and you didn't call me because you were too tired from all that hot, sweaty sex."

I scoffed, a bitter that sound that burst out of me in a huff. "Yeah, not so much." I sighed and pushed myself into a sitting position. My head throbbed, but the bed didn't spin, so that was absolutely an improvement.

"I don't understand." Mindy sounded confused. "If you weren't with..." Her voice trailed off for a moment and then she growled. "I'm going to kill him."

It took me a few seconds to put two and two together, but I got it and didn't have to ask for clarification. It seemed like the walls in Mindy's building were fairly thin too and that Steven had found someone to take home after all.

"Short version," I said. "Steven was more interested in talking about himself and trying to get me drunk enough to get into my pants than he was in actually being on a date."

"That bastard." She practically spit the words out and I knew she was seething.

I smirked. No way was she going to let Steven off easy, especially after I gave her the long version. Mindy was creative when it came to revenge. She'd told me and Adelle about a girl who had once cheated on Mindy's little brother, stringing him along for months. Mindy had snuck into the girl's driveway and hid bits of sushi in her rims and under the hood of her Astin Martin. Rumor had it, the girl had to completely scrap the car because no one had been able to get the smell out.

"Tell me everything."

I started at the beginning and went through all of it, including my own stupidity at drinking so much as well as my rescue, but when it came time to give the details of my stranger, I held back. I wasn't sure what I wanted to do about him and, for right now, I wanted to keep him all to myself. Once I shared him with Mindy, I'd have to share him with Adelle, and I didn't know how they'd react to me and my inability to stop thinking about my mystery man.

"I am so sorry," Mindy said as soon as I was finished. "I feel horrible. I'd always thought Steven was a good guy."

She continued to apologize for the next five minutes, occasionally promising to make him pay for what he'd done. I made appropriate noises in the right places and waited for the chance to end the call. I loved my friend, but I didn't want to talk. I wanted to be alone. There was wallowing to be done.

I showered after I hung up, then wrapped myself in my comfy robe and headed to the kitchen for some crackers to calm my stomach. Ice cream was really better wallowing food, particularly when it came to bad dates, but I didn't think I was ready for that. Crackers would have to do for now. Tomorrow, it would be ice cream time.

Ginger ale and crackers in hand, I headed for the couch. I curled up there, turned on the TV and let myself mope about how my love life sucked. If this had just been a single bad date, I might've just let myself have an hour or two of a pity party then moved on. But coming on the heels of my canceled wedding, it felt like a bigger rejection than it should have.

Although, I supposed if I thought about it, what had happened hadn't technically been a rejection. Steven hadn't walked away or stood me up. Sure, he'd been an asshole, but at least he'd wanted me. I laughed out loud, unsurprised at the bitterness of the sound. What did it say about me that I attracted guys like Ronald and Steven? Okay, it hadn't been like Steven had picked me out of a crowd, but still.

Did that mean my mystery man was just as much of a jerk as the others? Now there was a depressing thought. Someone who saved me, hadn't tried to take advantage of my vulnerable state, and had given me the best kiss of my life. Was it possible that it had all just been an act? I didn't want to think that. Somehow, that was worse than everything else.

I'd been a hopeless romantic once, believing in fairy tale endings. Sure, I'd understood that relationships were work, but I always thought that true love would figure it out in the end. After Ronald left me, I'd tried to cling to that same idealistic way of thinking and having a handsome stranger come to my rescue had fueled that belief. Now, I wasn't sure anymore.

My day progressed that way for several hours. I'd doze on and off, staring at the television in between naps, but not really seeing what was on. My head was full of questions and replays of all the shit that had happened over the past month. It wasn't until my stomach started to growl for more substance than crackers that I had a different thought.

I needed to prove that there were good guys in this world, and to do that, I had to find my hero. I went to the kitchen to see if I could find any soup, my brain starting to focus on my new task. If I could find him, I could ask him why he'd saved me. I could talk to him, thank him for what he'd done. If his intentions had been pure, it would be proof that there were still good men in this world, dashing heroes racing in to save a damsel in distress without any thought about what was in it for them.

It had nothing to do with the kiss, or how that one touch of the lips made my entire body hot. If a single kiss could do that, what would it be like to have more? To feel his body stretched out on top of mine, hands roaming over my clothes. Under my clothes. Against bare flesh.

I gritted my teeth and pushed the fantasies from my mind. I wanted to thank him for saving me, for restoring my faith in men. I didn't want a relationship, and I didn't do casual sex. What I did want was to believe in hope for the future, and finding my stranger would do that.

Now all I needed to do was figure out where to start.

# Chapter 6

I was pretty sure Mindy thought I was mad at her for setting me up with Steven because I barely spoke to her all week. Adelle, fortunately, had been busy enough with some charity fundraiser that she accepted my 'details on Friday' text without pushing for more. I hadn't been upset with either one of them though. I'd just been extra busy.

Aside from my classes and grading papers, every waking moment had been spent trying to find the stranger. When I'd made that my goal, I'd known it wouldn't be easy, but I hadn't realized how difficult tracking down someone without a name, picture or personal information could be.

I'd called O'Mallys first thing to see if they remembered the fight. The bartender who'd worked Friday night hadn't been in, so I'd tried again the next day. He'd remembered the fight and me, but he swore he didn't know the man who'd come to my rescue. After some coaxing, he admitted that Steven had told him to keep the drinks coming, but insisted he didn't know I'd get so drunk so quickly.

After that dead end, I hadn't known where to go. I considered going back to the bar and waiting to see if the man showed up again, but since I'd talked to the bartender and he'd remembered me, I didn't want him realizing why I'd come back. I told him I wanted to thank my rescuer, but I was pretty sure he hadn't believed me. If I showed up there, it'd look desperate, which I didn't want.

Instead, I parked my car in the O'Mallys parking lot for two nights, grading my papers as I watched people coming and going. Both nights, I'd gone home empty-handed. I wasn't sure which was more depressing, how much my romantic life sucked or how the only guy I really wanted to talk to had vanished.

On Friday night, I was ready for some girl time and wine. I'd already decided that I'd tell everything, including my mystery man. I just hoped my friends could either talk some sense into me, help me, or give me a distraction. I couldn't keep running in circles like this.

"Wow, you look awful," Adelle said as I took a seat to her right.

"Thanks," I said sarcastically.

She rolled her eyes. "Come on, Bree. The bags under your eyes have bags. You look worse than you did right after..." She let her voice trail off but I knew what she meant. Her gaze moved around, almost nervously. Then, suddenly, her face brightened. "Mindy! Perfect timing."

"Why? What's going on?" Mindy asked as she sat on the other side of Adelle.

"Adelle here was just telling me that I look worse now than I did after Ronald dumped me at the alter." I couldn't help but smile at the expression on Adelle's face. My friend was usually impossible to embarrass or make uncomfortable. I had to take advantage of it whenever possible.

Mindy gave me a small smile, one that told me she was still worried about me being mad at her. "I think you look fine."

Adelle's eyes narrowed and she looked from me to Mindy and back again. "All right, something's up. No way would Mindy say you looked fine the way you're dressed unless she knew there was some sort of extenuating circumstance. Spill it."

I took a deep breath and told my story. Mindy winced when I got to the part where Steven had tried to drag me out of the bar and I could see the guilt on her face. I didn't stop to reassure her though. Instead, I continued on with the part she hadn't yet heard, including the kiss this time. When I finished, Adelle and Mindy were both staring.

"Wait, so the reason you've barely talked to me all week is because you've been looking for your mystery guy?" Mindy asked. "I thought you were mad at me."

I shook my head and patted her on the hand. "It's not your fault Steven turned out to be an ass. You had no way of knowing. He came across all charming at first."

"Should've gone with my guy in the first place," Adelle said with a smug smile. "But now you have to."

"Yay, another blind date," I sneered, clapping in mock celebration. "That worked out *so* great last time."

"What are you going to do, then?" Mindy asked, changing the subject. "Hire some private investigator to track down a guy you kissed when you were drunk?"

She had a point. It wasn't like I had many options when it came to finding my rescuer. And no matter how much I wanted to find him, there was no way I was telling some detective about what had happened. No kiss was that good.

My body disagreed with that statement, but I ignored it.

"I have to ask." Adelle leaned forward. "What was it like? The kiss?" Her eyes were glowing with curiosity.

"It was a kiss," I said shortly. "You know. Lips against lips."

She grinned. "That good, huh?"

I glared at her.

"Come on, Bree, details." Adelle glanced at Mindy. "Was there tongue?"

"You're an ass." I threw a cherry tomato at her, laughing as it landed in her cleavage.

"Hey!"

I shrugged. "Shouldn't show it off."

She plucked the tomato out from between her breasts and set it down on her empty plate. "Seriously, though, Bree. Let me fix you up on a date." She threw a glance at Mindy. "I'll do better screening than she did."

"Bitch." Mindy stuck her tongue out at Adelle.

I laughed, my dark mood lightening as I let myself enjoy my friends.

"Please, Bree," Adelle begged, her face all puppy dog cute.

"I think I'm swearing off dating for a while," I said. I held up my hands. "No more men."

"So women now?" Mindy grinned.

I searched for another tomato to throw as she laughed. "I just mean that I've had bad luck with men this past month and I'm not sure I want to try again."

"It's not a commitment, Bree. I'm not asking you to marry the guy, just go on a date." Adelle slid her card into the bill fold.

"You're not going to let this go, are you?" I asked.

"Nope." She grinned. "You know me."

Yeah, I did know her. That's what concerned me. I had visions of her showing up at my house at random hours with strangers she wanted me to meet.

"Besides, you need something to get your mind off of your mystery man," she said. "You can't keep spending all your time looking for him."

She had a point. "All right," I agreed reluctantly. "One date." Maybe that would be the distraction I'd need.

Chapter 7

Adelle must've called half a dozen times over the next week to ask if I'd picked out an outfit to wear on my date for Saturday. Friday night at dinner, she and Mindy had both offered to come over and help me dress. I'd been half-tempted to snap at them both that I'd managed to clothe myself just fine since I was six, but I only smiled and let them know that I didn't need any help.

Now, however, as I stood in front of the mirror, I wasn't so sure that I hadn't been too hasty. Then again, I wasn't about to tell either of them where I'd gotten my new dress. Even though Mindy made pretty much the same thing I did, her parents had paid for her college, which meant she wasn't paying back school loans, leaving her with some extra spending money. She and Adelle might not have shopped in the same stores, but Mindy could afford the lower-priced name brands. The dress I was wearing was a name brand, but I'd picked it up at a thrift store earlier this week.

It was a dark, charcoal gray that fit me beautifully. I was slender enough that I didn't have much in the way of curves, but this dress highlighted what I did have. The neckline was lower than what I normally wore, but not so much so that I felt entirely uncomfortable in it. The hemline was the same length as the skirt I'd worn the other night, so I was at least used to that. My make-up was minimal, and my new haircut didn't require much in the way of styling. I didn't need my friends for any of that. No, I needed them to distract me from the fact that I'd chosen this dress because the color was the same as my stranger's eyes. I could only imagine what Adelle would say if she knew I was going to meet this Cade Shepard she'd set me up with wearing a dress that made me think of another man.

"What am I doing?" I muttered to my reflection. "This is not going to end well, and you know it."

I did know it, but that didn't mean I was going to flake out. I told Adelle I was going and I'd do just that. Since I'd been told to meet Cade at the Park Hyatt Hotel restaurant, at least I could get a free meal out of it. Maybe I'd get really lucky and the guy would at least be a good conversationalist. That was the most I was hoping for out of this evening, good food and a nice guy who didn't try to get me drunk or take advantage of me. I wasn't even considering the possibility that there could be anything else. No use going there and being disappointed.

With my expectations firmly in place, I grabbed my dress purse and headed for the door. I'd considered driving this time, as much to give me incentive not to drink so much, but I despised driving in heels so a cab it was. I winced as I thought of the fare, but my only other non-driving option was the train and there was no way I was doing that in a dress.

The cabbie was nice enough and didn't take any detours, which I appreciated. Sometimes, if they thought I was some naïve girl who didn't know my way around the city, they'd try to run up the meter. When we pulled up to the hotel, I couldn't help but stare. I'd seen it before, of course, but it was different getting out of the cab and knowing I was going inside. It was gorgeous.

I paid the cabbie, squared my shoulders and tried to look like I belonged at a five-star hotel. I walked slowly enough that I was able to find the restaurant without having to ask anyone and I headed inside. The hostess smiled at me as I came in.

"May I help you?" she asked.

"I'm meeting Cade Shepard," I said.

"Wonderful." Her smile widened. "Mr. Shepard is waiting for you. Right this way, please."

I followed her as she made her way around the tables, most of which were full. It didn't take long for me to figure out that we were heading toward a more secluded section of the restaurant. The lights were dimmer, the tables a bit further apart for added privacy. Then the hostess stepped to one side and everything else faded away.

It was him. Right there. My mystery man was sitting at the table directly in front of me.

My jaw dropped and I darted a glance toward the hostess to see where she was going to point me.

There was no way Adelle had found my savior and set us up on a blind date.

Then he was standing, his eyes brightening with recognition. He walked around to the other side of the table and pulled out the chair, the invitation clear.

"Your waiter will be here shortly with your wine selections."

The hostess may have been smiling at us before she walked off, but I didn't notice. I couldn't stop staring. I did, however, managed to shut my mouth so I didn't look like a complete idiot.

"Well, isn't this a small world," he said as he held out his hand.

I slid mine into his, still unable to believe this was real. He raised my hand to his lips just like he'd done last week. This time, I had no alcohol to blame for the way my stomach twisted and clenched as his mouth brushed against my knuckles. When he released my hand, my skin still tingled.

I sat down and let him help scoot in my chair before he walked back around to his seat. Before I could ask him how he knew Adelle, a waiter appeared with a wine menu.

He didn't even glance at it. "We'll have the Invictus Shiraz, two thousand four. And we'll need a few more minutes before we're ready to order." He turned back to me as the waiter walked away. "Now, Miss Aubree Gamble. It's nice to have a name to put to your lovely face."

"Likewise," I said. "My friends call me Bree."

"That's a shame." He smirked.

"Why do you say that?"

He ran his finger around the rim of his glass as he studied me. "Because Aubree is so much prettier. Suits you better."

Heat bloomed in my cheeks and I blurted out the first thing that popped into my head. "You didn't know who I was." I made it a statement rather than a question.

"When Adelle asked me to come here?" He shook his head. "No." He smiled. "I don't need to ask if you knew who I was. The expression on your face said it all."

I flushed and dropped my eyes.

"I admit it was a pleasant surprise," Cade continued. "When Adelle mentioned that her friend was getting over a bad break-up and needed to be reintroduced to the world of dating, I expected someone... different."

I raised my head. "Different how?" I tried to hide the hurt that went through me when I heard that Adelle had told him about what had happened.

He leaned back as the waiter returned with the wine. I resisted the urge to gulp half of mine just to calm my nerves. Once the waiter left, Cade turned his attention back to me.

"I assumed that Adelle's friend would be someone who was unable to find a date on her own, forced to rely on her friend's assistance. Shy, definitely. Most likely plain as well."

I blinked at the blunt statements. "Excuse me?"

He continued on without an apology. Either he hadn't realized I hadn't appreciated what he'd said or he didn't care.

"Women who've been scorned by men react in one of two ways. They either completely swear off men until they find that they're tired of satisfying their own desires, or they jump right back in the dating pool and find a nice rebound man." He gave me a once-over and I could see the admiration in his eyes. "Either way, the ones who rely on friends to find them men generally do so because they can't do it themselves."

I opened my mouth to tell him that I could find a man if I wanted to, but the waiter returned and I looked down at my menu, wondering if it'd be too obvious to order the most expensive thing on the menu.

"We'll have the duck served with a lime glaze on a bed of watercress salad tossed in a light vinaigrette."

"Very good, Sir."

My head snapped up as I realized he'd ordered for us both.

He spoke as he turned back toward me. "Adelle mentioned that you liked duck but weren't able to have it often."

I scowled. "Do you also know my bra size and bank account balance?"

His lips twitched like he wanted to laugh, but he didn't. "No." He raised an eyebrow. "I seem to have hit a nerve. Tell me, are you annoyed at me, or at your friend for sharing personal details with me?"

I inhaled slowly. He was right. True, I was discovering that my white knight was the kind of confident that was two steps past arrogant, but knowing Adelle had told him personal things about me, that was upsetting.

"Shall we start over?" He extended a hand. "I'm Cade Shepard. I have some lovely red wine here and duck on the way if you'd care to join me."

I shook his hand, trying to ignore the tingle that went up my hand and arm when we touched. This was a date to get Adelle off my back, nothing more. Okay, so I'd also met my rescuer, but I'd been telling myself for the past two weeks that I didn't want anything more than to thank him. I ignored the little voice in my head that reminded me how much I'd enjoyed that kiss.

"I'm Aubree Gamble. It's nice to meet you." I gave him a partial smile.

"Now, Aubree, since I'm not the type of man to ask questions about his blind date so as to ensure a pleasant evening, I must ask if you like duck or if you'd prefer to order something else?"

My face burned at his words. I suddenly felt petty and stupid. Adelle hadn't spilled secrets about me. Cade had asked because he wanted to know more about the person she was setting him up with. I'd never even thought to ask about him. Ironically, it had been because I'd been too preoccupied with trying to learn his identity.

"Duck will be wonderful, thank you." I put as much sincerity into my words as I could. I paused, and then apologized. "And I'm sorry for how I behaved. It's been a rough month."

He nodded and topped off both of our wine glasses. "So Adelle mentioned, though not the details. I suppose I can let you off with a warning this time." His eyes shone, but there was something in his voice that made me want to squirm. "After all, I witnessed firsthand part of the difficult month you've had."

"Thank you." The words burst out of me and more heat rushed to my face. If I kept this up, I was going to look like a tomato. "For helping me the other night. And making sure I got home safely."

He raised his glass. "You're welcome." He took a sip of the wine and then asked, "No thank you for the kiss?"

"Fuck." I closed my eyes as I realized I'd said the word aloud. This night just kept getting better.

"I don't believe we got that far." He sounded smug. "If we had, you'd be overwhelmed with gratitude."

I opened my eyes and glared at him. I wasn't sure which was worse, that he was teasing me or that he was so full of himself.

Our food arrived just then, providing me with enough of a distraction to regain my composure. Everything looked and smelled delicious. I thanked the waiter, then glanced up at Cade. He gestured toward my plate and then cut a piece of his duck. We ate in silence for several minutes. I wasn't sure if he was waiting for me to say something or if he was only enjoying his meal, but there were plenty of things I wanted to say. I just wasn't sure where to start.

Finally, I decided that I wasn't going to let tonight be a total waste. I'd found my mystery male. Or, rather, Adelle had somehow managed to find him for me, and that was a whole other set of questions. I'd thanked him, but there had been something I'd been wondering since I'd been able to think clearly about what had happened.

"Why'd you do it?" I asked.

He raised an eyebrow in question.

"Why did you intervene at O'Mallys with Steven?" I pushed at a bit of watercress. "And why did you take me all the way home? Just putting me in a cab after what you'd done would've been more than enough."

"Some people would've tried to take advantage of you in your inebriated state." There was no hint of judgment or mockery in his words.

"But you didn't."

"True." He took a drink of wine. "In fact, I seem to remember that if anyone was being taken advantage of, it was me."

I stabbed a piece of meat a little more viciously than was necessary. "You didn't seem to mind."

He laughed and the sound rolled over me, coating my skin. Arousal flooded me. Shit. I was getting wet just from his laugh.

"No, I did not." He leaned back in his seat. "And to answer your question, I stepped in because I don't like bullies, particularly when the person being bullied is a woman."

His tone was even, but I knew there was something deeper to that statement. I met his eyes, but they were mild and pleasant, betraying nothing of what had prompted his words.

"Enough about that horrible excuse for a date," he said, leaning forward. "I want to know more about you."

I blinked at the abrupt shift in conversation. I was glad he wasn't going to be like Steven and only talk about himself, but as we talked, I could feel him controlling the conversation, steering it where he wanted it to go. He answered some of my questions, but rarely in the detail he probed from me. I should have been annoyed; everything about him should have put me off. I liked confident men, but not ones who were cocky. I didn't mind charming, but I'd always been irritated by the men who seemed to think everyone found them as irresistible as they thought they were. Still, there was something about him that drew me to him. I didn't know if it was because he carried himself so differently than Ronald had or if it was just a reaction to the hero worship I'd been nursing for the past two weeks. Either way, the longer I stayed, the more I wanted to be here.

"Was the meal to your satisfaction?" he asked as I finished my wine.

"It was amazing." I'd purposefully only drunk a glass and a half even though it was probably the most expensive wine I'd ever have the chance to drink. The food, however, I completely devoured. It had been the perfect portion. Enough to make me not hungry, but not so much that I felt full. I wasn't sure, however, if dessert was on the menu. Cade had been an attentive date, not even looking at any of the women who'd checked him out over the course of the meal, but he also hadn't expressed any overt indications that he thought of this as anything but a single evening to please Adelle.

He stood and I tried to hide my disappointment. It seemed the night was over after all. When he held out his hand, I took it, believing we'd end with a shake. Instead, he curled his fingers around mine.

"I've already ordered dessert and champagne to my room. Join me?"

I almost couldn't tell if that last bit was a question or a command. "You have a room?" My mouth went dry and I considered pulling my hand away.

As if he'd read my mind, he squeezed my hand, then released it. "I'll be honest. When Adelle set us up, I was hesitant to accept. She was sure, though, that we would enjoy our time together. So much so that she insisted I rent a room. I'm glad now that I did."

He held out his hand again and this time the invitation was clear. "I promise that things will not go any further than you want them to. You say the word and I'll call a cab."

My expression must've been more skeptical than I felt because he continued.

"I hope you accept, but I have no problem spending the rest of the night gorging myself on chocolate and watching pay-per-view."

My eyes slid down his muscular torso. Somehow, I doubted he'd ever gorged himself on anything.

He took a step toward me, closing the distance between us to less than a foot. I could suddenly smell him, the clean scent of soap without any of the usual extras of aftershave or cologne. My stomach clenched.

He raised his hand and brushed the back of it down the side of my face. Heat bloomed across my cheek, but not from embarrassment this time.

"I can see the desire in your eyes, Aubree. I know what you want, and I can give it to you. Stop being so careful and give in to what you want." His voice was low and sensual, one hypnotic word after the next. "You do want it, don't you? You want me."

I swallowed hard. Damn. I had no doubt that if I went with him and asked him to stop at any point in time, he'd do just that. He wouldn't force me. It wasn't him I didn't trust though. It was me. I could tell myself I didn't want this night to end and if I went with him, we'd eat decadent desserts and maybe make out a bit, but I couldn't deny that I'd been fantasizing about seeing what was under that shirt of his from the moment I'd first looked into his face. If I went with him, I knew I wouldn't want to stop at a kiss or two, a caress or maybe a bit of skin. I'd want it all.

"Don't deny yourself." He palmed my cheek, his thumb brushing across my bottom lip. "Come with me."

A shiver went through me as I imagined him saying those words again, but with a completely different meaning.

Fuck it.

I nodded before I could change my mind. "Let's go."

# Chapter 8

He led me, hand-in-hand, to the elevators, and I envied the ease with which he carried himself. My heart was racing and only some of it was due to Cade. As I passed people, I felt like their eyes were on me, like they knew I was about to sleep with this man on the first date. I never judged anyone for the choices they made regarding their sex life, but I'd had it drilled into my head since childhood that I was a good girl, and good girls didn't have sex on the first date. My parents hadn't been the religious type where I needed to wait for marriage, but sex had never been a casual thing.

As the elevator doors closed, Cade pulled me against him so that my back was pressed against his front. He slid his arms around my waist, and put his mouth close to my ear.

"Don't overthink things."

His tone made it clear this wasn't a suggestion and my heart skipped a beat.

"If something feels wrong, then by all means don't do it, but if you're thinking about what other people will think, stop."

His tongue traced the outside of my ear and I closed my eyes. There was no way such a small touch should've been able to make my knees weak.

"It's not about anyone else. It's about you and what you want."

His hands slid up over my ribcage to rest just under my breasts. His fingers teased at the undersides of them and I felt my nipples tighten at his touch.

"What do you want, Bree?" When I didn't say anything, he tried a different way. "Tell me what you want, Bree."

I forced my eyes open and noticed our reflection on the gleaming door of the elevator. I watched his head tilt as he nuzzled his nose into my hair. I watched his thumb trace a path across my nipple. Then, he lifted his head and his eyes met mine in the mirror. My breath caught as a single word escaped me. "You."

He groaned, a sound of pleasure deep in his chest and then moved me away from him as the elevator doors slid open. Lacing his fingers through mine, he led me down the hallway toward his room. "Come."

That word again.

It was a nice room, not one of the highest priced ones with a mini kitchen and sitting room, but that wasn't surprising. He hadn't rented it for a vacation. Everything we needed sat against the wall to the right. He'd at least sprung for a king, and from the looks of things, the thread-count to those snowy white sheets was high. I took a moment to appreciate the decor and then turned my attention to the room service cart that sat next to the bed. A bottle of champagne chilled in a bucket of ice and next to it was a tray of chocolates. My mouth watered just looking at them and I glanced at Cade.

"Try one of the truffles," he said. "They're amazing."

I picked one up and took a bite, closing my eyes in pure enjoyment as the chocolate melted on my tongue. "Mmm," I moaned.

"There's a sound I want to hear again."

I opened my eyes and saw that Cade had taken off his jacket and tie, laying them on the chair on the far side of the room. The top two buttons of his shirt were undone and I felt a stab of desire. He walked back over to me and plucked the rest of the truffle from my hand. Holding it between two long fingers, he put it against my lips. I opened my mouth and he slid the chocolate inside. I let the tip of my tongue brush against the pad of one finger as I took the dessert and was rewarded with a sharp intake of breath.

"Champagne?" he asked, his voice rougher than it had been.

I nodded and watched as he poured us each half a glass. It was even more wonderful than the wine had been, a perfect complement to the chocolate. After taking a drink, he set down his glass and picked up a smaller truffle.

"Another?"

"Yes, please." I waited for him to feed it to me again, but instead, he opened his own mouth and set the chocolate on his tongue.

As he lowered his head, I realized what he was going to do and eagerly parted my lips to receive his offer. My tongue slid along his as it entered my mouth, the bittersweet flavor of dark chocolate bursting across my taste buds. My fingertips dug into his firm chest as I sucked on his tongue, savoring every last bit of dessert. He gripped my hips and pulled me tight against him. I felt him now, growing against my stomach as I released his tongue. I let myself get lost in his kiss until my lungs started to protest the little bit of oxygen they'd been getting and I had to pull away.

"Take off your clothes." He took a step back and ran his eyes over me, as if he was already picturing what I looked like naked.

I swallowed hard, the taste of chocolate and champagne still heavy on my tongue. This was it, I knew. Sure, if I changed my mind half-way through whatever was about to happen, I trusted that Cade would stop. But I also knew myself well enough to realize that if I made my choice here, I would see it through, no matter how terrified I was. It had been the same the first time Ronald and I had slept together.

I reached behind me, my stiff fingers fumbling with my zipper for a moment before getting it to slide along its track. Once it started coming down, I raised my eyes to meet Cade's. He was watching me with an intensity that was unnerving. There was an expectation in his gaze, as if he'd never doubted I'd do exactly what he wanted. Once the zipper was down, I started to pull off the dress.

"Slowly," he said, halting my motions.

I let the material slide from my shoulders and down, moving slightly when it caught on my hips. When it pooled onto the floor, I stepped out of it and bent to pick it up. For a moment, I thought he'd tell me to leave it, but he didn't and I was glad. It may have been a thrift store find, but it was the nicest dress I owned and I didn't want it to be accidentally ruined.

I hung it over the back of the chair next to his jacket and realized why he hadn't stopped me. He was enjoying watching me walk around in my heels, thigh-highs, panties and bra. My already damp panties grew wetter. I'd never had anyone look at me with that much heat in their eyes. I wished I'd had fancier underwear than white lace. My mind flashed to my honeymoon lingerie, but I pushed that thought aside. I still wasn't ready.

My heels went next and then the stockings. I rolled them down slowly without having to be told and set them on the seat of the chair. As I straightened, I realized he was still completely dressed.

"Aren't you going to...?" I gestured toward him, unable to finish the sentence.

"What?" He raised an eyebrow.

He was going to force me to say it. Fine. "Aren't you going to take off your clothes?"

His lips curved upwards into a sensual smile. "No."

A flush of embarrassment spread through me. Had this all been some kind of joke? A trick to get me naked?

"You are," he finished.

I stared at him.

"Unbutton my shirt," he said.

I swallowed hard and walked over to him. My fingers were trembling and I glanced up to see if he would laugh at my nervousness, but his expression was serious now. His hands stayed at his sides as I began to undo the buttons. The first time my fingers brushed against bare skin, I felt a shock of pure electricity move through me.

"Touch me, Bree." His voice somehow managed to be soft and firm at the same time. It wasn't gentle, more like quiet, but there was no doubt in my mind that he expected to be obeyed.

Not that I wanted to disobey. Not when his command was something I wanted to do anyway.

I slid my hands between the folds of his shirt, making a sound in the back of my throat as my palms skimmed over rock-hard abs and then up to a broad, muscular chest. My hands moved to his shoulders and pushed the shirt off them. Damn. He was like some sort of sculpture come to life. Well, except I didn't think Michelangelo's *David* had a tattoo of a Celtic cross over his heart, the letters RIP in fancy script above the word 'mom.'

"Now my pants."

I quickly looked away from his tattoo, feeling like I'd intruded on something personal. My hands had steadied and I didn't have trouble getting the button of his dress pants undone. The zipper, however, made me hesitate. I could see the outline of his erection and knew that if I unzipped his pants, I'd be touching him, albeit through another layer of cloth.

Cade cupped my chin and tilted my face up so that our eyes could meet. "Do you want me, Bree?" he asked.

I nodded.

"Say it," he commanded.

"I want you." My voice was barely above a whisper.

"I think it's obvious I want you." He gave me a crooked smile. "So you have nothing to worry about." He brushed his lips across mine, making me shiver. "Now, unzip my pants and pull them down."

I inhaled slowly, my face burning where his skin had touched mine. My head was spinning as I reached for his zipper. Sure, Ronald and I had undressed each other, but never like this. He'd never been this direct. I'd never felt so observed.

My fingers brushed against the bulge in the front of Cade's pants as I lowered his zipper. I could almost feel his flesh straining against its confines, begging to be released, and I suddenly wanted to be the one who freed him. I wanted to see him. But, I did as I'd been told and nothing more, crouching to finish lowering his pants. At some point earlier, he must've taken off his shoes because they were already gone, as were his socks, and he kicked his pants aside.

I stood, waiting for my next instruction. I wanted this to be perfect, and I wasn't about to let my lack of experience screw things up. I'd follow Cade's lead.

"Take off your bra."

I'd already mentally prepared myself that he'd ask for that next, so the nerves in my stomach only danced a little. I bit my lip to quell its tremor as self-doubt began to rear its ugly head. The biggest reason I was nervous was fear that he wouldn't like what he saw. My body was proportional, but that meant my breasts were a bit smaller than average, 'only a handful' Ronald used to say. I'd spent my life watching men ogle Adelle's much larger chest and I hoped Cade wouldn't be too disappointed.

As I dropped my bra onto the chair, I saw the heat flicker in Cade's eyes and my nerves quieted and then settled. The cool air made my nipples harden almost immediately and I flushed, the color spreading across my chest as well as my face.

"You have beautiful breasts," he said sincerely. He took a step forward and reached out, gently cupping them in his large hands. "Don't ever let anyone tell you differently."

I blinked. What had prompted him to say that? I knew Adelle never would've shared any conversations we'd ever had about body issues.

"Panties next."

I swallowed hard and slowly lowered the last thing that was keeping me from being totally naked. When I straightened, it took all of my willpower not to cover myself. When Ronald and I had been together, he'd watched me undress, but he'd never stared at me with this intensity, the burning passion I felt coming from Cade. I'd never been looked at by anyone the way he was looking at me now.

"Lie back on the bed." Cade's voice drew my attention.

I did as he asked, my curiosity piqued as he picked up my half-refilled glass of champagne. What was he going to do with that?

He moved carefully as he climbed onto the bed next to me, settling about halfway. Despite his previous words, I suddenly felt self-conscious about my breasts. Lying flat on my back, no matter how firm they were, made them seem smaller. Before I could overthink, however, Cade was tipping the glass and I gasped as a small amount cold liquid splashed across my breasts.

"What...?" I started to sputter half a dozen questions and push myself up.

"Stop."

I froze, my body automatically obeying the quiet command.

"Lay back down."

I did as I was told, shivering as the now-damp bedspread came in contact with my back.

"Trust me," Cade said. "You'll enjoy this. Just relax."

I flinched as another splash of champagne came down on my breasts. My nipples hardened even more, pale pink points jutting up from my flesh. The liquid ran down between them as Cade moved the glass down, spilling the expensive drink on my stomach and letting it pool in my bellybutton.

"Spread your legs."

Fuck. My stomach flipped as I parted my legs. I watched, knowing what was coming next, but still unable to completely prepare myself for the contact. I gasped as the champagne ran down my slit, coating my lips, beading in the thin layer of dark curls that I kept neatly trimmed. It was like nothing I'd ever felt before, tingling against my sensitive skin.

Once the glass was empty, Cade set it aside and looked down at me. I had a pretty good idea what he was going to do, but my heart still raced with anticipation. He lowered his head and began to circle my breast with his tongue. His lips joined in, cleaning every inch before taking my nipple into his mouth.

I cried out at the heat contrasted with the cool of my skin, then again as he began to suck. Each pull was slow and deliberate, as if he designed each one specially to send a jolt of pleasure straight through me. When he released my nipple, I made a noise of protest, but then he was moving across the valley between my breasts and starting over, first licking the drying champagne, then sucking on my nipple until I was shaking.

He sat up slightly, a curious expression on his face. I wondered what he was thinking, but didn't ask. My arousal was more important than my wanting to know. When he moved to kneel between my legs, he handed me a pillow and instructed me to, "Watch." I propped myself up, just enough to see what he would do next, curiosity and desire mixing to heighten my anticipation.

I'd never wanted to watch before, satisfied just to have Ronald go down on me. Those times had been few and far between, a reluctant act brought about by his inability to make me come any other way. Not that he managed to do it orally, I thought wryly. I'd just assumed I was broken, one of those women unable to have an orgasm very often. I'd fooled myself into believing that the physical closeness of sex was enough.

But now, as this man hovered over me, I knew this time would be different and my back arched at the thought.

He leaned over me, working his way down my stomach to my bellybutton. I laughed as he lapped up the liquid there, his tongue teasing a part of me that was extremely ticklish. He smiled, lingering a bit longer until I was gasping for air.

While I caught my breath, he stretched out between my legs, settling with his arms underneath my thighs, his hands resting on my hips. When I looked down at him, our eyes met and I knew that's what he'd been waiting for. He wanted to see my face when he did this. He didn't break eye contact as he pressed his mouth against me.

My hands fisted in the bedspread as his tongue cleaned every last drop of champagne before dipping between my folds to get what was now mixed with my own arousal. I cried out as his mouth found my clit, his tongue working over the little bundle of nerves until I was sure I was going to explode.

A finger slid inside me and my body jerked. Then he curled it, pressing against something that sent white-hot pleasure coursing through me. His lips closed around my clit and he gently sucked on it, making me cry out. My eyes rolled. It was too much. Tears ran down my cheeks as my body shook. I needed him to stop, but I never wanted it to end. Then, his finger was gone and his mouth moved. My muscles twitched and I felt his hands on my legs, slowly moving up and down, soothing me through the most intense orgasm I'd ever had.

When I was finally able to force my eyes open, I looked up to see him watching me and I flushed with embarrassment.

"There's nothing as beautiful as watching a woman come," he said, pushing himself up off the bed to stand.

"What was that?" I had to ask. His eyebrows went up and I quickly clarified so he didn't think I was a complete idiot. "I've had orgasms before, but nothing like that."

A look of understanding crossed his face. "A lot of women haven't had a g-spot orgasm before." He gave me a cocky grin. "It's one of the reasons I learned how to do that."

"Wow." I let out a breath. I'd heard of it before, of course, but it had always seemed so elusive. Something women like Adelle and Mindy talked about when they discussed the positives and negatives of certain lovers.

"We're not done yet," Cade said.

My stomach clenched at his words and I watched as he slowly lowered the black boxer briefs that appeared to have grown tighter since I'd taken off his pants earlier. I swallowed hard as the rest of his body came into view. He had a thin trail of black curls under his belly button, but the rest of him was either clean-shaven or waxed, leaving nothing hidden. If I hadn't been so distracted by his body, I might've worried that I should've shaven too, but as it was, the only thing I could think about was that long, thick piece of flesh curving up toward his beautifully defined abs.

Even though I only had Ronald for personal comparison, Adelle and Mindy were open enough about their sex lives that I knew my ex-fiancé had been average in length but a bit on the thin side. Cade was longer than Ronald by about two or three inches, but it was his thickness that made me wonder if he would fit inside me. He was easily twice as big around as Ronald, nearly three times at the base.

Cade ran his hand over himself, his hand moving up and down in an almost hypnotic rhythm. I licked my lips, wondering if I'd get the chance to taste him like he'd tasted me. I wasn't a big fan of giving head, but I didn't detest it either. Then he was rolling a condom over his cock and my heart skipped a beat.

"Spread your legs." Cade gave the command again.

I hadn't even realized I'd closed them, but I opened them, never taking my eyes off of that thick shaft.

"Trust me," Cade said as he climbed onto the bed. He knelt between my legs and gripped my hips, lifting them so that my ass rested on his muscular thighs. His cock brushed against my lips and I shivered. "Relax. I promise to go slow."

I nodded, still not looking at his face. His finger hooked my chin and raised my head.

"Aubree, what do you want?"

"You," I answered automatically. "Please, Cade."

He nodded and let me drop my gaze so I could watch as he slid the head of his cock inside me. My eyelids fluttered. Fuck, if just the tip felt that good, I didn't think I'd be able to deal with the rest of him. Cade reached out and took my hands, threading our fingers together as he began to move forward. He did as he'd said and moved slowly, stretching me inch by agonizing inch.

I moaned as he filled me, his cock rubbing against my walls with each bit of forward progress.

Then his dick pressed against the same spot his fingers had earlier and I gasped, my back arching from the bed. The sudden movement pushed him deeper and I cried out. He stopped, giving me a moment to adapt. My fingers tightened around his as my body tried to process the burn of being stretched too fast with the pleasure of everything else.

"I'm okay," I finally said. My eyes flicked up to his face and he nodded.

By the time he was completely inside of me, we were both panting, muscles straining. I was torn between wanting him to fuck me hard and fast to quench the fire burning inside me, and needing him to take it slow. I didn't know what to do, and so left it to him.

With careful deliberation, Cade pulled back, then moved forward. The stroke was slow, but steady and without pause. By the third one, any discomfort I'd previously felt was gone, lost in the delicious friction of his body inside mine. After another dozen or so, he shifted, leaning forward slightly as he released my hands. The base of his cock rubbed against my clit, sending new pleasure coursing through me.

"Yes!" I cried out. I slid my hands up his arms as he rested most of his weight on his hands. "Oh fuck." I could feel my climax approaching, something weighted and intense.

"Are you ready to come?" Cade asked.

I squeezed my eyes closed as I nodded.

"Look at me," he ordered. "Look at me, Aubree."

I opened my eyes and met his. I felt his hips flexing against my thighs as he began to move faster. His thrusts were deep, reaching parts of me I hadn't known could be reached. Each one took me closer to the edge. And then I was going over, calling out his name as I clung to his arms.

My back arched and my head tilted back. I couldn't keep looking at Cade. There were too many sensations to take in. My body had a mind of its own, every nerve singing, each cell on fire. I was coming and he was still fucking me. His cock pushed through my spasming pussy, sending new waves of pleasure crashing over me, pulling me under before I could come up for air. I wasn't sure if it was multiple orgasms or just one very long one, but I rode it.

After what felt like years of ecstasy, Cade drove deep, pinning me against the bed. I could feel him swell even more inside me and his body tensed. He groaned as he came, grinding down against me until I was writhing, needing to get away from the friction and pressure. And then he was pulling out and rolling onto his back.

My pussy twitched, suddenly empty. My legs fell apart, leaving me splayed across the bed, exposed, but I couldn't muster enough energy to move.

"Wow." I managed to say as I got my breath back. "I never...I mean...Just, wow."

Cade didn't say anything. It took more of an effort to roll over than I'd anticipated, but I managed to get myself onto my side and face him.

"Thank you," I said. "I hadn't know it could be like this."

He turned his head to look at me.

"My former fiancé, Ronald, he was the only person I'd ever slept with, and it was nice, but never like this." I wanted to reach out and touch Cade, take my time and explore those muscles with my fingers and my mouth. I glanced down at where his cock lay against his thigh, spent. And there was something else I wanted in my mouth.

Cade smiled at me and stroked my hair, gazing into my eyes. Then he blinked and the moment was over. He sat up and climbed off of the bed, pulling off the condom and tossed it into a nearby trashcan. "Do you want to use the shower first or would you prefer just to get dressed and shower back your own place?"

I wasn't sure what to say; I was surprised at the abrupt end to the evening. Then again, I could understand him wanting to make sure I wasn't angling to spend the night. Sure, he'd initiated things, but there hadn't been any commitments made. A line needed to be drawn, and this was it. I understood.

"I'll clean up a bit, but I'll wait to shower until I get home." As I stood, I was surprised by the ache between my legs. Cade hadn't even been close to rough, but I'd be feeling him for the rest of the weekend. The thought made me smile as I picked up my clothes and walked into the bathroom.

By the time I came out, Cade was dressed as well. That surprised me. I'd thought he'd shower and stay here, leaving me to get home on my own. Instead, without a word of explanation, he put his hand on the small of my back and went with me down to the lobby and then outside where he hailed me a cab.

He opened the door, but grabbed my hand before I could get inside. "Until next time." He gave me a dazzling smile and squeezed my hand.

Our gaze held for a moment and then I climbed into the cab and he closed the door behind me. I watched him walk back toward the hotel doors, admiring the view until he disappeared from sight. Then, as the cabbie drove me home, I pulled out my phone. It was midnight, but I knew Adelle would want to hear how my date went. Plus, I wanted details on how she knew him and what she thought about me seeing him again.

The call went straight to voicemail and I scowled. I should've known. It was a Saturday night. If Adelle's phone was off, it meant she was busy. I'd have to wait until morning.

At least I knew I'd sleep well tonight. My body was in that relaxed, boneless state that only occurred after a toe-curling orgasm. I smiled, I least that's what I'd always heard. Tonight I got to experience it. Maybe I'd be lucky and the events of the night would make an appearance in my dreams. I could do with reliving that.

# Chapter 9

His hands were on my breasts as I rode him, his fingers rolling and pulling on my nipples until I had to beg him to stop. But he didn't and I found that the pain and pleasure mixed, building into an orgasm that would make me scream...

A shrill tone cut through my dream before I could reach the end. I swore silently as I reached out and grabbed the phone. I squinted at the clock as I answered, ready to cuss out whoever had just woke me up at seven-thirty on a Sunday morning.

"How was it?"

I sighed. I couldn't get mad at Adelle. Plus, I'd asked her to call. I sat up and rubbed the sleep from my eyes.

"Come on, Bree, spill."

"It was amazing," I admitted, giggling like a school girl. "At first, I wasn't so sure, because he was kind of being a douche, ordering for me and stuff, but once we got to talking, we hit it off."

"I knew it."

As my brain fully woke, I remembered what should have been the first thing I'd said to her. "Adelle, did you know he was my mystery man?"

There was a pause and then a gasp. "The one from the bar with Steven? No fucking way!"

She wasn't pretending. She really hadn't known.

"I guess that means I don't have to ask if you thought he was hot," she teased.

"No, you don't," I said. I closed my eyes, remembering. "Shit, Adelle, he was even more gorgeous than I'd realized. That body... it just all seemed too good to be true. A random meeting and then an even more random second meeting. The fact that we actually ended up liking each other... it's like fate."

"And the sex?"

"It was fantastic." I paused, and then asked, "Wait a minute, how do you know we had sex?" Had I been that obviously desperate that she assumed I'd fuck whatever hot guy she sent my way?

"Come on, Bree. How do you think?" She laughed. "A great fuck was the entire reason I wanted you to date my guy in the first place. When you want something done right, hire a pro. Cade's a gigolo, Bree. A professional escort and lover. A damn expensive one, but worth every penny.

Consider it an early Christmas gift. Surprise!"

# Chapter 10

*Cade Shepard*

I grimaced as I pulled off the used condom and tossed it into the trashcan next to the massive king-sized bed where a curvy blond was currently sprawled. She was still coming down from the last orgasm I'd given her, her massive breasts heaving with every deep breath she took.

I looked away as I shoved a foot through the leg of my briefs, being careful to not look like I'm bolting from the room even though that's exactly my plan. It was always best to be up and getting dressed before the woman got the mistaken idea that I was going to stick around and cuddle. I didn't do that, not even when they begged for 'extra time.'

Most people assumed that someone in my line of work would do anything for money. That wasn't the case with me. I didn't really care what people think. If they weren't in my line of business, they'd never really understand what I did.

I offered a service to the lonely and rejected women who thought they weren't good enough, the neglected ones whose husbands or boyfriends either didn't care enough or were unable to fulfill their needs. And I didn't just mean a good fuck. Any man who gave a damn could get a woman off. Me, I did more than that. I showed them how to enjoy sex in ways they'd never dreamed possible. I taught them to surrender their thoughts, their beliefs and judgments... and just feel.

Some women came to me because they had insatiable appetites for sex and thought they wanted someone to basically fuck them senseless. I knew better. There's always an underlying need underneath the bravado and I had an innate talent for knowing what a woman needed. Not just sexually, but emotionally as well.

Not that I got all touchy-feeling. I don't do emotion. I don't believe in that shit. Sure, there's the basics of happiness, sadness, anger... but when it came to the whole notion of romance and love, that's where I drew the line. Romance was fine if it led to sex, but the idea of love was a joke. I'd learned that years ago.

In the almost ten years I'd been doing this, I'd had plenty of women tell me that they were falling in love with me. That was always where it ended. I didn't mind repeat dates, but I didn't need the headache of someone thinking this was anything more than a mutually agreeable transaction. Sure, it was a transaction I enjoyed, but that's all it ever was.

I felt the blonde's eyes on me as I buttoned my pants and then picked up my shirt. I had a bad feeling I was going to need to have that talk with this one. I'd seen Stella three times before, including once when I'd gone with her to the opening of an art museum. We'd fucked in the bathroom there because she'd wanted something daring. Tonight, she'd brought me back to her place instead of a hotel, and that was usually the first warning signal that a woman was going to try to get possessive.

Once I finished dressing, I picked up the cash from the bedside table and shoved it into the pocket of my perfectly-tailored suit pants. "Thank you for a lovely evening," I said with a polite smile and a quick wink to soften the rejection. "Until next time."

I left before she could ask if I wanted to spend the night. While annoying at times, having women wanting more of me just meant I was doing my job well. I grinned. Of course, the multiple orgasms generally told me the same thing. Nothing was as satisfying as hearing some high-society, well-educated woman screaming for me to fuck her harder.

I flagged down a cab and climbed in the back, giving the cabbie the address of my loft. I never understood why everyone looked down on people like me. I was better at my job than most people were at their mundane office work or retail sales. Hell, I did more good for women with my cock than half the psychologists and medical doctors ever could with all their drugs and therapy and procedures. Why should someone pay a shrink for a pill when they could get a ten-inch dick and a man who knew how to use it? I was a teacher, date, counselor and fuck buddy all in one, and worth every damn penny.

**End of Vol. 1**

# Casual Encounter Vol. 2

# Chapter 1

"Come on, Bree. How do you think? A great fuck was the entire reason I wanted you to date my guy in the first place. When you want something done right, hire a pro. Cade's a gigolo, Bree. A professional escort and lover. A damn expensive one, but worth every penny. Consider it an early Christmas gift. Surprise!"

My best friend's words still echoed in my mind even though I'd hung up on her more than a minute ago. I kept expecting anger to come to my rescue, to break me from this catatonic state. It might come later, but at the moment, I was numb. I sank back against my pillows and stared at my phone. It vibrated and began to ring. I didn't even have to look at the screen to know it was Adelle. Even if it hadn't been her ringtone, I would've known it was her.

I turned off the ringer and watched as her call was sent to voicemail. The second time she called, the anger came. Couldn't she take a hint that I didn't want to talk to her? Tears stung my eyelids and I squeezed them shut. I didn't want to cry. I'd spent too much time crying after Ronald had left. I'd shed enough tears over one bastard. I wasn't about to shed anymore over the one Adelle had paid.

I pressed my hands to my face as a stab of hurt pierced through me. I should've known better than to get my hopes up. I knew I idealized Cade as my mysterious white knight, but even after I forced myself to admit he wasn't perfect, I at least thought he liked me.

Heat flooded my face as I remembered telling him that I wanted him. Anger followed embarrassment when I remembered him telling me it was obvious he wanted me too. I'd just been foolish enough to believe it meant he felt something other than lust. And now I learn it was his job to get hard, to say pretty words. There probably hadn't been any lust there at all. I mean, I wasn't naïve. I knew it was more difficult for a man to fake arousal than a woman. A female prostitute could just lay there and make noises to convince her client that she wanted him. I wondered how Cade did it. Was it just the prospect of sex that got him hard? Did he cock respond to his commands like Pavlov's dog? Or had he been running through some fantasy in his head?

I suddenly felt sick. Who had he been thinking of when he was inside me? Had it been Adelle? And why had he pretended like that? If he'd treated it like some business transaction, I could've figured it out, stopped things from going too far. All he needed to do was make a single comment when he invited me back to his room for dessert. If he'd just said that the sex was already paid for, I would've been able to save myself a lot of pain and humiliation. I would've been embarrassed, but there was a huge difference between knowing I'd had dinner with a prostitute and knowing I'd fucked one.

My phone buzzed again and I was tempted to throw it across the room. Instead, I shoved it into my bedside drawer and crawled back under my covers. I pulled the blanket up over my head, closing myself off from the rest of the world.

When I'd been in seventh grade, my older brother had posted a picture of me on my locker at school. It hadn't been any picture though. It had been a picture of me modeling my mom's bra over my clothes, and it had been painfully obvious I'd never fill it out as much as she did. He'd gotten a detention from the teacher who'd found it, but by then, it had been too late. Every kid in the world had seen it, or so it seemed at the time.

My parents had grounded him for a month and made him apologize, but in my mind, my life had been over. I'd been convinced I'd never get over the embarrassment. For two days, I stayed in bed, my head under my covers, blocking out the world. I felt safe there, as if no one could hurt me. On the third day, my mom had forced me to come out and eat with the family. I'd gone to school the next day.

It was funny, I thought bitterly, how we grow up, but who we were as children never fully goes away. I hugged my knees to my chest and tried not to think about how much I hurt. What Cade had done had been bad enough, but he hadn't known me, and he'd just been doing his job. It hadn't been his fault that our first encounter had predisposed me to think of him a certain way.

I swore. Had Adelle set that up too? She'd sounded genuinely surprised when I said Cade was my rescuer, but she could've been acting. The idea that this entire thing had been a lie from moment one made it all the worse. It meant Adelle had no respect for me as a person or as a friend.

What she'd done had been so much worse than what Cade had done on many levels. Sure, she claimed she only had my best interests at heart, but what did it say about how she viewed me as a person—as a woman—if she thought I needed her to hire someone to go out with me, to sleep with me? How pathetic and stupid did she think I was? And she had to think I was both of those things because I couldn't think of any other reason that would've led her to believe I'd be okay with what she'd done.

Sunday went by far too slowly for me. Every fifteen to thirty minutes, Adelle would call. Every hour or so, I'd delete her voicemails without listening to them. I already knew what she said in every one. She apologized, but added something about how it was all for the best. She'd never admit she did anything wrong. I wasn't sure I wanted to forgive her even if she begged for forgiveness. I definitely wouldn't if she pretended she'd done something as simple as scratching my car or throwing up in my purse – both of which she'd done on more than one occasion.

When I finally had to get up to go to the bathroom, I decided to move my pity party into the living room where I ate half a gallon of Rocky Road ice cream and watched chick flicks for hours on end. By the time I showered and went to bed that night, I didn't feel any better but I knew I could at least pretend to be okay when I went into work tomorrow. I was just glad I didn't work with Adelle or Cade. I hoped to never see either of them again.

# Chapter 2

When my alarm went off on Monday morning, I didn't want to get up. I already knew how tough it was to slog through a day when I was emotionally devastated. It was strange how something like this could compare to being stood up at the altar. Most people would assume that having your fiancée run off with the wedding coordinator would be worse than finding out your best friend paid the man of your dreams to have sex with you, but it actually wasn't. I thought I loved Ronald, but in hindsight I could see all the ways we hadn't fit together. And this wasn't about Cade. He hadn't been the one who'd truly betrayed me. Adelle and I had been through so much together that her actions were worse than what Ronald had done.

I sighed and slapped the top of my alarm clock. I'd gotten through the humiliation of being left at the altar and I'd get through this. I was a stronger person than a lot of people thought I was, and I would move on. The first step was getting back to my normal routine. That meant school.

I dressed simply and then forced myself to eat an apple for breakfast. The only thing I'd eaten the day before had been ice cream, so I needed to get some food with substance inside me. That and coffee. I decided to treat myself to my favorite premium roast at the little café down the street, which brightened my mood enough that I was able to manage friendly greetings to my colleagues as I walked into the school.

My fake smile faltered when I saw Mindy heading my way. I hadn't even thought about her and how she'd want to know all about the date that had turned out even more disastrous than the one she'd sent me on. Heat rose to my cheeks as I wondered how much Adelle had already shared. Did Mindy know about Cade being my rescuer? Did she know what else he did? My stomach clenched. Was it possible that she'd even been in on it from the beginning? I shook my head. Mindy never would've gone along with deceiving me like that. Then again, I reasoned, I'd never have thought Adelle would've set me up with a gigolo either.

Gigolo. I winced at the word as humiliation washed over me and Cade's image flashed in my mind. That charming, cocky smile. His dark gray eyes. The way his blue-black curls had fallen carelessly across his forehead. Not exactly what I pictured when I thought of a male prostitute. He'd been authoritative, but never rude or cruel. He was comfortable with sex and his own body, but not crass. I supposed that's why he was a high-class escort.

I rubbed my temples. I could feel the start of a headache there.

"Bree!" Mindy's voice was cheerful.

I opened my eyes and reminded myself that her being a morning person and disgustingly chipper was not a valid motive for murder. I was already down one friend.

"So, how did it go?" She grinned at me and leaned against one of the front row desks.

I studied her for a moment and felt a stab of sadness that I didn't trust her completely. I forced a half-smile as I gave her a vague answer. "It went. Nothing worth talking about."

"Really?" She looked disappointed. "The way Adelle was talking him up, I was fully expecting you to come in here with a post-orgasmic smile from ear to ear."

I glanced at the door. "Not exactly school-appropriate talk."

She shrugged. "Fair enough." She straightened. "And there wasn't anything there between the two of you?"

I looked down at my lesson plan book as if it contained something I needed. "Nope. Not a thing."

In my mind's eye, I could see him as he moved above me. I felt him inside me again. His body thrusting into mine. Remembered how my skin had sung at his touch. I clenched my jaw and banished the thoughts. I wasn't going to do this.

"Well, if there's nothing to talk about." Mindy filled the awkward silence. "I guess I'll head back to my classroom. Those math problems aren't going to write themselves."

"See you at lunch," I said. I didn't want to eat lunch with her and subject myself to another round of questions, but if I didn't, she'd get suspicious and call Adelle right then. Now, if I was lucky, she'd at least wait until she got home and have the rest of the night to figure out how she was going to react to what had happened.

"Sure."

I caught her giving me a concerned glance before turning and leaving, but I didn't acknowledge it. Better to focus on the work and not think about anything else. I wasn't sure how well that would work, but I was going to try.

By the end of the day, I knew exactly how well that worked. The answer was: not at all. I was in the middle of a lecture about Romeo and Juliet's first meeting when the memory of Cade saving me popped into my head. I experienced my first pang of sympathy for Heathcliff and Catherine's angst. As I lectured on Austen, I wondered how her characters would have handled my situation. Well, not the escort part, but the friendship part. The books I'd spent my life escaping into no longer offered a place to hide.

A dashing hero with a dark secret. A lie. A betrayal and a broken heart.

My life had become one of those stories.

If you asked most teenage girls if they wanted their lives to be a romance story, they'd say yes, thinking of their handsome prince and the happily ever after. The problem was, they rarely remembered all of the shit the couple goes through to get their fairy tale ending.

And, of course, it is a fairy tale. Anyone who knows anything about the original stories knows that no one wants a real fairy tale ending. They want the Disney version. After all, who wants the version of Rapunzel where the prince gets his eyes poked out? Or how about the mermaid who chooses to die rather than the kill the woman the prince truly loves? And then there is my personal favorite... sweet little Snow White who ordered a pair of red-hot iron shoes onto her stepmother's feet, forcing the woman to dance until her feet bled. Most people don't know about the wicked queen crawling out into the snow and falling down a well after the princess's wedding.

With my luck, I would get a fairy tale ending, just not the Disney one. All I had to do was look at the kind of 'princes' I attracted into my life. Ronald was a real winner. And let's not forget Steven, the bastard who'd tried to get me drunk so I'd sleep with him. That, of course, led me straight back to Cade and how he'd come swooping in like Prince Charming rescuing the damsel in distress. Then he'd turned out to be a complete fraud, and not in a romantic Aladdin sort of way either. No, this was more the twist in the story where the guy everyone thought was the hero turns out to actually be the villain. And Adelle was the hateful step-sister who instigated it all.

I swore silently as I packed up my things. The day was finally over and I'd spent most of it thinking about Cade, both good and bad. I needed to get him out of my head. He wasn't a prince. I wasn't a princess, and this sure as hell wasn't a fucking fairy tale.

# Chapter 3

I was halfway to the front door of my apartment building when I realized someone was standing in front of it. I raised my head, ready to ask whoever was there to please move, and the words froze in my throat.

Cade.

"What are you doing here?" I'd intended the question to come out with anger and strength, but I heard a note of something else mingled in. A true desire to know why he was there and a hope that it was because he really cared.

"I need to speak with you." His voice was calm and even, with none of the arrogance or flirting that had been presence the other night.

I stepped past him, telling myself to ignore the flutter in my stomach and focus on the pain in my heart. I didn't want to hear a word he had to say. Unfortunately, he didn't seem to get that I was trying to blow him off.

"Aubree, wait."

I actually hesitated at the elevator, as if my body was programmed to obey. A flare of anger went through me which gave me the strength to move. I punched the third floor button harder than necessary and hoped the doors would close before Cade could slip in. But, my bad luck held and he stepped inside just in time.

He stood on the other side of the elevator, leaning against the wall in a casual pose I was sure he'd worked on for hours, perfecting it to draw the maximum amount of attention.

"I would like the opportunity to explain."

I refused to look at him.

"A cup of coffee. That's all I'm asking for. Give me the time it takes to drink a cup of coffee."

I folded my arms across my chest. In the time it took the elevator to go three floors, he had managed to weaken my resolve without even a real argument. I stepped out onto my floor and felt him follow. Fine, I thought. If he wanted to explain, then I'd let him. And then I'd tell him to get the hell out.

"One cup," I said as I unlocked my door. "That's it."

"Thank you, Aubree."

"I told you I go by Bree," I snapped as I walked inside.

"And I told you I prefer Aubree."

I scowled, but didn't argue. It didn't matter what he wanted to call me. Soon, I'd never have to hear him say my name again.

My stomach twisted at the memory of how he'd said my name, the way it had sounded when he'd asked me what I'd wanted. No, I told myself firmly. I wasn't going there.

"Take a seat," I said, gesturing toward the worn love-seat and faded armchair that were the only two places to sit in my living room. "I'll go get the coffee started. I wouldn't want to keep you from work."

I didn't look at him as I went into the kitchen. As eager as I was to get him out of my apartment, I took my time getting the coffeemaker going. I needed to compose myself. I couldn't let him see how much his being here upset me. He couldn't know the truth about how I felt about what had happened or any of the self-doubts it had fed into.

When I was convinced I could handle whatever was coming, or at least keep it together until he left, I went back into the living room. He was sitting at the far end of the love-seat, his arm across the back of it, his body angled so that he was facing me as soon as I entered. It looked so much like a carefully orchestrated pose that the serious expression on his face seemed out of place.

"You wanted to talk." I sat down on the edge of the chair. "Might as well get started."

"First, I have to apologize for what must appear like callous and deceitful behavior."

My jaw dropped and I couldn't stop the surprise from crossing over my face. I'd thought he'd either come on Adelle's behalf or... honestly, I didn't know what to expect, but a straightforward apology hadn't been it.

Cade straightened, leaning forward so that his elbows were on his knees. "I'm not ashamed of what I do, Aubree. And I didn't intentionally hide it from you. I assumed you knew about the arrangement. Adelle never mentioned she hadn't told you."

I laced my fingers together to keep myself from folding my arms again. I knew it was a protective gesture and I didn't want to appear weak. "Well, she didn't."

He frowned and something flashed across his eyes, darkening them to the kind of gray that a cloud turns just before a storm. "When she contacted me, she said she was hiring a perfect date fantasy for a friend. Everything else I told you was true. How I'd asked her for some details about you, how you didn't fit what I'd pictured in my head. I didn't lie about that."

I twisted my fingers until my knuckles turned white.

"She called me yesterday afternoon in a panic and told me the truth; that she'd surprised you and you were angry with her when you found out." His frown deepened. "I wasn't pleased with her myself."

That surprised me. He'd gotten paid. Why would he care what Adelle had done?

"Understand something." His voice was firm. "I don't do surprises and I don't lie about what I am or the services I provide. Fantasies are fine. They're role-playing, but both participants are always aware of the truth of the situation."

An idea was starting to take shape, a reasoning behind why he was offering an explanation and apology for something that hadn't been his fault. He cared about his reputation as an escort.

"I provide women with companionship when they need it, and often sex is part of that. I teach women how to pleasure themselves and their lovers, how to enjoy sex in ways they've never dreamed."

I almost shivered at his words as they flowed over my skin.

"I am not in the business of love and I don't believe in emotional attachments," he continued. "These are things my clients always know up front, and why I generally screen them personally. For Adelle, I made an exception and I regret it now. Not the events of the night. I don't regret those, but rather the circumstances surrounding them."

Tears burned in my eyes as a part of me died. I hadn't realized I'd been holding onto a small hope that he'd actually cared about me. I appreciated his apology, and any anger I'd felt toward him was gone now that I knew the full story. But I couldn't stop myself from thinking that maybe I'd been right before. Something was wrong with me.

"Aubree?" He gave me a puzzled look. "What's wrong?"

I shook my head, fighting back the sudden wave of emotion washing over me.

He crossed over to where I was sitting in two quick strides and crouched in front of me. "Tell me what's wrong."

I didn't know if it was the command in his voice or maybe I needed to tell someone how I was feeling; but everything started spilling out of me.

"What's wrong with me? I mean, first my fiancée takes off with our wedding planner, then the first guy I've gone on a date with in years tries to get me drunk." I wiped at my cheeks. "Am I so pathetic that my best friend thinks I need to pay to get laid? Is that the problem? Am I just such a lousy lay that it's a job to fuck me?"

"Stop."

I hiccupped and looked up at Cade, surprised. He didn't sound disgusted at my outburst, but there was something hard in his eyes that told me he wasn't to be trifled with.

"I have an idea, but I need to make a call first." He glanced toward the kitchen. "I'm going to step out and make a call. Pour us each a cup of coffee and I'll be back shortly."

My mouth opened, then closed again. My mind was spinning. What was going on?

"Coffee, Aubree," he said firmly.

I stood and started toward the kitchen, moving automatically. I heard my front door close as I retrieved two mugs from my cabinet. I could end this now, I knew. Go into the living room and lock the door. When he knocked, tell him I didn't want to see him again. But I didn't do any of that. I filled the mugs and went back to the living room. As hurt as I was, he hadn't been the one to do it. The least I could do would be to hear out whatever this idea of his was.

When he came back into the apartment, he looked pleased with himself. He sat back on the love-seat and took a drink of his coffee before speaking. "I spoke with Adelle."

I stiffened. If he said he thought I should forgive her, I was going to dump my coffee in his lap. See how well he could work with a burnt dick.

"I have a proposal for you."

I frowned.

"There's nothing wrong with you, Aubree."

He spoke like his statement was common knowledge. There was no hint of gentleness or flirtation in his voice. He was stating a fact.

"You're not bad in bed. You're a beautiful woman and you deserve better men than those jackasses you mentioned." He took another drink. "You just need the confidence to make everyone else see it. And I'm going to give you that."

My eyes widened.

"I'm going to teach you everything I know. Show you everything. For however long it takes, I'm offering my services. No fake dating or anything like that. A pure learning experience." One side of his mouth tipped up in that cocky grin I recognized. "Though an enjoyable one, I promise."

He stopped and looked at me, his expression clearly saying he was waiting for a response.

How the hell was I supposed to respond to something like that? "I-I," I stammered. "Thank you, Cade." I finally managed to find words. "I appreciate the offer, but I don't do casual sex."

He stood and grinned down at me. "Trust me, there's nothing casual about how I do sex." He reached into his pocket and pulled out a small, rectangular card. He held it out to me. "Like I said, this is all business, and Adelle is footing the bill." He winked. "The least you can do is make her pay. Literally."

I took the card. "Tempting as it is, I don't think I'll be using your services again." I stood. "Thank you very much for coming to set things straight. I really do appreciate it."

"But you're not interested in my offer," Cade finished for me.

"No." I shook my head.

"Well," he said as he headed for the door. "If you change your mind, give me a call. There's no expiration date."

As the door closed behind him, I looked down at the card in my hand. There was no way I was going to call him, I told myself as I carried our mugs back into the kitchen. I stuck the card under a magnet on my refrigerator.

No way at all.

# Chapter 4

I tried to be insulted by Cade's proposal but, in a way, I knew it was a result of what I'd said. I was annoyed at myself for sharing such personal thoughts, but I couldn't really be angry that he'd taken what I'd said and tried to help. He hadn't acted like I was pathetic and couldn't do things on my own, only that I needed more confidence or whatever it was he offered to women. I hadn't seen any pity in his eyes at least, and for that I was grateful.

Still, I couldn't consider taking him up on it, even if it would be nice to make Adelle pay for what she'd done. By Wednesday morning, she'd called half a dozen more times, leaving voicemails each time. When I saw Mindy waiting for me in my classroom, I knew Adelle had reached out to her.

"Bree, I don't know what happened between the two of you, but you need to talk to Adelle." She didn't even bother with a greeting or trying to ease into it. The annoyed expression on her face said that Adelle had either called her more than once or had woken her up early this morning.

"It's complicated," I said as I unpacked my bag.

She leaned against one of the front row desks and crossed her arms. "So complicated that you're not even going to give your oldest friend a chance to explain?"

"You're my oldest friend," I joked. She scowled at me. Apparently she wasn't in the mood for our group's way of reminding her that she was three years older than Adelle and me.

"What happened, Bree?" she asked.

I sighed. This was not a conversation I wanted to be having.

"Look, something's going on and you're obviously not talking to Adelle about it. You can't keep all this bottled up. It isn't healthy."

I rolled my eyes. "Seriously? You're going to go all school counselor on me?"

Mindy raised an eyebrow and got that stubborn look on her face that meant she wasn't going to let this one go. She wasn't pushy about everything, but she believed that once she chose to fight a specific battle, she stuck through it to the end.

I walked around my desk to face her. "Fine. You want to know why I'm not speaking to Adelle? Here it is. The date she set me up with wasn't a date. She paid for me to get laid."

I was satisfied to see Mindy's jaw drop. At least I didn't have to ask if she'd known. I continued, telling her all about how Cade was my mystery man and I'd gone through the entire date thinking he liked me for me. I forced myself to keep my head up and my eyes straight ahead. I hadn't done anything wrong. I didn't have anything to be ashamed of. Still, I couldn't stop the heat in my cheeks when I confessed to sleeping with Cade or the proposal he made. That was the only part of the story I wasn't entirely truthful about. By carefully choosing which piece of information I gave, I made it sound as if Cade's offer had come from wanting to help me 'get back on the horse' and not from any confessions of inadequacy on my part. I knew Mindy. If I questioned why I attracted men like that, she'd feel like she had to discuss it and try to make me feel better. I didn't want that right now. I wanted to get this done and over with so she could tell me it was okay for me to be mad at Adelle.

By the time I finished, Mindy's eyes were flashing. "I can't believe she did that!"

I went back around my desk and began setting out what I needed for my first period class. "Now you know why I'm not taking her calls."

"And then this Cade offers what, to 'teach' you?" She shook her head. "Well, you were definitely right to turn him down. You don't need to have anything to do with that."

"My thoughts exactly." I pushed aside the fact that I hadn't been able to stop thinking about Cade since that night. Mindy didn't need to know those details.

"But..." She hesitated.

My eyes narrowed. "But what?"

"But you and Adelle have been friends for such a long time." She held up her hand before I could argue with her. "I'm not saying she was right, and you have every right to be pissed at her. She deserves your anger, without a doubt." Mindy pushed her hair back from her face and I could tell she was trying to word this right. "My only concern is, after everything you two have gone through, do you really want to ruin your friendship over something like this? You know Adelle. Her heart's in the right place. It's her head that doesn't think straight."

I knew Mindy was right. I knew Adelle wouldn't intentionally hurt me and I knew I would eventually forgive her but today was not that day. I was still too wounded and raw right now and I didn't want to talk to the person who had done the cutting.

"I'm not saying you have to let it go and be all sweet to her," Mindy continued. "But I think you should at least talk to her. Let her tell you her side of things and if she truly did have your best intentions at heart, at least make an effort to understand where she was coming from."

I frowned but didn't say anything.

"I need to get back to my classroom," she said. "But if you need to talk some more, you know where to find me."

I nodded but knew I'd never take her up on her offer. A part of me was annoyed that she was trying to play peacemaker, but I could understand why. She and I worked together, so we had that, but she and Adelle had a lot in common too. If Adelle and I were fighting, Mindy would be caught in the middle. No matter how angry I was at Adelle, I wasn't going to force Mindy to choose.

Unfortunately, that meant I was probably going to have to see if I could at least be civil to Adelle. I glanced at the clock. The students would be arriving soon, so I couldn't do anything about it now. I'd call Adelle at lunch and see if we could salvage things between us. After more than twenty years of friendship, it was the least I could do.

I managed to focus enough on my morning classes that my students didn't notice anything was wrong. Then it was lunchtime and I knew I had to follow through with my decision to call Adelle.

She answered before the first ring had even completed. "Bree, oh, I'm so glad you called!" For the first time I could remember, there was a note of almost panic to her voice that competed with the hint of hope and relief. "I didn't think I'd get a chance to talk to you before Friday."

Friday. Shit. I hadn't even allowed myself to think about our Friday night dinners, or how much I would miss them. I closed my eyes. I didn't even want to think about having to be in the same building as her, much less at the same table.

Adelle kept talking, as if she was afraid I wouldn't let her get the whole story out if she paused even for a moment. "I know you're angry with me and you have every right to be. It was wrong of me to lie to you and trick you into thinking I was setting you up on a blind date. But I thought... no, I knew you and Cade would hit it off and it seemed like the only way I could get you guys to meet."

"You didn't think we'd hit it off," I interrupted. "You thought I needed to get laid and I'd think he was hot."

There was a moment of awkward silence. "I thought you two would really like each other."

"If you thought that, why didn't you ask him to go on a date with me? A real date. You know... boy meets girl; boy pays for dinner; boy and girl eat and decide if they like each other. Not boy gets paid to fuck girl because girl is too pitiful to get laid on her own." I struggled to keep my voice down, all too aware that there could be students outside my door.

"Bree–"

I cut her off. "Look, Adelle, I know you thought you were doing something nice for me, but you should know me well enough to know I wouldn't..." I sighed. "It's going to take some time for me to get past this."

"But you will, right?" Adelle actually sounded worried. "We're going to be okay?"

I honestly didn't know, but I couldn't tell her that, so I just ignored the questions. "I'll see you on Friday at L20." I hung up before she could try to say anything else.

By Friday, I still wasn't sure if my friendship would ever be the same between Adelle and me again, but I was determined to at least try. I'd lost the small hope I'd had for renewing my faith in love when I found my mystery man. I didn't want to lose my best friend too. And despite what had happened, Adelle and I had been through a lot together. If there was any chance we could mend this, I had to try.

For the first few minutes, things were tense, but as Mindy steered the conversation to safe topics that got us laughing and reminiscing, I found myself relaxing. If neither one of us talked about it again, maybe we could pretend nothing had happened.

"Can I get you ladies refills?" Our handsome waiter smiled at us as he reached for our empty glasses.

We all nodded despite having already reached our usual three drink limit. Well, three for Adelle and Mindy. Two for me. Three probably wasn't a good idea after the last time I'd had too much to drink, but I needed to take the edge off. Mindy would make sure I got home safely.

Of course, that made me think about how I'd gotten home before and all of my good humor vanished. What would it have been like if I hadn't been so drunk the first time we'd met? Would I still have slept with Cade after our date if I hadn't had that prior connection to him? What if I had asked him to come upstairs that first night? Would he have refused, citing my inebriated state, but really refused because I couldn't afford him? Or would he have taken me to bed, made love to me...

I closed my eyes and pushed the thoughts out of my head. Cade had made it perfectly clear that he didn't believe in emotional connections or love. Sex was a purely physical act. Granted, it was one he was extremely good at, but there wasn't anything real there. The only way things would've turned out good would've been if I'd never agreed to let Mindy or Adelle set me up with anyone.

"The waiter's checking you out." Mindy's voice cut into my thoughts.

I opened my eyes and looked over at her. "What?"

"The waiter," Adelle said. "He's been looking at you all night."

I frowned at her. Hadn't she learned her lesson? "He's probably still in high school."

Adelle rolled her eyes, a familiar gesture that once would've gotten an affectionate 'f- you' response from me. Now, it just annoying. It was her blatant disregard of my thoughts and feelings on things that had gotten us to this place.

"He's serving us alcohol," Adelle pointed out. "That means he has to be at least twenty-one."

"And?" I raised an eyebrow and took another drink. At this rate, I was going to end up with another bitch of a headache.

"And you should totally ask him out."

"Adelle," Mindy spoke softly as she threw me a glance.

"I learned my lesson," Adelle said. "I won't talk to him for you or try to give him your number. I just think you should find out if he wants to go out with you."

"I'm not interested in a relationship right now, Adelle," I said. "Or a fuck and run if that's going to be your next suggestion."

"I'm not saying you should move in together," she persisted. "Just go out for coffee, see where things go." She jerked her chin behind me. "He's cute."

I glanced over my shoulder as the waiter walked by. She was right. He was one of those gorgeous golden boys who looked like he'd be home on a California beach. "That's not the point," I said.

"It is so the point," she replied. "Ask him for coffee and then take him for a ride."

She was doing it again, pushing for me to do what she thought I needed to do and not listening when I gave my opinion. I didn't want to be here anymore. I raised my hand as the waiter walked by, signaling for him to come over.

"We're ready for our check," I said as he approached. Out of the corner of my eye, I saw Adelle open her mouth. I didn't know if she was going to protest me ending our night or if she was going interfere with my love life... again, but I didn't want to hear it. Words popped out of my mouth before I realized I was going to say them. "You have pretty eyes."

Oh shit. Had I really just said that? I didn't even know what the hell color his eyes were? Was that the best line I could think of? It sounded like the kind of cheesy pick-up line men like Steven Danforth used on drunk sorority girls to get them into bed.

"Thank you, Miss Gamble." The waiter smiled, but the expression on his face made it clear he was uncomfortable. "My boyfriend said you were a nice teacher."

"Excuse me?"

The waiter shifted his weight from one foot to the other. "My boyfriend. Kyle Jamison. You had him last year for senior English. He was behind a year because of some health problems and you helped him get caught up so he didn't end up getting behind again. He's at Stanford now."

Right. I remembered the young man. He'd been nineteen and desperate to prove he wasn't stupid. A sweet boy.

I forced a smile. "I'm glad to hear he's doing well. Tell him I said hello, would you?"

"Of course, ma'am." He glanced at Adelle and Mindy. "I'll be right back with the check."

I waited until he walked away, purposefully not looking at either of my friends. When he was out of sight, I stood. I felt a bit wobbly, but nothing I couldn't handle. "I think I'll be calling it a night."

"Wait, Bree–" Adelle began.

"No," I snapped. "I don't want to hear it."

"We just want you to be happy," Mindy interjected.

My mouth flattened into a line. "Right now, a long hot bath and a good night's sleep are what will make me happy." I didn't wait for either of them to try to make more excuses. I didn't run, but I walked as fast as a graceful exit would allow.

The cool autumn air felt nice against my overheated skin and cleared my mind. I wasn't as drunk as I'd feared and I didn't hail a cab right away. A walk sounded like just what I needed. I was too far from home to walk the entire way, but the direction I had to go was well-lit and still very public at this hour. The physical exertion would be good for me, help me burn off the anger starting to bubble up inside.

Nothing had changed. Adelle and Mindy both still thought it was their responsibility to 'help' me, but neither of them seemed to think that help meant supporting the decisions I made. I wasn't sure why it had taken me this long to realize my friends pitied me, but recent events had made it perfectly clear.

I could see now, as I looked back over the years, how they'd felt that way even before Ronald left me. They'd pitied how I'd only been with one man, as if my decision not to sleep with as many men as possible somehow meant I was broken and needed to be fixed. Maybe not that extreme, but they seem to think I couldn't manage on my own and I needed their help. When the hell did fucking equal being okay?

I scowled. I was tired of this. Tired of people thinking I was weak or couldn't do things on my own. I was tired of everyone acting like I needed to be coddled. The problem was, I wasn't sure I could do this on my own. I didn't want them to treat me like I didn't know what I was doing, but when it came to my personal life, I really didn't know. Tonight had been absolute proof.

I needed help, but I didn't want to get it from Adelle or Mindy. No, I needed it from someone who didn't have a personal stake in it. In me.

And I happened to know just the person.

# Chapter 5

I kept telling myself that I'd made the right decision, that this was the best way to get what I wanted. It still didn't keep my palms from sweating or my heart from racing as I walked toward the little café where I'd arranged to meet Cade. The little voice in the back of my head that had been telling me for years how a good girl was supposed to behave had been yelling at me since I'd called him last night and it wasn't getting any quieter.

I paused at the café door and asked myself one last time if I was sure this is what I wanted to do. If I did this, there would be no going back. I would have to own this decision, and since Cade's proposal had included Adelle paying for his services, it meant admitting to my friends what I'd done. There was no way I could afford him on my own, not on my budget, and I wasn't about to go to someone on the street. And as much as it pained me to admit it, I was attracted to Cade, and our night together left me certain I would physically enjoy the experience.

"It's time to take charge," I whispered to myself. "I'm a grown woman and this is a business transaction."

My little pep talk didn't ease my nerves, but it did at least quieten that voice and allow me to think.

I stepped inside and scanned the room. I was early, but Cade was earlier. I spotted him sitting at a table next to one of the massive glass windows. He nodded in greeting but didn't come to me. That was fine. I didn't want anyone mistaking this for a date. And by anyone, I meant me. I went to the counter and ordered coffee, but decided to forgo my usual caffeine and asked for decaf. I didn't need anything to make me more jittery. I didn't even actually want the coffee, but I'd feel better if I had something to keep my hands around and sip from to help stop me from fidgeting. I needed to appear in control. I was the one who'd initiated contact, the one who was calling the shots.

I slipped into the seat across from Cade, my best professional expression on my face. I met his gaze but couldn't read anything. His face was casually blank, not in an expressionless way, but rather like someone who was mildly interested in whatever was going on around him.

"You said you wanted to discuss my offer?" He broke the silence and I was grateful for that. I hadn't been sure how to best approach the subject, and it wasn't like either of us wanted to make small talk.

"I do," I said. Heat rose in my cheeks, but I refused to look down. "I'd like to take you up on it."

If he was surprised by my decision, he didn't show it. He did, however, ask, "What prompted the change of heart?"

"I'm tired of my friends acting like I'm some charity case when it comes to men," I said. "And I'm sick of attracting men like my ex."

Cade nodded and took a sip of his drink. "So what is it, specifically, you want out of this?"

I frowned, confused. Wasn't he the one who was supposed to tell me that? "Whatever it is you think I need."

For a moment, I could've sworn I saw something like desire flash across his eyes, but I dismissed it as a trick of light. I wasn't going to do that, read into little nuances and try to convince myself that I was different, special.

"All right," he said, his voice neutral.

"Everything having to do with payment goes through Adelle," I continued with the next point on the list I'd written down this morning. "Whatever you charge, extra expense, anything like that, you deal with her. I don't care how and when she pays you. It's between the two of you. I never want to hear about it. Ever." I couldn't stop myself from adding, "Considering you've dealt with her before with this kind of transaction; I figured you two already have an understanding."

"Makes sense," he agreed. He leaned back in his chair, the tight t-shirt he was wearing hugging his muscles.

I could see it now, how his every move was designed to draw attention to his body. Despite myself, a stab of arousal went through me. That was good, I supposed. I wouldn't want to get into this with someone whose touch I couldn't stand.

"Since I'm not discussing money with you," he said. "I suppose we should start on the other terms."

"Other terms?" I was confused, but curious.

One corner of his mouth quirked up in amusement. "Trust me, there's plenty we need to talk about before we get started."

I blinked. I hadn't expected this. I'd thought I'd come in, tell him to deal with Adelle for his payments, we'd set up a time to begin, and that would be it. I hadn't thought we'd need to have some lengthy conversation.

"First, there's one rule I have for clients who hire me for more than one session. No matter what verbal contract we've agreed to, this will end if you become emotionally attached."

"Good," I retorted. "And I expect the same if you become 'emotionally attached to me.' The last thing I need is you following me around like a lost little puppy."

A look of surprise crossed his face and I caught a flash of amusement in his eyes. Both were smoothed away in seconds, hidden behind his mask. "Since we've agreed on that, I need to know your sexual history," he said it so matter-of-factly it took me a minute to process it.

"Why?" I asked. "What does it matter? You know I'm not a virgin."

He ran his hand through his curls and I wondered if it was a nervous habit or a planned gesture. "During a normal session, part of the process of the night would be to learn what the client wants. I'm usually quite skilled at discerning needs. But, for what you're asking, it's different." He shifted in his seat and leaned his elbows on the table, clasping his hands in front of him. "You feel like there's something wrong with you."

I opened my mouth to protest, then snapped it shut again. He was right. This was why I'd come to him in the first place.

"I need to know what that something is," he continued. "Both what you think and the reality."

I mimicked his position, trying not to think about how close our hands were. "What do you want to know?"

"You said you've only had sex with one man other than me."

I nodded.

"How long had you and your ex been together?"

"Seven years," I answered automatically. "We started dating my freshman year of college."

"When did you begin sleeping together?"

This wasn't too bad, I thought. It wasn't like my choices were anything to be ashamed of. "My sophomore year."

"So you were, what, nineteen when you lost your virginity?" Cade gave me a searching look. "And you're in your mid-twenties now?"

I nodded again. "Twenty-five."

"So in those six years, you never had sex with anyone else?"

"No. I never cheated."

"What about threesomes? Or your ex watching you with someone else?"

For a moment, I thought he was joking, but then I realized he was serious. "Um, no. None of that."

"So you've never been with a woman either, right?"

Heat rose in my cheeks. "Adelle and I got drunk at a party in college and kissed, but I don't remember it. Does that count?"

Cade's lips twitched and I got the impression he was trying not to laugh. "No. Sorry."

I sat back in my seat and put my hands on my lap. "Is that it? You know my whole history now. One guy, period."

"We're not even close to done," Cade said. "I need to know what you've done so I can get an idea of your boundaries."

"What I've done?" I felt like an idiot even as I asked it.

"Was he strictly a lights-out, missionary style guy, or did the two of you at least try other positions?"

I glanced around, suddenly very much aware that I was in a public place. "We did it with the lights on and different positions, okay?"

Either Cade didn't sense how annoyed I was getting or he didn't care – I was betting the latter – because he got even more personal. "You've done oral? Anal? Toys? Any bondage? Spanking?"

"Shut up!" I hissed, my face flaming. "You have no right to ask me those things!"

He raised an eyebrow. "Aubree, you want me to teach you what I know but I can't ask questions?" He pulled his chair around the table so that he was sitting only a few inches from me. "You want me to wait until I'm balls deep inside your cunt, my finger in your ass before I ask if you've ever had anything in there before?"

My jaw dropped and I stared at him. He said it so plainly, I couldn't be offended. He wasn't trying to shock me or insult me. He was just proving a point. "Okay." My voice cracked but he didn't laugh. I tried again. "Okay. I get it. And I'll make it easier for you. The closest thing to kinky Ronald ever did was some dirty talk, and there wasn't really even much of that. Mostly just 'oh, baby' and 'you feel good.'" I dropped my eyes on the last one and hated myself for it. "And I went down on him once at a drive-in back when we were in college. So oral and regular sex. No kinky stuff."

"All right," Cade said. "That takes care of sexual history."

"I don't get yours?" The question shot out of my mouth before I could stop it. I looked up in time to see his look of surprise before he laughed.

"Hon, I've done it all." He winked at me. "But if you want details..."

"No!" I quickly said. "Are we done?"

Cade shook his head and the feeling of dread inside me grew. "Now we need to discuss how this is going to work."

I felt another snarky response wanting to escape and refrained.

"I'm your teacher, which means, entering into this, you are agreeing to do as I say."

"Hold on." I shook my head. "I don't think so."

"Would you tell a piano teacher that you don't want to follow his or her instructions?"

"No," I said. "But a piano teacher isn't going to tell me to spread my legs."

"If they're a good one, they might." Cade gave me his wicked grin again, the one that made me want to slap him and kiss him at the same time. "But seriously, you're asking for me to instruct you. That means you have to trust me to do my job." His expression became serious. "I promise I will never tell you to do something that isn't for your benefit."

"Really?" I let skepticism flow into my voice.

"I'm not saying I won't enjoy it, too," he said. "But it'll all be part of your lessons."

"So you want me to agree to do whatever you tell me, no matter what?"

"You'll have safe words. Red means stop. Yellow means you're uncomfortable and aren't sure if you want to go any further. Yellow's okay, but if you say red, I'll stop and we'll be done. I won't force you to do anything you don't want to do, but I'm not going to play either. It wouldn't be fair to either of us."

That actually sounded reasonable, I thought. Still, the idea of having someone bossing me around sexually made me anxious. "What kinds of things would you be telling me to do?"

"Well, we'd ease into everything, of course," he said. "But it might be something like me telling you to get down on your knees and put your hands behind your back." His voice was so low I had to lean closer to hear everything. "I'd tell you to open your mouth and I'd control how fast and how deep you took my cock."

I swallowed hard at the image his words painted.

"Or we might go to dinner and I'll have you leave your panties at home."

My hands curled into fists. He reached out and pushed back a curl that had fallen across my face.

"I'll tell you when you can come. When you can touch yourself or me. Every aspect of your pleasure will be mine to control." He paused, and stroked my cheek again, his finger brushing across my lower lip. And, Aubree... there will be pleasure. More than you've ever dreamed possible."

My pulse sped up at his words. I had no doubt he could deliver on his promise. The question was, could I do it? Could I give myself over to this man, allow him to take control of every aspect of that part of my life?

My eyes met his and he held my gaze, steady and sure of himself. He hadn't done anything to break my trust, I reminded myself. If anything, coming to see me after what had happened was evidence that he did have a degree of honor.

"All right," I said, my voice barely over a whisper. "I agree."

He pushed back from the table and stood abruptly. "Very good. I'll speak to Adelle about the monetary arrangements. Our first date will be tomorrow afternoon."

"Tomorrow?" I was thrown.

"I assumed you'd want to begin at my next available appointment. Would you prefer to wait?"

Part of me was saying I should wait, that I needed to carefully consider what I was doing. Up to this point, it had all been talk. But tomorrow? Tomorrow meant fantasy was speeding toward a reality I didn't feel ready for. If I agreed to see him tomorrow, he'd contact Adelle and there wouldn't be anyway to pretend like this exchange had never happened. I knew if I waited, even a week, there was a good chance I'd change my mind. And then... then everything would go back to the way it was.

My insides sank at the thought and I felt tears burn the back of my eyes. The 'way it was' sucked. The 'way it was' was merely existing. That, more than anything, made me agree.

"Tomorrow afternoon."

"Great." Cade held out his hand for me to shake.

I tried to ignore the heat going through me as we touched.

"I'll contact you with the place and time by this evening."

"Okay."

"Until tomorrow then." He released my hand.

Tomorrow, I thought as I watched him walk away. Tomorrow was when everything was going to change. A new chapter. A new life. I was going to be a whole new person. Brave. Adventurous. Alive.

I tried not to think about how much that idea terrified me.

# Chapter 6

I didn't know if it was Adelle's idea or Cade's to go to the Four Seasons Ritz-Carlton rather than the Park Hyatt Hotel where Cade and I had our first tryst, but I appreciated the gesture. I was nervous enough as it was. I didn't need memories of that previous night. The date itself hadn't been bad. It was actually because it had been so good I didn't want to be reminded of it. I didn't want to think about how I'd felt that night, full of hope and possibilities. Better I stick with what I knew to be true. Cade was going to teach me what I needed to know to make sure I never felt like a fool again. And if I enjoyed myself, then he was just doing his job. Nothing more.

His text had been succinct. The hotel name and room number, with a time. It surprised me a bit that he hadn't included any other instructions, like what I was supposed to wear or how I was supposed to behave. I'd spent the entire night trying to figure out what I was going to wear and had ended up not choosing any of the three outfits I'd picked out. Instead, I opted for simple and professional, a reminder for myself that this was a business transaction. Plain black skirt that reached my knees. White cotton blouse. Fitted black jacket. Sensible pumps. It had been the outfit I'd worn to interview for my position at Legacy.

And the moment Cade opened the door, I knew I'd made a mistake.

He managed not to laugh, but I saw the humor flash across his eyes before he could hide it. He opened the door and motioned for me to come in. I tried not to stare at him as I walked by. He was dressed simply in a pair of gray slacks and a long-sleeved white dress shirt, with the top two buttons undone. His shoes were plain but expensive-looking.

"What's so funny?" I hated the defensive note in my voice, but I couldn't seem to help myself. This wasn't my element. I wasn't a five-star hotel kind of girl.

"You look like a school teacher."

His comment was virtually identical to what Mindy had said about my clothes when I'd been trying to dress for my date with Steven. I found myself giving the same, automatic answer I'd given her. "I am a school teacher."

He grinned. "That's good to know for future reference." I must've looked as puzzled as I felt because he elaborated. "School teacher fantasies are always fun."

I glared at him. "Let me get this straight. My first lesson is to learn it's okay for you to make fun of me and my occupation, as long as you sexualize it in the next breath?"

His smile hardened and a muscle in his jaw twitched. "Most women coming to a hotel for a sexual liaison would dress in something provocative, something to seduce."

I folded my arms and raised an eyebrow. "I wasn't aware I had to seduce you."

He crossed into my personal space in just a few long strides and I gasped. His eyes were burning and I had a feeling I was glimpsing something beneath the calm mask he wore. He didn't touch me, but I could feel the energy vibrating off of him. The scent of him hit me, a rich masculine smell I'd noticed the first time I met him, and my pussy gave a throb.

"Lesson number one, Aubree: yes, men want sex and, yes, we don't really need you to seduce us." A finger lifted my chin until I was meeting his eyes. "But, if you want to be desired, want to be everything you think you're not, then you need to change the way you look at the world."

My eyes widened. His voice was even, but there was an authority to it that demanded I listen.

He took a step back, apparently satisfied to have my rapt attention. "It's not about showing skin or flaunting what you have. It's about how you carry yourself."

Okay, that hadn't been what I expected. I'd been prepared for a lecture about wearing something sexy.

"A woman can be seductive in anything, if she has the right attitude. You didn't dress in this outfit because it makes you feel powerful, respected, or confident in who you are as a person." Cade circled me and I fought the urge to squirm under the intensity of his gaze. "You chose it because you think it makes you look professional, which you feel automatically demands respect. You hide behind being a teacher, using it as an excuse for why you dress the way you do. It's not that this is your style or how you prefer to dress. You're comfortable in it not because you're comfortable in your own skin, but rather because you prefer to hide it."

"I wasn't aware you were a psychiatrist too." He was either a lot smarter and more observant than I'd given him credit for. Or he was a damn good guesser. Those weren't even observations Mindy or Adelle had ever made, though Adelle had gotten close.

"Take off your clothes."

It was abrupt, but at least that was a command I'd been expecting. I took a step toward the doorway I assumed led to the bedroom.

"Where are you going?" Cade asked.

"The bedroom?"

"I didn't say to go anywhere." He walked over to the burgundy love-seat on the far end of the room and sat down in the middle. He stretched his arms along the back of it, assuming a relaxed pose. "Take off your clothes. Slowly."

I shrugged out of my jacket and slipped off my shoes. Those were the easy ones and I took my time. This was too similar to our previous encounter and I didn't want it to be.

"Imagine the way you want to be undressed," he said as I started on my blouse buttons. "The way you would want your lover's hands to caress your body over your clothes. Think of the way your body would respond to his touch."

I was almost finished unbuttoning my shirt and I had no idea what he wanted me to do. Ronald hadn't been the caressing type. Sometimes he'd feel me up over my clothes, but that was generally because we weren't anywhere he could get them off or it was during the process of getting undressed.

"Take a deep breath, Aubree," Cade said. "Don't overthink it. Listen to your body. If it helps, for right now, close your eyes."

I closed them. That was better. I couldn't see Cade watching me. My muscles began to relax as I let myself fall into the head space I used when I touched myself. A place where it was just sensation, nothing else. Just me and my fingers; just pleasure. I concentrated on the way the soft cotton felt as it slid off my shoulders, then ran my hands up my sides to cup my breasts. My bra and panties were only plain white cotton, but it didn't matter. My hands moved to my hips, then around to the zipper at my back. I listened to it slide down its tracks, the whisper of the material as I pushed my skirt over my hips. I felt it pool around my ankles and stepped out of it.

"Much better. Now open your eyes."

Reluctantly, I did as I was told. I started to reach behind me to unhook my bra.

"Not yet," Cade said. "Touch yourself first."

I shifted my weight from one foot to the other. I wasn't sure which made me more uncomfortable, the idea of touching myself in front of a virtual stranger, or that I wasn't in a bedroom. Maybe it was because it was the middle of the day and the sun was streaming through the thin curtain covering the floor-to-ceiling window.

"Put your hands on your breasts, Aubree." Cade's knees parted slightly and I couldn't help but notice the way his pants showed off what he had to offer. "Do what you enjoy. Squeeze them if that's what you like. Play with your nipples. Not every woman likes the same things. How will a man know what you want if you don't even know it yourself?"

I cupped my breasts again and gave them a tentative squeeze. When my fingers brushed over my nipples, I felt a tingle of pleasure. I repeated the movement.

"Good girl. Now, touch your pussy through your panties."

I swallowed hard, but dropped my hand between my legs. The fabric was dry, but as I pressed my fingers against my lips, moisture seeped through. I made a small sound as I rubbed my fingers over the crotch of my panties, the cotton providing a different kind of sensation.

"Take off your bra."

It joined the rest of my clothes on the floor. This obedience thing wasn't too bad.

"Get your nipples nice and hard."

I rubbed my fingers over my nipples, feeling the carmel-colored flesh wrinkle and tighten. It didn't take much. I'd always had sensitive nipples.

"Look at me."

I didn't want to. I didn't want to see his face. The lie of desire, or worse, the absence of anything.

"Aubree." His voice was sharp. "Look at me."

I did and there was arousal in his eyes. My eyes burned with sudden tears. I folded my arms over my breasts, everything I'd been feeling vanishing. I didn't want to be here anymore.

"What's wrong?"

There was concern in his voice, but it wasn't a compassionate, tender sound. More like how my basketball coach in high school had talked to me when I'd gotten hurt. I half expected Cade to tell me to pull myself together and get on with it.

"I thought I could do this," I said. "If I came into it with my eyes open, knowing it was just business, but I can't take the lie."

"What lie?"

I lifted my chin and forced myself to meet his eyes. "I was okay with not having an emotional connection, but I can't stomach the thought that you're pretending to want me."

He chuckled and shook his head. "Seriously?" He dropped his hand to his crotch and my eyes involuntarily followed. "I'm already getting hard and I haven't even touched myself."

I hated that he made me so confused. "But Adelle's paying you to want to do this."

Cade sighed. "I'm going to explain this just once and then you're going to have to make a choice about whether or not you want to be here. Yes, I'm being paid to have sex with you. No, I don't do the whole emotion thing. But that doesn't means I don't find you attractive. I'm not some ten-dollar hooker who'll do anyone who has the cash. I'm choosy about my clients and I don't take on anyone I don't think I'd enjoy fucking. I don't fantasize about other women to get through a session. When I'm turned on, it's real."

A rush of relief went through me, chasing away the last of my lingering doubts. His words were sincere, I could feel it.

"Do we have an understanding?" he asked.

I nodded.

"Then slide your hand under the waistband of your panties and touch yourself." The hand on his crotch returned to the back of the couch.

I kept my eyes on his face as I ran my hand over my stomach and underneath the waistband of my panties. I didn't have to feel ashamed that I found him attractive or worry about what he was thinking when he looked at me. He wanted me, wanted my body. My middle finger slipped between my folds and I found myself wet. I shivered as I touched my clit, little sparks of electricity dancing across the thousands of nerves there.

"Roll your nipple between your fingers."

A moan escaped as I followed his instructions. The hand between my legs moved faster, falling into the steady rhythm I only used when I was alone. I applied more pressure to my nipple, my body jerking as a jolt of pain went through me.

"Stop."

I glared at him, but didn't argue.

"Take off your panties."

I slowly lowered them, enjoying the way his eyes dropped to my breasts as I bent over. When I straightened, I clasped my hands in front of me, not quite covering myself up, but not putting everything on display either.

"You'll find," he said "that there are just as many preferences for the appearance of a woman's pussy as there are for breast size, hips, and all the rest." His gaze slowly ran down my body and back up again. "I feel that a woman should choose based on what she enjoys."

I wondered if he was purposefully taking the time to have these little moments after working me up, just to keep me on edge.

"Did your ex ask you to keep yourself trimmed?"

I shook my head. "We didn't really talk about it."

"Have you ever shaved or waxed?"

"No." I'd had my legs waxed once. It wasn't an experience I wanted to repeat, especially on more tender flesh.

"Try it this week," he said. "Part of what I'll be doing is challenging you to try new things. After all, how can you know what you like if you don't experiment?" He shifted slightly. "Now, come here."

A thrill went through me. As much as I appreciated the lessons, I couldn't deny I was eager to feel him inside me again.

"Put one of your feet up here on the couch." He patted a spot next to his knee.

I gave him a questioning look, but did it. Heat flooded my face as I realized how this position opened me up to his gaze. His fingers curled around my ankle, holding me in place.

"Make yourself come."

Overly conscious of how closely he was now watching me, I moved my hand between my legs. The movements were almost automatic from years of practice, but this was different. Ronald had never watched me masturbate before. Hell, I was pretty sure he'd barely registered the times I'd helped myself along while we were having sex.

My embarrassment melted away faster than I'd anticipated, driven by the new flares of arousal brought about by Cade's rapt attention. He watched as I slid a finger inside me, pumping it a few times before adding a second. As my two middle fingers moved in and out, my other hand went to my breast, my fingers twisting my nipple until I gasped. I pressed the heel of my hand against my clit as I tugged at my nipple, pain mixing with pleasure.

Cade's hand tightened around my ankle, making me realize I'd closed my eyes. I opened them just as I came, my climax hitting me with an almost physical blow. My entire body shuddered, muscles tensing. My hands stiffened where they were, the fingers around my nipple tightening until I cried out.

I stayed where I was, letting myself feel the pleasure coursing through me. Then I heard a rustle and looked down. Cade had pulled a condom out of his pocket and set it on the couch cushion next to him.

"On your knees."

How he managed to make what should have sounded like a degrading command seem like a reasonable request, I didn't know, but I remembered him saying that everything he had me do was for my benefit. Besides, I'd be lying if I said I didn't want to do what I was pretty sure he was going to tell me to do.

"Unzip my pants."

The last time he'd told me to do that, my hands had been shaking. This time, they were steady. He shifted, spreading his legs so I could get between them and move closer.

"Pull out my cock."

I slid my hand into his open pants, my eyes widening as I met bare skin. I glanced up at him and he winked, a grin forming on his lips. We hadn't kissed, I realized. I filed that away for future consideration though. I didn't want any distractions from the thick piece of flesh my fingers had just wrapped around. I stroked him as I pulled him out. My fingers couldn't meet at his base and my pussy throbbed at the memory of how he'd stretched me.

"Suck my cock."

I didn't need to be told twice. I lowered my head to take the tip of him between my lips. I ran my tongue over the soft skin, then licked my way down his entire length, long stripes and little kitten licks, alternating pressure and speed until I heard Cade groan. I smiled and then took him in my mouth, letting the first few inches slide across my tongue, the taste of pre-cum surprisingly pleasant. I knew diet could change the taste of semen, but Ronald had never cared enough to even try.

"Take as much as you can." Cade's voice sounded a little strained.

I kept going until I started to gag and then pulled back. I repeated the move, opening my throat to take him further and established a slow rhythm as my hand worked the several inches of his length I couldn't take. I sucked hard, listening to his breathing increase. I raised my head and his hips jerked.

"Stop."

I let his cock fall from between my lips with a nearly obscene-sounding pop. When I looked up at him, his eyes were lidded, irises dark.

"Put the condom on me."

"Don't you want to get undressed first?" I asked.

He raised an eyebrow. "No."

I waited for an explanation, but there wasn't one. After a moment, I reached over and picked up the condom. I'd never done this before. Ronald had always been the one to put it on. I'd seen it done and knew how it worked, but this would be a first for me.

"You don't know how to do it."

"In theory," I said.

"Get it out."

I did and then waited for my next instruction. Instead of speaking, however, Cade put his hands over mine, sending a wave of heat through me. Together, we slid the condom over his erection and then he released my hands.

"Up on the couch," he said. "Put your knees on either side of my legs."

As I moved, I wondered if he would finally touch me. Aside from his hand on my ankle and then what had happened just now, he hadn't touched me at all. I remembered how his mouth had felt on my skin, the wet heat surrounding my nipples.

"You set the pace," he said. He folded his hands behind his head. "Ride me until I come."

My stomach clenched at his words. I'd been on top before, but Ronald had never stated so baldly what he wanted me to do. I reached beneath me and positioned Cade's cock at my entrance. I moaned as I slowly sank down on him, taking my time. The muscles in my legs quivered as I stretched to accommodate him. Had he been so fucking big before? Small whimpering sounds came out as I reached the widest part of him. It might've been the change of position, but I swore he felt bigger than before. I squeezed my eyes closed, gasping in shuddering breaths as he filled me completely.

"Breathe," Cade said softly, watching me intensely.

I wanted his hands on me, caressing my breasts, playing with my nipples, but there was nothing. Nothing to distract me from the nearly overwhelming sensations of being impaled on his hard cock. I shifted and he pressed against my g-spot, sending a bolt of electricity through me.

"Fuck!" My back arched and the motion rubbed him against that spot again.

"Damn," Cade spoke through gritted teeth. "You're even more responsive than I remembered."

I wasn't sure if that was a good or bad thing, but it wasn't something I cared about at the moment. I lifted myself an inch or two, then sank back down. The burn was still there, but it fed into the lingering pleasure and I liked it. I began to move, finding a rhythm I liked and letting my body relax into it, just like I did on a run.

"Play with your nipples."

The one I'd pinched before was still tender, so I focused on the other one, tugging and twisting it until it was swollen and sensitive.

"You enjoy that," Cade said. "You like things a bit on the rough side."

I flushed and my rhythm faltered.

Suddenly, Cade grabbed my hips, yanking me down hard enough that I cried out. He sat up halfway, enough that our faces were close together. His expression was fierce as he gripped me tight.

"There's nothing to be ashamed of, Aubree," he said firmly then realization dawned on his face. "That's it. Part of it anyway. You enjoy things you've convinced yourself you shouldn't." He released me and leaned back again. "We'll work on that, but for right now, make yourself come again. I'm getting close."

I tried not to think about his words as I started to move again, faster this time. My hands moved over my breasts, teasing with light scratches across my nipples until I felt the pressure inside me begin to crack. I dropped myself down on Cade's cock, biting my lip to hold back a scream as he hit something inside me that turned everything in my field of vision white.

The explosion rocked my body and I tightened around Cade. I heard him swear and his hips jerked, but all that was in the background. My body shook and arched before slumping against his chest. My overly sensitive nipples rubbed against his shirt and the extra sensation made me come again, a ripple effect of pleasure as my nerves still hummed from the previous wave.

When I started to come back to myself, I was surprised to find I was still on Cade's lap. I don't know why, but a part of me had fully expected him to push me off of him as soon as he regained his strength. Instead, he had his arms around me. As soon as I moved, however, he let me go and I sat up.

I winced as I climbed off of him. Whatever place deep inside he'd reached, there was an ache there now, mingling with what I had in my legs and pussy already. I had a feeling that tomorrow, I was going to regret agreeing to a Sunday meeting. I'd be feeling him for at least a day.

"I'll tell you this," Cade said as he removed the condom and tossed it into a nearby trashcan. "You can definitely forget about being bad in bed as a reason why your ex left. You're a natural."

I blushed, conflicted by the statement. Did being a natural mean I was some sort of slut?

"Aubree," Cade said my name. "It's a compliment. You have a natural instinct for sex. It's not something that can be taught. You just need some polish. And confidence." He pushed himself into a sitting position and tucked his now soft cock back into his pants. "When I'm done with you, no man will be able to refuse you."

That all sounded good, I thought. And I definitely wasn't going to say no to more sessions with Cade, especially not with Adelle footing the bill. In a short amount of time, he was tapping into parts of me that I'd hidden from everyone, even myself to some extent. No matter his methods, he was doing what I wanted him to do. He was helping me become who I wanted to be.

# Chapter 7

My session with Cade stuck with me into the beginning of the week. Part of it was the sex, the amazing sensation of him inside me, the pleasure of him filling me. Part of it was the memory of his eyes on me, his voice telling me what to do. But, what I found myself thinking about most of the time was how easily he'd been able to figure me out. He'd understood my insecurities, spotted kinks I'd barely acknowledged myself. I knew I wasn't easy to read since no one else in my life had seen those things before. He'd told me that this was what made him so good at what he did, knowing what women wanted and needed, but I couldn't help wondering if he was this accurate with everyone.

More than once, I told myself to let it go, to not read anything into it. This, I knew, was another lesson I needed to learn, and knew Cade would be the perfect teacher. I still believed in love, but I didn't want to equate sex with emotion all the time. I wanted to be able to have casual sex when I had an itch to scratch. I wanted to protect my heart until I found someone I could trust it with. To do this, I needed to learn how to separate physical pleasure from emotional intimacy. I refused to accept that I might just be wired that way. I had to be able to learn how to do it, and Cade was the perfect person to teach me.

The problem was, no matter how much I told myself to focus only on the physical attraction, I found myself drawn to him. I wanted to ask him personal questions, get to know him. There was someone very complex beneath the surface and I couldn't stop thinking about him. It was a bad idea to even entertain the thought. I considered this my own personal lesson. If I could keep having mind-blowing sex with Cade and not give in to my misplaced desire to explore a personal relationship, I could do anything.

During lunch on Wednesday afternoon, I was surprised to see a text from Cade. It was brief but still made things low in my stomach heat up.

Date Friday evening. I'll pick you up at your place at 7. Wear something elegant. No teacher clothes.

I immediately sent back a confirmation that I'd be ready at seven. It wasn't until the end of the day, when Mindy stopped by so we could walk to our cars together, that I realized by going with Cade meant I'd miss Friday dinner with my friends. I knew I should text him and reschedule. The only time any of us ever missed was if we were sick or out of town. The one I'd skipped after being stood up had been the first time I missed one of our dinners since a bad bout of bronchitis four years ago. We never scheduled dates on Friday nights, unless it was late and we weren't going out together afterwards.

"You know," Mindy said as we braved the early October wind. "I was talking to Stanley

Worthington, the guy who's subbing for Patrice while she's on maternity leave, and, apparently, he's not gay. And I know what you're thinking, but thirty-seven isn't that much older than you..."

"Thanks, Mindy," I interrupted, determination making my tone a bit sharper than I intended. Making the decision was easier than I thought it would be. "But I already have a date this weekend. Friday night, actually, so I won't be at dinner."

Mindy looked startled, and even a bit hurt, but I didn't apologize. This was exactly why I was going to Cade in the first place. I needed my friends to know that I could get a date on my own. I wasn't their charity case. A part of me knew I was being too harsh, but after all of the shit that had happened since August, I was tired of being nice all the time.

"Oh."

An awkward silence fell between the two of us and I sighed. "Look, Mindy, I appreciate what you've been trying to do, but I need you to back off. I'm perfectly capable of deciding who I want to go out with."

She nodded. "I'm sorry. I've just been worried about you."

"I know," I said, softening. "But I'm fine. Really."

She gave me a skeptical look, but didn't press the issue. "I won't do it again."

At least, with her, I knew I could count on what she said. Mindy had great self-control when it came to those types of promises. She wasn't like Adelle, who let her emotions take control. Mindy would take me at my word. With Adelle, I'd have to prove it, and with Cade, I would.

I spent the rest of the week eagerly anticipating my Friday night with Cade. I wondered what he had planned. Another tryst in a hotel? What new orders would he give me? Would he touch me this time? The only problem with these thoughts were they sometimes popped up at the most inopportune times. Like when I was lecturing on the symbolism in Paradise Lost.

When the final bell rang on Friday, I was as eager to leave as my students. I'd spent all of last evening scouring thrift stores for the perfect dress and had almost given up when I'd finally found it. It was the perfect shade of deep blue to complemented both my eyes and my skin tone. It clung to my body and was low-cut enough to show off what little cleavage I had but not so low it was sleazy. Unlike the dresses I'd worn before, this one was floor-length, making me look even taller than I was, especially once I put on my heels. A slit up my right leg, however, showed up to mid-thigh.

Then there was the fact that I'd followed Cade's instructions regarding... grooming. I'd gotten myself one of those home waxing kits and used it last night. The experience wasn't one I looked forward to repeating, but I had to admit that the sensation of my freshly waxed skin against the soft cotton of my panties was definitely something I could get used to. That, plus imagining the expression on Cade's face when he saw my bare pussy was enough to keep me uncomfortably moist nearly the entire day.

As soon as I got back to my apartment, I ate a quick meal and then headed for the shower. I took my time, lingering in a way I hadn't done since the morning of my wedding. I knew this wasn't a real date, but I liked the way Cade looked at me, how his eyes got dark when he was turned on. I liked being responsible for that.

By the time I was finished with my make-up it was almost six-thirty and time slowed to a crawl. My mind was racing with the possibilities of tonight. What kind of encounter with someone like Cade would require an elegant dress? Were we going out to eat first? It seemed too much like a date. And this wasn't about teaching me how to date. I could carry on an intelligent conversation over a meal once the initial contact was made. I knew how to do that quite well. Most of the help I needed wasn't outside the bedroom.

My face flushed. My previous encounter with Cade hadn't exactly been inside the bedroom. Was that what he was going to do tonight? Push my boundaries by us having some sort of tryst in public? My stomach clenched at the idea of Cade and me in a janitor's closet or a bathroom, desperately pulling at each other's clothes, eager to get off before someone caught us...

A knock at the door startled me out of my thoughts. I hurried to open it, my mouth already opening to offer a greeting. The words died in my mouth at the sight of Cade in a tux. He'd looked good in the suit he'd worn on our 'date,' and I was pretty sure he could pull off any outfit he wanted, but there was something about how a man wore a well-tailored tux. And Cade most certainly wore it well.

"Definitely not a schoolteacher dress."

I raised my eyes to see Cade smiling at me. A flush of heat spread across my skin, and it wasn't from embarrassment.

He held out his hand. "Shall we?"

I slid my hand into his and told myself that the tingle of pleasure going through me was acceptable. After all, Cade had said himself that physical attraction and enjoyment were part of his work.

"Why'd you pick me up instead of having me meet you at the hotel?" I asked, wording the question in such a way that it didn't sound like I was fishing for information on where we were going.

He wasn't fooled. "Because we're not going to a hotel." He glanced at me. "It's a surprise."

Knowing he was trying to surprise me caught me off guard. That sounded more like something a boyfriend would do. I kept my thoughts to myself though. I didn't want him to think I was thinking of him like a boyfriend. I wasn't. At all. It was just an observation and made me even more curious.

A town car sat at the curb in front of my building, looking distinctly out of place in this neighborhood. Cade opened the door for me and I slid in, conscious of the way the slit exposed quite a bit of leg before I gathered the fabric and pulled it back into place.

"You have lovely legs," Cade said. He closed the door before I could respond and walked around to the other side.

"Thank you," I mumbled as he sat next to me.

"You don't take compliments well, do you?" He brushed a curl off of my cheek as the car started forward.

I shook my head.

"Then that's one of the issues we'll have to work on. Modesty and gratitude are appreciated, but confidence when accepting a compliment is also attractive." He settled back in the seat, his body not touching mine, but close enough I could almost feel it. "Pay me a compliment."

"What?" I was startled by the request.

"Pay me a compliment." He winked. "Tell me I'm pretty."

"You're pretty." I blurted out the words, then flushed. "I mean – I – oh shit."

He laughed, a genuine laugh that soothed my embarrassment. There was nothing false about his amusement. "I suppose I asked for that." He reached over and squeezed my hand. "I just wanted to demonstrate a way to accept a compliment without getting flustered."

"Easy for you," I muttered, looking down. "Nothing throws you off."

"You do," he admitted.

My head jerked up.

"You're not like the other women I see," he said. "It's refreshing." His eyes twinkled. "And entertaining."

"Glad to know I amuse you," I said dryly.

"I just meant that it's rare someone can surprise me, and yet you manage to do it." He paused for a moment and I watched the professional mask slide back into place. "We're almost there. We'll work on compliments more later."

"Almost where?" I asked.

"Pritchard's Art Galleria."

Okay, definitely not what I'd expected. Maybe it was some sort of erotic art. I could see Cade thinking it was 'entertaining' to take me into a place full of nude or sexual photography or artwork. Trying to shock me seemed like something he'd want to do. I told myself that no matter what I saw in there, I wouldn't get embarrassed.

"The owner's a friend of mine," Cade said. "And tonight's the opening for a promising new artist Alejandro is particularly fond of."

I nodded. When the car stopped, Cade got out first and stretched out his hand to help me from the car. As I straightened, he wrapped my arm around his. I tried not to focus on his warmth but rather on the gallery in front of me. It was all glass and metal, but done in unique designs that weren't like any sort of standard architecture. I liked it.

Other well-dressed people were heading for the entrance all around us and I couldn't help but wonder how many of these women had purchased

Cade's services before. How many knew what he was, and by connection, why he was here with me? My stomach lurched as I thought of how they'd look at me, thinking the only way I could get a man was to pay for it.

"What's wrong?" Cade whispered. "You were fine a minute ago, but now you're stiff and tense."

Damn him and his annoying habit of being observant. I decided honesty was better than trying to deny that I was bothered. "Have any of these women hired you?"

If he was surprised by how blunt I was, he didn't show it, and he didn't seem offended that I'd asked. Instead, he scanned the crowd before answering. "I see two previous clients." He glanced down at me. I watched as first understanding, then something darker, moved across his features. Neither one stayed long. "You're ashamed to be here with me." It was a statement. Flat and without any indication as to the emotions behind it.

I lifted my chin. "This isn't exactly the kind of thing I want advertised." I felt his fingers tighten on my arm, just a fraction but enough to convey that what I'd said upset him. "Cade, it's not..."

"One of those women is here with her husband, who I doubt knows she hired me. The other is here with someone else like me." There was an edge to the last two words. "Neither one will say a word, and they can't very well look down on you because they were in your same position." His mouth curved into a humorless smile. "Or a variety of other positions."

An awkward silence fell between us as he led me into the gallery. We passed a waiter with a tray of champagne glasses and each took one. I drank half of mine at once and a glance at Cade told me he'd drained his and taken another. All of the positive anticipation I'd felt going into this evening had faded. I knew what I'd said had been horrible, no matter how I felt. And that itself was wrong too. How could I look down on Cade for what he did for a living? Was I really so awful of a person that I'd judge someone like him when I was the one paying for his services?

We stopped at the far end of the gallery. Most everyone else was crowded up front and the way the space was set up, we were hidden between a large sculpture and a wall that held a pair of paintings on either side. I turned to face Cade, but he kept his eyes on the painting behind me. I reached up and put my hands on his face, turning his head until he was looking down at me. I surprised myself with my boldness, but it was something that had to be done. He'd never done anything to hurt me and I'd treated him like shit. He didn't deserve it. He was a good man, no matter what he did to make money.

"I'm sorry," I said. "It's how I was raised, and that's not an excuse. It's just sometimes hard to shake off your childhood, you know?"

He nodded. "I know." His arms slid around my waist and my hands shifted to behind his neck. "And I'm used to the comments."

"That doesn't mean what I said was right." I pulled myself closer to him, feeling the heat from his body against mine. "I really am sorry."

"Thank you for apologizing. No one's ever apologized before." He bent his head and pressed his lips against mine.

It was a simple kiss, a chaste one, but I felt the warmth from it straight down to my toes. Then he released me and took a step back. His hand reached for mine and he laced our fingers together. He turned his attention back to the painting and gestured at it, drawing my attention to it as well.

"Alejandro told me about this piece. It's his favorite. Autumn Sunrise."

"Wow," I breathed. It was beautiful landscape, not one of those abstract paintings I never really understood.

"I understand why he likes it so much," Cade continued. "The artist managed to capture the juxtaposition between the beauty of the dying world at autumn and the new beginnings found at the start of the day."

I looked up at him, puzzled. "Okay, I have to ask. What are we doing here? I thought you were supposed to teach me about... you know." I glanced around to see if anyone was close enough to hear us. "Sex."

"Aubree, if you can't say the word, you shouldn't be doing it." His tone was mild. "That actually goes for pretty much anything when it comes to sex." He gave me a sideways look, something wicked glinting in his eyes. "If you can't ask me to fuck you or tell me you want me to spank you..."

"Cade!" I hissed, yanking my hand away from his. "We're in public."

He laughed. "Relax. No one's around." He took my hand again.

I scowled at him. "So why are we here then?" I went back to my original question.

"Part of your lesson is appreciating beauty."

"I appreciate beauty," I snapped. I didn't like how smug he sounded when he said it, like we were in some twisted, NC-17 version of My Fair Lady.

He led me around the wall to stand next to a sculpture. "What do you see when you look at this?"

I studied the figure in front of me. It was a man and a woman, carved from stone that I assumed was marble. She was nude, her hands partially covering her breasts, her legs twisted just right to still be considered modest. The man was also nude, but his hands were on her shoulders, his legs planted shoulder width apart so that everything was exposed.

"I'm not a prude when it comes to art, Cade," I said.

He pulled me in front of him, standing close enough to speak directly into my ear. "Look at them, Aubree. When you see something like this, do you just see line and symmetry? Can you only appreciate that it's well-formed, with graceful curves?" His voice slid across my skin, caressing it. "Can't you feel the desire between the man and his lover? How she wants him, but is holding back? The beauty of a piece like this, of any piece, isn't merely in what you see, but in the story it tells."

There was a passion in his voice that told me he wasn't just reciting things he'd read in a book or he'd overheard other people saying. And it wasn't just from a viewer standpoint either. I understood the difference. I taught literature. I loved literature. I could speak passionately about the subject, but I'd heard authors speak on the same subjects and there was a difference in their tone. Something very similar to what I was hearing from Cade right now.

"This isn't just about seeing art, is it?" I turned, feeling a pang of disappointment when he took a step back so that we were half a foot apart. I ignored the feeling and pressed the issue. "Are you an artist?"

The corners of Cade's mouth tightened.

"You are," I said. "Can I see some of your work?"

He was shaking his head before I finished asking the question. "I'm not an artist. I dabble. That's it."

"But you have finished pieces, don't you?"

His eyes were hard as he looked down at me. "That's not why I brought you here. This is a lesson in beauty. Part of what you're paying me for."

This time, I was the one who reached for his hand. I knew it wasn't a good idea to pry into his personal life, but I knew so little about this man with whom I was sharing so much of myself. "If this is about beauty, then show me what you find beautiful. Let me see the world through your eyes."

He held my gaze until I wanted to look away, but I didn't. He was searching for something in my face and I would remain steady until he found whatever he was looking for. After what seemed like forever, he nodded.

"All right. Come with me."

# Chapter 8

He asked the driver for the keys to the town car and gave the man what had to have been a huge tip, and then he acted like I was the crazy one for asking where we were going. I'd never seen someone leave their driver standing on the sidewalk. Then again, I wasn't exactly accustomed to having a driver, so maybe it was something rich people did when they got bored.

"Why didn't you just have him drive us?" I asked as he changed lanes.

"Because there's a slight chance that leaving this car unattended will result in it being stolen."

I gave him a sharp look, expecting him to laugh at the joke, but then I recognized some of the signs along the road. He wasn't kidding. We were heading into a not-so-good section of the city. It wasn't quite the kind of neighborhood where I'd be scared to walk by myself during the day, but at night, I'd be extra cautious and have my pepper spray ready. More vandalism and theft occurred around here than violent crimes against people, but it still wasn't a great place to live.

Why was Cade taking me here? I'd asked to see his work. This couldn't be where he lived. Even I made enough money to stay out of this neighborhood, and that was saying something. He had to live in a better part of the city.

We parked in front of what looked like some sort of abandoned warehouse. The bottom floor was boarded up and the front covered with graffiti and grime. He looked over at me, a half-smile on his face.

"You might not want to leave anything in the car. The insurance will cover it if it's gone when we come out, but it's a hassle." He got out of the car and walked around to open my door. His hand tightened around mine as he led me to a set of stairs at the side of the building. As we started up them, he spoke again. "It's not really dangerous here, but a sweet ride like that is a temptation few can resist."

I nodded. It was actually pretty quiet, which I found surprising. My neighborhood was much noisier than this at eight-thirty on a Friday night. A gust of chilly October air made me shiver and then I was following Cade into a dark space that flooded with light just seconds later.

It was an absolutely huge loft. It ran the entire length of the building, which made it almost three times the size of my apartment. The entire space was open, with the exception of what I assumed was a bathroom. A bed was shoved against the far wall, the mattress lumpy-looking even from where I stood. The blankets piled on it must've been a necessity during the winter. It wasn't cold in here since the wind was blocked, but it wasn't exactly warm either. A small kitchenette was in the other far corner with the basics. Fridge, sink, stove, none of which looked like they'd been used recently.

All of that, however, was peripheral. The majority of the room was taken up with what I now realized was the purpose for our visit. Canvases stood on easels and leaned against walls. A half-finished sculpture of some kind sat on a table among tubes of paint. It looked more like something formed from clay rather than chiseled from rock, but I couldn't tell what it was supposed to be. Among the paintings hanging on the walls were photographs, some black and white, some in color. A few were of people, but distant shots. Most were of nature or architecture.

"This is yours." I made it a statement instead of a question.

"You wanted to see my work." Cade took off his tux jacket and laid it across the back of a chair that looked like it had come from a thrift store.

"You don't live here, do you?" Somehow, I couldn't mesh the image of Cade in a tux with living here.

He shook his head. "I have a condo in the city." He smirked at me. "And much nicer furniture."

"Then what's this?" I gestured around me.

He hesitated and I wondered if he was trying to decide whether or not he wanted to tell me. "This is where I used to live."

My eyebrows went up, but I didn't say anything. If he wanted to tell me more, then he would.

"Once I began in my current occupation, I could afford a nicer place, but I kept this place for my... hobby."

The way he said the last word made me think he didn't exactly like thinking of art as a hobby. Instead of pushing, I walked over to the closest painting. It was a portrait of a sad-looking woman with dark brown curls and dark gray eyes. I didn't need Cade to tell me she was his mother. In addition to her curls and eyes, he had her nose and cheekbones. She was young in the picture, not too much older than Cade was now.

"She's beautiful," I said.

"She was." His words were clipped.

I suddenly remembered his tattoo, the letters RIP above 'Mom.' I didn't know the story or how long she'd been gone, but I turned to offer my condolences all the same.

"I work with different mediums, as you can see." Cade turned his back to me and walked toward a stack of canvases, the gesture telling me we were venturing into forbidden territory. "I'm never sure which one's my best, so I try them all. Experiment and see what I can do with each one."

"Do you develop the photographs yourself?" I followed his lead away from emotionally personal things.

"There's a space downstairs I use for a darkroom," he said. "It was easier to convert that than try to add one up here. Photography's a fairly new thing."

"Well, they're really good." I cringed at my words. Couldn't I come up with something better than 'really good'?

"Thank you." Cade picked up something from a cluttered table. He moved several easels out from the center of the room and then opened up the cloth he'd picked up and laid it on the floor. "You know," he said. "I never bring clients here."

A thrill went through me at his words and I told myself to stop being silly. We just had a different arrangement than he had with other women. It was an on-going teaching relationship, nothing more.

"I appreciate the chance to see your work," I said, unsure how I was supposed to respond to his statement.

"You're the only one who ever asked," he said simply. He didn't look at me as he picked up some paint and brushes and set them on the drop cloth. "But now, I think you need to do something for me in return."

The atmosphere in the room shifted.

"Let me paint you."

I swallowed hard, visions of every movie I'd ever seen where a woman reclined on a couch, nude, and allowed a man to paint her. It wasn't the idea of Cade seeing me that made me hesitate. Once it was done, it would be there, available, for anyone to see.

"Cade, I–"

"It's part of your lesson for the night," he said. "I was going to conduct this in a slightly different manner, but now that I have you here, this is what I want to do." He took a step toward me. "Everything off. You can put it on the chair over there."

Since he hadn't given me specific instructions about how he wanted me to undress, I did it quickly and efficiently. I was surprised at how easy it was to take off my clothes in front of him now. It had taken me months to not want to turn out the lights or undress under the blankets when I'd been with Ronald. Now, I easily resisted the temptation to cover myself as I turned back to Cade. My heart thudded painfully against my chest as I saw he was stripping as well. The man was a work of art himself.

It wasn't until he walked over to put his clothes on the chair that I thought to wonder why he was naked as well. Before I could ask, he was giving me new instructions.

"Go stand in the center of the drop cloth."

I did as I was told, but couldn't stop myself from flicking my eyes down to catch a glimpse of his cock. I licked my lips as I remembered how he tasted and I wondered what it would be like to take it now when it was still soft, feel it grow in my mouth until I couldn't take it all. My pussy grew wet at the thought.

When I turned to face Cade, he was walking toward me with a paintbrush in one hand and a palette of different colors in the other.

"My dry cleaner would kill me if I got paint on my tux," he said. "And this is going to get messy." He dipped the paintbrush into a dark red color.

I gasped as the cool paint spread across my breast. Definitely not what I had in mind when I agreed to let him paint me. But, as the soft bristles moved over my skin, spreading the paint in circles, I had to admit that I liked the sensation. It wasn't quite tickling, but close enough that I wanted to squirm as the brush started down between my breasts. Cade switched to a deep blue that mixed with the red to make purple, and that was the color he ran down my stomach to my belly button. The brush moved over my hips and around my back.

When it dipped into the top of my crack, my hands clenched. The brush began to zig-zag across my left cheek, then my right until most of my skin was covered. Then it was gone and I heard it drop to the floor. A moment later, Cade's hand was in the middle of my back, the paint slick between our skin.

He walked around me so that I could see him again. His eyes met mine for a moment and then he dropped to his knees and put his hands on my hips. The paint on his palms was black, but it only registered for a moment before he was kissing me.

I cried out as his mouth pressed against me, his tongue delving between my lips to find my clit. I'd never considered how waxing would change the way oral sex felt. It was like there were nerves I'd never known existed and Cade's mouth was finding every single one.

I reached out to put my hands on his shoulders to steady myself and he pulled back. I made a sound of protest, my fingers flexing.

"Get paint on your hands," he said. "Touch your breasts."

I cupped my breasts, covering them with my hands and squeezing to make sure my palms were covered with paint. My nipples were hard, aching for attention, and I obliged, rolling them between my fingers until Cade pushed my legs further apart and ran his tongue down to my core. My hands dropped to his shoulders, smearing color across his tanned skin.

My nails dug into his flesh as he thrust his tongue inside me, teasing around the entrance and then moving back up to circle my clit. I squeezed my eyes closed as a wave of pleasure hit me. The wet heat of his mouth sent me over the edge and I called out his name as I came. My knees tried to buckle and Cade's arms slid around me, supporting me as he lowered me to the drop cloth.

He put his lips against my ear. "Feels different bare, doesn't it?"

I nodded. It felt like every inch of skin between my legs was tingling. Being that sensitive might make the pain of waxing worth it. I heard a ripping sound and looked down to see Cade rolling a condom on his now-hard cock.

"I imagine it must feel amazing bareback," he said as he rolled me onto my side, facing away from him. "That is the one thing I don't do." He stretched out behind me and ran his hand down my leg. "But when you find a man you trust enough, I encourage you to try it."

His statement hit me. I'd almost forgotten the reason we were doing this. To make it possible for me to have the confidence to seduce and fuck other men. He lifted my leg slightly and began to slide inside, bringing my thoughts back to the present. None of the other stuff mattered. What did matter was the pressure and burn of him slowly filling me. I bent my knee, letting my ankle rest on his calf, and the change of angle pressed his shaft against my front wall.

"Fuck." The word barely made it out, the sound strangled. He was rubbing right against my g-spot with every inch he moved and the lower part of his cock was stretching me wider at the same time. The duel sensations made it impossible for me to think clearly.

"Each position has its advantages and reasons behind it." Cade brushed his lips against the side of my neck. "Some allow for deeper penetration, some provide stimulus right where you need it." He sucked at the place where my shoulder and throat met. "But for a man, the visual is always important. And what we can do with our hands."

His hands moved from my hips as his body came to rest, flush against mine. One hand went to my breasts, alternating between the two, rolling my nipples between his thumb and forefinger. The other hand slid over my stomach and down between my legs. His finger parted my folds and found my swollen clit.

"If your man doesn't know what to do with his hands, show him." His teeth scraped my ear lobe and I shuddered. "Put your hands over mine."

I did, my fingers not even close to covering his.

As he began to thrust into me, he gave me further instructions. "Show me how to touch you, how you like your clit rubbed. Show me how hard to pinch and twist your nipples."

It was odd, I thought, as I moved our hands together, how he was in control, but showing me how to take command. Our fingers moved together over my clit; my hand setting the pace and showing his how to move in circles, sending pleasure coursing through me. The hands on my breast were working my nipple until it began to throb, each tug making my body jerk against his, pushing him harder and deeper.

"Pleasure is beauty, Aubree," he whispered in my ear. "Every sensation has its own unique beauty, even pain." He twisted my nipple hard and I cried out. "Each person is wired to find it in their own way."

I was panting now. My fingers slipped and slid against Cade's as we rubbed my clit, our skin slick with paint and my own juices. I didn't know I could be this wet.

"Give yourself over to every sensation." He nipped at my neck. "Learn what you love and don't be ashamed of it."

He moved faster, his hips slamming into me with enough force to make me cry out. I didn't want him to stop, I wanted this to go on and on and on. I knew there was a lot I still had to learn, but I knew I liked this, the merging of pain and pleasure. I liked him taking me so hard that I knew I'd feel it the next day.

"Come for me, Aubree," he said. His voice was harsh. "Come for me now or you won't get to."

The thought of being so close to the edge, only to be denied brought memories flooding back of all the times Ronald had taken care of himself and never even thought to ask me if I'd come.

"I want you to come," Cade said. "I want to feel your pussy contracting around me, squeezing me until it hurts. I want to hear you scream your pleasure."

My head fell forward, my eyes closing as his thrusts forced away the past.

"Every decent partner wants to see and hear his woman climax."

I could feel it getting closer, the pressure inside me threatening to boil over. And then he was pushing my hands away. I whimpered, unable to believe he was going to deny me, but then his hands were there, taking care of me. His fingers knew exactly how to move; the right amount of friction to apply.

"A real man wants to be responsible for making sure his woman is satisfied."

I could hear the strain now and knew he was close.

"Never fake it," he said. "Never settle for anything less than this."

His fingers tightened around my nipple even as he drove himself deep. My back arched and I would've screamed if I'd had enough air. Wave after wave of pleasure washed over me as Cade thrust into me over and over again, his thick cock pushing through my spasming pussy even as his fingers kept rubbing my clit until I was almost sobbing, pushing at his hand. It was too much.

My limbs went limp, twitching as he buried himself inside me one final time and came without a sound. He stayed there, his arms wrapped around me, tucking me against his chest as my brain tried to remember how to function.

I vaguely wondered how much of a pain it was going to be to get the paint off, but I didn't care. The two orgasms I just had were worth having to scrub myself raw.

"There's a shower in the bathroom." Cade broke the silence. "Do you want to go first?"

I shook my head. "I don't think my legs are up to working yet."

Cade laughed and I could hear the note of pride in the sound. I wondered if he felt that way with every woman he fucked. My stomach twisted, and I pushed the thought aside. I watched him walk across the room, appreciating the way his muscular ass flexed with each stride. I'd never met anyone who was as confident naked as he was. As he disappeared into the bathroom, I rolled onto my other side so I was facing the wall with most of Cade's work. I thought I understood it now, what he'd said about appreciating beauty. It was strange. I'd come to Cade to teach me about sex but he'd already done more than that. Who would've thought hiring an escort would've changed the way I looked at myself and the world?

I pushed myself into a sitting position, grimacing at the way the paint clung to my skin. The sound of running water came from the other end of the loft and the image of Cade came into my head, water washing the paint off of his body, running down over the dips and curves of his muscles.

My stomach clenched with desire. It didn't matter that I'd already come twice or that just one round of fucking was enough to leave me sore the next day. I wanted him again. I ran my hand through my sweaty curls and looked at the bathroom door. I was willing to bet it didn't have a lock on it, and if it did, I doubted Cade used it.

Could I do it? That was the question. Did I have the guts to walk in there, step into the shower and tell him I wanted to fuck him again? And what if I did? How would he take it? Aside from our first kiss, he'd initiated everything between us, taken charge and told me what to do and how to do it. Then again, I reasoned, wasn't the entire point of our teaching sessions for me to learn confidence? For me to be secure enough in who I was to get what I wanted?

I stood up. My knees were a bit shaky still, but my legs stayed under me as I walked across the loft. Doing this completely naked proved how far I'd come in such a short period of time. I reached for the doorknob and told myself that if it was locked, it meant he didn't want me in there with him.

The door opened easily and I slipped inside. The shower was like the rest of the place. A ratty plastic curtain hung on a rod running the length of the tub. It was clear with little swirly designs that did nothing to hide the muted outline of Cade's body. I took a deep breath of the hot, humid air and reached for the curtain.

Cade half-turned as I climbed into the shower behind him and, for once, he didn't even try to hide his surprise. He tilted his head back as he finished turning, letting the last of the shampoo rinse from his hair. My eyes followed the suds down his body and I tried not to let my gaze linger on his tattoo. He'd made it clear that his mom was off limits.

"Decided you wanted to go first after all?" he asked.

I shook my head. Now that I was here, I found I didn't have the words to say why I'd come. I supposed that meant I'd have to show him. I took a step toward him, the warm spray caressing my body and sending rivulets of paint running down me. I reached out and ran my hand over his chest. I felt his breathing hitch as my fingernails scraped across his abs, and then my hand wrapped around his cock and he swallowed hard.

Ronald had been the kind of guy who needed at least eight hours of sleep before he could manage to get it up again, but considering what Cade did and how well he was paid, I had a pretty good feeling he could handle a second time. After just two strokes, I had my answer. I felt him begin to thicken in my hand.

"Not that I'm complaining," he began. "But what prompted this?"

I looked up, blinking against the water. "One of the things you're trying to teach me is to get what I want, right?" My hand continued its steady up and down movement and he continued to grow.

He nodded.

"Well, this is what I want." I lightly squeezed his cock.

He made a sound that was very much like a growl and grabbed my upper arms, pushing me back until I was against the cool tile wall. I stared up at him. I had a moment to glimpse a wild expression on his face, a look so foreign it should have frightened me, but then his mouth came down on mine and nothing else mattered.

His body leaned against mine as his tongue pushed past my lips to plunder my mouth. I moaned as my nipples rubbed against his chest and he swallowed the sound. His tongue curled around mine, drawing them both back into his mouth. I dug my fingers into his wet hair as he sucked on my tongue, sending a bolt of pleasure straight through me. The wet between my legs had nothing to do with the shower.

He was hard against my hip and I knew I had to have him inside me. I hooked my leg around his waist, shifting our position so that his cock was rubbing against my bare pussy. My eyelids fluttered. Fuck that felt amazing.

Cade groaned, his mouth tearing away. He rested his forehead against mine as he grabbed beneath my knee with one hand and reached between us with the other. I braced myself, but even knowing what was coming didn't stop me from wailing as he entered me with one swift thrust. I started to shake as my body tried to adjust. It was too soon after the last time and every nerve ending was still raw. I cried out as he withdrew, then slammed back into me. The base of his cock rubbed against my too-sensitive clit and I whimpered. I was on total overload. Each sensation was too much.

The cold tile on my back and ass.

The water pounding down on us.

The feel of skin against skin as he drove into me.

My eyes opened.

Shit.

"Cade." I pushed against his chest but he was solid muscle. I grabbed the back of his neck, pulling him toward me, and said the only thing I could think of. "Yellow! Yellow!"

He instantly froze and looked down at me. "What's wrong?"

I could hear the stress in his voice, but I knew as soon as I told him, he'd understand why I'd stopped. I lowered my leg and he let me go, taking a step back. I watched his eyes flicked down as his bare cock slid out of me.

"Oh, fuck." He took another step backwards, his eyes wide... disbelieving.

For the first time since I'd met him, there was no mask and I could see how horrified he was to have lost control.

"I'm sorry, Aubree," he apologized as he struggled to regain his composure.

I shook my head. I wasn't going to let this end. I closed the distance between us and grabbed his cock. His entire body shuddered. "We're not done yet," I said.

"But I don't have any condoms in here," he started to protest.

"There are other ways we can finish this." I smiled up at him as I reached for his hand with my free one. As I moved his hand between my legs, I felt a rush of power. This was what he'd been talking about. This was what it was like to know what I wanted and take it.

As I stroked him, his fingers slid between my folds, finding me slick and open and ready. Two fingers slipped inside as his thumb began to circle my clit. I looked up at him, my breathing quickening as I saw the lust in his eyes.

"What do you want, Aubree?" He spoke in a low voice.

Not second-guessing myself, I leaned forward and ran my tongue over his nipple. He moaned and I smiled against his skin. When I scraped my teeth over it, his cock jerked in my hand and he swore.

"Do that again." His voice was hoarse.

I nipped at the dark flesh and his breathed whistled from between his teeth. His free hand buried in my hair, holding my head in place. As he pushed a third finger into my pussy, my hand tightened around his cock and he groaned. His dick pulsed in my hand and felt him spurt between us, his warm cum coating my hand. His fingers twisted in my hair, sending a jolt of pain through me as he ground the heel of his hand against my clit.

I cried out as I came, my pussy clamping around his fingers hard enough to make him swear again. The hand in my hair dropped as he wrapped his arm around my waist, holding me up as my climax rolled over and through me.

As we came down, he moved us further under the spray, letting the water wash away everything. When I could finally stand on my own, he released me and then handed me shampoo. We finished showering in silence and while I knew Cade had enjoyed himself, I couldn't help but feel that something about what happened was bothering him. I didn't ask about it though. If it was something I needed to know, he'd tell me. Otherwise, I was going to just keep on with what we were doing. As unconventional as it was, it seemed to be working.

# Chapter 9

When Adelle called me Saturday morning and asked if I wanted to come over for brunch, I hadn't been sure it was a good idea. I pushed aside my hurt and remembered I was trying to work past our issues. I didn't agree with how she'd done things, but I could no longer deny that hiring Cade had been a good idea.

Still, things were awkward between us as we ate the crepes and strawberries her chef prepared. I'd asked her once, shortly after Morgan had died, why she kept the huge house in Chicago's most affluent neighborhood as well as the entire staff. She'd always told me she felt uncomfortable having people do things for her, and she'd always thought the house too opulent. Her answer had surprised me. She told the staff that if they wanted to look elsewhere, she'd give them a great recommendation, but that she wouldn't leave any of them without a way to care for themselves and their families. Everyone had stayed and I knew they all thought of each other more like family than employer and employees.

Adelle had a good heart, no matter how her plans screwed up her intentions. It's part of why we remained such good friends through the years, and I hoped it would be enough to get us past this current obstacle. I was pretty sure it would. Adelle felt horrible about what she'd done and she was doing a great job of keeping her thoughts about my hiring Cade to herself.

"Morgan's step-father called me this morning." Adelle broke the silence.

"What does he want now?" I asked, grateful for a topic that wouldn't lead back to Cade.

Adelle rolled her eyes. "What do you think?"

Her late husband, Morgan Dane, had lost his father when he'd been a kid. The man his mother had remarried had been a real piece of work. He made Ronald look like a saint. She'd actually caught him hitting on one of the bridesmaids at the reception. Morgan's mother had died when he was fifteen, leaving him in his step-father's custody. The old man had shipped Morgan off to boarding school and hadn't wanted anything to do with his step-son until Morgan had made his first million. When Adelle and Morgan first met, his step-father had been awful, coming on to Adelle to the point where she'd had to file a restraining order. After Morgan's death, when his step-father found out Adelle had gotten everything, he'd started harassing her with everything from legal threats to marriage proposals.

"Which was it this time?" I asked. "Does he want to marry you or sue you?"

Adelle laughed and we fell into the familiar pattern of discussing how cruel fate was to have taken Morgan so young while leaving his asshole step-father to clutter up the world. Right after Morgan's death, it had been an emotional catharsis for Adelle, often ending in her smashing something expensive, but over the last year, it had become more of a thoughtful musing with fond memories mixed in.

By the time we were done eating, the tension between us had eased and I was beginning to feel better about where things were going between us. Maybe it wouldn't take as long as I'd thought to get our friendship back to normal.

"I'll be right back," Adelle said as she picked up my plate and carried both of our dishes into the kitchen.

Her phone rang before she'd gone more than a couple steps and she quickly tapped the screen to send it to voicemail. She gave me a bright smile and hurried off to the kitchen.

It was nice of her to not want to interrupt our time together, I thought, but the expression on her face had been strange when she'd looked at the phone. My curiosity got the best of me and I reached over to tap on her screen.

Cade.

I frowned. Was there some issue with her paying him? I thought he received his payments up front in case he needed to pay for something for our sessions. Maybe he was scheduling another date for us. I knew it was dangerous to think of our time together as dates, but after the other night, it was hard not to.

"Jocelyn made fresh cinnamon rolls, complete with her famous butter cream icing," Adelle announced as she came back into the kitchen.

"Is there something wrong with Cade's payments?" I blurted out the question. If Adelle didn't want to pay him anymore, I needed to know. I needed to be prepared to have it end.

Adelle's eyes flicked down to her phone and then back to me. "No, everything's fine." She sat down across from me and put the plate of delicious-smelling rolls between us. Her smile was tight and it didn't reflect in her eyes. Something was up.

"What's going on?" My eyes narrowed. My trust in Adelle was thin at the moment, so maybe I was reading too much into this, but I didn't think so.

"Nothing," Adelle said too quickly.

I grabbed her phone, ignoring her protest. If I spoiled some surprise Cade was going to give me, I'd feel bad, but at least I'd know Adelle had been telling the truth. The way she couldn't look at me as I went to her voicemail made me think, however, that I was right. I put it on speaker so she could hear it too.

"Adelle." Cade's voice was smooth. "I'm just calling to confirm our session for tomorrow night. If there's anything specific you want to use, please bring it with you."

One look at my best friend's face told me I hadn't misunderstood the message at all. I understood it perfectly. She was still fucking Cade.

# Chapter 10

## *Cade*

I looked down at my phone as I ended the call. It was second nature to me now to leave messages like that, reminding clients of sessions, letting them know to bring toys or whatever specific things they wanted to use. I put my phone in my pocket and walked over to the window. I looked out at the city, remembering when the view I'd seen hadn't been so nice. At twenty-seven, I had an expensive condo in one of the nicest neighborhoods in all of Chicago, but I'd only lived here for a couple of years. And the road to get here hadn't been an easy one.

I could still remember the first time I'd booked a client on my own. How nervous I'd been taking that leap. It hadn't been my first time doing what I did, but it had been the first time I'd been the one in charge.

Heather Benedict.

I still remembered her name, everything about her really, down to her peach-colored toenails.

I'd spent nearly a year planning how I was going to break away from the situation I'd been in, how I was going to branch out on my own. I'd saved money, set up a budget and carefully planned everything possible. The one thing I hadn't been able to plan, however, had been client response. If I hadn't been able to find clients on my own, the entire thing would've crashed and burned. And it hadn't been just finding any woman. I'd needed ones I found attractive who'd be willing to pay a fairly steep price. My starting prices had been much lower than they were now, but they'd still been expensive for someone without any backing.

I'd gone into the Ritz-Carlton hotel bar, convinced I'd get thrown out before I could get a seat, and I'd waited there, scouting potential clients. When I'd seen Heather, she'd been sitting by herself, her shoulders hunched as she nursed her drink. I'd approached her, struck up a conversation, and then offered my services. For the first few seconds after I'd said the words, I'd been terrified that she'd laugh or call for security. Instead, she'd slipped a hotel key card into my hand and had told me to wait ten minutes before following.

Looking back, I could see how unsure I'd been, hiding it all behind swagger. I'd spent three hours with her, using everything I'd learned over the previous four years to make her scream, and she'd paid me everything I'd asked. Plus a bit of a bonus. As I'd left her hotel room, I'd felt none of the guilt or disgust that I'd felt before when I'd been with a client. Instead, I'd felt a new kind of freedom, the kind that had come with knowing that I'd regained control of my life. From that moment on, I'd been in charge and I'd never looked back.

I fucked who I wanted to fuck, and I got paid an obscene amount of money to do it. I never had to go through the hassle of dating or even working to get a woman in bed. Instead, they came to me and paid for my time. I never lacked for sex, and I never had to deal with the emotional shit storm that inevitably came from relationships.

I loved my life.

My phone vibrated against my leg. I frowned as I looked down at the screen. Catherine. One of my repeats who I'd had to cut off a few days ago. She'd been getting clingy, talking about leaving her husband for me. I didn't want to talk to her, but I knew her type. If I didn't answer, she'd keep calling.

This was exactly why I made it clear to every client that an emotional attachment meant the end of our business transactions. That was my number one rule. No one fell in love.

## End of Vol. 2

# Casual Encounter Vol. 3

## Chapter 1

Without thinking about it, I reached out and tapped the touchscreen again, letting Cade's voicemail play through a second time. I stared at Adelle's phone, unable to bring myself to look at my friend. Not that it mattered. I knew she wasn't looking at me. She hadn't been able to since I'd taken her phone. The fact that she was acting embarrassed was proof that she knew she had been caught.

It wasn't that I didn't think Cade had other clients. And it wasn't because I thought Adelle shouldn't hire an escort. I couldn't exactly judge her for that. I even knew and was pretty much okay knowing that Adelle had probably used Cade's services in the past. Getting mad at her for having fucked him before would've been as useless as getting angry at anyone for their previous relationships.

No, it was because she'd scheduled a session with Cade just two days after he and I had been together. And she'd done it knowing he was my mystery savior, the man I couldn't get out of my head. She'd done it following my devastation from learning he'd slept with me out of contract instead of desire. I'd gotten past that. I'd forgiven her. I'd placed our friendship as more important. But considering how her deceit involving Cade had nearly destroyed our relationship, I couldn't believe she'd involved him again. That was the part that really left me stunned.

The thing about this entire situation that hurt me the most had nothing to do with Cade. It had been how my friends viewed me, how little they truly knew me. Adelle, who I'd known as long as I could remember, hadn't been able to understand why I'd been furious with her for hiring a prostitute without telling me. And now, it seemed like she understood what she was doing would hurt me, but she didn't care.

As the message ended for the second time, I stood. I pushed her phone across the table. "I'll be going." My voice was harsh. "I don't want to keep you from getting together all your little toys for your session with Cade."

She opened her mouth but I didn't want to hear anything she had to say. Apology. Excuse. Angry retort. I was through listening to her shit.

"Feel free to schedule a few more sessions this week. You'll both have plenty of free time. I'm done." She called my name, but I ignored her and hurried down the hall and out the door.

As I got into my car, I was glad I'd driven instead of letting Adelle send a car to pick me up like she'd wanted to. I just wanted to get away as quickly as possible. My tires screeched a bit as I drove down the driveway and I kept the speedometer rising even as I turned onto the road. My heart was pounding, my head chaotic, and there was still one more thing I needed to do. I waited until I was at least a mile from Adelle's house before I pulled into a store parking lot. This wasn't the kind of call I wanted to make while I was driving, and if I waited until I got back home, I'd either lose my nerve, or Adelle would've interfered. There was still a good chance I wouldn't be able to avoid that as it was.

I pulled out my phone and made the call. I was torn between wanting it to go to voicemail so I could avoid what I knew was going to be an awkward conversation and hoping Cade picked up so he could tell me it was all a horrible misunderstanding.

I scowled. It was that kind of thinking that made me need Cade in the first place. I tried too hard for the romance, for the emotional connection. I was blinded by how I felt. That had been why I hadn't seen what had been going on between Ronald and the wedding coordinator before they ran off together. There was no misunderstanding this situation. Adelle had hired Cade to do his job. That was it.

I tapped Cade's phone number and closed my eyes as it rang. I had tears in my eyes and desperately didn't want to cry or sound as if I was.

This part was a business decision, nothing more. I breathed a sigh of relief when it went to voicemail. I hoped it meant Adelle was talking to him already. She could explain what happened so he'd understand my message.

I kept it short and professional. "Cade, I don't believe I can continue with our arrangement. I'm sorry for any inconvenience this may cause or disruption to your work schedule. I wish you all the best."

It wasn't until I hung up that I realized I hadn't said my name. I assumed he'd recognize my voice. Knowing he might not realize who I was broke the last of my resolve not to cry. My face crumbled and with a sob that torn through my soul, I put my face in my hands and let go.

# Chapter 2

I turned off my phone for the rest of the Saturday. I didn't feel like having to go through the whole dance of sending calls to voicemail and deleting them. I would deal with them tomorrow. I had papers to grade and I wanted to avoid gorging myself on ice cream again. I'd had enough over the past couple months.

Unfortunately, while I did manage to avoid the ice cream, I wasn't able to concentrate enough to get much grading done. At one point, I'd had to refrain from going on a rant on one student's essay regarding the friendship between Mercutio and Romeo, and how Romeo's relationship with Juliet betrayed Mercutio. That was when I realized I needed to just go to bed.

When I showered, I tried not to think of the last time I'd been with Cade and the shower we'd taken together, but it wasn't easy. I could almost feel him against me, the way he pushed me against the wall and thrust inside me, making me wail. How hard it had been to make him stop when I'd realized, in the heat of the moment, we'd forgotten a condom. How we'd finished each other off with our hands.

I closed my eyes and rested my forehead against the shower wall, cursing myself for the memories. I didn't want to think about them. I didn't want to think about him. I told myself that I'd ended things because it was too weird with Adelle involved, but a part of me had already been thinking I was getting too attached. Even now, my body was craving his. I needed his hands on me, his mouth, his cock...

"Dammit, Adelle!" I slapped my palm against the shower wall. "Why'd you have to fuck everything up?"

I let myself cry again in the shower, but once I was out, I was done. No more dwelling. I was going to move on. I sighed as I dressed for bed and climbed under the covers. I was getting tired of having to give myself those 'moving on' pep talks. Maybe, I thought, I needed to consider actually moving. My brother and sister-in-law had been trying to talk me into moving to Texas for the past couple years. I could visit them for Christmas and take a look at the schools in the area. I wouldn't leave until after this year was done, but if I had that plan all set up, I could get through until June.

I fell asleep wondering if I could meet a nice cowboy, who would sweep me onto his black stallion and steal me away.

When I woke on Sunday morning, I didn't exactly feel good, but I was clear-headed enough to see things for how they were. I wasn't going to leave a job I loved and move hundreds of miles away. I would eventually forgive Adelle because I wasn't going to throw away a lifetime of friendship because we'd hit a rough patch. I'd learned enough from Cade that I could manage, and not continuing with him would make it easier to get things smoothed out between Adelle and me. I would miss the sex, of course, because he was the only lover who'd been able to make me climax like that. He was easy on the eyes and not bad to talk to, but that didn't mean anything. I could think fondly about our time together, but from a clinical perspective. It was all physical. Nothing else.

With all of that firmly sorted out in my head, I ate breakfast, turned my phone back on and started to work on my papers. Adelle had called twice yesterday, but hadn't left any messages. I was surprised, but decided to let it go. I would forgive her, but I wasn't going to make the first move. Not now anyway. The pain was too fresh and sharp.

I fell into the rhythm of grading and let literature essays purge everything else from my mind. Grammar corrections came automatically and my red pen marked the mistakes. I stopped around noon to make myself some lunch and then kept working while I ate. If I stayed busy, I didn't have time to think. That was a very good thing.

I finished my work shortly after making a grilled cheese sandwich for supper and wondered if I should clean the apartment to stay busy. It wasn't exactly dirty, but I didn't want to spend the rest of the evening sitting on the couch watching TV or finding some chick flick to cry through. If I cleaned the kitchen and bathroom, I could then shower and go to bed. There was a new murder mystery I'd been meaning to read, but I'd been too distracted recently to get started on it.

I was still debating the merits of scrubbing my bathroom floor versus cleaning the oven when my phone rang. It was Adelle. I looked down at my screen, unsure if I had it in me to talk to her. By the time I decided I didn't, she'd already gone to voicemail. I waited a few minutes, trying to decide if I was even ready to hear her voice before finally playing the message.

"Bree." Her voice was shaking. "I know you're pissed at me and I hope you'll eventually give me a call back so we can work this out. Until then, I want you to know that I canceled my session with Cade. Your friendship means more to me than anything else. Especially sex."

She inhaled like she was going to say something else, but didn't. The voicemail ended and I deleted it, softening as the full impact of her confession ran through me. Adelle had canceled her time with Cade because of me. She hadn't argued that she had every right to see him, especially since she'd been with him first. She hadn't told me it was none of my business who she or Cade fucked.

I touched 'call back' and she answered on the first ring. There was a moment of awkward silence and then we both started talking at the same time.

"Bree, I'm so sorry..."

"Adelle, I get it..."

We fell silent for a moment again and I let her break it.

"I wasn't thinking; at least not thinking with my brain," she said. "But I understand why you're upset."

"Don't worry about it," I cut her off. I didn't want to get into the reasons why I'd had an issue with her seeing Cade. I knew Adelle. She'd read too much into it and we'd end up arguing again. "It doesn't matter."

"It does," she insisted.

I sighed. "Adelle, I don't want to fight with you and I don't want to have this talk over the phone. I think we can get past this, but we're going to need to have a very frank discussion at some point."

She was quiet for a moment. "All right," she said. "I really don't want to lose you, Bree."

"I know," I said. "I don't want to lose you either. We just have to deal with what's happened."

"Do you and Mindy have the day off tomorrow?"

I looked at my calendar and silently swore. She was right. I'd completely forgotten that we didn't have school tomorrow. I was going to have to find something to keep myself busy for the day. "Yeah, we do."

"Let's meet for lunch. We can talk then."

At least that'd give me something to think about other than Cade, plus I wouldn't have to spend days trying to figure out how to keep things from being awkward on Friday. "All right," I said. "How about the café around the corner from my place?"

"That sounds good," Adelle said, the relief evident in her voice. Just hearing it made me feel better.

"And, Bree, um, there's something else I have to tell you."

That didn't sound good.

"Cade's on his way to see you."

"Shit."

"I'm sorry," Adelle said. "When I called him this afternoon to cancel our session, I told him why and he said he was going to see you."

I didn't ask her why it had taken her until today to decide to cancel her session. I was too busy trying to figure out how I was going to handle things when Cade showed up. Especially considering I was wearing my bum-around-the-house outfit: a pair of gray yoga pants and a baggy t-shirt... with no bra.

There was a knock on my door.

"I have to go." I hung up before Adelle could say anything else and hoped she wouldn't think I was still mad at her. I just couldn't deal with her on the phone and Cade at my door at the same time.

"Aubree, open up." His voice had that quiet, authoritative tone that made me automatically move to obey.

I was half-way to the door before I even realized I'd moved. I stopped before I could unlock it. I took a deep breath and closed my eyes. I could do this. It wasn't personal. It was business. Once Cade understood that, he'd leave and we'd never see each other again.

I ignored the pang going through me at the thought. I opened the door and took a couple steps back. Without meaning to, I crossed my arms, hating myself for feeling so self-conscious.

Cade shut the door behind him. His face was blank as he turned toward me. "Would you like to explain why I received a voicemail from you canceling our contract, and then a call from Adelle canceling her session because you were upset I was seeing her?" His words were even and carefully devoid of any inflection.

"I didn't ask her to cancel her session," I said.

"That wasn't the question," he said as he took a step toward me.

It was all I could do not to back up. There was a tension radiating from him and I could feel my body wanting to respond.

"Did I ever give you any indication that you were my only client? That we were somehow exclusive?"

I shook my head. I needed to explain before he thought I was jealous. Ending our deal was one thing, but I didn't want him to be mistaken as to why I'd done it. It had to be very clear that I didn't have feelings for him. Because I didn't.

"I know you see other clients," I said. "It wasn't that."

"Really?" He raised an eyebrow, clearly not believing me. "Then what was it?"

He was starting to get that smug tone that was equal parts annoying and sexy. I scowled at him. "It was weird thinking of you fucking my best friend and then fucking me, okay? Comparing us." The last two words came out before I could stop them. That was it, I knew, the main reason the idea of Adelle and Cade together had freaked me out. The truth.

"Comparing you."

I lifted my chin. "Yes. Comparing us. Our bodies. How good we are in bed." I forced the words out. "I've been friends with Adelle my entire life. I know what it's like to stand next to her, to have guy after guy walk past me to get to her. I shared a room with her in college, so I got an earful of her social life, okay? I know you'd been with her before, but it's different thinking you'll fuck me one day and her the next. I'll always be wondering how I measure up. If you're thinking about her—"

He closed the distance between us in two quick strides, his eyes blazing. "I told you before, I don't think of anyone else when I'm with you... with any client. And I never compare."

I swallowed hard. "That's bullshit. You're a man, not a machine. Besides, I didn't say you'd do it on purpose, but I know Adelle." My lips tried to curve into a smile, but didn't quite manage it. "And when we're next to each other, I'm not the one who stands out."

"First of all." Cade's voice was harsh. "Adelle won't be hiring me again until after I'm done with you."

Done with me? I started to shake my head, to tell him it didn't matter now. We were done. I wasn't doing this anymore.

"And second," he continued without even acknowledging my negative response. "I'm not done with you."

# Chapter 3

His mouth was on mine and I was drowning in his kiss. He hadn't let me say anything after declaring he wasn't done with me. I'd barely had time to process the words. His lips came down with bruising force, taking my breath away, and his arms had wrapped around me, crushing me against his chest. When his tongue teased the seam of my mouth, I'd been unable to resist and parted my lips with a moan. I couldn't deny how my body responded to him.

When he pulled away, I was breathless and trembling, my knees weak. I expected him to let me go and distance himself, reminding me with his body language that this was professional. He wanted this because I was guaranteed repeat business for weeks. Adelle was an occasional fuck and she'd probably go back when he was done with me. I was a steady paycheck, at least for a while.

He kept one arm around me though, his hand at the small of my back. The other hand came around to push a few stray curls from my face.

"I don't compare you to anyone, Aubree," he said. "There's no comparison."

I blinked. What did he mean by that? Before I could ask, he was releasing me, his stance shifting.

"If you're drawn to a dominant man, he may feel the need to punish you from time to time, particularly when you do something that displeases him."

My head spun as Cade switched into his teaching mode. What the hell?

"If you're a submissive, you may even ask him to punish you." His voice lowered. "You may need him to." He undid the button on his jeans. "Or you may just wish to please him. Get down on your knees. It's time for you to learn a few things about using your mouth to get your partner off."

I stared at him. How had we gone from that to this?

"Aubree," he said my name sharply. "Use your safe word to end this, or get down on your knees."

I swallowed hard. I should do it, scream the safe word at the top of my lungs. I told him we were done and he'd refused to accept me as being serious. But, if I said 'red,' I knew he'd listen. We'd be finished and he'd walk out the door. Which was exactly what I wanted.

I opened my mouth to say the words and took a step toward him for emphasis. Then, all thought fled my mind and I sank to my knees before him. His eyes filled with heat and my stomach clenched as his pupils dilated with desire. He unzipped his jeans and pushed them down to mid-thigh, taking his boxer briefs with them. My pussy throbbed at the sight of him, already half-hard and bigger than average.

"You have a very talented mouth, Aubree." Cade cupped my chin, tilting my head up so that I was looking at his face rather than his cock. He brushed his thumb across my lips, then pressed it inside my mouth.

I flicked my tongue across the pad of his thumb and then sucked on it. His fingers tightened on my chin and his eyes darkened.

"That's good, but there is more to a blow-job than a single piece of anatomy." He pulled his hand back, moving it down to stroke his cock as it stiffened. "This isn't the only thing that enjoys the wet heat of your mouth." He dropped his hands and cupped his balls. "We're going to work on your attention to these too. And we're going to see how much of me you can take."

I nodded.

"Not today, but by the time we're done together, I expect you to be able to take me right down that pretty little throat of yours."

Fuck. I bit my bottom lip. I didn't know if it was actually going to be possible, but when he said it like that, I definitely wanted to try.

His hands dropped to his sides and I took that as my cue. I started like I always did, running my tongue along every inch of him, circling the tip as I wrapped my hand around his base. He still wasn't fully erect, but he was big enough that my fingertips couldn't touch.

"A man's balls are just as sensitive as his cock," Cade said. "Take them in your hand."

I cupped them. The skin was softer than it looked, the texture smoother than what I expected.

I'd felt them against my legs when having sex, and I was sure I'd brushed against them when I'd given Ronald a hand job or blow job, but this was the first time I'd deliberately paid direct attention to them.

"Use your mouth. Lick them, suck on them. All the things you do to my cock, do to my balls too."

I bent my head, the angle awkward, but as soon as I ran my tongue along them, Cade moaned and I forgot about how uncomfortable the position was. I took one of his balls into my mouth, rolling it around on my tongue, feeling it shift and move within its sack. When I switched to the other one, I heard Cade mutter something that sounded like an encouragement, but I couldn't quite make out the words.

His hand rested on my head, his fingers massaging my scalp as if he was restraining himself from pulling my hair. I moved back up his cock, letting my hand take over on his balls as I paid attention to the thick shaft that was now curving up toward Cade's flat stomach. When I lowered my head, I took the first couple inches into my mouth, savoring the weight of him sliding across my tongue.

"That's it," Cade breathed. "One hand playing with my balls while you suck my cock."

The pleasure I heard in his voice spurred me on. I was glad he was pleased with what I was doing, but I'd have liked it even more if he hadn't been able to talk. I hollowed out my cheeks every time I pulled back, determined to prove I could make him lose control. I wanted it more than I wanted anything. To hear and see him come apart and know I was the cause.

He pressed down on my head, wordlessly encouraging me to take him deeper. I opened my mouth wider, ignoring the brief pop in my jaw. The head of Cade's cock reached the back of my tongue and I felt myself starting to gag. I pulled back, half-expecting him to shove me back down, but he didn't.

"Again," he said. "Breathe slowly through your nose."

I did as he said, concentrating on taking air in as his cock slid back into my mouth. This time, when I automatically started to gag, Cade's hand tightened in my hair. He held me just a split second longer than I would've stayed, not enough to make me panic, but enough to remind me who was in control. I coughed as he slipped out of my mouth.

"A partner who enjoys control may want to control the speed and depth of a blow-job." Cade used the hand in my hair to tilt my head up. "But always remember that it is the illusion of control."

I frowned at him, not understanding.

"It is your mouth that can make him come. Your hands holding one of the most sensitive parts of his body. It is an exercise in trust." He brushed his fingers across my lips. "Now, make me come."

I took his cock back in my mouth, wrapping one hand around the base and using the other to cup his sack. I used what he'd just taught me, taking him as deep as I could as my fingers rolled his balls. I sucked hard, letting the way his fingers twisted in my curls tell me what he liked. He swore and his cock twitched in my mouth.

"I'm close," he warned me and I knew he was giving me a choice of where I wanted him to finish.

It wasn't a choice, really. I'd known what I wanted from the first moment I'd seen him. I'd known then that I wanted to feel him come in my mouth. I could feel his balls tightening, ready to empty, and I went as far as I dared, fighting the urge to gag as more than half of him filled my mouth. I couldn't hold it for long, but it was enough.

Cade's fingers curled into a fist, pulling my hair hard enough to hurt, but I ignored the pain and focused on swallowing every last drop as he climaxed. A stream of obscenities spilled out of his mouth as I sucked and licked the sensitive piece of flesh in my mouth until he was pulling me away, breathing hard. I looked up at him, desire flaring sharply at the near-wild look in his eyes.

He grabbed my shoulders and pulled me to my feet. One hand cupped the back of my head, holding me in place as his mouth covered mine. He thrust his tongue between my lips, twisting around mine. His other hand pushed under the waistband of my pants and underwear. As his fingers roughly parted my folds, I moaned, my hands fisting in his shirt. A finger rubbed against my clit, almost too hard and I cried out. He swallowed the sound, then nipped at my already swollen lips. He rested his forehead against mine, panting with his need for air. As his fingers dropped lower, two slid inside me.

"Fuck." I closed my eyes, giving myself over to the pleasure spreading through me.

"Never." His voice was low and fierce. "Never let anyone make you feel like you're less than who you are."

A small whimper fell from my lips as he ground his palm against my clit. My legs shook as a thousand sensations trilled through me.

"Do you hear me, Aubree?"

I nodded, unable to speak. I was pretty sure only my grip on his shirt was keeping me from falling. That and his hand between my legs.

"Good girl," he said. "Now come." He curled his fingers and pressed against my g-spot. "Come." He rubbed in a small circle as he scraped his teeth along my jawline.

I did.

I came with a shudder, silently, wordlessly, my body too overloaded with all that had happened to process anything as complex as sound. The hand on my neck dropped to my back, holding me as his fingers continued to slide in and out of me, drawing out my orgasm until I wasn't sure I could take anymore.

When he pulled his hand from my pants, my legs almost gave out and I had to lock my knees in order to stay in a standing position. I took a step back, leaning against my table as I focused on regaining my breath. Cade pulled up his pants, tucking himself back inside before zipping up. His eyes met mine as he raised his hand and slowly licked the fingers that had been inside me. My stomach contracted almost painfully as I watched.

"We're not done until I say we're done," he said. He turned to go, saying one more thing before closing the door behind him. "I'll be in touch."

# Chapter 4

When I walked into the café late Monday morning to meet Adelle for lunch, I had a much different attitude than when I'd last talked to her. Cade's confrontation made me realize that while there was an element of being justifiably upset, my emotional upheaval had more to do with my own personal insecurities. And those were something Adelle could never be responsible for.

"Hi," she said nervously as I approached the table.

When I smiled, I saw the relief cross her face. I sat across from her and placed my usual order with the waiter who came by just a few seconds later. This was my usual go-to place when I didn't feel like making a meal, so they knew me pretty well.

"So, how do you want to do this?"

I didn't think I'd ever seen Adelle look so uncomfortable, so out of her element. As long as I'd known her – which was as long as I could remember – she'd been this confident, unstoppable force. It was that, the uncertainty in her eyes that raised my resolve to make sure we worked this out. There was no doubt our fighting was hurting us both.

"How about no bullshit?" I said bluntly. Her eyes widened slightly and I understood why. While I was a generally honest person, I also tried to be tactful. When she nodded, I continued, "I wasn't jealous. I mean, I'm not jealous. I know Cade has other clients. It wasn't that. Part of why I was so hurt..." I paused, exhaling the pain the words wanted to bring back. I needed to think with the rational side of my brain, not the side that wanted to scream and throw a tantrum. "I was hurt because you didn't realize or care that I'd be upset for you to hire Cade while he and I were still sleeping together. Plus, you were clearly hiding it from me."

I paused as the waiter brought out our salads and water. We ordered the same thing without thinking about it, a reminder of how connected I'd always thought we were.

"That's one of the reasons I was so angry with you when I found out what Cade was, too." I picked up my train of thought. "Did you really know me so little that you thought I'd actually want you to pay someone to have sex with me?" I ignored the irony of how I'd ended up doing just that. "It was more about how you seemed to think I'd be okay and accepting with all of it."

She reached across the table and put her hand over mine. "I am so sorry, Bree. I do know you better than that. I was just thinking of what I wanted instead of you."

I covered her hand and let us have a moment before I continued with my confession. She deserved to hear it all. "It wasn't all your fault," I said. "A big part of the blame is mine, especially this last time."

She gave me a puzzled look, but didn't ask me to explain. She knew I would.

"The reason I was freaked out by the idea of you and Cade sleeping together while he and I were still having sex is because I was scared he'd compare me to you."

The look on her face was real. She was surprised, shocked even, to hear this confession. I could tell she'd never had a clue how things had always been for the two of us. I had to smile at that. She was completely confident in who she was and how she looked, but she'd never seen herself as more desirable than me.

"That doesn't matter." I waved my hand dismissively, while her open mouth continued to find words of rebuttal. "The point is, I was upset with you for something that was, in large part, my issue. Not yours. And I'm sorry I took it out on you."

Adelle got up and walked around to where I was sitting. She crouched down and wrapped her arms around me. "Let's never do this again, okay?" She sniffled. "This has been awful, having you mad at me."

I nodded and felt my own eyes welling up with tears. I'd decided to be with Cade because of how my friends treated me, but I could see now that I was partially responsible too. And none of it was worth losing my friends over. "Never again."

Her arms tightened around me for a moment, and then she stood up. She wiped at her eyes as she went back to her seat and I took a moment to compose myself as well. After a few seconds of silence between us, Adelle took a bite of her salad and looked thoughtfully at her glass of water. "Do you think it's too early to order wine with lunch?"

I chuckled and the tension between us disappeared as if it hadn't ever been there to begin with. By the time I left the café, the weight I'd been carrying since the end of August was gone. Adelle and I were okay. Cade was still going to teach me. And I was going to show everyone that I wasn't who they all thought I was.

When I went back to school on Tuesday, more than one of my students commented on how much happier and more relaxed I looked. Even the other teachers noticed and I got quite a few knowing looks from the staff. Well, knowing in the sense that they suspected I had a new man in my life. Mindy was the only one who knew the whole truth.

By the time Wednesday came around, I found myself wondering if it was the sex that had made the difference... or the companionship. I constantly found myself thinking about Cade, which was nothing new. From the moment he'd rescued me from that horror of a date, I'd been unable to stop thinking about him. The thing was, it was less and less the sex that popped into my mind. More often, I found myself thinking about his smile, the way his hair fell across his face. The artwork in his loft and the way he'd talked about the painting at the gallery.

And, of course, what he'd said to me on Sunday, how there was no comparison to me. I told myself that he was speaking professionally and with an artist's eye. Each person was beautiful in their own unique way. He'd told me before that he never took on a client he didn't find physically attractive. He was all about beauty and confidence. His statement meant all of that.

By mid-morning, however, I asked myself if the problem was that I wanted what he'd said to be real. Did I want it to be a declaration of feelings? Was I reading so much into it because I was doing what I knew I shouldn't do? Was I falling for Cade? As the morning progressed, I told myself that wasn't the case. It was physical attraction, an enjoyment of his company and mind-blowing sex. No emotions involved. I was safe.

Shortly before the bell rang for lunch, I heard my phone buzz with an incoming message. The students in the front row giggled and exchanged looks. I always made a point of making sure all of my students followed the rules about no phones on in the classroom. Catching me with my phone on, even on vibrate, was a reasonable source of amusement. Despite my curiosity, I waited until I finished the lecture and the students were either working on their homework or wasting time chatting before pulling out my phone. I kept it under the desk, not wanting to set a bad example, and hoped it wasn't an emergency, though I couldn't imagine why anyone would text me when they knew I was in class.

My heart skipped a beat when I saw Cade's name. Then my eyes skimmed the first sentence and heat rushed to my face. Fuck! I turned off the screen and shoved my phone back into my bag. What the hell was he thinking sending me a text starting with "Take off your panties..."?

"Are you okay, Miss Gamble?" One of the students, a cheerful girl named Tracy, spoke up.

All eyes turned toward me and my flushed deepened. "I'm fine, Tracy." I forced a smile, reminding myself that there was no way any of the fourteen juniors sitting in my classroom could know what I'd just read. "Just overly warm."

She gave me a look that said she didn't believe me, but fortunately didn't press the issue. As soon as the bell rang, the kids hurried away and, as the last one left, I put my forehead down on my desk and breathed a sigh of relief. My phone buzzed again and I pulled it out, double-checking to make sure I was alone before opening the message.

You have three minutes.

What? I frowned at the screen, then scrolled up to read the previous message in its entirety.

Take off your panties and come to the parking lot. You'll be having lunch with me. A car will be waiting.

Shit. I stared at the message. He couldn't be serious, could he?

Another message came through.

Two and a half minutes. Better not be late. Tardy girls get spanked.

"Fuck," I said softly. Things low inside me tightened. There was no way he meant any of this, right? He had to be messing with me, seeing how far he could push.

Two minutes. If you don't tell me you're on your way, I'll come in there, and I doubt you want to risk anyone catching me bending you over a desk.

Oh, shit. He was serious.

I quickly typed "coming." I jumped from my seat and practically ran out of the classroom. I was halfway toward the exit before I realized I hadn't done the first thing he'd told me to do. I was still wearing my panties. I looked around and quickly ducked into the janitor's closet. I leaned against the door as I reached under my skirt and yanked them off. Cool air brushed against my bare pussy and I shivered. This was so wrong.

I reached for the door before I realized my underwear was still in my hand. I had two choices: hide my panties in here and hope no one found them before I could sneak back in. Or I could try to hide them under my clothes. I swore, feeling time ticking away with every second I hesitated. Swearing, I shoved my panties down the front of my shirt and folded my arms across my stomach. I felt ridiculous and exposed as I walked out of the closet, but that didn't stop the coil of heat inside me. As much as I hated to admit it, knowing I was in public without underwear was turning me on.

A gust of cold wind hit me as I stepped outside and I suddenly realized I'd left my jacket in my room. It was too late now to go back inside and get it. Besides, I could see the Bentley Cade used sitting at the edge of the parking lot. I hurried toward it, hugging myself now because of the cold. A particularly icy breeze went up my skirt and I gasped. My nipples were hard already, chafing against the soft cotton of my bra.

The back door of the car opened and I gratefully climbed in, keeping my knees tightly together even though my skirt was long enough that I probably wouldn't flash anyone. Cade sat less than a foot away, but didn't say a word as I closed the door. He reached up and tapped on the divider between us and the driver.

I smoothed down my skirt nervously as the car pulled out of the parking lot. "I only have a half hour for lunch, but I do have a planning period right after, so I can be a little late, but not too much." I snapped my mouth shut, realizing I was getting dangerously close to babbling.

Cade still didn't speak. He wore that blank mask that meant he didn't want me to know what he was thinking. The car drove less than a quarter mile and then turned into the driveway of a small tech business. We moved around to the space in the back and parked.

When the silence continued for nearly a minute, I couldn't take it anymore. "What are we doing here?"

The mask cracked and Cade's eyes glinted. "Well, first, I'm going to have to punish you for being late, and I think you know what comes after that."

Oh fuck.

# Chapter 5

My heart was hammering against my ribs so hard I was surprised Cade couldn't hear it. My eyes darted from him to the divider. There was no way he was going to spank me, and definitely not in the backseat of a car with the driver in the front seat. Then his hand closed around my wrist and he pulled me to him and I realized that was exactly what he intended to do.

"Don't worry." He pushed some hair away from my face. "The driver can't hear a thing up there."

I wasn't sure I believed him, but I had the feeling I didn't really have much of choice in the matter.

"Now, for your punishment." His free hand slid up my thigh and under the hem of my skirt. "Did you do as you were told?"

I nodded, unable to speak as I tried to accept what would happen next. The anticipation was nerve wracking and I was having a difficult time concentrating with Cade's hand on my bare thigh.

His hand moved higher and I parted my legs without having to be told. Cade chuckled and my arousal spiked. His laugh was quickly becoming one of my favorite sounds. His fingers brushed against my bare pussy and I sucked in a breath.

"I guess that means I only get to punish you for being late."

"You sound disappointed." I found my voice, breathless as it was.

"Oh, I am." Cade's voice dropped. "Do you have any idea how long I've wanted to bend you over my knee?"

I tried to swallow but my mouth was suddenly dry.

"Remember your safe words?" he asked.

I nodded.

"Good."

I let out an undignified yelp as he pulled me across his lap, easily manhandling me into place. I would've been completely mortified at the position I was in, but Cade was pushing up my skirt to expose my ass and my poor brain didn't know what to deal with first.

"You were five minutes late," he said, running his palm over my bare cheeks. "So I think five swats would be fair."

"Five?" Butterflies fluttered in my stomach. I knew it wasn't much, but this whole thing was playing hell on my nerves.

"Would you prefer ten?"

I shook my head.

"Relax," he said. "Close your eyes."

I did.

"Let yourself feel."

I took a slow breath and as I let it out, Cade's hand came down. I heard the crack of his palm before I felt it, and then pain blossomed on my behind. I made a sound the second time, my hands tightening as it hurt more.

"Give yourself over to it, Aubree. Don't fight it. Surrender." Cade's voice was firm, but hypnotic. "That's two."

I cried out when his hand came down again, this time on the same spot as the first. I could feel the heat spreading across my skin this time, a warmth moving through me in a way that wasn't entirely unpleasant. On the fourth, the contact made my pussy throb. The sound that came out of me was half-moan.

"Hmm, I think someone is enjoying this." Cade sounded pleased. His fingers dipped down between my legs. "You're wet."

My cheeks flamed, but I couldn't deny the way my body tightened when his hand came down for the last time. I dropped my head, embarrassed at how much I liked what he'd done.

Cade pulled me up, positioning me on my knees in front of him. He cupped my chin and raised my face so that our eyes met. "Did you like it?"

I tried to look away, but he wouldn't let me.

"Aubree, did you enjoy being spanked?" The hand not holding my chin pushed between my legs. "Don't lie to me. I can feel how wet you are."

"I liked it," I admitted. More heat flooded my face.

"Say it," he demanded.

When I hesitated, he slid a finger inside me. I moaned.

"Say it."

"I liked you spanking me." A rush of shame washed over me. How had I gotten to this point?

"And I liked doing it." Cade's voice was harsh. "Never feel guilty for what you enjoy." He released my chin and removed his hand from between my legs. "Do you want me to fuck you?"

I nodded.

"Say it."

"I want you to fuck me." I blushed, but didn't drop my head so that was an improvement.

"And I want to fuck you," he said. He pulled a condom from his pocket and set it on the seat next to him. "But I'm not going to touch you until you tell me what you like."

I gave him a puzzled look. Hadn't I done that already?

"What are the things you enjoy that you feel like you shouldn't?" he asked. "The things that make you feel guilty when you fantasize or masturbate. The ones you'd always wished your ex-fiancé would do, but never had the courage to ask."

After all the things we'd done together, this would be the one to break me. I couldn't do it. I couldn't confess those hidden things. My hands curled into fists.

He tilted his head, the expression on his face making me feel as if I was being studied. "Do you know what I would love to do to you?"

I nodded, hoping this meant he was being lenient about making me answer his question.

"I'd like to spend hours on your nipples." His gaze flicked down to my plain cotton blouse. "Pull and twist and nibble on them until they were sensitive and swollen."

I took a shuddering breath as my stomach twisted.

"Would you want me to do that?" he asked.

I nodded.

"And what else?"

I knew what he was doing, but I accepted it, let his question take me where he wanted me to go. I couldn't go back to work like this. I needed him. "I like it when you use your teeth."

Cade's eyes darkened and he nodded, encouraging me to continue.

"And I like using mine." It was the first time I ever admitted any of this out-loud. "I think I might enjoy toys. I don't want real pain, but a little edge..."

"Makes things more intense," Cade finished the sentence.

"Yes," I said.

"What about now?" he asked. "What do you want me to do to you now?"

"I want you to fuck me," I repeated what I'd said before, but this time I went one step further, forcing myself out of my comfort zone. "Hard. I always felt like Ronald thought I was going to break or something. Everyone thinks I'm some fragile thing, but I'm stronger than I look. I'm not breakable." I put my hands on Cade's thighs and felt his muscles tense. "I need you to fuck me like you're trying to break me. I want to feel you for the rest of the day."

"Fuck, Aubree," he groaned. He was reaching for me even as I moved onto the seat.

I sat on his thighs as my hands worked open his pants. By the time I'd freed his cock, he had the condom ready and rolled it onto his hard shaft. Before I could slide down on him, however, he flipped us so that I was sitting on the edge of the seat and he was kneeling on the floor in front of me. His hands gripped my hips so hard I knew there was a good chance I'd have bruises, and then he was burying himself inside me with one quick, hard thrust.

I screamed, my back arching, hands scrabbling at the seat for some sort of purchase, something to hold or tear, an outlet for everything I was feeling. Every nerve was on fire, a blaze of pain and pleasure. He stilled inside me, and I could feel his muscles trembling with the effort it took to keep from letting loose. But I didn't want him to hold back.

"Please," I begged. "Please, Cade."

He drew back and snapped his hips forward, drawing another wail from me as another wave of painful pleasure washed over me, more pleasure than pain this time. He didn't wait for me to ask him before he began to pound into me, using my hips as leverage to pull me toward him as he surged forward.

"Yes!" I cried out, my eyes closing. I could feel an orgasm approaching, something big. Then Cade's thumb brushed against my clit and I came so hard that, for a moment, it felt like everything had stopped, like the world was nothing but white, blinding pleasure.

When I opened my eyes, Cade was leaning over me, his breathing heavy. I hadn't even felt him come. When he pulled out, a shudder ran through me. I'd asked him to make me feel it for the rest of the day, and he'd certainly complied. I was probably going to be sore tomorrow too, but the good kind.

After a moment, I pushed myself up, grimacing at the wetness between my legs. Cade reached over to a small bag I hadn't seen before and opened it. He tossed me a pack of wet wipes and then got one out for himself. We cleaned ourselves up in silence and then he tapped on the window. As the car began to move, he returned to the seat next to me.

We pulled back into the school parking lot and I knew there was something else I had to do before I could go inside. Cade was probably going to laugh at me for this, but it was better than walking into the school without underwear. I unbuttoned my shirt.

"What are you doing?" He sounded mildly curious.

"I had to put my panties somewhere," I said as I retrieved them. "And that was the best I could do on short notice."

He laughed as I pulled on my panties and I had to smile too. After I'd done up my blouse again, I reached for the door.

"One more thing," Cade said.

I paused, waiting for him to continue.

"We're going away for the weekend. I'll pick you up at your place on Friday at eight. You'll need to bring at least one dress appropriate for a night out... and some sexy lingerie."

I smiled at him. I knew exactly what to pack. It was time.

# Chapter 6

When I went back in to the school, I felt like every eye was on me, like everyone knew what I'd spent my lunchtime doing. It was ludicrous. No one had even been in the parking lot when I'd gotten in or out of the car. No one was in the hall when I swiped my card to go inside. In fact, I didn't see anyone the entire walk to my classroom, but Mindy was sitting at my desk waiting for me when I entered the room.

"Decided to step out for lunch?" A smirk played over her lips.

I glared at her but didn't respond. I wasn't the best liar, especially not to my friends.

"Might've helped if you actually took your lunch with you." She gestured toward the container I'd put in the fridge that morning.

I glanced up at the clock and opened my fruit salad. The lunch period would be ending in just a few minutes which meant Mindy would have to leave for her next class. I stayed standing as I began to eat, grateful that Mindy was in my chair so I didn't have to try to explain myself if I happened to wince when I sat down. The spanking hadn't been bad, but combined with Cade's roughness, it was probably going to make sitting for the next couple hours a bit awkward.

"You were with him, weren't you?"

I chewed on a piece of cantaloupe and refused to answer, though I was sure my face was bright red and answer enough.

"Damn, girl." Mindy shook her head as she stood. "I just hope this guy isn't ruining you for real men. Because, trust me, this whole fairy tale thing is not realistic. Soon, you're going to have to come back down to the real world with the rest of us."

Mindy's words stuck with me for the rest of the day. Was it possible that Cade's instructions would make it harder for me to have a relationship because he'd become what I'd expect from a boyfriend? From a lover? Would anyone be able to measure up to Cade? And I didn't just mean sexually, though there was that. The question that really hit me as I was walking to my car, however, was: did I want anyone else to try to measure up?

When I got home, I went to my closet and pulled out the clothes I'd packed away. I set the box on my bed and opened it, my heart hammering in my chest. I wasn't sure why I was so nervous, but my hands were trembling. The first thing I'd thought when Cade said we were going away for the weekend was the contents of this box. Now, I wondered if I had been thinking about wearing these clothes not because I was ready to move on but because these were the clothes I would want to share with a boyfriend.

Those were dangerous thoughts. Especially when Cade was concerned.

I took out the garment on top. A brand-new, dark purple bikini I'd bought specifically for lounging around the cruise ship pool. I set it aside and went on to the next. A sheer black teddy with a series of laces down the sides so that it could be unlaced and easily removed. The deep blue dress I'd planned on wearing on the plane to the coast where Ronald and I would board the ship. Under that was the matching bra and panty set I'd intended to wear under the simple, but cute dress.

I felt a pang of sadness as I remembered how I'd picked out these items, wondering what Ronald would think of me in each one. I remembered how pretty I'd felt. These were clothes I felt comfortable in, not because I thought they hid me, but because I genuinely liked the way I looked in them. And I hadn't gotten to wear them for anyone.

They were special and the fact that I'd thought of them first meant I was thinking of this weekend as something more than just sex. Cade hadn't said or done anything to make me think that spending a couple days together was anything but business, but the idea of uninterrupted days and nights with him had me thinking along lines that were best left alone.

Problem was, my brain didn't want to leave things alone. All Wednesday night, all day Thursday and into Friday, I found myself wondering about the non-sexual things Cade and I would do together, the things we would talk about. Would I finally be able to get beneath that mask and get to know the man? Would we talk about things that had nothing to do with my sex life? More than once, I imagined what it would be like to fall asleep in his arms, to wake up next to him. Almost like we were a real couple.

By the time I was staring at the clock and wishing the bell would just ring already, I was forced to admit that I was in deep. I tried to convince myself for the past couple days that the only reason I was fantasizing about this trip was because I'd been so excited about my honeymoon and I hadn't gotten to take it. I told myself I wanted to know more about Cade because he was actually a decent guy. But while there was some truth to that reasoning, I knew it wasn't all there was.

Despite what I'd told Cade, despite the warnings I'd given myself and the promises I'd made that things between the two of us would only be business, I could no longer deny that I was falling for him.

I'd always known this was a possibility. For me, sex and emotion had always been linked. This arrangement with Cade had been, in part, an effort to change that for me. But I couldn't say I was surprised I was having a problem separating the two. Even after I'd learned what Cade was, I'd been drawn to him. Sure, I was physically attracted to him, but it had always been more than that. It was his confidence, the way he was so sure of himself. But there was also a part of him hidden, a part of him I wanted to know more about. I'd glimpsed that man on a few occasions, usually when I'd done something to catch him off guard, and what I'd seen just made me want to know him more.

I knew I couldn't act on it. First, because I knew he didn't feel the same way. He didn't do love or emotions. There was physical attraction and pleasure, but nothing more. And, second, because any mention of my feelings would result in Cade ending our arrangement.

Eventually, the way I felt would either go away or they'd reveal themselves, but for right now, I was going to pretend nothing had changed, that I was emotionally unattached. I knew that meant I'd end up getting hurt in the long run, but I couldn't help it. If I confessed, he'd leave me, and I didn't think I could handle losing him. Not yet.

So, after the final bell rang and the last of my students left, I packed up my things, reminded Mindy that I'd miss dinner because I was going on a trip, and then headed home to finish packing and grab a bite to eat.

I dressed in the outfit I'd intended to wear to the ship, knowing it would travel well. I was also wearing the matching bra and panty set I'd bought to surprise Ronald. I just hoped Cade would like what I'd picked. The dress was more conservative than what he'd had me wear before, but what I had on underneath was sexier. It reflected who I was more than anything I'd ever worn. An attractive exterior that didn't get much attention, but with desires that were a bit on the wild side. Just how wild, I was still figuring out.

Cade knocked on my door at five till eight and I was ready to go. He gave me an approving once over as he stepped inside the apartment.

"I forgot to tell you to bring your passport."

My stomach flipped. My passport. I knew where it was, of course. It was in the same place it had been since the end of the second week in August when I'd learned I didn't need it after all.

"I'll go get it." I went back into my bedroom and opened the top left drawer of my dresser. It was empty except for my passport. It had seemed fitting to put it in that specific drawer, the one Ronald had used when we'd been together. I'd packed his shit up after I'd received a box delivered with all of my things that had been at his place.

"Is there something wrong?" Cade's voice came from the doorway. "You do have a passport, right? When I made the arrangements with Adelle, she said you had one."

"I do." I picked it up and pasted a fake smile on my face. The anticipation I'd felt about this trip had been dampened by the memories. "Let's go."

Cade crossed his arms, the expression on his face saying he wasn't going to move until I talked.

"Ronald and I were going on a Caribbean cruise for our honeymoon," I explained. The words came out in a rush. I just wanted to get it over with so we could get on with the weekend. "That's why I got it. I didn't have one before." A pain went through my heart as I remembered how excited I'd been when

I'd seen it for the first time. "I've never even been out of the state before."

Cade came into my room and took the passport from my hand. His eyes locked with mine as he tucked it into the outside pocket of my bag. His fingers curled around mine. "Let's see what we can do about that."

I nodded, willing myself to ignore the way my heart skipped a beat when he took my hand. He led me back through my apartment, pausing only to pick up my bag. The town car that was waiting for us looked like the one from earlier that week, and even though I knew the chances of it being the same car were slim, I still flushed at the memory.

"We're not going on a cruise," he said as we settled into our seats. "And Toronto might not be as exotic as the Caribbean, but I think you'll enjoy yourself."

"I'm sure I will." If he was with me, I wouldn't have cared if we were just going down the street.

"The flight's only an hour and a half." His voice took on that business tone he had. "And a car will be waiting to take us to our hotel. It won't be very late when we check in, but I hadn't planned on us going out tonight." His last few words warmed.

I smiled, a genuine one this time. "That sounds good to me." I glanced at the divider and hoped the driver wasn't listening. "Because I followed your directions on what I was supposed to wear." I took the hem of my skirt, waited until Cade's eyes dropped, and then quickly flashed my sheer lace panties.

Cade's hands curled into fists against his thighs and the way his eyes darkened made my heart skip a beat.

"And the bra matches."

He made a sound in the back of his throat and my panties went from dry to wet in seconds.

"If we didn't have a flight to catch, I'd make you strip for me right here." Cade's voice was rough. "And if we have any delays, I can't promise I won't fuck you on the plane."

I tightly pressed my lips together. A part of me said there was no way I wanted any of that, but another part, the newer part, said it might not be such a bad idea.

Fortunately – or unfortunately depending on how I wanted to look at it – everything went smoothly. We got through security with plenty of time and didn't have to rush to board. We departed on schedule and had an uneventful flight. We made small talk and Cade ignored the flight attendants who flirted with him, keeping his attention solely on me.

This was the kind of thing that would spoil me for a real relationship. I'd never had anyone listen so attentively to what I had to say or carry on a conversation where they didn't seem the least bit distracted. I didn't know how Cade managed to keep things from getting too personal, but still allowed us both to talk about things we loved. Great sex wasn't the only thing that made him so good at his job.

The ride from the airport to the hotel was relatively quiet though. I kept my attention focused on what was outside the window, enjoying the skyline of a new city. I'd seen other cities in movies and on TV of course, but it wasn't the same as actually being here.

Then we pulled in front of this massive building with the kind of stone architecture that reminded me of a medieval castle. In fancy script, above the large front doors, were the words Windsor Arms Hotel.

Cade left our bags for someone to carry in and offered me his arm. The doorman gave us a polite smile and nod as we walked past. The inside was gorgeous. A massive chandelier hung in the center of the lobby and, as I looked up, I could see the second floor. My low heels clicked against the gleaming tile, sounding loud in my ears. This was the kind of place that made me feel like I needed to whisper.

Less than fifteen minutes later, we were getting off the elevator on one of the top floors and Cade was opening the door to our suite. Two bedrooms, two beautiful bathrooms, one with a walk-in shower and separate tub. A sitting room and small kitchenette. One of the bed rooms had a massive floor-length mirror with an ornate frame, as well as elaborate landscapes covering the walls. The other had a piano. In the bedroom.

Oh, yeah, he was definitely spoiling me for other men.

# Chapter 7

After I'd freshened up, I wasn't sure what I was supposed to do next. I stepped out of the bathroom and found Cade stretched out on the bed, his shoes and socks gone. At least that answered one of my questions. I'd already taken off my shoes and the carpet was soft and thick beneath my feet as I walked further into the bedroom.

Cade folded his hands behind his head. "Lovely room isn't it?"

I nodded, looking around. After all this time with Cade in these fancy hotels, I'd never feel the same about staying in some three-star place.

"Let me see what you wore for me."

I reached behind me and lowered the zipper. Without taking my eyes off Cade, I slowly let my dress slide off. Remembering what he'd told me during our first lesson together, I ran my hands over my breasts and then down to my hips, warming as Cade's eyes followed the movements. I waited for him to tell me what to do next.

Instead of giving me instructions, he climbed off the bed and stripped down to a pair of tight, dark gray boxer briefs. He walked over to where I stood at the foot of the bed and looked down at me.

"Turn around."

I did and found myself face to face with the mirror. It framed us perfectly, almost looking like a picture. Cade's eyes met mine in our reflection. He ran his hand down my arm and then back up again, his touch feather light against my skin.

"Watch," he said and pressed his lips against the hollow under my ear.

Out of all of the instructions he'd given me, this one seemed deceptively easy to follow. My stomach tightened as Cade's hands slid around my waist, his palms burning against my bare skin. When they moved to cup my breasts, I shivered. Even through the thin lace, my body responded to his touch.

"Your breasts are absolutely exquisite," Cade murmured in my ear as he ran his thumbs over my nipples. They hardened instantly. "Every man has his preference, but believe me when I say yours are perfect."

He pressed an open-mouthed kiss on the side of my neck and I moaned, my eyes closing. They flew open again as he tweaked my nipples, sending a little jolt of pain through me.

"Watch," he repeated firmly. His fingers found the front clasps on my bra without fumbling. He made short work of them and slipped his hands under the loose fabric to palm my bare breasts. "I want you to look at yourself and see how beautiful you are."

I swallowed hard as I watched our reflections in the mirror. It was different, seeing myself being touched in the mirror rather than just looking down at my body. In a way, it was almost like watching someone else, like it wasn't me.

Cade let my bra fall off of my shoulders and onto the floor. His fingers rolled my nipples and I moaned. I watched a pleased smile flicker across his face. "Do you want me to pull on them?" His voice practically dripped sex. "Do you want me to make these pretty little nipples of yours stand out, make them sensitive to the slightest touch?"

"Yes." The word was little more than a whisper, but I cried out when he did what I wanted. His fingers twisted my nipples, tugging on them until I was squirming against him. Each pull was just the right combination of pain and pleasure and I started to feel that familiar pressure building up inside of me. The moment he touched my clit, I was going to come.

"I'd love to see how you'd react with nipple clamps," Cade said. "I bet I could make you come from just those. The sharp little teeth bite into your flesh, and then, when they're taken off, all the blood rushes back and it's like thousands of tiny little pinpricks."

I made a sound. I wasn't entirely sure I'd like that, but when Cade said it, I was game for pretty much anything. He'd proven time and again that he could make me see stars.

One of Cade's hands settled between my breasts while the other dropped lower, sliding down my stomach and over my panties. I parted my legs as his fingers ran along the lace.

"You're soaked." He pressed his fingers hard against me and I moaned. "So aroused."

He released me long enough to slide my panties off, pausing only to press his lips against my left cheek. I wondered if he was thinking about how red he'd made my ass when he'd spanked it. The color had faded by the time I'd gotten home, but I'd been pretty sure it had at least been a deep pink when he'd finished.

"Do you see yourself?" Cade asked as he took his place behind me again. "Do you truly see yourself?" He ran his fingers through my hair and then moved his hand between my legs again. "Too many people are ashamed of the human body, of the way it's made." He ran his finger between my lips, brushing against my clit and making my hips jerk. "Look down."

I dropped my eyes to where his fingers were spreading me apart. My face flushed. I knew what things looked like down there, at least in a general sense, but I'd never had this view.

"See the beauty in yourself." His middle finger made circles over my exposed clit and I moaned. "Every part of you is beautiful." When he slid his finger inside me, my knees almost buckled and I came.

He kept steady, even strokes as waves of pleasure washed over me. Just as I was starting to come down, he added a second finger, sending new tremors through me. He twisted and scissored his fingers, stretching me for what was coming next. Then, suddenly, his fingers were gone and he was taking a step backwards.

I wanted to turn toward him, but he hadn't told me to do that yet and I had a feeling he had something very specific in mind for tonight. In the mirror, I watched him climb onto the bed, pull off his underwear, and rolled on a condom. How he managed to do any of it with that much grace, I didn't know. Practice, I supposed.

"You can look away to get on the bed," he instructed.

I walked toward him, feeling a rush of power as his eyes were drawn to my breasts. He really hadn't been lying when he'd said he liked them. When I reached him, he held out a hand to stop me from getting any closer.

"Turn around."

Not really a surprise there. I wondered if he'd specifically requested a room with a mirror across from the bed. I did as I was told.

"On your hands and knees."

A flare of arousal went through me. I'd been honest when I'd told Cade that Ronald and I hadn't just had sex in the missionary position, but I hadn't given him details. The truth was, there really hadn't been much variety. Him on top, me on top. That was pretty much it. Secretly, I'd always wanted to try other ways, the kinds of positions with names like reverse cowgirl and doggy-style. I just hadn't known how to bring any of it up without sounding like some kind of slut.

"Don't close your eyes," Cade instructed. "I want you to watch yourself the entire time I'm fucking you. I want you to see how amazing your body is, the way your face changes with ecstasy when you come. You need to see all of it."

I nodded.

Cade ran his hand down my spine and I arched up into his touch. A finger slid down my crack toward my pussy and I shuddered. I needed him inside me so badly it almost hurt.

"I don't know if it was the idiots who bypassed you for Adelle when you were younger, or someone else who made you feel like you were less than what you are, but tonight, you are going to see yourself the way I see you."

I moaned as the head of his cock nudged at my entrance. I started to close my eyes, then remembered my instructions.

His hands slid up over my hips and over my ribs, moving down beneath me to cup my breasts. He looked into the mirror, our eyes meeting. "See what I see, Aubree."

I watched his body curl more tightly around mine and his hips moved, pushing the first inch or so of his cock inside me. I shivered with pleasure. I wondered if I'd ever feel the same way when it was another man's body on mine...

Cade straightened and put his hands on my waist. His hips snapped forward and I keened. He'd stretched me enough that there was no pain, only the intense sensation of being filled so completely that it was as if we'd been made to fit together.

"Look at yourself," Cade ordered as he slowly drew back. "What do you see?"

I watched this time as he thrust back into me. The way my breasts swayed. How my lips parted. The blush across my skin that was more arousal than embarrassment.

"Do you see?" he asked.

My gaze slid up to him, watching the way his muscles flexed as he began to set a steady rhythm, each stroke reaching the very end of me. His strong jaw, those amazing lips, his eyes. How his dark curls fell across his forehead. I saw beauty, but it was all him.

He reached down and grabbed me by the shoulders, pulling me onto my knees. One of his arms wrapped across my shoulders, above my breasts, holding me so that my back was flush against his chest. His free hand splayed across my stomach.

"Your body is amazing, Aubree." Cade's lips were against my ear. His knees pushed at mine, somehow managing to spread my legs while still keeping his balance. "Look at our bodies together."

My eyes fell to where I could see his thick shaft buried inside me. I whimpered as he thrust up into me. The hand on my stomach slid down until it found my clit. My body jerked as his fingers brushed against the throbbing bundle of nerves and I moaned as the motion pushed Cade deeper.

"I love the way your body responds to me."

My stomach clenched and my heart thudded in my chest.

"How can you not see it?" His fingers were moving in time with his thrusts now, driving me closer and closer to the edge. "Every inch of you is any man's dream. Soft skin." He pressed his lips against the side of my throat. "Firm breasts. A tight, hot pussy. A body that quivers with the slightest touch."

His touch, I wanted to say. I didn't want to be any man's dream, only his. I didn't want any other man touching me.

"See yourself how I see you, Aubree Gamble." He was starting to breathe harder, every stroke coming faster. "See the exquisite sexual creature you are and... come."

He bit down on my earlobe and I cried out, my body tightening around his. Wave after wave of pleasure washed over me, spurred on by Cade's hand between my legs and his voice in my ear, telling me how gorgeous I was when I came, how much he loved watching me come.

At the height of my orgasm, there, for just a split second, I caught a glimpse of what he was talking about. Tears burned in my eyes and I reached behind me, putting my hands on his thighs. My nails dug in, the only release for the enormity of what I was feeling. I felt his muscles tense, then he groaned my name. His arms tightened around me and his cock pulsed inside me, sending new ripples of pleasure through me.

He sat back on the bed and pulled me onto his lap, holding me as we caught our breath. "Don't let anyone tell you that you don't deserve everything you want."

A pain went through me. Would he still say that, I wondered, if he knew he was what I wanted?

He shifted me off of his lap, hissing as he slid out of me. He tossed the condom into the trash and then rolled back to face me. "Why don't you go ahead and grab a shower?"

I nodded and climbed off the bed. Getting away from him seemed like a good idea. My mind was buzzing with too many thoughts and my entire body was sticky with sweat and other things. I'd think more clearly once I was clean.

I sighed as the hot water beat down on me, washing everything away. I took my time, shampooing my hair and scrubbing myself clean. I tried not to think about anything. I didn't want to read too much into what Cade had said tonight, but as the events kept popping up for replays, I couldn't quite quash the hope that maybe Cade meant some of those things in ways that went beyond the physical. Maybe this weekend was his way of telling me I was different from his other clients. I was special.

I pulled on the thick, fluffy hotel robe without bothering to put anything on underneath. I stepped out into the bedroom, wondering if Cade and I were finally going to talk about how things were changing between us.

The bed was empty. I frowned. Had he decided to use the other bathroom because I'd taken too long in the shower? I walked over to the bedroom door and looked across the hall into the other room.

I couldn't see details, but I could see the lump in the middle of the bed where Cade was sleeping.

In the other bedroom.

Alone.

Fighting back new tears, I walked back to the bed. I turned off the light and crawled under the covers. I pulled them tight around me and told myself it was all for the best. I really didn't want to get involved with someone like Cade anyway. I wanted all the things he didn't believe in, including love. At least, this way, I didn't make a fool of myself and end our contract before we were through.

The thoughts were little comfort as I fell into a restless sleep.

# Chapter 8

When I opened my eyes, the clock said it was almost nine o'clock but I felt like I'd barely slept at all. I pushed myself into a sitting position, slightly disoriented. The hotel curtains were thick, preventing most light from coming into the room. I sniffed. Now there was something that could wake me up. Coffee. That was what I needed to chase away the bad sleep.

I stood and stretched. The bed had been comfortable, but my head was too busy for me to be able to get any real rest. I trudged into the bathroom for some basic morning business, but didn't bother to get dressed before heading out into the kitchenette area.

Cade was sitting at the table already, newspaper in hand. I couldn't help but feel a pulse of lust as I looked at him. He wore jeans and a plain long-sleeved shirt that emphasized his broad shoulders. His hair was tousled and seemed longer than usual, though I quickly realized it was because he hadn't put any product in it. His feet were bare and he looked so at ease that I wondered if this was how he always looked in the morning.

"Morning." He gave me a dazzling smile. "I wasn't sure when you usually woke up on the weekends, so I took the liberty of ordering a bit of everything so you could eat whenever." He gestured toward the table.

"Thanks." I smiled back but bypassed the table in favor of some coffee. I inhaled deeply as I poured it into a mug. Oh, this wasn't just coffee. This was the good stuff. Hazelnut. And the choice of creamers was like something out of a dream.

I drank a third of it before I made my way back to the table and took a look at what all Cade had ordered from room service. There was an assortment of fruit, bagels and muffins. Pancakes and waffles with three different kinds of syrup. Far too much for two people to eat.

"Whenever you're done, I'll call room service to come pack all this up," Cade said as he turned the page.

"Pack it up?" I asked as I put a blueberry muffin and some grapes on a small plate.

"There's a church a few blocks away that will give the leftover food away to people who need it."

The muffin was half-way to my mouth when it stopped. I stared at Cade, or the bit of him I could see over the top of the paper. "A church?"

He bent the paper down, the expression on his face annoyingly blank. "Surprised that I would contact a church? Or that someone like me didn't burst into flame even thinking about it?"

"No, I... that's not..."

He cracked a smile. "Relax, Aubree." He set his newspaper aside. "When you grow up with nothing, you tend to know where to go to get help." He gestured to the tray. "Or in this case, where to give it."

I didn't say anything as I broke a piece of muffin off and popped it into my mouth. Just when I thought I had Cade Shepard figured out, he went and did something like this. I wanted to probe, ask about how he'd grown up. There was so much about him that was a mystery and so much I wanted to solve. I mused over it as I ate my food and drank my delicious coffee. Was there a way I could get to know him better without revealing that I was starting to get attached? Was that even a good idea? Would learning more about him make me want him less or more? What if I found out bad things and that made me not want to be with him? Wouldn't that actually be better? And what if it went the other way? What if who he was, his past, touched me more than he already did? He could have been a Boy Scout turned orphan for all I knew. Could I really afford to get more involved than I already was?

"You're going out tonight," Cade announced suddenly.

I blinked. Had he said 'you' and not 'we'?

"I've been working with you for almost a month now and it's time to see you put into practice what I've taught you," he continued. "You'll have all of today to prepare. Your date will meet you at La Vecchía Ristorante at six."

"My date." I found my voice.

Cade folded his hands in front of him and gave me all of his attention. "The entire point of this has been to teach you to be the woman you want to be.

You're beautiful, sexy and, I hope, beginning to see yourself that way."

A few minutes ago, hearing him call me beautiful and sexy would've been the best thing he could've said. Now, his words felt cold and empty. My stomach twisted.

"What better way to determine how far you've come than to set you up on a date that you have to seduce and fuck."

I leaned back in my chair, numb with shock. When he'd said we were going away for the weekend, at the very least, I'd expected a couple days of toe-curling sex, complete with lessons about what I needed to do to please him. I'd never considered that Cade would want me to have sex with another man.

"He's not a pro," Cade continued. "I found him on a dating site and told him that I wanted to set him up with a friend of mine."

Friend. The word was bitter in my mouth. We weren't friends, and I didn't want to be friends. I wanted everything or nothing from him.

"Are you trying to make the transition from escort to pimp?" I asked. "Because you're doing a bang-up job."

"I didn't pay him, Aubree," Cade said mildly. "I told him about you and said that you'd lost a bet. The stakes were, you had to go out with a guy I chose."

I crossed my arms. "What if I've had enough of blind dates? They don't always go very well for me."

"I'll remind you that you agreed to do as I said." Cade paused, and then added, "Unless you've decided you no longer wish to continue with our agreement."

I frowned. "So basically, you're telling me I have to fuck a complete stranger, whether I want to or not?"

"I'm telling you that you're going to go on a date with a man who could possibly be everything you're looking for, or just a good lay. I'm telling you to seduce him and fuck him, yes, but it's not about you doing something you don't want to do." Cade pushed his chair from the table and rested his ankle on his knee. "It's about you having the confidence to know what you want and going for it. Proving that you've learned from what I've been trying to teach you."

An idea came to me and it was both perfect and dangerous. I didn't take the time to analyze or assess the risks. No overthinking, just action.

I stood and reached for the belt on my robe. "You want to know if you're a good teacher? How about I show you?"

Cade shifted in his chair. The movement was slight, but I knew that even the smallest break in his facade meant I'd caught him off guard. That was good.

I untied my robe slowly, giving him the time to wonder what I was wearing underneath. As the belt came undone, I let the robe fall naturally, giving Cade a glimpse of pale flesh. I walked toward him and was gratified to see his eyes locked on my body, darkening as each step hinted at what was beneath the soft cotton.

When I was standing directly in front of him, I reached down and removed his ankle from where he'd had it resting on his knee. With his feet on the floor, legs parted, I could see the considerable bulge straining against his jeans. I smiled and let the robe slide off my shoulders, revealing my body inch by inch. As it fell to the floor, I went to my knees.

"Shit," Cade breathed.

I ignored him and went right for what I wanted. Button undone, zipper down and then I tugged his jeans and underwear down his hips until his cock was free. I lowered my head to take all of him while he was still only half-hard. Remembering what he'd taught me, I cupped his balls and then began to massage them. Cade moaned and a thrill of pride went through me. I licked my way down his thickening shaft and took his balls into my mouth, giving them the attention they deserved before moving back up to his cock.

His hand dropped onto my head and I responded to the pressure, letting him set the rhythm as I my headed bobbed up and down. When he pushed me down further, I didn't fight it, taking as much of him as I could. Then, suddenly, he was pulling me off of him and picking me up.

I barely had the chance to register the cool edge of the table under my ass before Cade was shoving his fingers inside of me. I cried out, my eyes closing as his fingers thrust into me, stretching me, preparing me. When they curled up to press against my g-spot, I nearly fell back. Only Cade's arm wrapping around my waist kept me upright.

He bent his head and wrapped his lips around one of my nipples. There was no slow build-up or licking. He just began to suck, hard. I dug my fingers into his hair, moaning as each pull of his mouth corresponded to his fingers rubbing against that spot inside of me. I'd never gone from zero to sixty this fast before and my body was shaking as it struggled to process how rapidly my orgasm was approaching.

He bit down on my nipple, and my hips jerked, forcing his fingers harder and deeper.

"Yes!" I ground down on his hand. "Yes, Cade!" I came calling out his name. I heard him swear as my pussy tightened around his fingers and then his hand was gone, leaving me gasping.

Pleasure was still racing along my nerves when, a moment later, I felt the head of Cade's cock against my pussy. Latex slipped against my skin and I had the absurd thought that Cade must've been a Boy Scout because he definitely lived by the 'always be prepared' motto when it came to sex. Then he was pushing into me and I thought about nothing but him inside me.

I was stretched enough from last night and his fingers that he was able to slide in smoothly, but my body was still sensitive from the previous pounding I'd received and the orgasm I'd had only seconds ago. I could feel every inch of him. I wrapped my legs around his waist, my arms around his neck. One of his hands went to the small of my back, the other between my shoulder-blades, giving him the leverage he needed.

His eyes locked with mine as he began to fuck me. I could feel his ass flexing against my calves with every stroke, the muscles in his arms hard and tight as he held me in place. Our breathing was harsh, mingling with the sound of our flesh coming together over and over.

I tilted my head, bringing our mouths together. Cade's fingers curled against my back as I thrust my tongue into his mouth. He made a sound in the back of his throat and I curled my tongue around his. They danced together, chasing back and forth between our mouths, sliding against each other as our lower bodies came together with greater intensity, working us both toward the inevitable.

I caught his bottom lip between my teeth and worried at it until Cade growled. He pulled out of me, yanking me off of the table and spinning me around so that I was bent over the table, my hands the only things keeping me from falling. I cried out as he grabbed my hips and slammed into me. My nipples rubbed against the smooth wood of the tabletop as each thrust pushed me forward.

"Touch yourself." The command was harsh. "I'm close. Make yourself come."

I shifted my weight so that I could move one hand beneath me. I was close enough that it wasn't going to take much. I wondered if I could come on his cock alone, but I didn't want to take the chance of him finishing before I could find out. I needed to come. My entire body was humming with tension, ready to explode. Cade's rhythm faltered as he drove into me and I knew he wasn't too far away. My fingers found my clit engorged and throbbing, begging for attention. I closed my eyes as I rubbed my clit, shutting out everything but the pleasure coursing through me. When Cade shoved himself deep inside me, the end of him hitting against the end of me, I let out a breathless scream and came.

White spots danced behind my eyelids as Cade came with a shout. He slumped over me for a moment, his hands on either side of my body. I was limp, barely able to hold myself upright as I gasped for air. I waited for him to say something, to help me up, anything.

I made a small pained sound as he pulled out. If this was what it was like after two days in a row, I could hardly imagine how I'd feel after a whole weekend of getting fucked by Cade. I'd need a full day to recover.

"I'm going to get cleaned up," Cade said. He continued speaking as he walked toward his bedroom. "You have a spa appointment at one if you want to soak in the tub before you go. It's a whole exfoliating, waxing thing. You'll be done in plenty of time for your date."

I pushed myself up off of the table and reached down for my robe. My hands were shaking as I pulled it on, suddenly feeling used and exposed. My eyes burned with tears and I hurried toward my bedroom, needing the privacy of my bathroom before I gave in to the dark emotions filling me.

Humiliation.

Rejection.

I'd offered myself to him and he'd taken what I'd given, but he didn't want me. I was a job. A body he found physically attractive and enjoyed fucking. Nothing else.

# Chapter 9

The spa treatment was wonderful. Even the waxing hadn't been an entirely unpleasant experience. There'd been a facial and a massage that had left my skin tingling and my muscles relaxed. The only thing that would've made it better would've been if I had been getting ready for a date with someone I cared about. I refused to put a name in there. He'd made it perfectly clear where I stood with him.

The hotel room was empty when I got back, but I went straight to my room anyway. I didn't want to risk running into Cade as I was unsure how to handle what had happened. I couldn't tell him I was upset or that would bring up questions as to why I felt that way, and that would lead to the end of everything. I wasn't sure I was ready for that just yet.

I laid out all of the clothes I'd brought with me and began to look through them to find something perfect for tonight. I didn't really want to go through with it, but it was the only way to keep up the pretense with Cade. Besides, I thought, there was always the off chance that I could actually have fun. And hadn't that been the entire point of this whole thing? For me to prove I wasn't some pathetic loser who needed her friends to set her up on pity dates? Granted, Cade had set this one up, but this was a test, not pity.

I picked up the teddy I'd bought for my ex-fiancé to enjoy. I'd brought the clothes, thinking that using them with someone other than Ronald would somehow fulfill the promise of that missed opportunity. I saw the whole truth of it. This whole trip, I'd been trying to make it a replacement for what I hadn't gotten with my ex. An out-of-country trip. A five-star hotel. Hot sex.

This wasn't a romantic getaway, though. And nothing that happened this weekend would have any sort of special meaning. If anything, what I was doing with Cade just cheapened everything. I put on the teddy and then looked through the dresses I'd brought. There was no use saving any of this.

Most of the clothes I'd bought for my honeymoon had been for a Caribbean cruise in August, not Toronto in October, but I had purchased a couple warmer outfits, not knowing how cold it would get on the ocean at night. I picked one of those now, a clingy deep blue sweater-dress. The deep v-neck showed off the tops of my breasts and the hemline was mid-thigh, revealing enough leg to get some attention. It was attractive without promising too much.

I was ready early, but stayed in my room. At five-thirty, a text came through. It was Cade letting me know that a car was ready to take me to the restaurant. I scowled at his message and then shoved my phone into my purse. The entire ride down to the lobby, I told myself that I needed to focus on having a good time, on proving I could do this. I needed to prove it to myself as much as anyone else.

The driver didn't try to talk to me on the ride, which I was grateful for. I didn't want to make small talk at the moment. I had enough of that in my near future. When I walked into La Vecchía Ristorante, for a moment, I forgot about the circumstances surrounding my being there. The place was gorgeous. Warm lighting, stone walls, just the right combination of romantic and chic so that it was perfect for any sort of date. Grudgingly, I admitted that Cade had done well in choosing it.

"Ms. Gamble?" The hostess interrupted my thoughts.

"Yes?" I was surprised she knew who I was, but I didn't ask. I had a feeling Cade had taken care of it and I didn't want to think about him anymore for the rest of the night.

"Your table's right this way."

She led me to a table near the back. I perused my menu while I waited, but I didn't have to distract myself for very long. A few minutes after I'd been seated, one of my quick glances toward the doors showed the hostess coming my way again, a man close behind her. I set aside my menu, deciding I didn't want to try to play coy and pretend to not be watching. I let myself study my date as he came closer.

He was tall, even taller than Cade, and more muscular. Cade's build wasn't quite thin enough to be lean, but my date was almost too big for my tastes. His hair was golden blond and cropped short. Not military, exactly, but in that same vein. As he drew closer, he smiled and I saw straight white teeth, a dimple and warm brown eyes. His features were cute rather than handsome or pretty. All-in-all, a nice package. I found myself wondering what had prompted Cade to pick someone like this guy. It wasn't like we'd discussed the types of guys I found attractive. As far as I knew, he didn't even know what Ronald looked like, so he couldn't have used that as a template. Not that my date looked like my ex. What made me so curious was that it seemed like Cade had purposefully picked someone who didn't look anything like him.

As my date sat down, he extended his hand across the table. "Jason Lowe."

"Aubree Gamble," I answered automatically as I shook his hand. "Call me Bree." I didn't want anyone else calling me Aubree, especially not someone I was supposed to seduce.

"It's nice to meet you, Bree." He flashed another charming smile and then looked at the waiter who'd appeared. "I'll start with water, but if my date is amenable, we'll be ordering wine with the main course."

Amenable. And used correctly. That earned points from the English teacher. Another point for not ordering for me. He was doing well so far. "That sounds lovely."

We chatted about menu choices and wines while we decided what we wanted. Once we'd put in our orders, the conversation shifted to the usual introductory small talk. I tried not to tense as I remembered how this had been the point in my last date where things had started going south. I hoped Jason wasn't as self-absorbed as Steven Danforth had been.

"Your friend didn't tell me much about you except that you were gorgeous."

"Thank you," I said. Surprisingly, I didn't blush. I wasn't sure if that was because I'd gotten used to the compliments or if it was simply the difference in who was saying them. I really hoped it was the first. "He didn't say anything about you at all." I smiled and sipped at my water. "But if he had, I'm sure he would've been equally complimentary."

Jason laughed, a nice sound without any innuendo or double-meaning attached to it. "So, Bree, do you mind if I ask what you do for a living?"

"I'm a teacher."

As the questions went back and forth, I realized why Cade had chosen for this date to be outside of Chicago. Both Jason and I were giving ambiguous enough answers that, while we were learning about each other, we also weren't providing enough information that could be used to find the other. Our names alone wasn't sufficient.

The conversation flowed more smoothly than I'd expected and I found myself relaxing a bit more. Jason was a charmer, but not in a sleazy kind of way. He seemed to be genuinely interested in what I had to say, but not so much so that I didn't find out he was divorced, worked for a pharmaceutical company and traveled a lot. He didn't take himself too seriously, but wasn't flippant about things either. He was sweet, humble with just the right amount of confidence. He was everything I should've been looking for in a first date. In a relationship, even.

Except I couldn't stop thinking about the ways he wasn't like Cade. His looks. His smile. The way he carried himself. Even how he spoke. It wasn't that I didn't think Jason was attractive, but he wasn't the one I wanted. It didn't matter that Cade had made it perfectly clear that there wasn't anything between the two of us but business.

I barely tasted any of the delicious food in front of me, spending more time pushing it around on my plate so I looked busier than I was. The more time that passed with Jason, the more I realized this wasn't going to work. I should've been enjoying Jason's company and trying to figure out if I wanted to invite him back to my room, but instead, I was wondering if Cade would be there when I went back.

"If you'll excuse me," I said abruptly. I stood and gave Jason a smile. "I just need to use the ladies' room." I took my purse and headed toward the restrooms.

The bathroom was empty and I breathed a sigh of relief. I went to the sink, wishing I could splash cold water on my face without ruining my make-up. Instead, I settled on washing my hands and then pressed a damp paper towel against the back of my neck. I couldn't do this anymore. It wasn't fair to

Jason. I knew the date hadn't been set up under the most honest of explanations, but he at least deserved someone who wasn't thinking about another man.

I could tell him I wasn't feeling well. The fact that I'd hurried away to the restroom would support a lie. And it wasn't entirely untrue. The thought of having a one-night stand with a virtual stranger was turning my stomach. If I couldn't have Cade, that was one thing, but even after all of his 'teaching,' I still wasn't the type of woman to have sex with someone I felt nothing for.

My phone rang and I dug it out of my purse, answering without even bothering to see who it was.

"Don't do it."

The sound of Cade's voice sent my pulse racing. Had he just called to tell me not to sleep with Jason? A small flare of hope perked up inside me.

"You're thinking of walking out, aren't you?"

"What?"

"Did you really think I'd send you on a date with a perfect stranger and not keep an eye on you?" His voice was flat. "I've been watching you, Aubree, and you're faking it. Badly. Running to the bathroom was an excuse to back out without hurting poor Jason's feelings. I bet you were planning to lie, planned to tell him you were sick, weren't you? Because Aubree Gamble is too nice to tell the truth and too chicken shit to follow through."

"You're watching me?" I hissed the question, looking around the bathroom to make sure no one could hear my side of the conversation.

He didn't even bother to answer my question, though I supposed the answer was obvious in the first place. "If you leave without at least finishing the date and initiating something physical, we're done. You promised to obey–"

I hung up the phone before he finished the sentence and then switched it off so he couldn't call back. "Son of a bitch!" I slapped my hand on the counter. Who did he think he was, ordering me to fuck someone like I was the prostitute in this relationship?

I looked at my reflection, anger burning in my eyes. Anger at Cade for telling me to do this. At myself for what had happened at the hotel earlier, for allowing myself to feel something. And now he was watching me, telling me to fuck a total stranger?

"Fine," I muttered. "If that's what you want." I straightened, smoothing my dress and making sure my hair and make-up were flawless. If Cade wanted to watch me seduce Jason... I'd give him a show he'd never forget.

# Chapter 10

## *Cade*

I wasn't sure which would've been worse, sitting at a table and watching everything going on but not being able to hear it, or having to suffer through whatever numbingly boring conversation Aubree and Jason were most likely having without being able to direct where it went. All I knew was that Aubree's pleasant demeanor was becoming more forced by the minute and I didn't think she was going to go through with it. That would be a problem.

I sighed and ran my hand through my hair. Things were more complicated with Aubree than any other client I'd ever had. Usually, the only complication was when someone got attached and I had to cut her off. With Aubree, things were... different.

A tall woman with chestnut brown hair passed my table and I caught a whiff of some sort of fruity-scented body spray. I tensed, not relaxing until I caught a glimpse of the stranger's profile. The nose was all wrong, but the rest of the similarities brought forward memories I'd rather have forgotten.

*****

I looked up at the house doubtfully. It was my last hope to make at least enough money to get something to eat. My stomach contracted painfully. My last meal had been at the hospital two days ago, and it wasn't like hospital food was filling to begin with.

As I started up the driveway, the rain that had been threatening all day finally broke free of the clouds. I was already too miserable to do much more than frown as the chill quickly soaked through my ragged clothes. I clutched my side as pain shot through my cracked ribs, but I didn't slow down. If I paused every time I hurt, I'd never get more than a couple feet. Every wrong movement twinged something injured, and there were plenty to choose from. Aside from four cracked ribs and serious bruising that had left my entire torso a mass of black and blue, I also had cuts and bruises on my knuckles, at least one cracked knuckle, two black eyes, a split lip, bruised cheek and a nose I was lucky hadn't been broken. There were also scrapes and cuts covering pretty much every inch of my body. Walking was painful, but so was sitting and laying down. It was beyond a no-win situation.

I straightened as best I could and hoped that whoever lived in this insanely huge mansion would pity me enough to give me something to do for a couple bucks. How far had I fallen, I wondered as I rang the doorbell. Less than a year ago, the idea of someone pitying me would've pissed me off.

"Can I help you?" A tall brunette opened the door, the expression on her face showing only the slightest surprise at finding someone who looked like me standing there.

"I'm looking for work," I spoke carefully and tried not to wince when the movement pulled on my lip.

The woman opened the door further and motioned for me to step inside. "Come out of the rain and we'll talk."

As I stepped into the lavish foyer of the house, I realized the woman who'd come to the door wasn't a maid or one of the servants like I'd been dealing with at the other houses. She wasn't dressed in anything fancy, but I could tell her clothes were expensive, designer-label shit. Her haircut alone was probably worth a week's paycheck for most people.

"What's your name?" she asked.

"Cade." I watched as she circled me, her eyes running over me with a critical light in them. I didn't know what she was thinking, but if it meant I got to eat today, I didn't care.

"Are you hungry, Cade?" She stopped when she was standing in front of me again. "You look hungry."

"I'm just looking for work, ma'am," I said stiffly. "Not charity."

"How about this," she said. "I fix us both something to eat and then you clean the kitchen for me? I was going to have some fried chicken, pasta salad and biscuits. How does that sound?"

I wanted to protest that it didn't sound like an even trade, but my stomach let out a loud growl. I flushed. "That would be great, ma'am."

"Please," she said. "Call me Penny."

I followed Penny into her kitchen where she produced all of the food she mentioned and then some. I was hesitant at first, but she kept insisting I eat until I wasn't hungry anymore. Neither one of us talked while we ate, but I felt her eyes on me almost the whole time. When I finished, I immediately set about cleaning things up. I hoped that if I did a good enough job, she'd offer me something else and I could get a bit of money out of the deal too. Either way, it was better than anything I'd had in a long time.

As I filled the sink, Penny asked, "How old are you?"

I thought for a moment, debating whether or not I wanted to be honest. "I'll be eighteen in a month." I waited for the inevitable follow-up questions, the ones that started with what had happened to me and why I wasn't with my family.

"Are you just looking for work today, or would you like something a bit more regular?" Penny asked.

I glanced behind me and saw that she'd tucked her foot underneath her. The gesture made her seem younger than I'd originally pegged her. "I'll take what I can get," I answered honestly. "I'll do anything you need."

Her green eyes gleamed. "I was hoping you'd say that." She gestured toward a set of French doors leading to a backyard that was bigger than the entire house I'd grown up in. "I have a guest house out back that needs some work. Cleaning, painting, some minor repair stuff."

I was nodding before she finished. That sounded like at least a week's worth of work, maybe more if I was lucky.

"I'll let you stay in the guest house and provide meals in exchange for you getting it into tip-top shape." She slid off of her chair and walked toward me. "I inherited the house from my great-aunt, and she let some things go." She stood next to me, close enough that I could feel the heat radiating from her. Her expression was thoughtful as she looked out the window over the sink. "Once the guest house is done, I'm sure I can find plenty of work for you to do for room and board, maybe even some cash too."

I almost didn't believe her, but I couldn't see any reason for her to lie. If anything, a single woman alone in a big house like this should've been more wary of letting in a complete stranger, especially one as beat-up as me. "I'd really appreciate it," I said.

"Good," she said. "That's settled then." She smiled brightly up at me. "As soon as the rain lets up, we'll go have a look."

The next few weeks were the best I'd had in a long time. With food and rest, my body began to heal and I was getting my strength back. I ate meals in the house with Penny and we talked about everything except how I'd ended up on her doorstep. I slept in the guest house and worked there too. Penny had been right; it had needed some work, but I knew this job wouldn't last forever. I kept my eye out for things I could suggest to her I do when I was done with the guest house. I wanted to keep this arrangement going as long as I could.

The morning of my birthday, I was woken by a knock on the guest house door. When I opened it, Penny was standing there. I stepped aside so she could enter and tried to rub the sleep out of my eyes. It wasn't until I closed the door that I realized Penny was wearing only a thin silk robe and I was in my boxers... complete with morning wood. My face burned as I tried to figure out a way to keep Penny from noticing.

"Today's your birthday, right?" She asked.

"Yeah." I side-stepped so that I was standing behind an arm chair.

She smiled at me but didn't say anything. Her hands went to the belt of her robe, but I didn't realize what she was doing until the robe was falling to the floor and she was naked. Large, full breasts, a little bit of hair between her legs... fuck.

My jaw dropped and, for a moment, I was speechless. When I recovered my voice, I still stammered, "Penny, I... this... I mean..."

She took a step toward me. "I have work for you to do, Cade. And I'm willing to pay very well."

My brain buzzed as it tried to comprehend what she was saying. Was she seriously offering to pay me for sex? Why would a rich, good-looking woman have to pay for sex?

"You know, Cade." Her tone was conversational, like she wasn't standing there, nude, propositioning me. "It's difficult to meet men who aren't after my money. And there's always the emotional attachments that form from a long-term relationship. When I want a good fuck, I find it better to enter into a... business transaction with someone." She stepped around the chair so that we were less than a foot apart. "What do you say, Cade? I'll give you a hundred dollars to bend me over this chair and fuck me."

A hundred dollars. To have sex with a thirty-something woman with no strings attached. I'd already been hard from the usual process of waking up and this wasn't doing anything to help matters.

She ran her hand down her stomach and between her legs. As I watched, she started to play with herself. I swallowed hard, unable to look away.

"You're not a virgin, are you?"

I shook my head. I didn't tell her I'd only had sex with my girlfriend twice before everything in my life had gone to hell, my relationship with it.

"Then what's the problem?" She seemed more amused than annoyed as I stood there in a state of shock. "Two hundred dollars, then. And if I can get you hard again, we have another go."

That was more money than I'd seen the entire time I'd been on the streets. When Penny leaned over the arm of the chair, her ass the air, I found myself walking toward her.

I put my hands on her hips, a sense of surreality washing over me. I was really going to do this. She told me to just fuck her, hard, and I obeyed. She was hot and wet, an enthusiastic partner. She moaned and cursed and gave instructions on what to do to make her come. I did everything she asked, barely registering her reactions to each touch.

It wasn't until after I came that I realized we hadn't used any protection. She laughed when I stammered an apology, assuring me it wasn't an issue. She took my hand and led me to her bedroom where she took me in her mouth until I was hard again. This time, I had enough presence of mind to insist on a condom. I may have sold myself, but I wasn't going to do it unprotected again. She thought it was cute, but complied, then rode me until I came again. I wasn't sure how many times she climaxed, but I was pretty sure she enjoyed herself because when she flopped back on the bed and lit a cigarette, she gave me an appraising look.

"For someone without a lot of experience, you're a good fuck," she said. She half-turned toward me and scraped one of her fake nails against my nipple. "You're worth a hell of a lot more than two hundred dollars for a day."

I wasn't entirely sure how I was supposed to take that. Was it a compliment I should thank her for or should I have been insulted that she was treating me like some sort of commodity? I was saved having to figure it out when she said the words I knew would change everything.

"I have a few friends who would love to spend some time with you." She wrapped her hand around my cock and I winced. Still too sensitive. "For a price, of course. You and me, Cade, we can make a lot of money off of your cock."

***

I shook my head, pulling myself out of the past. I didn't want to think about Penny or her friends. I'd spent the next few years fucking whoever Penny told me to fuck, whether I wanted to or not. But I wasn't that kid anymore. I did things my way, by my rules...

And it looked like Aubree was about to break those rules. She was getting up to go to the restroom, and I knew that look. She was trying to figure out a way to run. I took out my phone. Someone needed a reminder of our agreement. I needed her to see this through.

I wasn't done with her yet.

### End of Vol. 3

# Casual Encounter Vol. 4

# Chapter 1

As I left the restroom and headed back into the dining room of La Vecchía Ristorante, determination competed with the rage flowing through my veins.

Fuck Cade, that controlling bastard. He wants follow through? I'll give him follow through. I was sick and tired of Cade acting like he was in control of everything, including me.

Fine... I'll do what he said. I'll flirt and seduce Jason Lowe, but only because Cade will be watching. If he's really as distant and cold as he seems, it won't bother him at all and I'd at least get an enjoyable experience out of it. But if he feels even the tiniest fraction of emotion for me, I'll make sure he regrets ever giving me this... command.

"Miss me?" I asked as I slid into my seat. I looked directly at my date, resisting the impulse to look around to spot Cade's hiding spot. He was still watching, I felt his eyes on me but I didn't want to give him the satisfaction of knowing I thought about him at all.

"Desperately," Jason said with a laugh. He reached across the table and placed his hand on top of mine. "I took the liberty of pouring you a second glass of wine. I hope that was okay."

"More than okay," I answered honestly. I used my free hand to pick up my glass and take a drink. Just because I'd decided to go through with this didn't mean taking the edge off with some wine wasn't a good idea.

Jason picked up the conversation where we'd left off and I fell back into it. This time, however, instead of keeping up just enough to not be rude, I engaged in the interaction. I laughed and teased, remembering all of the ways Adelle and Mindy had gotten guys over the years. I kept making excuses to touch his hand, his arm. I even brushed my foot against his a few times, eliciting a flare of heat in his dark eyes.

He really was quite good-looking, I thought as he told me about a trip he'd taken with Habitat for Humanity. He had a solid job, did charity work, and could hold an intelligent conversation. And, best of all, he was a virtual stranger who didn't live near me, which meant whatever happened here wasn't in danger of spilling over into my real life.

Our plates were empty and I saw the waiter coming toward us. It was now or never time because once the waiter got here, he'd ask if we wanted dessert or the check. It was the deciding moment of where the rest of the evening would go.

"I have a room – a suite actually – at the Windsor Arms." I hoped Jason couldn't tell how nervous I was. I didn't want him to think this was my first time inviting a man back to my room. "What do you say we head back there for dessert?" I gave him a sly smile. "Room service has quite a selection."

He didn't even look at the waiter as he said, "Check, please."

Jason was a complete gentleman as he hailed a cab and opened the door. I kept my hands folded on my lap, unsure what to do with them. I didn't know how this transition worked, how to get from date to bed. Jason continued the small talk we'd made at dinner as if we really were intending to just share some pie or cake and then call it a night.

When we reached the hotel, he extended a hand to help me out of the cab and then kept hold of it as we walked into the lobby. My heart was racing as I led Jason toward the elevators. I was really going to do this.

"You know," Jason said suddenly. "I think maybe I need a little taste of dessert."

He used my hand to pull me against him and bent his head to kiss me. His mouth was hard against mine as he parted my lips with his tongue. I tried to give myself over to him, to enjoy the way his tongue was exploring my mouth, but part of my mind was protesting at such a thorough kiss in public. Then I felt his hand on my breast, cupping and squeezing through the dress. I grabbed his wrist without breaking the kiss and brought both of our hands down to our sides. I was in charge, in control. That was the point of this entire exercise.

Jason broke the kiss but didn't step back. His eyes gleamed as he walked me backwards until my back was against the wall. The elevator next to me dinged open, but Jason made no move for us to enter. The hand I had restrained twisted and now my wrist was in his grasp. I frowned. This wasn't how Cade behaved when he was forcing me out of my comfort zone. I trusted Cade. I didn't trust Jason. I didn't trust this.

"What's wrong?" he asked, dragging my hand between us. He pressed it against his crotch. "Don't you want to give the other guests a bit of a show?"

"No," I said firmly. "I'm not into that." I yanked my hands free and pushed against his chest. He barely moved. "I think we need to call it a night."

He scowled. "I don't think so." He pushed his hips against mine so that I could feel his cock hard against my stomach. "You can't just make promises and not deliver."

My temper flared. I'd had enough of men telling me what I could and couldn't do. "Get the hell off of me!" I pushed at his chest again, but he had the leverage to keep himself from moving.

"Cocktease!"

All of the good humor vanished from his face and I found myself wondering why no one was coming to help me. I knew there were guests around, but were we hidden enough from view that no one could see what was happening?

I jerked my knee up, but Jason shifted at the last moment, taking the blow against his thigh. He pulled back, his hand coming down before I could register it heading my way. The slap caught me across the cheek with enough force to snap my head back. I cried out, more from shock than the pain. My eyes filled with tears as the sting quickly followed.

Jason glared down at me, his face red. "You little bitch!" He raised his hand again and I tried to remember the self-defense moves I'd learned in college.

A hand wrapped around Jason's wrist and he was spun around, just as a fist connected with his jaw. I silently cheered as the creep's head swung to the side then Jason stumbled backward, and I saw Cade swing again. This time, the blow was accompanied by a crunch as bone yielded to the blow, followed immediately by a shriek of pain.

Cade stepped in front of me, but not before I saw his face. Gone was his usual calm demeanor. He was enraged as he spat in Jason's face, "Get out of here before I seriously fuck you up."

My eyes widened. I'd heard Cade's voice with an edge before, but I never imagined he could sound so fierce. He meant it, there was no doubt and I wondered if that was the real man behind the mask. I couldn't stop myself from flinching as he turned toward me and a flash of pain went across his face. He reached out and took my arm, pulling me to his side.

"Come on," he said, looking around. "We don't want to make any more of a scene than we already have." He led me away from the elevators, carefully stepping over the drops of blood on the pale tile.

There were people moving toward us, hotel guests and a few people I assumed were security. Before I could get a good look at any of them, Cade ducked through a doorway, taking me with him.

"Sir, we're not open–" A young man hurried toward us.

"Here." Cade stretched out his free hand, a bill folded between his fingers. "We just want some privacy."

The young man looked at me, and I saw doubt cross his face. I could only imagine how we looked. My cheek had to be red and I could feel it starting to swell. Cade's knuckles were bloody and neither one of us looked very happy.

"I'm fine," I said and forced a smile. "I had a misunderstanding with someone who didn't take it well." I jerked my chin at Cade. "He protected me."

The young man nodded. "This way."

We followed him through what I now realized was the Courtyard Cafe. It was light and airy, the kind of place I would've enjoyed coming for a light meal. The young man motioned to a table that was tucked behind a heavy curtain. It would shield us from view of anyone who might happen to glance in here.

"Cade," I asked as I took a seat. "Are you okay?"

"Am I okay?" Cade let out a bitter laugh. "Are you kidding me?" He pulled his chair around until we were just a few inches apart. He reached toward my cheek, stopping just before his fingertips touched it.

"Thank you," I said. "For what you did, but why are we hiding in here? We didn't do anything wrong?"

Cade dropped his hand and I saw it was shaking. I met his eyes and saw the storm still raging inside. "We're hiding because I'm not sure if I want to report him to the police or go find him and beat the shit out of him."

I put my hands over his; something in my stomach twisting as his hands jerked under the touch. He was almost more rattled by what happened than I was. "I'm okay," I said softly. "We can just let it go."

"Let it go?" Cade's hands curled into fists. "Sure. Just forget it ever happened. Put it behind us until it happens again and again."

His voice was shaking and, with a start, I realized it wasn't just from anger. What happened triggered something in Cade, something he'd hidden for a long time.

"It's my fault," he said. His expression was raw and open as he looked at me. "I'm so sorry, Aubree. I didn't know he was that kind of man. I should've seen it. Stopped him."

"You couldn't have known," I said.

He shook his head. "I should have. I spent seventeen years watching a man like him charm my mother one minute and beat her the next."

My hands tightened over his, but I didn't make a sound.

"She married the abusive bastard when he knocked her up with me. And she stayed with him because she loved him."

The anger and bitterness he put into that single word made me wince.

"Stayed with him and loved him right until he beat her to death for burning dinner."

"Oh, Cade." My heart broke.

"I couldn't stop him. I tried, but he beat me up and locked me in a closet. I listened to her scream and beg him to stop. Every time she told him she loved him, he hit her harder." Cade shuddered, his head dropping. "By the time I broke through the door, he was gone and she was dead."

I put my hands on Cade's cheeks and raised his head until we were face-to-face. I didn't try to tell him that it wasn't his fault. He'd heard it a million times, I was sure, and he'd never believe it, no matter who said it. I did the only thing I could do. I gave him a distraction, something he could lose himself in.

I covered his mouth with mine, teasing at his lips with my tongue. I felt him stiffen in surprise for a moment before he took what I offered. His arms wrapped around my waist as my tongue slid into his mouth. I kissed him to forget what happened to me.

To help him forget what he'd been through. I kissed him because my heart was aching for him and it was the only form of comfort I could offer for us both.

When I broke the kiss, his hands flexed on my back and I saw desire in his eyes. I stood and held out my hand. "Come on," I said quietly. "Let's go to bed."

# Chapter 2

We managed to avoid the crowd still gathering around the spot where the fight had occurred. The ride to our floor was silent, but this was different from other moments of quiet between the two of us. Something had shifted, at least for the moment, and I wasn't going to risk breaking it. I doubted it would last, but I was going to enjoy what I had as long as I had it.

I led the way off the elevator and down the hall, and I was the one who unlocked the door. This whole thing with his past had taken something out of Cade. I kicked off my shoes and urged Cade to do the same. We walked back toward my bedroom and, once inside, I took charge.

The shirt came off first. Cade lifted his arms like a little boy and allowed me to pull it over his head. He looked down at me as I tossed the shirt on the floor and reached up to brush his hair away from his eyes. For a moment, I almost forgot that this was business, that while I might have been offering him my body for comfort, it was, at most, a friendly gesture.

I looked down at his chest, running my hands over the solid muscle, exploring the dips and curves. I scraped my nails over his nipples and he hissed. The darker flesh wrinkled and I bent my head to cover it with my mouth. Cade moaned as I sucked on his nipple and I ran my hands up and down his back, enjoying the feel of his smooth skin. I flicked my tongue across the tip and dropped my hands to his ass, squeezing the firm muscles until I felt one of Cade's hands in my hair. I bit down on his nipple.

"Fuck, Aubree!"

Cade's body jerked and I smiled. When he pushed down on my head, I let him guide me to my knees. I wasn't sure if he was completely taking control back, but as long as I got what I wanted, I didn't care. I tugged down his pants and boxer briefs together and he stepped out of them, leaving him gloriously naked. I ran my hands up his calves, then his thighs, until I was right at the level he wanted me.

I looked up at him through my lashes and he tugged on my curls, an encouragement to take the thick shaft in front of me into my mouth. I gave him a wicked grin and darted out my tongue, licking along his full length, then stopping. He applied pressure to my head again and, this time, I shook my head.

His eyes darkened and something low and deep inside me twisted. It wasn't until that moment I realized what I'd been doing without even knowing it. I wanted him to be in control because that's what he needed. I needed to be what he needed. And at this moment, it wasn't slow, gentle lovemaking that would help him. And it definitely wasn't what I wanted either.

Something flickered across his eyes and he touched the cheek Jason had hit. I could see the question in his eyes. He needed to know I understood the difference between what Jason had done and what Cade wanted to do to me. My pussy throbbed in response and there was no doubt in my mind that I knew the difference. And I wanted what Cade had. I nodded, letting him read the desire in my eyes. I couldn't let him see the emotion behind it, but the lust…that I could allow.

Something clicked in Cade's face and he was back. He took half a step closer to me and let the tip of his cock brush against my lips, but I didn't open my mouth. He tugged on my hair, half pulling me to my feet. I caught my breath at the heat in his eyes and then he was pulling my dress over my head.

He made a sound in the back of his throat as he saw what I'd been wearing underneath. The black lace was so sheer that my nipples were clearly visible, as was my freshly waxed pussy.

"You were wearing this for him?" The question came out in a near growl and my stomach flipped at the possessive undercurrent I could hear. I didn't let myself read too much into it. That was dangerous territory.

"I wore it for whoever got to undress me." The words didn't come out quite as cocky as I'd meant them to, but I knew he got the gist of what I meant. I slowly turned, letting him see the way the back of the garment exposed most of my back and barely covered my ass.

"Bend over."

I didn't even consider disobeying. I knew what was coming. I put my hands on the edge of the bed and planted my feet shoulder-length apart. I shivered when Cade's hand ran over my ass, but it was all anticipation.

"You disobeyed me," Cade's voice was soft, but far from gentle. "Do you think you should be punished for that?"

I nodded, then yelped as his hand came down on my ass.

"Do I need to repeat myself?" he asked sternly.

"No," I said. A smack to my other cheek made me gasp.

"Then I believe you need to answer me."

"Yes. Yes, I should be punished."

I flinched as his hand came down again, this time across both cheeks. I closed my eyes, absorbing the sting and heat as he spanked me again. My ass began to burn and I lost count of the strokes. Just as it threatened to become too much, when painful pleasure would lose itself to pain alone, he stopped. I let out a shuddering breath, my body trembling as he ran his hand over the too sensitive skin.

"Are you wet, Aubree?"

I nodded, crying out as he smacked my ass again. "Yes!" I blurted out. "Yes, I'm wet."

His hand slid down between my cheeks, then underneath me to rub across the crotch of my panties. "Oh, yes, you are. You're soaked."

I moaned at his touch, the heat from my skin merging with a different warmth spreading inside me. His fingers slipped beneath the thin material and my head fell forward as a single digit slid inside. I made a sound of protest when he slid it out again, but then stiffened as his finger trailed up between my burning cheeks.

"Fuck," I swore as his finger lightly traced over my asshole. I hadn't had that in mind at all.

"Don't worry," Cade said, a hint of amusement in his voice. "That doesn't happen without preparation." His hand moved and air hissed from between my teeth as his hands slid over my burning skin. "But it will happen. I will have your ass."

The thought sent another rush of arousal through me. I'd never considered anal sex before, but I remembered what Cade had told me, that he'd make sure everything we did was to my benefit.

"Tonight, though," he continued. "I'm just going to fuck you until you see stars, until your legs buckle and your eyes roll back."

Oh, I liked the sound of that.

His hands slid up my sides, working open the laces that held the lingerie together. I stayed bent over until he cupped my breasts and pulled me into a standing position. He pressed his lips against my neck as he worked down the teddy, no finesse or sensual caresses. Instead, he was rough, practically manhandling me as his lips and teeth sucked at the skin of my throat until I knew I was marked. I had the tenuous thought that I'd have to wear a scarf; a hickey wasn't a good example to set for my students. Then Cade's hands were squeezing my breasts, his fingers rolling and twisting my nipples, and everything else dropped away.

"One of the things most men truly love is knowing they can bring their lover to climax." Cade sounded in control once more. "Multiple orgasms are, of course, a wonderful thing for both partners. But, there is the opposite end of the spectrum as well."

I had a feeling I wasn't really going to like where he was going with this.

"Orgasm denial."

Yeah, definitely not going to like this.

"Having control over when your partner comes is a heady thing."

My nipples were starting to ache from how rough he was being and each new pull or twist added to the pressure building inside me.

"Lie down on the bed."

I started to climb on the bed and then realized I had a choice to make. I glanced over my shoulder and from the smug smile on Cade's face, he knew exactly what my problem was. If I laid on my back, my ass would feel every movement. If I laid on my stomach, my nipples would chafe on the bedspread. Ass or nipples... which one would win?

I sighed and stretched out on my back, wincing as I tried to make myself as comfortable as possible. I hadn't chosen this position because I thought it would hurt less. I'd chosen it because whatever Cade was going to do, I wanted to watch.

He crawled onto the bed, spreading my legs as wide as they could go without causing discomfort. He kissed the inside of my thigh and then looked up at me.

"Sometimes, the longer a person is made to wait to reach their pleasure, the more intense it is when it's finally achieved." He ran his tongue along my slit but didn't dip inside. "It's not about hurting the other person or leaving them wanting, though some dominant partners enjoy prolonging the experience to days or weeks."

"Weeks?" I nearly squeaked the word.

He grinned. "I never go to that extreme," he assured me. "But you are going to get a little taste of what it can be like."

I opened my mouth to ask him to be more specific, but that was when he chose to bury his face between my legs and all the air rushed out of me at once. His tongue danced around my pussy, delving into my core before moving to my clit. Around and around it went. Light little flicks. Short thrusts. Long licks with the flat of his tongue. Each one pushing me closer and closer to the edge.

It didn't take long before I was writhing against him, desperate for that last little push. He laced our fingers together so that I couldn't do anything with them but cling to his hands. I was so close.

And then he raised his head, stopping just before I could get to where I needed to be.

"No," I groaned. "Please, Cade. Please."

"The trick is," he said "to know how to read your lover so well that you know right when they reach the point where they're ready to explode. Too far, and they come. Not far enough, and it's not quite as effective."

Effective? Effective for him maybe, but not for me.

"And, of course, you have to know how long it takes them to lose that edge so you can start the process all over again." He lowered his head again, his mouth resuming its previous ministrations.

I moaned as he sucked on my clit. I wanted to be annoyed at him for stopping, but it was difficult to feel anything but pleasure when his talented tongue was at work. I tried to pull my hands away from his, wanting to bury my fingers in his curls, make sure he didn't stop until the job was finished, but he held tight.

I was almost there and I bit down on my bottom lip, desperate to keep back any sounds that would tell him how close I was, but it didn't matter. Just as I was ready to tip over the edge, Cade's mouth was gone and he released my hands. On instinct, I started to move them, ready to give myself the last nudge I desperately needed.

"No." Cade's voice was sharp and I froze. "Tonight, that's mine."

I looked at him with wide eyes. There was that edge again, a note of possessiveness that almost made me think he felt the same for me as I did about him. He was half-turned away from me though, picking up a condom from who knows where and tore the wrapper open.

"Tonight," he continued as he rolled the condom over his swollen shaft. "I'm going to make you come."

I nodded in agreement even though I was only half-listening. All I wanted was for him to fuck me and give me what he'd promised.

He settled himself between my legs again, but didn't enter me right away. Instead, he lifted both of my legs, stretching them out until my ankles were at his ears, my calves on his upper chest and shoulders.

"Do you want to come?" he asked as the head of his cock pushed against my entrance.

I nodded, my breath coming in short pants. This position was going to make things even tighter than usual and my body was still recovering from earlier today and last night. He'd essentially promised to make me come harder than I'd ever done before and I had no doubts about whether or not he could do it.

"Aubree." My name held a warning note.

"Yes," I said, immediately understanding that he wanted me to speak. "I want to come."

"How badly do you want to come?"

The tip of his cock entered me and I whimpered. "Please."

He smiled and leaned forward. The backs of my thighs burned a little as they stretched, but another inch of him slid inside. "Tell me, Aubree, what would you be willing to do if I let you come?"

"Anything," I answered automatically.

"Would you let me fuck your mouth?" he asked. "Make you take me deeper than you thought possible?"

"Yes." I nodded. I started to reach for him, but he grasped my wrists and held my hands at my sides.

"Would you let me fuck your ass?" Another inch and he pressed against my g-spot.

I swallowed hard, nodding before I knew how I was going to answer.

"Say it."

"I'll let you fuck my mouth, my ass. I'll do anything you want, just please let me come." I struggled against his hands, knowing that if I said a single word, he'd let me go. I didn't say it though. As much as I wanted my hands free, I wanted him to fuck me more.

"Are you ready to scream, Aubree?" Another inch and he was almost half-way inside.

The tension inside me felt like it was going to tear me apart if I didn't get a release soon. "Please, Cade," I begged.

"Imagine," he said as he slowly pushed the rest of the way into me. "If I'd denied you four or five times. If I'd taken you to the edge so many times that you lost count."

"Fuck," I groaned as he filled me. The stretch and burn of him inside me wasn't enough to make me climax, but it was enough to ratchet up the pressure another notch. My nails dug into the bedspread.

"You can come whenever you want," he said.

I started to say something, but the thought was lost the moment he leaned forward, bending my legs so far back my knees almost touched my chest. His hands tightened around my wrists as his arms bore most of his weight and he began to move.

His thrusts were hard and fast, each one pounding into me with enough force to make me cry out. Or they would've been if I'd been able to get enough air. Cade shifted slightly as he pulled back and my legs slid partially down his shoulders, giving me enough room to breathe. This time when he slammed into me, I keened, a high-pitched sound I'd never made before. He hit something deep inside me that sent sparks of pleasure and pain racing across my nerves, the last little bit I needed.

My body began to shake as I tipped over the edge. I cried out his name and Cade responded by fucking me harder and faster, sending wave after wave of pleasure over me until it was almost too much and I couldn't do anything but try to scream. The sound was breathless, every muscle in my body straining to find a way to release what I was feeling. There was no end to it. I couldn't tell if I was having multiple orgasms or if it was just one that kept going and going, but whatever was happening, my brain decided to shut down. My eyes rolled back and my vision began to gray. Then Cade was saying my name, his hips jerking against me. He slumped down and I wrapped my arms and legs around him, instinctively holding on to something solid as my surroundings seemed to have liquefied.

I hovered there on the edge of consciousness, waiting for my world to normalize. At some point, Cade rolled off me and then, a few minutes after that, I watched as he got up, gathered his clothes and walked out. He didn't go into the bathroom and he didn't say a word.

I frowned as I pulled the blankets around me, but I was too exhausted, both emotionally and physically, to dwell on it. There was always tomorrow.

# Chapter 3

I wasn't sure what to expect the next morning, but at the very least, I assumed things would just go back to the way they had been... a professional relationship without emotions involved. A part of me hoped, no matter how much I tried to tell myself not to, that things would be different, that what had happened meant Cade cared about me, at least somewhat.

As I came out into the main sitting area, I realized something had changed, but not for the better. Cade stood by the door, his bag on the floor at his feet. He glanced at his watch.

"We need to leave for the airport in thirty minutes." His face wasn't just blank; it was cold. I didn't see a hint of warmth, not even the lust I'd grown accustomed to when he saw me. Considering I was wearing only a robe and it wasn't even belted, his lack of attention spoke volumes.

I frowned, puzzled, but didn't say a word. He didn't seem in the mood to talk and I didn't want to overstep the boundary that seemed firmly back in place. I nodded and went back into the bedroom.

"I'll meet you in the lobby," Cade called after me. "Don't be late."

Now I was really confused. Had I done something to upset him? Or was he embarrassed for having told me about his past? I could understand that. But this coldness seemed more significant than that. If he'd felt like his actions had been unprofessional, why hadn't he just apologized or owned up to the mistake? Or simply told me it was a lapse in judgment to share something so personal? Why act so distant? Or, the thought struck me, had I been too obvious? Had he been able to tell that my feelings for him went beyond the physical?

The questions nagged at me as I packed my things and got ready to go. I was done with time to spare and headed down to the lobby, hoping Cade would be in a better mood when I arrived. Instead, I found the lobby empty and I looked dumbly down at my phone. No text messages, no calls. I was five minutes early, so maybe he'd gone to the restroom or stepped out for something, but not finding him here made me nervous.

I considered asking the front desk, but I didn't want to seem like the kind of girl who was checking up on her boyfriend. Cade was not my boyfriend. I knew that.

So I waited and tried to appear calm, not wanting him to see how upset I truly felt. I wasn't so sure I succeeded, but when I saw Cade walking toward me from the direction of the hotel restaurant, I was pretty sure he didn't suspect I'd been worried. I hadn't thought to check to see if he was getting breakfast. I didn't have much of an appetite.

"Our car's here."

As Cade walked by, I caught a whiff of alcohol and frowned. He hadn't been eating. He'd been drinking. And it was way too early for that. I held my tongue though. It wasn't my concern. He was an adult and we weren't together. But while both of those things were true, neither of them stopped me from worrying as we climbed into the car.

The ride to the airport was tense and silent, but not the good kind of tension, the kind that meant once it was unleashed, amazing things were going to happen. I kept glancing at Cade out of the corner of my eye, trying to will him to look at me, but he kept his gaze straight ahead. I'd expected at least a hint of a smile when I winced as I sat down, but there was nothing. My ass was still tender, my pussy sore, and sitting wasn't exactly the most comfortable thing in the world – all things that should've been of interest to Cade. Instead, I was getting the cold shoulder.

By the time we landed back in Chicago, I was a bundle of nerves. Something was wrong and I didn't know what it was. I promised myself that as soon as we got in the car, I'd ask him, and I wouldn't let up until he told me the truth. Whatever it was, we'd get past it. He'd told me he wasn't done with me yet and I intended to hold him to that.

As we walked out of the terminal, however, he handed me my bag. "You'll be taking the car back to your place."

"What about you?" I hoped I sounded much more casual to him than I did to myself.

"I have some business to attend to." He didn't meet my eyes. "The driver's waiting."

I stared as he walked off. The entire time Cade and I had been together, he'd had his moments where he'd kept his distance, but he'd never been rude. And he'd never made me feel cheap. Until now. I lifted my chin. I wasn't going to let him do this to me. I would go home, spend the rest of the day relaxing and grading papers. I wouldn't think about Cade until the next time he called. And I certainly wouldn't spend the time in between worrying over him.

That resolve lasted exactly three hours. As much as I tried not to, I wasn't able to stop myself from being distracted. Every so often, I found myself staring at a test and realizing I'd been looking at the same question for five minutes. Sometimes it was a specific thought that caught my attention, or a theory about what could've happened. Other times, it was just a general feeling of unrest.

I waited for him to call, to set up a meeting for the upcoming week, but he didn't. Monday came and went with nothing. Mindy asked about my weekend and I gave her a few unimportant details. Good food. Good sex. Nothing much else. I didn't like lying to her, but until I was sure what was happening with Cade, I didn't want to speculate. There were too many variables in play, too many things I didn't understand.

I considered calling him, but every time I took out my phone and started to tap on his number, I began to wonder if maybe this was a test. Maybe he was teaching me patience. I remembered his lesson on orgasm denial and wondered if this was just another way for me to learn delayed gratification.

Even the idea that this isolation was intentional didn't mean any of it sat well with me. It was one of a dozen scenarios, each one with its own sets of pros and cons. I didn't know what to hope for, which meant I didn't have a single possibility on which to fix my mind. Instead, I jumped from scenario to scenario.

When Friday rolled around, I was more than ready for a night out with the girls. Adelle and I were good again, which meant there wouldn't be any awkwardness. Neither she nor Mindy would expect me to give them details about my weekend since they both knew the whole Cade thing was a sensitive subject. Whatever I did share, they'd take at face value. Plus, there'd be alcohol, which was always a good thing. Okay, not always, but in this instance, it would be. Plus, I was hoping Adelle and Mindy would be able to provide me with some distraction.

When I arrived at L20, the other two were already there and Mindy was practically bouncing in her seat. That was good. It meant she had something exciting she wanted to share. Whatever it was, I hoped it would be big enough to keep us going most of the night.

"I'm so glad you're here," Adelle said. She sent a pointed look in Mindy's direction. "I think she's going to burst if she doesn't get to share her news soon."

I smiled as I sat down. Mindy didn't even wait for me to get my coat off before letting loose.

"I met someone!"

"That's great!" The enthusiasm in my voice was genuine. Mindy wasn't quite like Adelle when it came to the love 'em and leave 'em mentality. She enjoyed her flirtations and her one night stands, but she also wasn't opposed to having a relationship like Adelle was. Not that I could really blame Adelle for not wanting to get into anything serious. Losing Morgan had been tough on her.

"All right, then, spill." Adelle signaled to the nearby waiter. "Champagne, please. The best you have."

"Well," Mindy began. "I met him two weeks ago..."

"Two weeks and you're just sharing now?" Adelle shook her head. "What's his deep dark secret?"

Mindy rolled her eyes. "It was a chance meeting a coffee shop one morning before school, and that turned into a second meeting and then a third. We chatted in line, waiting for our orders and he confessed that after our first meeting, he'd deliberately gone back at the same time, hoping to see me again."

I really was interested in what Mindy had to say, but I found myself having to concentrate to pay attention. Random things made me think of Cade, and I didn't want that. I focused on each word, occasionally following Adelle's lead and putting in a comment or two. I let the atmosphere of friendship and warmth surround me and began to relax.

By the time I was walking out to get a cab, I was feeling better than I had all week. I could do this. I didn't need Cade.

As I slid into the back seat of the cab, my phone rang. My stomach flipped when I saw his name on the screen. Maybe I wasn't as completely over him as I thought. I answered the call, keeping my voice cool and clipped. I didn't want him to know how worried I'd been. Better he think I was either annoyed or indifferent.

"Yes?"

There were no apologies, no explanations. He didn't even bother with a greeting. All that came were instructions. We had a date for tomorrow night, and it was going to be a surprise.

# Chapter 4

Saturday morning, I woke to someone knocking on my door. I ran my hand through my hair as I stumbled out of bed.

"I'm coming!" I called, then stifled a yawn. It had taken me a long time to fall asleep last night. I was just glad I'd worn a pair of sweats and a t-shirt to bed instead of something more pajama-like.

The guy at the door didn't even bat an eye as he handed me the clipboard to sign for the package. He wished me a good day and handed me what was obviously a garment box. It was light, making me think I knew what was inside. Or, at least, I had a pretty good idea.

When I opened it, I saw that I was right. In general, at least. I'd guessed that Cade had sent me lingerie, but what was laying on the tissue paper wasn't like anything I'd ever owned. I'd saved up to buy the lingerie I'd gotten for my honeymoon, but even then, I'd gone to a regular department store. One look at this, however, and I knew it had to have come from some high-end boutique. The kind of place that didn't bother putting their prices on things because if you had to ask, you couldn't afford it.

I didn't take it out right away though. There was an envelope sitting on top, my name written in strong, masculine script. Opening the creamy linen, I pulled out a piece of stationary; my breath caught in my throat as I unfolded it. Inside was the same handwriting with a list of instructions.

Tonight, you are to come to the loft at eight. Wear the enclosed garments under a coat. Only a coat.

I shivered at the idea of being out in public in a very skimpy pair of bra and panties with only a coat to cover me. Although it was almost the end of October in Chicago, it wasn't the chill outside that prompted my response. I'd felt exposed walking a few feet across a parking lot, fully dressed sans underwear. I could only imagine what it would be like to walk outside, take a cab, walk up the stairs to Cade's loft, all while nearly naked.

I swallowed hard as my stomach squirmed. I couldn't deny that the idea turned me on. I was nervous, of course, but my arousal more than covered it.

I kept reading.

For tonight's lesson, you must follow my instructions exactly. First, you are to completely shave or wax. Legs, pussy, ass. Everything. Second, there is something new you have to do...

My face flamed as I read his directions. I wasn't an idiot. I had a pretty good idea why he wanted me to do... that, but it didn't make the thought any less embarrassing. Now I understood why he'd sent this today. I wouldn't have to rush, but I was going to need most of the day to follow his instructions. I'd even have to run to the store for a few things.

I set the note aside and picked up the lingerie one piece at a time. First, there were a pair of sheer purple-black thigh-high stockings. That was good. At least my legs wouldn't be completely bare. The stockings looked like they connected to the panties with garter belts. The panties almost looked like they could be boy-shorts... if they hadn't been sheer purple. And crotchless.

Fuck.

The bra was strapless, with barely enough of the same filmy material to cover my nipples. All three pieces of the outfit – if it could be called that – had a dusting of glitter making them sparkle and shimmer in the light.

Something glinted inside the box and I set aside the bra to see what else Cade had sent. Whatever it was had slipped underneath the tissue paper. My fingers closed around something cold and as I lifted it out, I gasped. If I hadn't known how meticulous Cade was, I would've thought it was a mistake.

The gold chain was delicate and the setting for the stone simple. It wasn't a diamond. It was amethyst, a deep purple that went perfectly with both my eyes and the lingerie. I'd never seen a necklace quite so exquisite.

I set it back down in the box, my head swimming. I understood the clothes and the instructions. He was still in teacher mode. But I didn't get why he'd given me the necklace? It seemed like such an odd gesture, especially after how we'd left things. I closed my eyes and tried to regroup.

This was business. Pleasure too, but no attachments. Cade had his reasons for everything he did and I was sure I'd learn what they were tonight. For right now, I had to do all of the things on his list, and they were going to take me a while.

After several hours of grooming in ways I'd never imagined, I was dressed – or as close to dressed as I was going to be – and ready to go. I'd had to dig into my closet to find my longest coat, but it actually ended up being the perfect choice. The bottom of it hit just above my knees and it closed tightly enough that I didn't have to worry about flashing anyone. One accidental slip and I could end up in jail for indecent exposure. I could only imagine having to call one of my friends to bail me out for that.

My stomach was in knots as I headed out. I was sure someone would figure out what I was doing and what I wasn't wearing, but no one gave me a second glance. The cab driver barely looked at me until I gave him the address to the loft, and then it had hardly been lust or admiration in his eyes. He definitely didn't think a woman should be alone in that neighborhood at this time of night. After I reassured him that, yes, that's where I wanted to go, we set off.

It was a bit noisier than it had been the last time I'd been here, but no one bothered me as I got out of the cab. I was pretty sure someone was watching me, but when I looked around, I saw only a few kids across the street and a guy standing on the corner, smoking a cigarette. He looked a bit rough around the edges, like he'd done some time, but he wasn't doing anything threatening. No one looked my way.

After taking a calming breath, I headed up the stairs. It was showtime.

# Chapter 5

I knocked on the door, then pushed it open when I heard Cade call for me to come in. I stepped inside, remembering the last time I'd been here. The lighting was dimmer than it had been, casting the edges of the room into shadows. The center of the room was still well-lit. In fact, in the same spot where Cade had literally painted me, was a ring of bright lights, all pointed down at what looked like a fleece or velvet blanket of some kind. There also appeared to be some padding underneath it, making a vague, sort of shapeless cushion that looked big enough for two people to enjoy.

"Did you do as I instructed?" Cade stepped out of the shadows and I caught my breath.

I nodded in answer to his question, too distracted by him to answer properly. He was barefoot and bare-chested. He wore a pair of dark blue jeans that hung low enough on his hips to show off the deep v-grooves that pointed straight to his cock. His hair was wild, a mass of untamed curls.

"Come here."

I walked toward him, until I stood at the edge of the light circle. When I stopped, I noticed he had something in his hands. A camera. Not a digital one, but the kind real photographers used. The butterflies in my stomach doubled.

He raised the camera and pointed it at me. "Slowly walk toward me, unbuttoning your coat as you come."

My fingers shook as I reached for the top button. My steps, however, were steady. I could hear the camera clicking as I undid a new button with each step until the coat hung open.

"Take it off."

I didn't need him to tell me he didn't want it to just fall off. I took a step and let the jacket slide off of my shoulders. Then fall to my elbows. By the time it was on the floor, I was standing only a few feet away from Cade, dressed only in my skimpy lingerie.

He put the camera on a tripod facing the cushion at the center of the circle and picked up something from the floor. He crossed into the circle and stood next to the cushion. "Come here."

I moved to stand next to him, curious as to where things were going next. I heard the snap of a cap and saw him squirt something into his hand. A moment later, cool gel slid across my skin as he ran his hand over my arm. I looked down and saw glitter. It wasn't too thick, but enough that the light caught it, throwing sparkles into the air.

He didn't speak as his hands worked over every bit of exposed skin, sending little tingles of pleasure across my nerves. When he knelt in front of me to rub down my legs, I saw lust flash across his face when he caught a glimpse of the panties framing my bare pussy.

In what seemed to be an uncharacteristically impulsive move, he leaned forward and pressed his lips against the exposed skin. I bit back a moan, hoping he'd do it again, but he didn't. He stood, our bodies mere inches apart. His fingers brushed just under the necklace and warmth spread out from the place he touched.

"Sit on the cushions," he said as he took a step back.

I did as he said while he retrieved the camera from the tripod. It was funny, I thought, how I never even considered the danger of letting an escort take pictures of me in what I was sure would be provocative poses. As a teacher in a private school, I should've been worried that the pictures would leak and I'd lose my job. I knew it wouldn't though. I completely trusted Cade to never let that happen.

"Lean back."

I leaned back on my elbows. I wasn't nearly as self-conscious as I probably should've been, but I still kept my knees pressed together. At least, I did until Cade spoke again.

"Open your legs."

I slowly let my knees fall apart. Cade moved around me, snapping pictures, having me shift and pose in various ways. Some sexual, some not. The more pictures he took, the more comfortable I became. I should've known that would be when Cade changed things up again.

"Lie back with your legs spread," he instructed. "I want you to touch yourself. Make yourself come."

Nerves threatened, but I pushed them down. I stretched out on the cushion and closed my eyes, focusing on the feel of the soft fleece against my skin. I ran one hand down my stomach and then slipped it between my legs. It was a strange sensation, going from material beneath my fingertips to skin without the usual methods of going under or taking off.

I shivered as my fingers brushed over my sensitive flesh. I'd followed all of his instructions, including a fresh wax. I found that each time I did it, I found it less unpleasant. I wasn't sure I'd do it consistently, but I had to admit I did enjoy it in moments like this.

"Tonight," Cade said. "You're going to orgasm more times than you've ever dreamed possible."

I swallowed hard and let my fingers slide between my folds. They found my clit easily, the little bundle of nerves already throbbing, ready to be touched. The pad of my index finger brushed across it and I shivered as a rush of arousal went through me. I was getting wetter by the second. Cade had to be able to see it, exposed as I was, his camera capturing every moment of it.

I dropped my hand and let a finger slide into my pussy. I moaned as I slowly pumped it in and out. A second one joined and I pressed down with the heel of my palm on every stroke, the base of my hand rubbing against my clit with just the right amount of pressure. My free hand moved to my breasts as I found myself growing closer to climax. Through the thin material of the bra, I caressed my breast, then began to tug on my nipple.

"That's it, baby." Cade's voice was quiet.

The endearment, however general, spoke to a hidden part of me that wanted more from him and I cried out, shoving my fingers deep inside me as I came.

I heard movement as I came down and I opened my eyes, propping myself on my elbows again. Cade had put the camera back on the tripod, a timer making it click at evenly-spaced intervals, and was standing over me. I watched as he knelt next to me, the angle perfect to allow an unobstructed view of me while keeping him mostly out of the way.

He held up his hand and showed me the smooth rubber phallus he was holding. Last summer, I would've thought it was big because it was thicker than Ronald's, but it looked small compared to what I knew was straining against Cade's jeans. Still, when he pressed the head of it against my entrance, my body had to stretch around it. I moaned as it entered me, the cool material strange after the warmth of my fingers.

The strokes were even and deep, perfectly angled so that each one pressed against my g-spot and made me writhe. Cade's free hand roamed across my body, adding to the sensations, as his fingers rolled my nipples, then danced down my belly to rub circles on my clit. When his mouth covered my nipple, the wet heat instantly soaking through the thin material, I cried out. He pushed the dildo into me and held it there as he increased the suction on my nipple until I exploded again.

I gasped for air as he straightened and removed the toy from me. He set it aside and I waited for him to take its place between my legs. Instead, he rolled me onto my stomach and shifted the cushion beneath me until my ass was higher up. I flushed at the thought of him spanking me on camera.

"Did you follow all of my instructions?" Cade asked as he ran his hand over my ass.

For a moment, I thought he was trying to find an excuse to spank me, but then, as his finger teased between my cheeks, I realized what he wanted to know. One of his directions, the one that had embarrassed me the most, would prepare me so that he could make good on a promise he'd made while we were in Canada.

"I did," I said softly. I tensed as his finger brushed against my asshole.

"Have you ever had anything in here?"

I would've laughed at how casual his question sounded, but I was starting to get nervous. "No," I said.

"Just relax," he said. "Trust me."

I made a surprised sound when I felt something cold and wet between my cheeks, but the sound turned to a moan when Cade slipped a finger into my pussy.

"Relax," he murmured. "I promise, this is going to feel amazing."

After a few moments, he removed his hand. Then I felt something hard and cool at my hole.

"Breathe and relax," he instructed as he slowly pushed it into my ass.

I closed my eyes and focused on my breathing. It didn't hurt, but the pressure was unique. I felt a strange quick stretch and then the sensation was gone, replaced by something new. There was something inside my ass; I was still trying to decide how I felt about that. A moment later, a second object started to work its way in. This time, I figured out what Cade was using. I may not have been as sexually adventurous as my friends – at least not until recently – but I wasn't completely naïve.

"I chose these particular beads," Cade said, confirming my suspicion. "Because they're all the same size, and since you're a virgin, we don't want to risk stretching you out too fast."

"I'm not a–" I started to disagree and then realized what he meant.

"Do they hurt?" Cade asked. I thought I heard a note of concern in his voice.

"No," I answered honestly. There was a feeling of fullness that was odd, and they rubbed against my insides in unfamiliar ways, but there was no pain.

"Now," Cade said. "I'm going to show you exactly why these little beauties are so good."

He slid two fingers into my pussy and I instantly felt the difference. I moaned as his fingers thrust into me, the motion causing the beads to shift, sending ripples of pleasure through me.

"Imagine," he said. "If it was my cock inside you. Imagine how full you'd feel."

"Fuck." I pressed my face against the blanket. I was pushing back into his hand, driving him deeper. The duel sensations were almost too much. I didn't think I could handle both his cock and the beads inside me. Then he pushed another finger inside and I cried out, my body stiffening with an unexpected orgasm.

He stilled, holding his fingers inside until my muscles relaxed and he could move his hand again. This time, he worked his fingers inside me, rubbing against my g-spot with his knuckles before pressing against the thin wall of skin separating his hand from the beads. As his fingers twisted inside me, he slowly began to pull the beads out of my ass. My body jerked with each one, the sudden pressure and pop as they passed sending a jolt through me.

"One more time," he said as his thumb rubbed against my clit. "Come on, baby. One more time for me."

I started to nod, wanting to tell him I was almost there, but it was lost in a wail as he pulled the last six beads out all at once. I'd never felt anything quite like it, the electricity shooting across my nerves, muscles twitching and fluttering as I exploded again, this one harder than before.

When he pulled his fingers out of me, I shuddered, another wave of pleasure washing over me. I rolled onto my side, looking up at him. His face was smooth, unreadable, but his eyes were heated. I ran my gaze down his sculpted chest and abs to where I could see the outline of his cock through his jeans.

I reached for his zipper, determined to show him just how much I enjoyed what he had done, but he stopped me. His hands curled around mine.

"Not yet," he said.

There was something strange in his voice and I frowned. This wasn't his commanding tone letting me know we weren't done. This was something different.

"There's something I need to tell you."

# Chapter 6

I sat up, feeling more exposed than I had just moments before. Cade didn't say anything as I pulled the blanket from behind me and wrapped it around my shoulders. I was glad for the few minutes of silence. I wasn't sure what he was going to say, but I had a feeling it was going to change everything.

"I always know the right thing to say," he began.

I looked up at him, but he wasn't looking at me. His eyes were on his hands as they sat on his lap.

"For the past six years, I've always had the right words to say to every woman I've ever met. I know what she wants and what I need to do to give it to her." He ran his hand through his hair. "But now, here... I can't find the words I need."

"Just say it, Cade." My voice sounded harsher than I meant it to be. My heart was pounding painfully against my ribcage, my palms sweaty. He knew. That had to be it; had to be the reason he'd withdrawn so suddenly. He'd figured out that I had feelings for him and he was trying to find a way to let me down easily.

He took a deep breath and my heart clench as I waited for the words to come. Instead he said the last thing I expected. "I fucked up."

"How?" I said the word slowly, trying to understand what was behind this confession.

"I made a big deal about how I keep things professional and how, if there's the slightest bit of emotional involvement, everything ends." He looked at me now. His expression was still guarded, but I could tell it was a struggle for him. "But I fucked up. The things I'm feeling for you, Aubree..." He reached out and brushed his fingers across my cheek. "They're anything but professional."

I caught my breath and told myself to calm down. I needed him to explain because if this was some sort of test, I didn't want to make a wrong move.

"When I'm with you." He shook his head. "I can't think straight. I lose control." He gestured toward the back of the loft where the bathroom was located. "When we were in the shower and you stopped me because we weren't using a condom... that was the first time in nine years I've forgotten to use one."

The memory of that night warmed me. I hadn't even thought of it that way.

"I tried telling myself it was because you were – and please don't take this the wrong way – more submissive than any woman I'd been with in a long time. Women who want me to dominate them, they still consider themselves in charge. They don't fully give themselves over to me." A ghost of a smile played at his lips. "But you, even when you're fighting with me, you trust me."

I wasn't even tempted to protest him referring to me as submissive. I hadn't explored that part of me yet, but this wasn't the time to try to figure it out. I didn't want to speak, didn't want to risk breaking whatever spell it was that had him talking so freely.

"I pretended everything was a physical reaction, because how you responded to me was something I hadn't gotten from other women I'd been with." He put his hand on my cheek. "And then I saw you with Jason."

I pulled the blanket more tightly around me. It wasn't a memory I wanted to dwell on.

"The reason I was so adamant about you going through with fucking him was because I thought it'd break this hold you have on me. I thought it would help me see you as just another client, but it didn't." He ran his fingers through my hair. "Even if he hadn't hit you, I would've stopped things." His hand slid down my neck, stopping before it went under the blanket. "I can't stand the thought of another man touching you."

I couldn't breathe.

His voice grew rough and I could see the struggle on his face as he tried to maintain control. "I know this means we're done, and I'm sorry I didn't tell you this before..." He gestured around us. "I had to look at you one more time. See that expression on your face when you came." He brushed his thumb across my bottom lip and then pulled his hand away. "But I knew I couldn't take my own pleasure in you, not like this."

I put my finger on his lips, stopping the flow of words. "When you said you had to tell me something, I thought you were going to say this was over... because of me." He frowned and I continued. "I feel the same way. I've been trying to lie to myself, to deny the feelings I have for you, hoping they'd go away. They haven't."

He started to shake his head. "Aubree, that's... I..."

"Hey, usually when someone confesses that they care about you too, it's a good thing." I tried to keep my tone light, but I didn't understand why he was protesting.

"You don't know," he said, looking away. "There are things about me..."

"Cade," I spoke slowly. "I know you have sex for money. Kinda how we met." I reached up and turned his face back toward me. "Whatever it is, you can tell me."

After a moment, he began, "I told you about my mom, but I didn't tell you what I did." I paused and watched the guilt slide into grief on his face. "I ran. I knew she was dead. There was no point in calling an ambulance and I knew that if I called the cops, they'd arrest my dad. I knew they'd want me to testify against him. And I knew he'd just charm his way out of it like he did everything else. They'd make me go with him, and he'd spend every day until I was eighteen reminding me that it was all my fault. If he didn't just kill me too."

"Cade," I started to speak but he cut me off.

"I was on the streets for a few months, doing odd jobs here and there, trying to stay under the radar." He paused for a moment, like he was trying to decide if he wanted to tell me what came next.

During that silence, I realized I was about to discover how he'd gotten involved in prostitution in the first place. My throat grew tight as I understood the level of trust he was placing in me.

"There was this rich woman, maybe thirty or so, and she hired me to do some work around a house she'd inherited. She fed me, let me stay in the guest house... and then she offered me money to fuck her."

I was glad my hands were under the blanket and he couldn't see me twisting my fingers together. What kind of woman propositions a kid she should've been helping? Okay, so he may have been eighteen by then, but it didn't mean she hadn't taken advantage of him and his situation.

"For three years, I serviced her and her friends." Cade was looking away from me again. "They were the ones who taught me everything. How to please a woman physically, how to see what they want, give them what they don't even realize they need."

I reached out and wrapped my hand around his. He looked over at me.

"I hadn't been a virgin when I'd met her, but I'd only had sex with one person." He gave me a sad smile. "I'd been like you. Innocent. Not like I am now."

"Did you lie to me?" I asked and he looked startled at my question. Good. I needed him to understand what I was going to say and catching him off guard was the best way to get his attention. "All of the things you told me about how I shouldn't be ashamed of who I am or what I want? Were those lies?"

"No." He shook his head.

"Then why are you ashamed of who you are?"

Anger flashed across Cade's face. "Because, while I was fucking Penny and her socialite friends, my father was beating the shit out of his new girlfriend and her kid."

Now I got it.

"I should have stopped him," he said fiercely. "It took almost two years of domestic abuse claims and putting the kid in the hospital half a dozen times before the girlfriend finally had enough and shot him. She got off on self-defense, but it never should've happened."

I could feel his hand shaking beneath mine.

"If I'd called the cops, testified, she never would've been put in that position."

"You don't know what would've happened," I said. "She could've met another abusive man. He might have gotten off even if you'd testified. At least he can't hurt anyone else."

"I should've been the one to do it. Not her." He pulled his hand away and turned until his back was to me. "That's the kind of man I am, Aubree. A coward. That's why you should leave now and never look back."

I sat up on my knees, letting the blanket fall off my shoulders. I wrapped my arms around him from behind, the feel of his bare skin against mine sending a shiver through me. I pressed my lips against the side of his neck.

"I know what kind of man you are, Cade. You saved me, and not just from Steven or from Jason. You saved me from myself." I spread my hands out on his chest, one over his heart. "You showed me who I could be."

"Aubree, I–"

I ran my hand down his flat stomach, not stopping until I was cupping him through his jeans. He'd gone soft while we talked, but I heard his breathing hitch when I squeezed him. "No," I said firmly. "No more putting yourself down." I flexed the hand on his chest, letting my nails dig into his skin. "I want you. I need you." I put my mouth against his ear and spoke in a low, sultry voice. "Fuck me."

# Chapter 7

Cade spun toward me and I gasped at the heat in his eyes. He scooped me up and stood as I threw my arms around his neck. Before I could make a sound, his mouth covered mine. I parted my lips, my tongue running out to meet his. I played with the curls at the base of his neck, lightly tugging at them until he growled. His teeth scraped at my bottom lip and I moaned. It still amazed me that I had spent years with Ronald and he'd never once done this to me, and Cade had known almost from moment one what I liked. Being with someone who used to be a professional was definitely going to have its advantages.

He carried me to the bed in the corner and laid me down. It was darker back here, the lights from the photo shoot offering barely enough to see by. It was perfect lighting, softening everything but the way his eyes were blazing. I flushed, warmth spreading across my skin.

He stood next to the bed and stripped off his jeans, revealing a pair of snug black boxer briefs. He kicked the jeans aside and smiled down at me as he hooked his thumbs in the waistband of his underwear. Anticipation coiled in my stomach. I wondered if I'd ever get tired of this, of the slow reveal of each inch of tanned, muscular flesh. In the time it had taken him to walk me to the bed and take off his clothes, his cock had started to swell. My mouth watered at the memory of how he'd felt sliding between my lips, across my tongue.

"I said that I felt like you trusted me." Cade reached over to a battered stack of drawers and opened the top one. "Am I right?"

I nodded, wondering where he was going with this. Wherever it was, I was positive I was going to like it. "I trust you."

The smile that spread across his face was equal parts seductive and pleased. He pulled a strip of fabric from the drawer. By the wicked glint in his eyes, I could tell he was either going to blindfold me or tie me up. I was hoping for the latter, my heart skipping a beat as I thought about how it would feel, my hands restrained, unable to move.

"Do you remember your safe words?" he asked. "There are some things I want to do with you... to you, and I don't want to freak you out."

I stretched my arms above my head, hoping he'd understand that I wasn't just agreeing to do what he wanted... I wanted it too. "I remember them." I stretched my body out, my breasts pushing against the bra until my nipples almost popped free. "Do what you want to me. For me. With me."

"Fuck, Aubree," he groaned. "Do you have any idea how hot you are?"

I grinned at him. "Very. Or so I've been told."

He knelt on the bed next to me and leaned close. His cock brushed against my ribcage, drawing my attention for a moment. Then his hands were at my wrists. He crossed them, one over the other, and then wrapped the strip of cloth around them. It wasn't tight, but I could tell it would limit my movement. I couldn't see what he was doing, but when he sat back, I gave a tug and confirmed my hands had been tied to something.

"Here."

Something soft slid into my palm. I wrapped my fingers around it.

"Two quick pulls and it'll release your hands."

I nodded to show I understood, then moaned as his hands ran across my ribcage and up to cup my breasts. The little push he gave them caused the material to slip down enough to expose my nipples. The cool air caressed the already hard points, raising goose bumps along my skin.

Cade's fingers teased at my nipples, eliciting little gasps of pleasure from me as he tugged and rolled until I began to squirm. When he released them, he leaned back and reached for one of the drawers next to his bed.

"I once told you that I wanted to use nipple clamps on you," Cade said. "But when I lived here, I couldn't afford any of the toys I have now." He held up two wooden clothespins. "These, however, can work in a pinch." He smirked at his play on words.

Shit.

He moved until he was straddling me, a knee on either side of my waist. I stared up at him, appreciating the magnificent picture he made above me, choosing to focus on him instead of the medieval torture device he held in his hands.

The first clothespin clamped down on my nipple and I sucked in a breath as the pain caused me to arch and twist on the bed. It wasn't too dissimilar from his fingers twisting me when it came to pain level, but it felt very different otherwise; a harsh persistence that finally faded into numbness. I bit my lip as Cade held the other one close to me, teasing me, threatening me with its presence. Finally, it was attached and my breath hissed through my lips as the pinch seared through me.

"Feel it," he whispered as his fingers traced around my breast. "Accept the pain, don't fight it. It's only reminding you that you're alive. Welcome it."

One part of me wanted to twist his balls in my hands and ask him to embrace the pain. Now, I understood why he'd tied me up. Another part, though, felt the pain morph into something deeply sensual. My body was on high alert. I could feel everything.

He slid down my body, using his knees to push my legs apart until he was laying between them.

"I think I'll want you to wear these out in public some time." Cade ran his finger down the length of my slit. "We'll go someplace nice and I'll take you right there, slide inside you while people are all around us."

I made a noise as his finger dipped between my folds. It circled my entrance, then moved up to move around my clit, never quite touching it.

"I can imagine it," he said. "The sounds you'd try to keep in." His finger slid inside me and my body jerked, still sensitive from the previous play. "The way your pussy would grip me."

My back arched as he ran his tongue over my sensitive flesh. I tugged at the restraints, wanting to bury my hands in his hair and press his face against me. Still, I didn't even consider freeing myself. There was something to be said for relinquishing control.

"Would I be able to make you lose control?" He added a second finger. "Make you forget everything but the sensation of me inside you? Filling you, pressing against all those places inside of you that make you scream my name."

He curled his fingers and rubbed against my g-spot. I cried out, my hips bucking up. He chuckled as he put a hand on my stomach, pushing me back down against the mattress. His tongue flicked the top of my clit and I swore. The restraints tightened around my wrists, sending a twinge of pain along muscles that were starting to burn. The sensations mingled with the dull ache in my nipples. Then there was the pleasure coursing up through me from his fingers and his mouth on my clit. I closed my eyes, unable to process all of the varying forms of stimulation.

I hovered on the edge of an orgasm and then the hand on my stomach slid up to my breasts. He flicked one of the clothespins, sending a jolt of pain down through me.

"Fuck!"

A second flick knocked it off and I whimpered as the blood rushed back into my nipple. It hurt in that pins and needles way, like when a foot or hand fell asleep but more intensely. I barely had time to adjust before the second one was knocked off and Cade's fingers were massaging the swollen flesh. I didn't know if his touch made it worse or better, but then his lips closed around my clit and he started to suck.

I yelled his name as I came, waves of pleasure washing over me. Even while I was coming, his fingers slid out of me and then I felt one, slick with my own juices, rub against my asshole. The suction on my clit increased as he pushed his finger inside. My body convulsed, not knowing where to go or what to do. Pain and pleasure exploded and a second orgasm hit me hard enough to knock the wind out of me.

When I recovered enough to start dragging in deep breaths, Cade was leaning over me and untying my hands. He sat back on his knees as he began to massage my wrists and hands.

"That wasn't too much?"

I could hear the concern in his voice but couldn't manage more than a weak shake of my head. I felt similar to how it had been after the first time he'd spanked me, like I'd finally found someone who got it, who understood a side of me I hadn't really understood myself.

"Good," he said. "Because we're not done."

He helped me roll over and I winced as my sore nipples rubbed against the blanket. A definite downside to the things I liked was how uncomfortable certain parts of the anatomy got as the endorphins faded.

"One day," he said. "I'm going to put you in this position and fuck your ass." His hand ran down my spine and over the swell of my buttocks. "Not tonight though." I heard a condom wrapper being opened. "I'm so hard, I wouldn't last more than thirty seconds inside your ass, and when I do it, I want you to enjoy it."

If someone had asked me a few months ago about having anything in my ass, I would've turned red and sputtered something about how I didn't think so. Now, my world was being expanded and Cade's words were making me even wetter.

"Do you have any shoulder issues?"

The question startled me. "No, why?"

"Because if you did, this wouldn't be a good idea."

Cade took my arms and brought them behind my back. My wrists crossed at the base of my spine and I felt the strip of fabric wrapping around them again.

"It's not tied," he explained. "But it will hold. Say yellow if it's too much."

"I will," I promised.

I wasn't sure I understood why he thought this might be too much, but then his hands were on my hips, raising me onto my knees. I turned my head as my upper body remained on the bed. When I felt a hand curl around the tie linking my wrists together, I realized what he was going to do.

He yanked me up by my wrists as he snapped his hips forward and buried himself inside me with one thrust. My mouth opened but no sound came out. I couldn't think, couldn't breathe. And then he was pounding into me, each stroke harder than the last as he used my arms for leverage.

I wasn't sure when I started talking, but I became aware that words were mixed with the moans of pleasure. Cade. Fuck. Yes. More. Harder. There didn't really seem to be any sort of order, but they all boiled down to one thing. Every cell in my body was on fire and I never wanted it to stop.

"Come for me, Aubree," Cade said, his voice breathless. "I want you to come from just my cock."

If it happened it would be for the first time, but I was so worked up from everything that had come before that I could feel myself getting closer to the edge. The muscles in my arms were quivering, burning. My shoulders begged for relief. My throat was sore. My nipples ached and my pussy was feeling every thrust. I was aware of every inch as he moved inside me, rubbing against my walls, stretching me to the limit.

"Come, Aubree."

I could feel Cade fighting against his body to maintain control. I could feel him thicken inside me.

"Please, baby."

I didn't know if it was the 'please' or the 'baby' that got me, but everything coiled together inside me burst at his words. Every muscle tensed and Cade pulled back hard enough on my arms that it was almost too painful. I rode the sensation, letting the waves take me where they would, into the light and the dark, hovering at the edge of consciousness.

"Fuck, yes!" I groaned as my body went limp.

Cade let my front half slump onto the bed as he slammed into me, grinding against me as he came, roaring out his release. He stilled for a minute, his fingers digging into my hips as his cock throbbed inside me. Then he was easing out and lowering me to the blanket. I whimpered as he withdrew, my muscles still spasming as electrical impulses fired from overloaded nerves.

I closed my eyes, hearing Cade moving around before he settled behind me. He wrapped the blanket around us and pulled me against him. I could feel his heartbeat against my back and pulled his arm more tightly around me.

"Thank you," Cade said as he kissed my temple.

"I think I should be thanking you," I said, opening my eyes. "That was amazing."

"Thank you for trusting me," he said. "Even after everything I told you."

I tilted my head back until I could see his face. "None of that matters. The past is the past."

He kissed the top of my head. "I like having you here. It's special. A place just for us."

"I like that I'm the only person you've brought here," I admitted. "No ghosts."

"I don't take clients to my condo either," he said. "So we have two places where it's just us."

I like that even better. I may be getting better with the whole not comparing me and Adelle thing, but as a girlfriend, I would be self-conscious in places where Cade had fucked other women. I wanted to put as much distance as possible between that part of his life and where we were headed together.

"Guess this means I have to drop Adelle permanently from my client list."

I rolled my eyes. "Funny."

"We'll have to work out some sort of schedule," he said thoughtfully. "We definitely don't work the same hours and while I can afford to cut back, I will need most weekends..."

I pulled out of his embrace and rolled onto my back so I was looking at him. A knot was forming in the pit of my stomach. This wasn't funny anymore. "What are you talking about?"

Cade gave me a puzzled look. "How we're going to schedule time to see each other between your teaching and my clients, of course. I don't exactly work a nine-to-five, Aubree."

# Chapter 8

I stared at him for almost a full minute, waiting for him to give me the punch line, to confess he'd taken his joke too far. Then his eyes met mine and I saw he wasn't kidding. My heart twisted, pain mingling with anger. I sat up, pulling his blanket over me.

"You're still going to be an escort?" The question sounded even harsher than I'd meant it, but I didn't take it back.

"It's my job, Aubree," Cade said. He sat up, frowning. "I wouldn't ask you to quit your job."

"My job doesn't involve me fucking other people!" I snapped. I climbed out of bed, yanking the blanket from underneath him. My eyes burned with tears but I refused to give in. Cade would think I was trying to manipulate him by crying. "You said you couldn't stand the thought of another man touching me. How do you think I'd feel, knowing you were doing a hell of a lot more than touching other women?"

He scowled, his eyes flashing. "Well, I'm sorry I don't have a college degree and a career as a lawyer or doctor to fall back on. You knew what I was. Should've just said then that I wasn't good enough for you."

My jaw dropped and it took me a moment to find my voice. "When the hell did I ever say that?"

"Right now." He climbed off of the bed and folded his arms across his chest. "You tell me you care about me, but you're just like the rest. You want me to be something I'm not. To pretend."

I took a step toward him, my anger curbed by the pain I could hear in his voice. "I don't want you to be something you're not. I want you to be the man I see in you."

He gave a bitter laugh. "Right, the man you want me to be."

"Who I know you are," I said firmly.

"You don't know me," he snapped. "You think because we fucked and I told you some shit about my past that you know everything there is to know about me?"

"I know enough to know that you're better than this."

"Bullshit." He practically spat out the word. "You want to believe that because you think you're too good to fall for a whore. Too precious and pure for someone like me. So you convince yourself that there has to be more to me. The hooker with a heart of gold, right? Some fucking Hollywood fairy tale."

I clutched the blanket more tightly to me. Why was he saying these things? What had happened to the man who'd told me that he cared about me? The one who'd made me feel things I'd never felt before?

"If I'd wanted to, don't you think I could've figured something out after nine years?" Cade's face was a cold mask, his words equally as icy. "Don't you think if I had any sort of marketable skill I would've used it to get out of this life years ago?" His mouth twisted. "This is what I'm good at. The only thing."

"That's not true," I protested. "You could do anything you want."

"What if this is what I want?" he asked, his voice flat.

I took a step back. I hadn't even considered that. I'd assumed he'd kept being an escort because he didn't have a reason to stop. My heart gave a painful thump. I thought I would be that reason. I turned away from him so he couldn't see the tears spilling over.

I picked up my coat and pulled it on, wishing I had real clothes to wear. My bra was somewhere around here, but I wasn't going to look for it. I just needed something to cover me. I felt too exposed. It didn't, however, stop me from feeling the slick wet on my inner thighs, or prevent my sensitive skin from chafing against the coat. I wiped the back of my hands across my cheeks and took a deep breath before turning around.

I had to make him see what I saw. There was no way he wanted this. No matter what he said, I did know him. "You're a talented artist, Cade. And you're smart and sweet..."

"Smart and sweet?" He sneered. "How fucking naïve are you?"

I flinched but didn't back down. He was scared. That had to be it. "You could sell your work and I could help you until you get on your feet—"

"Get out."

"What?" I shook my head. I couldn't have heard him right.

"We're done. Contract ended." Cade took a step toward me, but there was no desire, no emotion in his eyes. "You got what you wanted, Bree."

I caught my breath. He'd never called me Bree. Not once.

"I taught you how to fuck, how to seduce a man." He gave me a tight, humorless smile. "And you got to try to save the whore. Too bad the whore doesn't want to be saved."

I stepped back. I didn't want to hear this.

"I like who I am. What I do. Why would I want to give up fucking hundreds of gorgeous women and getting paid obscene amounts of money to do it?"

Each word was a blow and I couldn't stop the tears this time.

"Just get out."

"You bastard," I whispered. I turned toward the door, using all of my self-control not to run. I had to preserve at least that much of my dignity. I didn't have much left. Not after I'd bared my heart to him, let him do things to me I'd never considered doing. Shame and humiliation flooded me, mixing with anger and hurt until I wasn't sure I could handle feeling anything else. I needed to get as far away from here as possible. And I needed to forget I'd ever heard of Cade Shepard.

# Chapter 9

I barely got out of bed for the rest of the weekend. I didn't curl up on the couch and watch chick-flicks or finish off the half-gallon of ice cream that was in the freezer. I didn't eat anything. I'd taken a shower when I'd gotten home, desperate to rid myself of the smell and feel of his body. I scrubbed myself harshly, trying to get him off, making my outside feel as raw as my insides. I'd taken out my comfy pajamas but then remembered what had happened the last time I wore them. Finally, I'd ended up just crawling into bed naked and rolling myself in my blankets until I'd been unable to move. I got up only when it was necessary and then just fell back into bed and burrowed under the covers.

When I finally crawled out of bed Monday morning, I felt worse than I'd ever felt before. Worse than when I'd had to face the wedding guests and tell them Ronald had left. Worse than when I'd found out my best friend had paid Cade to have sex with me. Worse, even, than finding out Adelle had still been sleeping with Cade. I'd thought I'd had my heart broken by Ronald, but this was beyond broken. I was shattered. It had taken me falling for Cade to realize what I'd been missing with Ronald for a long time. I'd trusted Cade with everything and had been prepared to walk away because he said he didn't get emotionally involved. But then he'd gone and gotten my hopes up. He'd made me think I was something more than a job to him.

I closed my eyes and took a slow, deep breath. "Pull yourself together, Bree. He isn't worth it."

A pang went through me as I realized how much that sounded like what he'd said about me and about how he saw himself. It wasn't true though. I didn't think he wasn't good enough for me because of what he did. Good enough had nothing to do with it. He wasn't worth my tears not because of what he'd done, but because he'd chosen other women over me.

I looked in the mirror and winced. My eyes were bloodshot and swollen, my face puffy. My hair was a tangled mess that was going to take me twice as long as normal to get through. Worse, though, were the things I couldn't see. The way my body ached as if I'd spent the weekend doing an intense work-out. The phantom feelings of his hands on me. The memory of how he'd felt inside me.

I climbed into the shower, letting the hot spray beat down on my aching muscles. I didn't really have the time to linger, but I pushed it anyway. The sound of the water was soothing white noise, helping to drown out thoughts I didn't want to entertain. I kept my mind virtually blank as I got ready for school, pushing back the thoughts as they came forward, memories of how Cade had commented on my wardrobe. I wished I had enough money to buy new clothes, not because I felt like I needed them but because I couldn't quite stop myself from thinking about how Cade had said I hid behind my work clothes.

"Fuck him," I said the words to my reflection. I dabbed on a bit more concealer. "He doesn't know me."

When I was finally convinced that I looked presentable, I was running late, but it had been worth it. I didn't want anyone knowing what had happened over the weekend, and I needed to be able to fool not only the kids and faculty, but Mindy as well. If she saw how completely miserable I was, she'd call Adelle and the two of them would have some sort of crazy intervention or something. I knew Mindy wasn't exactly thrilled about my arrangement with Cade, and while she'd never say 'I told you so,' it'd still be there. And, of course, I had no clue how Adelle would take things. Ever since the whole incident with her canceling her appointments with Cade, things had been a bit fragile between us. We were moving past it, but it didn't make things any less uncomfortable at times.

Maybe, I thought as I quickly gathered my things and headed out, me being finished with Cade would speed up the process. And that, I'd decided, was what I was going to tell them. Cade and I had ended our arrangement because I was done. There wasn't anything else he could teach me. And if Adelle asked if I minded her calling him again, I'd tell her to go right ahead. Cade would never tell her the truth about what had happened and if she wanted to fuck him, who was I to say no? In the end, I wasn't any different than his other clients. I ignored the pain in my chest at the thought.

Mindy was waiting in my classroom when I arrived, the expression on her face saying I was later than I thought. I almost always got in before her, and she was never ready before me. She was visibly worried.

"I overslept." I gave her a smile I hoped was more convincing than it felt.

"Long weekend?" She raised an eyebrow suggestively.

That was a perfect segue to share the latest about me and Cade. Even better, there was the possibility that she would tell Adelle for me. I just had to manage to say it without any emotion.

"Cade and I were finishing up our arrangement," I said nonchalantly. "He says I'm ready to go out and have some fun."

"That's great!" Mindy practically squealed. "We're so having a girls' night out Friday after dinner. We're going to a club and we're going to get you laid."

I rolled my eyes and tried to not grit my teeth. "The entire point of this... this adventure was to prove to myself that I could get my own men and don't need help."

"Of course," Mindy hurriedly agreed, her eyes falling to the floor. "Adelle and I will stay out of it completely." She threw her arms around me. "We just want to see you work it."

Wonderful. Terrific. That's exactly what I wanted. Dancing and flirting with random guys while my friends watched to see if I'd been 'fixed'. I so didn't want to go to a club this weekend. I didn't even want to go to dinner, but I knew Adelle and Mindy would get suspicious if I tried to call off.

I gritted my teeth and hugged Mindy back. "That sounds great," I said. "Some girl time sounds like exactly what I need." That was such a lie, but Mindy bought it.

"We'll talk more at lunch," she said as she released me. "We'll want to go someplace special."

I nodded and then made a show of looking at the clock. "Best get back to class. Who knows what the hellions will do if you're not in there."

She grinned at me and headed for the door. "Lunch. Don't forget."

"I won't," I promised. I wouldn't want to go, but I'd do it to prevent her from asking why I bailed. I could do this. I could get through lunch pretending to be happy. I could get through the entire day being fake. And then again tomorrow, and the day after that, and however long I had to fake it before it became real.

It was harder than I thought, but I managed. By the time I entered my apartment building, I was exhausted, but no one had suspected a thing. I was so tired I didn't even see the person standing just inside the door until I ran into him.

"Oh!" I stumbled and my hands came in contact with a hard, muscular chest. I looked up into a pair of twinkling green eyes. "I'm so sorry. I wasn't watching where I was going."

"It's okay," he said. He put his hands on my upper arms to steady me. "Are you okay?"

"Fine." I nodded and took a step back to put some distance between us. "Just lost in my thoughts."

"It happens." He flashed a brilliant smile at me, a dimple appearing in his cheek. He held out a hand. "Finn Colson."

"Bree Gamble," I answered. I didn't even consider introducing myself as Aubree. That name wasn't one I wanted to hear again anytime soon. I shook Finn's hand and tried not to think about how his grip lingered.

"You live here or are you visiting someone? A boyfriend maybe?"

My smile was actually half-genuine. "Three E," I said. "What about you?"

"Not visiting a boyfriend."

I surprised myself with a laugh.

"I just moved here. To the city, not just the building. All the way from Sacramento." He gave me a shy smile. "In fact, I was just thinking how I needed to find someone who could show me around."

I started to shake my head.

"Or maybe just show me where to get a cup of coffee," Finn continued, holding up his hands in a gesture of surrender. "But I don't need an answer right away." He stepped around me. "I'm running late for a business dinner, but I hope to see you around."

"I'd like that," I answered automatically. I meant to be polite, but as soon as I saw Finn's eyes light up, I knew I'd come across as flirtatious. It looked like Cade had done a better job than I realized. I gave Finn a wave and then headed toward the stairs. The physical exertion would help keep my mind off things.

I opened the apartment door and turned on the light, just in time for my foot to kick something across the room. I looked down and saw an envelope. I frowned. Sometimes the super would leave notes, but they were usually taped to the outside of the door, and I couldn't think of anything he'd need to tell me. If it wasn't him, who else could it be?

A thrill of hope went through me and I dropped my bags, snatching the envelope from the floor. Was this some sort of ploy from Cade, a note telling me he was sorry? My hands were shaking as I tore it open and pulled out a single sheet of paper. It was folded in half, writing only on one side. The moment I opened it, I knew it wasn't from Cade. The handwriting was all wrong. My disappointment, however, was immediately overshadowed as I read...

Back off, bitch. Cade is mine. Stay away from him. I know where you live and I know people who'd love to hurt a pretty little blonde thing like you. Go near him or contact him again and you'll regret it.

## Chapter 10

*Cade*

My heart was racing, adrenaline coursing through my veins. My entire body was flushed and hot. I curled my hands into fists, my breathing harsh and fast in my ears. Strangely, my mind was blank. Well, not blank, but not exactly thinking in clear and coherent thoughts either.

When the door slammed behind her, my stomach lurched. She was gone.

I'd never fought with anyone before. Not like this. Whenever women got too attached, I cut them free and whatever protests they made, I ignored. I didn't care what they thought of me. But, Aubree's final words, the expression on her face when she'd called me a bastard... I'd never been cut so deeply. Not that she wasn't right, I knew.

I was a bastard. A bastard for breaking my own rules, a bastard for thinking I deserved anything more. A bastard for setting my sights too high.

That's what I got for letting someone close, I told myself as I stomped to the bathroom and turned on the shower. I had known better than to fall for her, but after nine years, she'd been the only one who'd tempted me to break my own rule. I stepped under the water without waiting for it to warm. I shivered as the cold hit my overheated skin. I hated cold showers, but at the moment, it was the wake-up call I needed.

I closed my eyes as the temperature started to rise but all I could see was her face. The hurt in those beautiful violet eyes.

"Fuck!" I yelled and slapped my hands against the wall. I rested my forehead between my hands. What the hell had I done?

Actually, I knew the answer.

I sabotaged myself on purpose. As I'd told Aubree before, I always knew what to say. Sure, I had a hard time telling her how I felt, and it had been difficult to share details of my past, but only an idiot wouldn't have known my little announcement wouldn't be taken well. And I wasn't an idiot. I'd known before I spoke that if I told Aubree I was planning on continuing my work as an escort, it'd drive her away.

Pain laced through my chest and I went to my knees. I never should have told her how I felt. Never should have acted on it. I should have just told her she was ready and cut her loose. Free to pursue relationships with whoever she wanted. I buried my hands in my hair as water poured down my face. The thought of her being with anyone else made me sick to my stomach.

But it had needed to be done. I'd gotten caught up in the moment, in the idea that she and I could have a life together. The moment we were done, however, real life had come crashing back down and I'd known it wouldn't work. Not because I didn't feel anything for her, but because I felt too much. She deserved better than me.

"...piece of ass... all you're good for..."

I squeezed my eyes shut, as if it would keep me from hearing the thoughts from my past. I was in enough pain. I didn't need those memories coming forward, reminding me of exactly how little I was worth.

"...pretty skin... tight ass..."

I moaned as the memories came flooding forward. I couldn't help it. I'd been telling the truth about my mother's murder, but that wasn't my only dark memory. As horrible as that had been, these memories were almost worse.

I could hear myself screaming, begging. I heard the laughter, that deep masculine laughter that promised pain. And, as always, I could hear his voice. It had been nearly ten years, but I still remembered every word, every action.

***

"What do you think gives you the right to say no to me, you worthless piece of shit?"

Pain exploded across my face and I cried out. The second blow came so fast I didn't have the chance to defend myself. I dropped to the floor, my head ringing. A third punch and I whited out. As hands tore my shirt from my body, I wished for darkness to take me. I knew what was coming, and I didn't want to be awake when it did.

"You're just a piece of ass. That's all you're good for."

I could feel his hands on me, pulling off my pants and boxers. I tried to hit away his hands as he wrapped his fingers around my soft cock, but he laughed and squeezed. A flare of pain went through me and I cried out, even as the pain started to clear my head.

He released me and manhandled me onto my stomach. His knee pressed against my spine, keeping me in place as he bound my wrists above my head, then tied them to something I couldn't pull free from. He moved off of me and ran his hand down my back and over my ass.

"Pretty skin and a tight ass."

I tried to get away, pulling against my restraints until I felt them cutting into my wrists. He kicked my side and I gasped, losing my breath. Another kick, and I screamed as something cracked. I pulled my legs up, trying to protect myself, but the gesture only pulled and twisted my shoulders. He laughed again and pulled my legs down, tying both of them apart.

The gravel scraped and tore at my chest, my stomach, my cock, sending pain shooting through me, but still, I struggled. I screamed for someone to help, anyone, and he didn't care. My head knew that meant no one would hear me, but I screamed just the same.

He slammed his fist against my temple and I saw stars. He slapped my ass, then dropped his hands to squeeze my balls until I whimpered, unable to make a louder sound.

"Did you really think you were so special that you could just waltz out of here because you don't swing this way? I don't give a fuck if you're straight. Just means I get to be the first one to take that cherry."

He released my balls and slid his hand between my cheeks, his finger pressing against my asshole. I began to beg, my pride shredded away. My only thought was to stop the inevitable.

"And when I'm done with you, I'm going to leave you here, let whoever wants have a crack at you. Maybe then you'll realize that no one gives a fuck what you want or who you are."

I began to pray that he'd just kill me and get it over with.

***

I rubbed my wrists as if I could still feel the ropes around them. I stood, shivering. I turned the cold water almost all the way off, scalding my skin. It still couldn't chase away the ice inside me. With the cold came the hopelessness and worthlessness I worked so hard to keep at bay. When I blocked out my past, I could almost pretend I was as confident as everyone thought I was. But when it hit me, it was a struggle to beat it.

As I felt the hot water starting to cool down, I turned off the shower and reached for a towel. I turned my face away from the mirror as I dried off, not wanting to see my reflection. In my head, I knew I'd see the same thing I'd seen for years. Hair that might've changed style according to current trends, but was still basically the same. Skin that was still smooth and tanned. A body unmarked with the exception of the tattoo I'd gotten for my mom with my first real paycheck.

But a part of me was afraid I'd see that same scared seventeen boy who'd gotten the shit beaten out of him on the streets. The boy who'd had everything his father had ever told him solidified in a brutal fashion.

And that's why I couldn't be with Aubree, why I'd had to pretend to want to keep being an escort. This was the only thing I was good at. I hadn't been lying about that. But it wasn't just because there wasn't anything else I could do. It was also because she deserved someone who wasn't broken, someone who was worthy of her. And that wasn't me.

I wrapped the towel around my waist and headed to the main area. I quickly turned away as I saw the bed. Fuck. Now I was looking at the center of the room where the cushion, blanket and lights were still set up. That wasn't any better. My stomach knotted at the thought of Aubree stretched out on the cushion, following my every direction. The toys we used were still on the blanket.

"Dammit," I muttered, running a hand through my hair, flicking droplets of water onto my bare shoulders and chest. I needed to get out of here. I couldn't stay, not with reminders of her everywhere. My safe haven wasn't here anymore.

A knock at the door pulled me away before I could get lost in my head. I walked across the room, not caring that I wore only a towel. Most people thought that nudity didn't bother me because I was confident in my body. The simple truth was that I didn't care who saw me naked. It didn't matter.

"Who is it?" I asked as I reached for the doorknob.

"Open up, Cade."

The voice sounded vaguely familiar but I couldn't quite place it. Still, I wasn't stupid enough to just open the door because someone knew my name. It hadn't happened often, but I had, on occasion, had a client's husband get pissed at me. How they would've found me here, I didn't know, but it wasn't impossible.

I put my foot against the base of the door and opened it a crack.

The shadows kept me from seeing much more than a profile, but it was enough for me to see the scar on the side of his cheek.

"Sammy?" I could barely breathe.

He turned toward me and I could see that it was him. Samuel Lehane. Sandy brown hair. Hazel eyes. Slim body that was thinner than I remembered. The last time I'd seen him, he'd been being shoved into the back of a cop car, his clothes covered with blood. Then I'd passed out and hadn't heard from him or seen him again.

"Hey, Cade." He gave me a ghost of a smile. "Good to see you again. Can I come in?"

I was frozen to the spot. This wasn't possible. How could Sammy be here when I'd just been thinking about that time? It was too strange. I had to be imagining him, right?

Sammy's smile tightened. "Come on, Cade. You gonna make your old buddy stand out in the cold?"

I took a step back and he walked inside.

"Nice place," he said. "Looks like you've done well for yourself in my absence." He turned toward me and gave me a once over. He reached out and brushed the back of his knuckles across my chest, running from my nipple down to my stomach. "And now you're going to repay me what you owe."

## End of Vol. 4

# Casual Encounter Vol. 5

# Chapter 1

I really wasn't having the best of weeks. After a shitty Saturday night, the rest of my weekend had sucked almost as badly. Monday hadn't been any better...with one exception. When I'd gotten home from school, I'd run into – literally – a new neighbor in my building.

Finn Colson was a nice guy. Good-looking, polite and sweet. He was exactly the kind of guy I'd always been looking for. So, when I happened to see him coming down the stairs on Wednesday morning while I was rushing to get to school on time, I smiled and asked him out to coffee.

I spent the rest of Wednesday being nervous as hell. So nervous, in fact, that I actually dropped my chalk twice while lecturing on Heathcliff and Catherine. I finally had to finally tell my students to take the rest of the class to work on their homework. I saw the kids exchanging looks and knew they were all wondering why I was acting so weird. Hell, I was wondering it. I'd been the one to ask Finn out, after all. And it wasn't like I was trying to seduce him. It wasn't about sex or power. Just coffee.

At least that's what I told myself when I left the school and headed for the café where we'd agreed to meet. My palms were sweating as I stood outside the building, trying to work up the nerve to go in. This was what I'd wanted, to be able to ask out men, to have men desire me. I wanted to be able to rely on myself when it came to romance, not to need my friends to set me up because I was so socially awkward and unsure of myself that I couldn't take matters into my own hands. So why, if this was what I'd wanted when I'd agreed to Cade's proposal to teach me, wasn't I jumping at the chance to prove myself?

Because it wasn't about not wanting to prove myself or being nervous that I couldn't do it, I was forced to admit. It was about the who. As perfect as Finn Colson seemed to be, he wasn't the person I wanted to be with. A pang went through me. I shouldn't want Cade, I knew that. He was one hundred percent the wrong guy for me, and that would be true even if he felt anything for me. Which he didn't. I still couldn't figure out why he'd lied to me that last time, but I knew it had to have been a lie. He couldn't care about me and still want to be an escort.

"Forget about him," I muttered under my breath. "You can do this." I took a deep breath and walked across the street.

Finn beamed when he saw me, a genuinely pleasant smile without expectation. Still, I saw the admiration on his face when I walked towards him. Someone liked my teacher clothes, I thought smugly. Mr. Know-It-All had been wrong about my wardrobe.

I didn't want to consider that, maybe, it wasn't my clothes that had truly been the problem but rather the way I'd worn them before. I could feel the difference in how I walked, how I carried myself. Even though I'd worn this outfit numerous times since I'd bought it, it wasn't until now that I felt comfortable in it. And that, I realized, was because I finally felt comfortable in my own skin.

"You look nice," Finn said as he stood.

"Thank you." I gave him a polite smile. I was proud of myself for not blushing or brushing off his compliment. Granted, it hadn't exactly given me the warm fuzzies like I would've gotten from one of Cade's compliments, but that was because he hadn't generally just said that I looked nice. Anyone would blush at some of the things he said. It had nothing to do with how the sound of his voice could turn me on, no matter what he was saying.

"I have to admit," Finn spoke, drawing my attention. "I was surprised when you asked me for coffee."

"Really?" I asked. "Why's that?"

"You backed off so quickly when I suggested you show me around. I figured you weren't interested."

He gave me a wry smile. "Unless I completely read this wrong and you're only trying to be neighborly."

"And what would you do if I said that was the case?" I asked.

"I'd try to convince you otherwise." Finn's eyes met mine.

They really were a pretty shade of gray...green. Finn's eyes were green. I didn't want to think about dark gray eyes.

The waitress came by and took our order, giving me a couple minutes to get myself focused again. It wasn't fair to Finn that I was thinking about Cade, comparing him to Cade. In all the ways he and Cade were different, there was one that was more important than the rest and the only one that matter. Finn chose to be here with me. Now, granted, with my luck in men so far, he probably had dates with half a dozen other women from our apartment building, but there was always the off chance that he really was a good guy. And it didn't matter if he was going out with other women. There were no expectations here, no commitments. Just coffee and conversation. If either of us wanted something more afterwards, we'd bring it up then. And if one thing led to another, then that'd be fine too. I wasn't looking for a relationship. Not after the back-to-back beatings my heart had taken. No matter how perfect Finn seemed to be.

"So, Bree Gamble of three E, are you a transplant like me or a native to the windy city?" Finn asked as the waitress walked away.

To his credit, he didn't even glance at her ass as she passed.

"Native," I said. "Born and raised in the suburbs. Moved into the city when my parents decided they wanted to retire to Florida."

"Your parents retired already?"

I nodded. "My mom always says that I wasn't an afterthought or late in life kid. I was the 'oh shit how did that happen' kid." I laughed, remembering all the times my mom had said that to get a rise out of people. "My brother was the late in life kid and she was almost forty when she had him. She was forty-four when I was born. My dad was forty-eight."

"Wow," Finn said. "My parents were the exact opposite. They were high school sweethearts, married right after graduation because Mom was already pregnant with my oldest sister. Had the rest of us one after the other."

"The rest of you? How many brothers and sisters do you have?"

He grinned. "I have one older sister, two older brothers, three younger brothers and two younger sisters. Lisa's a junior in high school."

I stared at him. "Nine kids?"

He shrugged. "What can I say? Very devout Catholic upbringing."

I really hoped he wasn't saying all this because he thought he was going to try to get into my pants and claim he couldn't use a condom for religious reasons. I'd been on the pill since Ronald and I had started sleeping together, but that had been because

I knew the failure rate of condoms. Plus, there'd always been the off chance that we'd get caught up in the moment and forget. Neither one of us had wanted to risk an accidental pregnancy.

"Myself," he continued. "I'm more of a C&E Catholic."

"C and E?" I asked.

"Christmas and Easter." He glanced over to where the waiter was bringing our drinks.

I blew on my coffee before testing it. Perfect.

"What about you?" Finn asked. "Were you raised religious?"

"Pretty much just Christmas and Easter Baptist," I said. "More spiritual than religious."

Finn nodded and took a sip of his coffee. "You said you have a brother?"

"Ian. He and his wife live in Texas."

"Do you have any other family in the city?" Finn asked. He laughed. "I just realized how completely serial killer that sounded. Totally 'will anyone notice if you go missing?'" He shook his head. "Sorry."

I laughed. As much as Cade's confidence had been attractive, I had to admit that it was a bit refreshing to see someone who wasn't the perfect conversationalist. "You said you were from Sacramento? Is your family still there?"

"I moved here from Sacramento," he said. "But I was actually raised in Boston. Business took me to California and then brought me here. Most of my brothers and sisters are still in Boston, but my oldest brother works an oil rig in the Gulf of Mexico."

"What business would that be?" I asked as I took another drink. At least I knew whatever Finn's answer was, there was no way it would be anything like Cade's.

"I'm a journalist," he said. "Technically, the business meeting I told you about the other day was me meeting a source about a story." He took a drink. "What about you?"

"I'm a teacher."

I felt myself starting to relax as Finn and I fell into small talk, the typical getting to know each other kind of thing that came with a not-quite-but-maybe-it-is-kind-of-a-date moment like this. Halfway through, he reached out and brushed his fingers against mine. The gesture was deliberate, but definitely the kind that was meant to feel out how someone felt rather than a promise of things to come. My skin tingled from where it had touched his, but it was a mild sensation, not the sort of knee-jerk reaction that my body had every time Cade had touched me.

No. I wasn't going to think about him. Or the way it had felt when his hands had run over my body...

Dammit, Cade!

Finn was a great guy and I should've been enjoying myself more than I was. I wasn't disliking the conversation we were having or his company, but I should've been more attracted. He wasn't anything like Cade or Ronald, which should've been what I wanted. It was what I wanted.

But I couldn't stop my thoughts from wandering to Cade. Wondering what it would be like if it was him sitting across from me. What he would say and do.

I had to get him out of my head. Had to do something to make myself stop thinking about him.

"Which apartment did you say you were in?" I asked at the next break in conversation.

"Four C," Finn answered as he drained the last of his coffee.

"I'd like to see it sometime." I smiled when I saw Finn's breath catch. I wasn't interested in being subtle at the moment.

"Really?" he spoke slowly, as if his brain was racing to figure out if I meant what he thought I meant. "When would be good for you?"

I emptied my cup and then reached into my purse for a mint. I held another one out to Finn. "Now works for me."

Finn popped the mint into his mouth, then reached into his pocket and took out his wallet. He tossed a couple bills on the table that would more than cover the drinks. He stood and held out his hand.

I didn't even hesitate as I took it. This was the perfect opportunity for me to get my mind off of Cade and show that I could do the whole casual sex thing. I'd make sure Finn knew there weren't any strings attached, but if I also wasn't going to say no if he wanted to try and make it more. That's what made him so perfect. He was physically attractive and nice, so perfect for a little fling, but I could also see us really having a lot in common and wanting to see where things went.

The two of us walked back to our apartment building hand-in-hand. The wind was brisk and I could smell a hint of snow in it. We usually didn't get snow until closer to the end of November, but it was definitely cold enough. This would probably be one of the last times I'd want to be walking much of anywhere and I enjoyed the chance to enjoy it with some easy conversation. Whatever was coming, we weren't talking about it, and I appreciated that. I wanted to see where things progressed naturally and it really felt like Finn was going to let me set the pace.

He unlocked his door and stepped inside, motioning for me to follow. I stepped inside and looked around. The apartment was virtually identical to mine except backwards since it was on the other side of the hall. Well, that and the fact that this one still had unpacked boxes against the living room wall while mine was obviously very lived in.

"I haven't gotten around to settling in all the way." He gave me a sheepish smile. "It's mostly kitchen stuff, so I can't offer you much more than a beer or leftovers from a box."

I chuckled. "I understand. It took me weeks to get everything organized."

He gestured towards the worn couch. It looked like he'd picked it up in a thrift store, which wasn't surprising. Most single people – especially men –

weren't going to spend the money for brand-new furniture. I walked across the room and sat down. Finn followed and took a seat next to me. He was close enough that it wouldn't be awkward to reach over and touch him, but he was far enough that I didn't feel like he was crowding me.

"I have to ask." The tone in his voice changed. It wasn't slick or anything like that, but there was a definite undercurrent of something else. "How is a woman like you still single?"

I paused, unsure about how much I wanted to tell him. I decided to keep it simple. "I wasn't up until a couple months ago."

"His loss." He smiled. He started to reach for me, then hesitated. When I didn't pull away, he tucked a curl behind my ear. "My gain."

"What about you?" I asked. I might not have been looking for a relationship, but I definitely didn't want to get involved with something complicated. "You're good-looking, kind and," I gestured around me, "you obviously don't live with your mother. How are you still single?"

"My job tends to send me on trips every couple weeks. I've found most women don't like it when their boyfriend has to leave at the drop of the hat and be gone for who knows how many days."

I really hoped I wasn't reading too much into what he was saying. It sounded to me like he wanted to let me know that he wasn't looking for something serious and that was good. No matter how nice he was, I was getting more and more sure that I didn't want to get right into something that could be a relationship.

"I could see how that'd be difficult," I said honestly. "I know my ex always got annoyed when I had school stuff that kept us from..." My voice trailed off and I shook my head. "You know what, I don't want to talk about him."

Butterflies fluttered in my stomach. I didn't want to talk about Ronald and I sure as hell didn't want to think about Cade. I knew of one way I could make sure neither of those things happened.

I leaned across the distance between us and brushed my lips against his. The kiss was tentative because I wasn't entirely positive Finn wanted this to go any further, but when I saw his eyes light up, I knew he did. He put his hand on my cheek and I could see him gauging my reaction. I met him halfway and this kiss was anything but hesitant.

His lips moved with mine, opening my mouth. I ran the tip of my tongue along his bottom lip and he made a pleased sound. I tried not to frown. I was glad he liked what I did, but the moan hadn't sounded quite right to me. Finn's hand slid around my back, pulling me closer to him and I tried to put out of my head that the warm palm on the small of my back belonged to the wrong person.

No. Finn wasn't the wrong person. He was the right person. My tongue slid into his mouth, tangling with his. Finn was the one who was going to help me forget.

He leaned into me and I knew what he wanted. I wrapped my arms around his neck and pulled, letting him lay me down on the couch. The hand on my back slid down my hip and he pulled my legs up before stretching out on top of me. I ran my fingers along the short hairs at the base of his neck, trying not to think about how I preferred longer hair. Soft curls. Dark...

Finn's hand moved back up over my ribcage and he cupped my breast through my shirt. I sighed. It should've felt good. The pressure was just right, and his thumb made circles over my nipple in a way that started to make it get hard. But there was no electricity, no arousal making me wet, no heat spreading through me. Only a faint friction that was mildly pleasant.

Dammit!

I pushed gently against Finn's chest and he sat back. His face was flushed, breathing heavy, but he didn't try to keep going. I gave him a smile to let him know I wasn't angry.

"I think I should go." I adjusted my clothes and stood.

"All right." Finn stood as well. He smiled at me, his eyes warm.

Relief flooded me. He wasn't angry.

"Should I call you?" he asked as he walked with me to the door. "Or would you prefer we stick with small talk in the elevator?"

I raised an eyebrow as I looked up at him.

He shrugged. "I don't want you to be uncomfortable around me."

"You really are a nice guy, Finn Colson." I opened the door. "I'll see you around."

"See you around."

As I walked towards the stairs, my head was spinning. I'd wanted a casual hook-up, something to take my mind off of Cade. Instead, I'd managed to push away a decent guy who could've ended up being a nice fling, maybe more as we saw how much work would be an issue.

I knew why. I just didn't want to say it. I had to though. I had to admit it.

I wasn't ready to move on.

I wasn't over Cade.

# Chapter 2

When I went to school on Friday, I'd completely forgotten that Mindy had mentioned that we were all going to go out to a club after dinner, so when she came bouncing into my classroom, I couldn't figure out why. Then she announced that she and Adelle had planned the perfect night out. After L20, we were going to a club opening. It was supposed to be the hottest new thing, so it was guaranteed to be a blast. At least that what Mindy kept telling me. I really didn't want to go, but I didn't want to let her down either, so I didn't say anything. Instead, I went home after work and picked out one of the sexy dresses I'd gotten with Cade. Even if I knew I wasn't going to have fun, I could at least pretend.

When I showed up at L20, I knew I'd chosen my outfit well. Adelle let out a low whistle and I felt eyes following me as I walked by. Mindy's eyebrows shot up when she saw me and I just smiled.

"Damn, Bree," Mindy said. "If you weren't my friend, I'd be all over you right now."

"What about your guy?" I teased as I sat down.

"Oh, I'm sure he'd be very interested in joining us," Mindy shot back.

"Man, Cade did an amazing job with you," Adelle said.

My smile tightened and I looked down as I put my napkin on my lap. I didn't want her to see how hearing his name bothered me.

"Mindy said you and Cade are done," Adelle said.

Her casual tone didn't fool me though. I could see the interest in her eyes.

I nodded. "We ended our contract. I'm ready to go out on my own."

"So." Adelle leaned across the table, a smile playing across her lips. "Did he spank you?"

"Adelle!"

Mindy sounded horrified so I didn't have to say anything. That was good, because I wasn't entirely sure I could trust myself not to be rude.

"Sorry," Adelle said, though she didn't sound sorry. "Come on, Mindy, you can't tell me you're not interested in knowing what kind of kinky stuff our girl learned."

Mindy gave Adelle a stern look while I took a sip of the wine that had already been poured for me. I was starting to regret having agreed to this. I changed the subject. "So, Mindy, how are things going with your guy?"

She smiled at me and I could see that she knew what I was doing. She immediately went along with it. For the rest of the meal, she steered the conversation, purposefully keeping it away from my sex life. I knew she thought it was just because I wasn't comfortable telling them about the things Cade and I had done together, but whatever worked.

By the time we were ready to head to the club, I was feeling much more relaxed, though that might've had more to do with the extra glass of wine

I'd had with dinner than anything else. Still, Adelle had dropped the subject of Cade and that helped.

When the taxi dropped us off, the line to get in to the club was down to the corner. I looked doubtfully at Adelle and Mindy, but neither of them seemed bothered by it so I followed them in silence. They walked to the front of the line where a massive man stood, arms folded and a forbidding expression on his face.

"Nolan McAllister put my friends and I on the list," Adelle said as she smiled sweetly at the man. "Adelle Merriman-Dane."

His expression didn't soften, but he did unfold his arms and look at a list. After a moment, he looked at the three of us, then shrugged. He gestured towards the door. "Go on."

I waited until we were inside before I asked the question. "Nolan McAllister?" I had to practically shout to be heard over the music.

"He's the owner," Adelle shouted back. "We had a thing for a while."

I didn't push for details, but instead focused on my surroundings. Flashing lights pulsed in time with the music and the bodies on the dance floor below writhed to the beat. The DJ was good, keeping things riding that knife's edge between just enough and too much. Where we'd entered was like a balcony of sorts, a raised area where tables and chairs lined the space next to a metal railing. On the far side was the bar and at regular intervals were staircases that led down to the dance floor.

"Drinks first?" Mindy asked.

I nodded. As we walked, I felt eyes on us and, for the first time, I knew they were looking at me as much as they were my friends. I put a little extra swing in my hips and resisted the urge to look around. I was curious to see who was watching, wondering if any of them would be someone I'd want to take home, but I didn't turn my attention from my friends until we had our drinks and were all three turning to survey the crowd.

"He's cute." Mindy pointed to a tall blond man with practically no neck and arms bigger around than my thighs.

I shook my head. "Not my type."

She gave me a look.

"I like muscles," I said. "But that's a bit extreme."

She shrugged. Mindy's taste in partners was wide and varied for both sexes.

"What about him?" Adelle nudged me and gestured towards a tall man with dark curls. I couldn't tell under the lights if they were brown or black, but I immediately shook my head. I didn't want anyone who could remotely remind me of...*him*. I didn't even want to think his name tonight.

After getting another suggestion from each of them, I wanted to snap at them both that I was perfectly capable of doing this myself. Instead, I decided that words weren't going to do any good. I needed action. At the end of the bar, I spotted a guy with reddish hair downing the last of a beer. He was ruggedly handsome, only an inch or two taller than me and lean. All things that were nothing like Cade, which made him perfect.

I threw back the rest of my drink and started towards the other end of the bar without a word to either of my friends. I didn't have to look behind me to know that they were watching. I ignored the butterflies in my stomach as I approached my target. He saw me coming a few feet before I reached him and flashed a smile. He was definitely attractive.

"Can I buy you a drink?" he shouted the question when I was close enough and I appreciated that he hadn't automatically leaned close to speak in my ear. Too many guys used loud music as an excuse to invade personal space.

I shook my head and held out a hand. "I want to dance."

His smile widened and he let me lead him down the stairs to the dance floor. I put just a few inches between us and began to move to the music. He did the same and if his dancing was any indication of how well he moved in bed, he was definitely a candidate for my first one-night stand.

We danced well together, and my body was definitely into it, but my heart wasn't. I kept remembering what it had felt like to move with Cade, our bodies more like a single entity than two separate people. I closed my eyes and forced myself to focus on the music. When I opened them again, the guy had taken a step forward, but he still wasn't touching me. He leaned down so that he was closer to my ear, but kept our bodies a respectful distance apart.

"I'm Damian," he said.

"Bree." I gave him just my first name back.

We danced for a few more minutes before I decided I was going to politely excuse myself. I'd head back to my friends, tell them that I'd proven myself and now I wanted to go home. The buzz I'd had was starting to wear off and I just wanted to go home and go to bed before I risked a nasty hangover. As we turned, however, I changed my mind.

There, standing at the railing just a few feet away, was Cade. His face was shadowed, but it was him, and he was watching me. I couldn't see his expression, but it didn't matter. Next to him was a gorgeous blonde with massive amounts of cleavage nearly falling out of her dress. When she put her hand on his arm, I looked back down at Damian and reached for his hands. He looked pleasantly surprised when I put his hands on my hips and moved closer, pressing my body against his. If Cade was going to be here with one of his clients, I was determined that he see me having a good time with some other man. He probably didn't care enough to be jealous, but at least he'd see that I wasn't at home moping over him. I was out with a new guy, putting all of those lessons to good use.

I could feel the sweat trickling down the small of my back. Despite the fans I knew were blowing, the press of bodies generated its own heat. Damian's hands tightened on my hips and pulled me more firmly against him. I saw his head bending towards me and knew what was coming next. This was decision-making time. I could pull away and leave or I could let him kiss me. Kiss him back. See if that turned into more.

I glanced up to where Cade had been. He wasn't there, and neither was the blond.

I tilted my head to meet Damian's kiss. His lips were firm as they came down on mine. The kiss was brief and he didn't even try to make it open-mouth, but it was definitely pleasant. I compared it to Finn's kiss earlier this week and it was definitely on par with it. I didn't bother to put it up against Cade's.

A flare of jealous anger went through me as I thought of what he and that blonde must be doing right now. Had he taken her to a hotel where he'd bend her over the couch and fuck her senseless? Or maybe into the bedroom where he could pay attention to her huge breasts while she was splayed out underneath him? Or, even better, had they not even bothered to leave? If I went back to the restrooms, would I find them fucking there?

I grabbed the front of Damian's shirt and pulled him closer so I could speak into his ear. "Wanna get out of here?"

He turned his head, his bright blue eyes lighting up when he saw I was serious. I wondered what he'd do if I reached down and grabbed the front of his pants to find out how much his cock liked that idea.

"Hell yes." He put his arm around my waist, resting his hand at the small of my back, and we walked towards the closest set of stairs.

When we reached the top, I paused. I needed to let my friends know I was leaving. I wondered what the chances were I'd find them in this crowd, but when I turned towards the bar, they were both still standing there, watching me with wide eyes. It had only been a couple of songs, so I supposed it shouldn't have been that strange they hadn't moved. I smiled at them and gave a little wave. I gestured towards Damian and then pointed to the door. I laughed when Adelle's jaw dropped and Mindy's eyes widened even more. Apparently they hadn't really believed me when I'd told them I could take care of myself. I waited until they had gotten over the shock enough to nod in acknowledgement, and then I took Damian's hand and led him outside.

# Chapter 3

We took a cab back to my apartment building rather than the town car Adelle, Mindy and I had arrived in. I knew Adelle wouldn't have minded if we'd taken her car service, but I preferred the cab. The town car seemed a bit pretentious.

Damian had his arm around me in the cab and I leaned against him, but he didn't try to kiss me. I wasn't sure if he was trying to be a gentleman or if he was waiting for me to initiate things, but either way I appreciated it. The cab driver seemed a bit too interested in the amount of leg I was showing and I really didn't want to put on a show for him.

When we reached my apartment building, I glanced at Damian, wondering if he'd make some comment about the neighborhood, but he didn't. Based on the designer clothes he was wearing, he definitely lived in a pricier part of the city, and my dress made it look like I belonged with the rest of the classier set at the club. This place might've been a disappointment.

"My apartment's kind of small." I felt the need to make the excuse before he even saw it.

He grinned as he helped me out of the cab, and he didn't let go of my hand. "Then it won't take long for you to give me the tour and we can get started on more interesting things."

A flutter of arousal went through me. That was good. It probably meant I wouldn't push him away like I had Finn. Only a few days had passed since then, but seeing Cade with that other woman had done wonders for me getting over him. I wasn't stupid. There were still things I had to deal with, but I was definitely sure I wanted to sleep with Damian.

Probably.

I was so deep in thought that I barely noticed we'd entered the building and had walked past a couple other tenants on our way to the elevator. When the door dinged, I made up my mind. I was going to do this.

I turned towards Damian and grabbed the front of his shirt, pulling him into the elevator and covering his mouth with mine. I felt surprise stiffen his body for a moment, and then he was kissing me back. This wasn't a hesitant kiss like the one he'd given me at the club. I was taking control of this one. I parted his lips with mine and thrust my tongue between them as I pressed my body so tightly against his that I could feel his cock start to harden. I was just starting to really enjoy the kiss when, suddenly, Damian was torn out of my arms.

My eyes flew open to see a shocked and confused Damian being pulled out of the elevator and shoved back into the lobby. I started to take a step forward when a body entered the elevator, blocking my way. A hand hit the button and the doors started to close.

I looked up into a pair of stormy gray eyes and my stomach flipped.

Cade's eyes flashed as he walked forward, moving me backwards without laying a hand on me until my back was against the wall. He cupped my chin, his grip almost painful. "I meant what I said before. I don't want any other man touching you." His mouth came down on mine, hard and possessive.

My head told me I should push him away, but my body was already responding. I moaned as his tongue plundered my mouth and my fingers tangled in his curls, tugging at them until he growled. His body pressed against mine and I could feel his thick shaft against my hip. When he raised his head, he kept our bodies together.

"You're mine, Aubree." He nipped at my bottom lip. "Only mine."

When he pushed back, I barely stopped myself from protesting. This wasn't real, I told myself. This was some sort of test. It had to be.

Without taking his eyes off of me, he pushed the emergency stop and then crossed that short distance again.

"Mine," he repeated as he claimed my mouth again.

The moment his lips touched mine, I was gone. It wasn't smart. In fact, it was probably one of the stupidest things I'd ever done, but I couldn't help myself. My body craved his. The need to have him touch me was almost physically painful. I sighed when his hands slid down my sides to cup my ass. I didn't care what happened next, if he was going to simply walk away, having proven that I wanted him but he didn't feel the same or if this was going to keep going until I was coming so hard my eyes rolled back into my head. All I could think about was how his tongue was twisting around mine and how close his hands were to bare flesh.

Then his mouth was gone and I was gasping for air. I blinked, confused. I didn't know why he'd stopped. And then I saw him kneeling down in front of me.

Shit.

Heat flooded my body and I hoped I wasn't wrong about what he was going to do.

He looked up at me as his hands slid up my calves, over my knees and then to my thighs. When he reached the hem of my dress, I half-expected him to hesitate and ask if it was okay. He didn't and I realized he was trusting me to stop him if I didn't want it.

Fuck that.

I swallowed hard as his fingers curled around the waistband of the silk panties I was wearing. He pulled them down and I started to step out of them. I only managed to get one leg out, however, before he was shoving my legs further apart and pushing up my skirt, exposing my bare pussy.

My eyes rolled as his tongue made a long pass across my folds before dipping between them. I moaned as his talented mouth pleasured me. The shock of seeing Cade and my body's instinctual reaction to his possessiveness had already set me on edge, so it wasn't long before I felt that familiar sensation twisting low in my belly. I ran my fingers through his hair and he looked up at me without taking his mouth away.

The sight of those eyes darkened with desire, that gorgeous face pressed against me...he sucked on my clit and I came. I made a breathless sound and closed my eyes, my hips twitching as he continued to work over my sensitive flesh.

A finger slipped inside me and I jerked. Cade groaned as my fingers tugged at his hair, but he didn't let up. He made slow, even strokes with his finger even as he licked around my opening, caressing the quivering flesh until I cried out and came again. My eyes closed as I struggled to absorb the myriad sensations coursing through me.

"Fuck!" My hands slapped against the elevator wall as a second finger was slid inside my pussy. I gasped in air, each breath deep enough that, if I'd been able to think about it, I might've worried that my breasts would pop free of the top of my dress. At the moment though, I could care less. I could've been stark naked up against that wall as long as Cade didn't stop.

He crooked his fingers and I wailed. I clapped a hand over my mouth, stifling the sound before it got too loud. It didn't stop my climax from crashing over me, making my knees buckle. Cade put his hand on my stomach and his shoulders against my knees, holding me in place as his tongue circled my clit, then dropped down to tease around where his fingers were stretching me.

"Please," I gasped, dropping my hand. "Please, Cade, no more. It's too much."

He looked up at me again and shook his head. He took my swollen clit into his mouth and gently sucked it as I thrashed and writhed, nonsensical sounds falling from my mouth until another orgasm rocked through me. This time, however, he granted me relief, removing his hand from between my legs and standing, wrapping his arms around me and holding me until I stopped shaking.

I clutched his shirt, pressing my face against his chest and breathing in his scent. I knew I was going to have to deal with this soon, but at the moment, I needed to regain my composure before I could do anything that required coherent thought. And I just wanted to enjoy the feel of Cade's arms around me, his hand running through my hair.

"That's my girl," he whispered. His voice sent a shiver down my spine. "My Aubree." He kissed my forehead.

Reluctantly, I pulled away from him. I caught a flash of something across his eyes, but I didn't say anything. No matter what I said, it'd start a conversation that I didn't want to have in the elevator. I pulled my panties off of my other foot, then tugged down my dress. As I reached around him to hit the button to get us going again, I shoved my panties into Cade's back pocket. I felt him tense and when I straightened, I saw his eyes were warm again.

I tried not to sigh out loud. What the hell had I just let myself get into?

# Chapter 4

Neither one of us said a word as we walked the short distance down the hall to my apartment. My hands were shaking and my head spinning, but I didn't ask him for help. I wasn't sure I could handle him touching me, even just a brush of fingers by accident. Not until I knew what was going on.

I felt his eyes on me as I struggled to get the key into the lock, but I didn't look at him. I needed to be in the safety of my own place before I could risk it. What had happened in the elevator was proof I couldn't control myself around him.

I walked inside and left the door open behind me, hoping he'd read that as an invitation. When I heard the door close, I knew he had. I walked over to the far side of the room before turning towards him. He stopped a few feet away, and I was grateful for that. My insides were in knots and every inch of me was tense again. Despite everything that had happened, I wanted him, but I wasn't sure my heart could take it. The only thing I did know was that I wasn't going to speak first.

"I don't know any other way to say this than to just come out with it."

It took me a moment to realize why his voice sounded strange, but when I did, I was surprised. He was nervous. My strong, confident Cade was nervous. My heart did a little somersault when I realized I'd referred to him as "my" Cade.

"I tried to go back to how things were before, but I couldn't." He ran his hand through his hair, pushing it back off of his face. "I even had a client earlier this week."

I looked down. I didn't want to hear about that.

"But I couldn't do it."

My head came back up and my eyes met his. There was no mistaking the honesty I saw there.

"And I don't just mean mentally," he said. "I kept looking at her, trying to convince my body that I found her attractive, but it wasn't happening. I couldn't see anything but the ways she wasn't you."

I felt a flare of hope and tried to squash it. I needed to hear him out. He'd told me he cared about me before. For all I knew, this was just going to be him talking about how he needed to get me out of his system.

"For the first time since I started doing this, I couldn't...perform." He took a step towards me. "I didn't want her. I wanted you."

I swallowed hard. I couldn't do this. I couldn't wait for him to give me hope that things had changed, then crush it. "I want you too." His face lit up and then crumpled as I continued, "But it's not enough." Seeing the pain I brought to him made my heart ache, but I had to make sure he understood I wasn't going back. "I tried too. I tried to do the casual sex thing. And not just tonight."

His mouth tightened and I saw the jealousy burn in his eyes, mixing with the hurt there. Heat flooded me as I remembered what he'd said before about how he didn't want any other man touching me.

"I couldn't go through with it then," I said. "We went back to his place and when he was kissing me, all I could think was that he wasn't you."

"And tonight?" The question was soft, as if he wasn't sure he wanted to know the answer.

"I was planning on sleeping with him," I admitted. "Because I saw you with that woman at the club and figured you'd be having sex with her."

He frowned for a moment. "The woman at the...oh, her. She's a pro." He must've realized that didn't really help matters because he quickly added, "When I told her I was too, she left me alone. No money in trying to seduce another escort."

"It doesn't matter," I said. "Because this isn't what I want." He flinched and I had to force myself to continue. "I can't do the casual sex thing. That's not who I am. And I still can't be with you, no matter how much I want to, not while you're with other women."

"I'm not." His voice was firm. "That's what I came here to tell you. I'm done with that life. After experiencing with you what it's like to have that emotional connection, I couldn't have sex with some random person. Not anymore."

I folded my arms across my chest. No, I wasn't going to dare to hope. I'd let my guard down in the elevator, but he'd surprised me. I hadn't had time to shield myself, to prepare. Now, I'd pulled myself together.

"I haven't been able to stop thinking about you, Aubree." He moved closer, his gaze holding me in place. "The way you look. The sound of your voice. Your scent." He reached out and wrapped a curl around his finger. "How you feel."

I closed my eyes as he ran the back of his hand down my cheek. I couldn't deny the way my skin warmed under his touch, how the heat in my stomach spread through me at the mere thought of his hand in more intimate places.

"Tell me you haven't thought about me," he said. "Tell me honestly that this isn't what you want and I'll go. That you don't feel the same way I do. You do that and, I promise, I'll walk away and never bother you again."

Tears burned against my eyelids and I bent my head. I couldn't tell him any of that because it wasn't true. I cared more about him than he did me. I'd been lying to myself when I'd said that seeing him with that blonde had gotten me over him. I wasn't over him and I didn't think I'd ever be. I wasn't just falling for him. I was in love with him.

And that was why I had to let him go.

It hurt now, but it would be so much worse if I let him in and then he realized what he felt for me wasn't that strong. I knew myself better because of him and that meant I knew if I allowed it, I would give myself over to him whole-heartedly, without reservation. I was already his and to admit my feelings would be the final step. Look at how long I'd stayed with Ronald because I'd refused to consider that things were done. And I'd never felt for my ex even a fraction of what I felt for Cade. How depressed I'd been this past week was proof of that. If I let him, he'd own me.

So I stayed silent and let him read into it what he would.

His hands rested lightly on my shoulders and I felt him kiss the top of my head. "Okay then. I'll keep my promise." He released me. "Good-bye."

The tears spilled over at the pain I heard in those words and I pressed my hands against my chest. I heard him start to walk away. And then, so quiet that I might have imagined it, I heard him speak.

"I love you, Aubree."

# Chapter 5

I felt my heart thump wildly against my palms. He loved me. He didn't just care about me or want to be with me. He hadn't even said that he was falling for me. He'd said he loved me.

My head jerked up, tears streaming down my cheeks. The door was open and he was stepping into the hallway, but I couldn't move. I couldn't even speak. He was going to close the door and disappear. I'd never see him again and he'd never know that I loved him too...

"Cade!" His name ripped out of me and I saw him freeze. "Don't leave me."

A shudder went through him but he didn't turn. The fingers curled around the doorknob tightened until his knuckles turned white. "Aubree."

The agony in that single word, in my name, the name only Cade used, it broke through my paralysis and I ran to him. He must've heard me move because he started to turn, getting enough around in time to catch me as I threw my arms around him and buried my face against his chest. His arms closed around me, tentatively at first, as if he was still trying to process what had happened, then tighter.

"Please don't leave me." I was crying, as the realization of how close I'd come to losing him hit me.

"Shh," he murmured as he smoothed down my hair. "I'm not going anywhere." He moved us both so he could shut the door and give us privacy, but we didn't go more than a couple steps. He rested his cheek on my head as his hands moved up and down my bare back, but there was only comfort in his touch, nothing sexual.

Slowly, I calmed down. He'd stayed. I hadn't said those words yet, but he'd stayed because I'd asked him to. I pulled back until I could look up at him. His expression was blank and I understood why. He'd opened himself up to me and I'd been the one who'd fucked up this time. Well, I wasn't going to wait any longer to fix it.

"I love you, Cade." I reached up and put my hand on his cheek. "I was just too scared to say it. I didn't think you felt the same way."

I saw cautious hope in his eyes and vowed that I'd never again do anything to make him think I didn't care.

"You don't have to say it," he said. "It's okay. If you want me to stay, I'll stay." He ran the tip of his finger just under my bottom lip. "You can have as much of me as you want and I won't ask for anything in return."

"I want all of you, Cade," I said firmly. "My Cade."

I had a moment to see desire and love blaze across his eyes and then his mouth was on mine. His tongue pushed at my lips and I parted them willingly, running my tongue out to curl around his.

His teeth scraped against my lips and I moaned. He buried a hand in my hair, cupping the back of my head as he deepened the kiss. I could feel the desire radiating out from every part of him and knew it was so much more than physical. I pressed my body even closer, rubbing my hip against his crotch until he moaned into my mouth.

I didn't know how long we stood there, only that when he finally broke the kiss, we were both gasping for air and my knees were trembling.

He rested his forehead against mine. "My Aubree?" He made it a question, so tentative that it tore at my heart.

"Your Aubree." I smiled and pulled him down for another kiss.

Any hesitation that had lingered must've been chased away by my answer because I felt him shift back into that confident, dominating man I'd first met less than two months ago. His hands slid down over my ass as his tongue plundered my mouth. I tugged at the hem of his shirt, eager to get my hands on bare skin. When my palms skimmed across his sides, his muscles twitched and he groaned. His hands moved further down and he picked me up. Without breaking our kiss, I wrapped my legs around his waist, my arms around his neck.

He began to walk us back towards my bedroom as I moved my lips down his jawline, the light stubble there rough against my mouth. He swore as I latched on to a spot just under his jaw, sucking the skin into my mouth and worrying at it with my teeth until blood came to the surface.

"Mine," I whispered fiercely in his ear.

Cade spun us so fast that I barely processed it. Suddenly, my back was against the wall and his mouth was on my neck. My head fell back, granting him easier access as he nipped and sucked every inch he could reach. I was sure he was leaving hickeys all over, but I didn't care. In fact, I wanted him to mark me, something to remind me that I was his.

"Mine," he growled as he ground himself against me. "My Aubree." His hands ran up my sides and squeezed my breasts. "Only mine."

"Yes," I gasped as his jeans rubbed against me, the thin material of my dress instantly soaking through. When he pulled down one strap of my dress, baring my breast, his fingers immediately went to my hardening nipple, rolling it and sending a ripple of pleasure through me.

"Come again," he demanded. He tugged at my nipple and rotated his hips, rubbing against my already sensitive clit.

He didn't have to tell me. I was already there. My head fell forward and I called out his name as I came. Even as I was still riding out my orgasm, he pulled away from the wall and finished carrying me into the bedroom.

We fell onto the bed and he twisted so that I landed on top. Not that I would've minded. I only cared that he never stopped touching me. His hands tore at my dress, pulling at the zipper and tugging it up over my head. I winced as it caught in my hair, but didn't let it distract me from trying to get his shirt off.

Before I could, however, he flipped me over onto my back and went up onto his knees, pulling his shirt over his head and tossing it behind him. I greedily ran my eyes over his sculpted torso. Damn, he was hot. I had the sudden desire to run my tongue over every inch of him. Then I saw the look in his eyes and knew that would have to wait. We may have had a bit of give and take, but I had no doubt that was over for now, and he was taking charge. My stomach twisted. I definitely wanted that.

My eyes dropped as his hands went to his jeans. He undid the top button and pushed the jeans down his hips, revealing a pair of gray boxer briefs and an impressive bulge that made my pussy throb with anticipation. He gave me a wicked grin and stood. He stripped off the jeans and then reached down into the pocket. He pulled out a condom and tossed it up by my pillow.

"Always prepared," he said as he pulled off his underwear. His cock curved up towards his flat stomach, thick and swollen. He crawled back onto the bed, his eyes darkening as he ran them over my body. He stayed on his knees next to me as he spoke again. "Up on your hands and knees."

I sat up. Before we started this, there was something I wanted to tell him. I got onto my knees facing him and reached out to wrap my fingers around his cock. He groaned as I lightly stroked the hard flesh. "If you go get tested, preparation won't really be a problem."

His eyes narrowed and he grabbed my wrist. "That's a naughty thing to tease about."

I winked at him, my stomach clenching. "I can't wait to feel you inside me, nothing between us."

His fingers flexed around my wrist, not hurting, but enough to remind me of just how strong he was.

"Feel you come inside me, filling me..."

Cade grabbed my waist and spun me around. A hand between my shoulder blades bent me towards the bed and I caught myself on my elbows. I'd barely settled when a hand came down on my ass with a loud crack.

"Ah!" My body jerked. I closed my eyes as I let my body absorb the sensation. A second blow made me gasp. This was harder than it had been before and my ass was already stinging, but my pussy was throbbing and it wasn't from pain.

He ran his hand down between my legs, fingers probing at my pussy. He slid a finger inside and I shivered.

"All I can think about now is being inside you, skin against skin." He removed his hand and smacked my ass again. "Now I need a distraction. Can you distract me?"

I nodded, then yelped as he slapped my ass again. "Yes!" I said, remembering how he'd always insisted I speak, not just nod.

"How?"

My brain raced through all of the different things Cade and I had done during our time together and decided to keep it simple. I rolled onto my back, grimacing as the sheets rubbed against my sensitive skin. He sat back on his heels, his hand wrapping around his cock as he waited to see what I'd do next.

I ran my hand over my stomach and then down between my legs. I moaned as I rubbed my fingers on either side of my clit.

"Oh, fuck."

A thrill went through me as Cade swore. I loved that I could make him do that. His hand dropped to the base of his cock and I saw him tighten his fingers around it. I dropped my hand lower and slid my two middle fingers into my pussy. I worked them in and out, avoiding putting any direct pressure on my clit. It was still sensitive from the elevator and I had a feeling it was going to get more attention before the night was over.

"Lick your fingers clean." Cade's voice was rough.

I raised my hand to my mouth, my eyes locking with his as I licked my juices from my fingers. I'd never tasted myself before, but it was strangely erotic, knowing that this was what Cade had tasted when he'd gone down on me.

He slid his hand up over his cock, nice and slow and I watched, remembering how it had been to have his dick in my mouth, the way it had felt when it slid over my tongue.

"Turn over," he said, his voice hoarse.

I rolled onto my stomach.

"Grab the headboard."

My stomach fluttered. I wrapped my hands around the cheap wooden rails. I heard the condom wrapper rip, then felt the bed dip as Cade moved behind me. He stretched his body out on top of mine, not putting his full weight on me, but enough pressure that I felt it.

"Have you ever done it like this?" His tongue traced the outside of my ear.

"No." My fingers flexed around the headboard.

He raised his hips and, a moment later, I felt the head of him nudge against my soaking wet entrance. We both groaned as he slid inside me with one smooth motion.

"So perfect," he said. He slid one arm under me until his hand rested at the base of my throat. "We fit together so perfectly."

My eyes closed as he pulled back, then slid forward. Fuck. I sighed.

"You okay?" He sounded concerned.

"Just never thought I'd feel this again," I admitted.

He pressed his lips against my temple. "I love you, my Aubree."

"And I love you, my Cade." I tried to push back against him, but the position didn't allow me any leverage against the larger body covering me.

He chuckled, the sound sending a shiver through me. "Is there something you want?"

"You," I said. "I want you."

"You've got me." He kissed my shoulder and then began to move.

His thrusts were slow and deep, pushing me forward so that my clit rubbed against the sheets, sending ripples of pain and pleasure through me. His fingers twitched against the base of my throat and his breath was hot against my ear.

"I'm not going to last long," he said. "You had me too worked up, watching you come in the elevator, then playing with that pretty little pussy of yours."

"I'm close again," I panted. And I was. My clit was so sensitive that the friction was almost painful. I was going to come again, and if he kept going after that, it was going to hurt.

He scraped his teeth against the place where my shoulder and neck met. "What do you want?"

"Bite me," I answered automatically. "Mark me."

"Fuck," he groaned. "You're gonna be the death of me."

He began to move faster, pushing deeper than he had before, reaching places inside me that made me see stars. I began to shudder, ripples of pleasure washing over me. Then Cade's teeth were in my shoulder, not hard enough to draw blood, but enough to make me cry out. And then he was coming, crushing me against him.

It was different this time, not just a physical joining of two bodies fit perfectly together. This was more like I couldn't tell where he ended and I began.

Like every cell in my body was merging with every cell in his. I'd never felt anything like it, not once. And, as I heard him saying my name over and over again, I knew he felt it too.

He wrapped his arms around me and rolled us onto our sides. "Thank you." He pressed his lips against my neck and I shivered.

"For what?" I was still half-floating.

"For loving me, despite everything."

I picked up his hand and kissed the back of it. "You're mine," I said simply.

"Yes," he said as he nuzzled behind my ear. "I am."

# Chapter 6

We made love two more times before we finally fell asleep, exhausted and satisfied. And that's what it had been, making love, not fucking, no matter how rough we had been with each other. Cade may have been the dominate one, but I wasn't exactly gentle. I hadn't seen it, but I had a feeling his back was going to be covered with scratches. I knew he had hickeys on his neck and chest to match the ones he'd left on me. And, of course, every inch of me ached in a pleasurably used kind of way. I could only imagine what it was going to be like to have him as much as I wanted.

These were the thoughts buzzing about in my brain when I woke. I smiled a sleepy smile and rolled over to greet Cade. My hand hit the pillow and I frowned. I told myself not to freak out as I opened my eyes. He was probably just in the bathroom. Then I saw a piece of paper on the pillow. I grabbed it and sat up, ignoring the throb of pain in my ass as I did so. No matter what had happened the night before, an empty bed and a note immediately made me think about Ronald and my wedding that hadn't been.

I relaxed the moment I read the first line.

My Aubree.

I settled back against the pillows and pulled the blankets up to cover my breasts as I read the rest.

I wanted nothing more than to wake you so I could make love to you again, but you looked so peaceful sleeping there that I couldn't bring myself to do it. I just went to my place because I have to call all of my FORMER clients and let them know that I'm no longer in business. I didn't think those were conversations you wanted to hear. Plus, I kind of needed a change of clothes, though I'm hoping not to be wearing much the rest of the weekend. When I'm done, I'll come back and we can talk about where things are going next because I don't know anything about my future except I want you in it. Well, first I plan on ravishing you. Then we can talk.

Heat coiled in my belly at the thought of him taking me again. I closed my eyes. Fuck. I'd never felt like this before. How was I supposed to get anything done when all I could think about was Cade's body, his hands and mouth on me? How could anyone function like this?

I opened my eyes and forced myself to look at the note again. There were only a couple more sentences left.

I'm going to stop by the loft too. I developed those pictures and want you to see how amazing you look. I shouldn't be long. I love you. Your Cade

I'd almost forgotten about those pictures he'd taken. I flushed and turned over the letter even though there was no one else around to read it. What would it be like, I wondered, seeing myself in those pictures? Cade had made me watch myself in a mirror while we had sex, but I didn't think it'd be the same. That had been in the middle of things, the heat of the moment where I hadn't exactly been thinking clearly. The pictures were still frames of me in explicit positions, doing things and having things done to me that only Cade had ever seen. Even my ex hadn't seen me do any of that. He'd been very much a 'get in, get off, get out' kind of guy. Not in a rude way, but more of a 'that's how it is' way of thinking. And since he'd been my only other lover, I hadn't thought anything of it until I'd met Cade.

I glanced over at the clock and sighed. I needed to get up. I had papers to grade and if I wanted to be done by the time he got back, I needed to get started. And I definitely didn't want anything to get in the way of my time with Cade. My stomach growled. Besides, I was ready for breakfast.

I didn't know how I did it, but somehow I managed to concentrate enough to get my papers done in record time. I actually went back and checked the first couple just to make sure I hadn't gotten distracted and missed things, but no. They were done and I had nothing to do but wait. It was getting close to noon, so I decided to tidy up and then took a shower, figuring Cade would be back by the time I got out. When he wasn't and it was now past one, I considered eating lunch but couldn't quite stomach it. I started pacing by one thirty and by two I was getting really worried. Even if he'd left just minutes before I'd woken up, he should've been back by now. He didn't have that many clients. Even if he'd talked to each one for ten minutes, packed a bag, then loitered around the loft while collecting the photos, he should've been back by now.

A mean voice in the back of my head suggested that maybe this had been the way he'd decided to get rid of me. That he'd left me too. I put my hand on the place where my shoulder and neck met. The bruise there was dark, a reminder that I was his and he was mine. Nothing else mattered. He wouldn't have left me. If he hadn't wanted to be with me, he never would've come back, never would've said he loved me. All he'd had to do was walk away. And he wasn't the kind to play games. If I knew nothing else about him, I knew that. He was straightforward, had been from the moment we'd met.

No, something was wrong. I could feel it in my gut.

I called his cell and, after several rings, it went to voicemail. I frowned, but refused to let myself panic. He might've been in the middle of something. I waited five minutes and then called back. Same thing. Now I was getting really anxious. I couldn't see him letting it ring and ring twice in a row. It wasn't like he'd sent it to voicemail after a single ring because he was busy.

I might've been overreacting and I hoped that I was, but something deep inside me said that I wasn't. I needed to find him. I didn't know where he lived, but he'd also said he was going to his loft. That's where I'd start. If he wasn't there, I'd have to figure out a way to get his address.

I practically ran down the stairs, unable to stomach being in the elevator, just standing there while it went down, the memories of the previous night playing in my head. No, I needed to be moving. To my relief, I spotted a taxi almost immediately and waved it down.

I quickly gave him the address and promised a big tip if he got me there in ten minutes. The driver glanced at me and I could tell he was doubtful that I could afford a tip that would make that kind of driving worth it. Then he saw my face and realized that I wasn't asking for the fun of it. He nodded and pulled away from the curb fast enough to throw me back in my seat. I spent the entire trip with my nails digging into the seat, my knuckles white, my stomach churning. I didn't usually believe in premonitions or anything like that, but I couldn't deny this horrible feeling that Cade was in trouble and I was going to be too late to stop it.

When I got to the loft, I quickly paid the cabbie and gave him a big enough tip that he asked if I wanted him to wait. I thanked him and told him if I wasn't back in five minutes to go ahead and leave. It'd take me less time than that to see if Cade was there. The loft was spacey, but it was only one room and a bathroom. And it wasn't like he was going to hide from me.

I took the steps one at a time, but it was all I could do not to run up them. I knocked on the door, then sucked in a breath when the knock pushed the door open. My heart was in my throat as I pushed the door open even further, my hand shaking. I tried not to think about what could've happened here as I took my first step inside. This place held a lot of good memories, but I wasn't thinking about any of those when I saw the mess.

At first, I couldn't figure out what was covering the floor, but when I took a closer look, my blood ran cold. They were my pictures. The ones Cade had taken of me last week. The ones he'd come back here to get. I pressed my hands together as I forced my head up. Cade wasn't lying on the ground with what was left of my pictures.

I scanned the room, stopping when I saw a shape on the bed in the back. I reached over and switched on a light. It confirmed what I'd thought. Cade was lying on the bed and the knot in my stomach eased. He'd just fallen asleep. Not surprising. We'd had a long night. Maybe the pictures had been the result of a break-in and he'd fallen asleep waiting for the cops.

I was halfway across the room, already thinking of enjoyable ways I could wake him up, when I realized he wasn't alone. But it wasn't a woman in bed with him. A sandy-haired man with a scar on his cheek had his arm thrown over Cade's stomach.

I almost bolted, sickened by the thought I'd been lied to. Then I realized what was really wrong with this picture.

The man's arm wasn't moving.

Cade wasn't breathing.

# Chapter 7

I forgot about what this looked like. Forgot my questions as to why Cade was in bed with a man. Forgot about everything but the fact that the man I loved wasn't breathing.

"Cade!"

He didn't respond when I yelled his name.

I ran the rest of the way, nearly falling as my feet skidded on the torn photographs. With each step, another detail of the scene imprinted in my mind, seared there in such a way that I knew I'd never forget any of them.

Cade's skin was pale, too pale.

The man wrapped around Cade was stretched out, like he'd lain down, but Cade wasn't laying. He was slumped like he'd been sitting and fallen over.

There was a glass on the floor, pieces of it broken, drops of liquid splashed across the wood. The smell of alcohol was in the air.

I reached the bed, my heart pounding. "Cade!" I said his name again before reaching out to touch him. I almost didn't want to, afraid that his skin would be cold, that I'd waited too long to look for him. No, I told myself. I couldn't lose him, not when we'd just found each other.

I shoved the stranger's arm off of Cade, barely glancing at the other man as he rolled onto his back. I heard him exhale and then ignored him. If he was breathing, I wasn't about to pay any attention to him. I didn't know if I would've anyway. All of my attention was on Cade.

I reached out, my hand shaking. I pressed my fingers against the side of his neck and nearly sobbed with relief when I felt his pulse. It was weak, but it was there. Then I put my hand on his chest and my heart skipped a beat. My first assumption had been correct. He wasn't breathing.

I dug my phone out of my pocket and dialed 911, putting it on speakerphone as I leaned over Cade, trying to remember what I'd learned about CPR during my freshman year health class.

I tilted his head back, opened his mouth and pinched his nose shut. I blew in a single breath before a woman's voice came over the air.

"Nine one-one, do you have an emergency?"

"I need an ambulance." My voice trembled. "Something happened to my boyfriend. He's not breathing."

"Okay, ma'am, what is your location?"

I rattled off the address, then leaned down to blow another breath into Cade's lungs. I could barely see through the tears burning in my eyes.

"I've dispatched an ambulance to your location."

"Two," I said, suddenly remembering the other man. "There's someone else here too."

"There are two people who need assistance?"

I gave him another breath before answering. "I got here a couple minutes ago and found my boyfriend and...a friend of his." I wasn't about to try to figure out who this person was or why he'd had his arms around Cade. "They were both unconscious. The other guy, I don't know who he is or why he was here. He's breathing. Cade isn't."

"Are you doing CPR?"

I wanted to snap at her that I was trying to but she kept asking me stupid questions, but I focused on giving Cade air and just gave a short answer. "Yes."

"The paramedics are on their way, miss." Her voice took on a soothing tone that grated on my nerves. "Everything's going to be okay."

The tears spilled over onto Cade's cheeks and lips as I kept breathing for him. It wasn't going to be okay, not if he didn't wake up. I didn't look at his mouth as I tasted the salt from my tears. If I looked, I might see that his lips were blue from lack of oxygen. If I saw that, I wasn't sure I'd be able to hold it together. And if I fell apart, Cade would definitely die.

And there was no way in hell I was going to let that happen.

I was vaguely aware that the operator was going on in the background, telling me all of the encouraging things that her job told her she was supposed to say, but I wasn't listening to her. There were only two sounds I wanted to hear right now. Ambulance sirens and, more than that, Cade taking a breath.

"Please, baby," I whispered, my lips brushing against his as I spoke. "Please don't leave me."

I gave him another breath and then took a shuddering breath of my own. I wasn't sure how much longer I could hold it together. Then, in the distance, I heard the wail of sirens. They were coming. I just needed to hold on.

"I love you," I said before covering his mouth again.

I had to keep going. I couldn't even bear to think about what would happen if I stopped. I'd been living my life in the dark before I'd met Cade, barely knowing myself, not knowing everything the world could offer me. I wasn't going back to that. I couldn't go back to that. I wouldn't.

"Damn you, Cade." I hit his chest with my fist. "Don't do this to me!"

He gasped and I gave a little cry.

"Cade?" I shook his shoulders harder than I probably needed to, but he took a shuddering breath, then another. I almost cried with relief, but then I heard footsteps behind me.

I spun around, spreading my arms out as I took a defensive stance in front of Cade. It took my brain a moment to process what I was seeing, and then I moved out of the way to let the paramedics through. I stumbled, then put my hand down. I felt a sharp pain in my palm, but I didn't acknowledge it. Cade was my only concern.

"Do you know what happened?" The male paramedic asked.

I shook my head as I straightened. "I came in and saw them like this." I gestured towards the stranger. "I don't know who he is or why he's here."

The female paramedic leaned over the stranger. "His pulse is weak."

"Him too," the man said. He glanced at me. "You know this one?"

I nodded, fighting back tears again. "He's my boyfriend." My hip bumped against the bedside table and I realized my phone was still on. I reached down and hung up, then slid my phone into my pocket.

"Does he do any drugs?" he asked. "Be honest."

"No," I said firmly. Glass crunched under my feet and I remembered the liquid I'd seen on the floor. "He might've had a drink."

"Does he have any allergies?"

"I don't know." I pressed my hands against my chest. "Please, don't let him die." I whispered the plea over and over as the paramedics worked.

As they moved Cade onto a gurney, the first paramedic who'd come in looked over at me. "You said you did CPR?"

I nodded.

"If he lives, it'll be because of you."

I barely heard the praise. All I heard was the "if." My heart clenched. No, please, no. Not "if."

"Come on," the paramedic called as they started to take Cade down the stairs. "You can ride with us." His eyes flicked down to my hand. "And you're going to need to get that looked at."

I looked down, puzzled. Blood was dripping from my hand. When had that happened? I raised my hand and wrapped the bottom of my shirt around the wound. It'd do until I knew Cade was okay.

I climbed into the ambulance, taking the seat that the paramedics offered. I started to reach for Cade's hand, then hesitated, unsure if I should touch him. He'd always looked so strong and invincible. Now, with oxygen being given to him through a portable tank and mask, his skin pale and gray, he looked so weak. Almost frail.

"It's okay," the paramedic said. "You can hold his hand." He reached for my cut on. "Gives me a chance to take a look at this."

"I'm okay," I said absently as I took Cade's hand with my good one. I hissed as the paramedic started looking at the cut.

"You're lucky is what you are," he said. "It's deep, but I think you'll be good with just a bandage. Unless you want stitches."

"Bandage is fine," I said. Especially if it meant I could stay with Cade. I hardly felt the paramedic doing his work or heard the sirens as the ambulance raced through the streets. When he said I was done, I put both hands around Cade's. "Come back to me," I said softly.

The ride to the hospital and the rush that followed became like a dream. The doctors pulled me away from him and led me to seats to wait. Time lost all meaning as I waited. Nurses and doctors walked past, ignoring me as much as I did them. The only one I wanted to listen to was the one who'd tell me that Cade would be okay.

It was late evening, however, before that one came out.

"Are you here with Cade Shepard?" An older man walked towards me.

I nodded and stood, adrenaline flooding through me. "Is he okay?"

The doctor nodded and the relief that washed over me nearly made my legs buckle.

"He's resting now," the doctor said. "You can sit with him."

"Thank you," I said. I followed as the doctor led me back through the doors. "What happened?"

The doctor gave me a sideways glance. "Are you family?"

"Yes," I said without hesitation. And as far as Cade was concerned, that was true. He didn't have anyone else.

Something about the way I answered must've convinced the doctor not to inquire any further. "There was a high quantity of narcotics in his system."

"What?"

"Along with some alcohol. Not a lot, but still a dangerous combination." He opened a door and motioned for me to enter. "And," he hesitated, then continued, "the other young man had the same in his system."

"You think they were partying," I said with a scowl.

"It's not my place to say," he said. "But you should know that the police will probably want to investigate."

"That's good," I said. "Because there's no way Cade did this to himself." I walked towards the bed, my eyes fixed on Cade's pale face. "When will he wake up?"

"I don't know," the doctor said. "But I'll let the nurses know that you can stay here as long as you want."

"Thank you," I said. I glanced up at him, curious. "Why?"

He gave me a partial smile. "Because I saw you sitting out there, waiting for him, and I think he needs you to be here when he wakes up."

I thanked him and turned my attention back to Cade. When I heard the door close, I put my head down, resting my forehead on the edge of his bed and finally let myself go. The tears poured out of me and my shoulders shook. This wasn't some delicate, romantic crying. This was full-on ugly crying and I didn't care. I'd almost lost him. Someone had tried to take Cade from me and if that had happened, I wasn't sure what I would've done. I'd known I loved him and I'd know how scared I'd been of him walking out of my life, but the idea of him being gone completely was almost more than I could bear.

I cried until I'd released everything and was left with that empty feeling that came only after something intensely emotional had passed. I pressed my lips against the back of his hand. "I'm here, my Cade. I'll be here when you wake up." My fingers tightened. "Just wake up, baby. Please."

# Chapter 8

There was a crick in my neck. The first thought I had as I started to climb my way towards wakefulness didn't make any sense. Why did my neck hurt? Then I realized I was slumped over. My back bent and my head down, like I'd fallen asleep sitting up. Why would I have done that?

Even as I thought the question, everything came back in one excruciating rush. Cade telling me he loved me. Waking up with a note saying he'd be back. The hours of worrying. Arriving at the loft. Seeing the torn pictures. Then Cade on the bed with a man next to him. Realizing Cade wasn't breathing. Performing CPR. The ride to the hospital.

I was in the hospital, sitting next to a bed. I must've fallen asleep at some point while I'd been waiting for Cade to wake up.

Then I felt fingers tighten around mine and my heart stuttered. Cade.

I opened my eyes and looked up to find a pair of dark gray ones staring at me. Relief rushed through me so sharply that tears formed in my eyes. I grasped his hand tightly.

"Hey there, Sleeping Beauty." His voice was weak, but it was there and that's what was important.

I threw myself at him, heedless of the wires and tubes connecting him to monitors and bags of whatever. I didn't care about any of that. I just had to have my arms around him, feeling him breathing, his heart beating. I pressed my face against his chest.

"I'm okay," he whispered as he stroked my hair.

I didn't cry. Not really. A couple tears escaped, but that was all. I'd spent everything last night. Now, I was just exhausted. The little sleep I'd gotten was only enough to keep me from passing out, and this weariness wasn't just physical. Between everything that had happened the night before and then today, my emotions had taken me on a roller coaster ride like nothing I'd ever experienced before.

"Don't ever scare me like that again." My voice was muffled against his chest.

"I won't," Cade said. "Believe me."

I let myself relax against him for a few more minutes, not wanting to break the silence with the questions I was trying to avoid. No need to create more drama. We'd had enough to last quite a while. I just wanted to listen to the steady beating of his heart, echoed by the beeping from the monitor. I couldn't even find the sound annoying. Not when it was reassuring me that he was okay.

"There are some things I need to tell you," he said softly.

I sighed. Apparently my questions were going to be answered whether I wanted them to be or not. I could only hope that I could survive what he told me. I sat up and then back in my chair. Until I knew how this was going to go, I didn't trust myself to be touching him.

"But first I need to know what happened. How I got here."

"Didn't the doctors tell you?" I asked.

He shook his head. "I haven't seen any. I woke up about ten minutes before you did."

"And you didn't call anyone in here?"

"I didn't want to wake you."

I managed a weak smile that I knew didn't reach my eyes. I gave him the short version of what had happened, starting with me being worried when he didn't answer my calls. My voice hitched when I got to the part where I'd realized he wasn't breathing, and he reached for my hand. I let him take it, needing the comfort more than I needed the distance.

"I'm so sorry, Aubree." He pressed his lips against the back of my hand.

"What happened, Cade?" I couldn't stop myself from asking the question. "Who was..." My voice trailed off.

"The man you found with me is named Samuel Lehane. Sammy."

The familiarity in the way Cade said the name made my stomach turn to ice. I forced myself to keep my hand in his. I'd trusted him this far. I would hear him out before I acted.

"I told you before about how a woman I'd worked for propositioned me and that was how I got started as an escort," he said.

I nodded. I remembered. A flare of anger went through me at the thought of the people who had taken advantage of a hurting young man.

"That was true...to an extent." His fingers tightened around mine. "There was a time between me running away and ending up in that woman's bed."

I could see the struggle on his face. He didn't want to share this, and it wasn't because he wanted to hide things from me. He was in pain. "It's okay," I said. "You don't have to tell me."

"Yes," he countered. "I do. You deserve to know."

Maybe that was true, but I wasn't sure I wanted to know.

"I was on the streets for weeks after I ran, trying to find ways to eat, to survive, and I was losing. And then I met Sammy. He was the first friend I had. When he realized that I was working odd jobs for barely enough money to keep me alive, he told me I should do what he did. Turn tricks. I kept telling him no, but he persisted and, finally, when I was hungry enough, I agreed."

His fingers twitched and suddenly, I was holding his hand and not the other way around.

"He took me to meet his pimp who told me I was perfect, that I'd been made to fuck."

My lips flattened into a thin line but I didn't speak. I knew how hard it was to re-start a painful story once stopped. I wasn't going to interrupt.

"He told me that he had the perfect client for me to start with and gave me an address. That simple. All I had to do, he said, was do what I was told and I'd get sixty bucks and get to keep half."

Thirty dollars. I really didn't want to know what he'd had to do for that money.

"When I got to the address, it was a warehouse and the client was a man."

My eyes widened.

"I tried to leave, told him I wasn't gay, but he grabbed me. Hit me." Cade's hands were cold. "I'd barely eaten for weeks. I wasn't strong enough to fight back."

I felt like I was going to be sick. I didn't want to hear what happened next, but if he could tell it, the least I could do was listen.

"He tied me up, took my clothes." Cade's voice was flat, emotionless, but his eyes told a different story. "He touched me, told me how I was only good for one thing, told me what he was going to do to me. I knew he was going to rape me and leave me for others to do the same. And I hoped that in the end, I would die."

Oh, my Cade. I had to bite my bottom lip to keep from saying it out loud.

"Before he could..." He paused, and then continued. "Sammy showed up. He hit the guy with a brick. Killed him."

The man I'd found with Cade had saved his life. I didn't understand.

"I went to the hospital. The man went to the morgue and Sammy went to jail. I tried telling the cops what had happened, but all they could see were two hooking street kids who'd killed a respected schoolteacher. Sammy pled out on a self defense charge and got out last week. He showed up at the loft after you left the other night..." His voice trailed off and I knew he was remembering the fight.

"It's okay." I put his hand on my cheek. "I'm here."

He nodded. "The night I was almost...the night Sammy saved me, it was one of the worst nights of my life. And he rescued me from it being something even more horrible. I owed him my life."

The image from when I'd first seen Cade and Sammy popped into my head. I couldn't help but wonder if Sammy's reasons for saving Cade that night hadn't been just because they were friends or Sammy was a good guy. The way the other man's arm had been draped over Cade had looked an awful lot like a romantic embrace.

"So when he asked me if he could stay with me, I said okay." Cade rubbed his thumb over my knuckles. "We were fine the last couple days. We talked. I tried to help him find a straight job. I know some people who owe me favors so I told Sammy I could get him work." He looked at me. "And I told him about you."

I suddenly remembered the note that I'd found slipped under my door. I had a sneaking suspicion that Sammy had been the author of that note. The one that had told me to stay away from Cade. The pieces fit together. I wasn't about to tell Cade any of that though. Not when he clearly wasn't done with whatever he had to say.

"He was fine at first, listened to me when I talked. I thought he was being a friend." He sighed and ran his free hand through his hair. "But then, before I went to the club last night, I got your photographs developed. They made me realize how much I needed you. I told Sammy that I was going out so I could clear my head. Then I got back this morning and saw that he'd torn up all of the pictures."

That at least explained the mess I'd found.

"When I confronted him about it, he told me that he was in love with me."

I was more surprised about the fact that he seemed surprised. I'd suspected that much after hearing only part of his story and couldn't figure out how he hadn't at least had some idea.

"Sammy said that he'd protected me because he'd loved me back then too, that he thought I had to have known how he felt." Cade looked at me with wide eyes. "But I didn't know. Not until he said it."

I nodded and squeezed his hand. I had a feeling we were getting into what had happened in the time before I arrived at the loft.

"I told him that we were friends, that I appreciated what he'd done, but that I was in love with you. And that we'd made up. That I was going to quit hooking because I wanted to be with you. He told me that it was an infatuation, that I'd just fallen for the first trick who didn't treat me like trash. He said it was common, that it happened to everyone like us." His expression was earnest when he looked at me. "But it's not."

"I know it's not." I felt a strong urge to wrap my arms around him, to protect him from things that had already happened to him. "I know you love me." And I did. Even when I'd initially freaked out seeing Sammy with his arm around Cade, deep down, I'd known that there had to be an explanation. And I was also certain now that Sammy had been the one to threaten me.

Relief passed over Cade's face and then he continued his story. "Sammy started getting worked up, so I told him to sit down, that we should have a drink together. I poured us both a drink and then went to the bathroom. When I came back out, he was calmer and I thought things were better."

I looked down at my hand. The glass I'd cut my hand on, it had been from a broken glass, something with liquid in it. I had a bad feeling that I knew where this was going.

"We drank together and then Sammy leaned over. He tried to kiss me. I told him 'no,' but it came out garbled. He said it was okay, that it didn't matter anymore. That we'd be together forever soon enough. Things got really hazy after that. I remember sitting down on the bed. Feeling Sammy sitting behind me. Then…nothing until I woke up here and saw you sleeping."

I stood, considered it for a moment, then climbed onto the bed. The nurses would probably have a fit when they came in shortly, but I didn't care. Cade wrapped his arms around me as I curled against him. I rested my head on his chest as my fingers traced patterns over his flat stomach.

"I am so sorry I put you through that," he said. He kissed the top of my head.

"Promise me that you'll never scare me like that again." I squeezed him.

"I promise." He ran his fingers through my hair. "There is one upside to all of this."

I looked up at him, confused. What the hell kind of good could come out of all this shit? We hadn't needed this to confess our feelings for each other.

He smiled at me and traced my lips with the tip of his finger. "Since Sammy destroyed all of those pictures, I get to convince you to pose for me again."

I started to roll my eyes, but his mouth came down on mine and I forgot about everything but kissing him.

Until the nurses came in.

# Chapter 9

The weather was warm for the middle of May, but I didn't mind. In fact, I was glad that it was warm. It gave me the chance to wear the dress I'd picked out especially for this occasion. It was just the right combination of sexy and appropriate for this kind of event. A deep, rich purple, it showed off cleavage and leg both, getting me admiring looks from men and jealous ones from women. But I didn't care about how everyone else looked at me. There was only one set of eyes I cared about and those were currently looking at me with enough heat to make my panties wet.

Or would have if I'd been wearing any.

"What are you thinking?" Cade's voice was low in my ear and a shiver of pleasure went down my spine.

I smiled over my shoulder at him and pitched my voice at the same volume as his. "I'm thinking how much fun it's going to be to watch you squirm all night."

"Oh really?" He raised an eyebrow. His gaze ran over my body. "That dress is amazing, but I think I have more self-control than that."

"It's not the dress," I said softly. "It's what's under it."

"And what's that?"

I took a step towards the gallery door, then looked over my shoulder at him. "Nothing."

"Fuck."

I chuckled and walked through the double doors into the large, airy space where the exhibit was showing off the city's newest talent.

An arm slid around my waist, pulling me back against a hard body. "That was naughty." Cade's voice was rough. "I should punish you."

"I'll hold you to that later," I replied. "For right now, let's just enjoy the show." Cade made a sound that was suspiciously like a growl and my stomach twisted. I twisted out of his embrace, knowing I wouldn't be able to control myself much longer unless I moved. I reached over and took his hand. I threaded my fingers through his. "Show me my photos."

It had taken me weeks to convince Cade to talk to his art gallery owner friend about perhaps taking on a couple portraits. When he'd shown his friend his work, the response had been even better than I'd hoped. Cade had gotten his own show.

It had taken him almost two months to convince me to pose again. I had no problem posing for Cade. The idea of him photographing me in erotic positions or while we were making love turned me on, but I hadn't been sure I was ready for others to see me like that. But, Cade had been very persuasive and the evidence of that was being displayed at the back of the gallery.

The front was all paintings since those could be seen through the front windows, but once we made our rounds and greeted those admiring the work there, we stepped around a divide and I saw myself from all angles.

The photographs were all black and white, though highlights of color had been applied in various places. In some, the elaborate mask covering my face had been given back its rich red velvet. In others, the crimson lingerie. The only things that were never colored were my hair and eyes. While plenty of women had dark brown hair, my eye color was unique enough to identify me. Somehow, I doubted my school would appreciate the artistic value of one of their teachers posing half-naked. And then, of course, there were the ones where Cade and I were making love. He always took full shots and then cropped down to the elegant lines and curves he wanted to show. Never obscene, but definitely erotic.

He'd titled the series "The Claiming of Her," though he assured me that, in his mind, I was the one doing the claiming. I wasn't sure who was more nervous about their first reveal to the public, him or me. Sure, it was my body, but when it came to art, that was a matter of soul.

Still, my skin flushed as I saw on the walls what I'd only seen before in Cade's studio. I reached up with my free hand to self-consciously pat down the up-do I'd managed to wrangle my curls into. I'd started letting my hair grow out again just before I'd done the photoshoot and it was now long enough now to pull back. I'd originally started growing it because Cade had asked if I would, but I had to admit that it helping to disguise me from the woman in the pictures was an additional benefit.

"Relax," he murmured as he squeezed my hand.

I didn't get a chance to respond as Alejandro, the gallery's owner, approached. He was a handsome older gentleman, probably in his mid-sixties, thought I was too polite to ask. He'd also made no bones about the fact that he found both Cade and I extremely attractive. I'd almost been put off by his open comments when we'd first met, but it hadn't taken long for him to put me at ease, and the flirting was just part of the usual banter now.

"Bree, darling!" He kissed both my cheeks, letting his hands linger on my shoulders until Cade glared at him. "Cade, darling!" He repeated the embrace. "Have you decided to allow me to paint you?"

Cade rolled his eyes and I laughed. From the moment we'd met, Alejandro had been trying to convince Cade and I to pose nude for him, a process that they both informed me would result in the three of us sleeping together. We'd declined and he'd respected our decision, but he still liked to tease us with it every once in a while.

"Looks like a great turn out," I said as I looked around, trying not to think about what all of the people around me were looking at.

"It is," Alejandro said, his dark eyes sparkling. "Everyone has been practically breathless with anticipation over this exhibit."

"Only because you promised them the most sensual pieces they'd seen in years," Cade countered.

My blush deepened and I hoped Alejandro would mistake it for anything other than what it was. Judging by the way his eyes widened ever so slightly, my wish hadn't been answered. He knew. To my surprise, however, he didn't say anything about it, but continued on as if he hadn't just figured out who Cade's model was.

"I did," he admitted. "And these are. Everyone admired your paintings and I've already had offers on three separate pieces."

"Really?" Cade sounded completely caught off guard.

Alejandro smiled. "I told you that you're quite good."

"See," I said. "It's not just me who thinks it." I wrapped my arm around his waist and he put his arm around my shoulders. I leaned against him, enjoying the solid warmth of his body.

"As for these," Alejandro continued, gesturing to the pictures all around us. "I've been hearing words like 'alluring,' 'seductive' and even 'captivating' being thrown around." His eyes sparkled. "And more than one person wondering just who these amazing models could be."

Cade stiffened slightly. He'd just realized that Alejandro had figured it out.

"I tell them that the anonymity is what makes them so wonderfully mysterious."

My boyfriend relaxed. "Thank you."

Alejandro made a dismissive gesture. "Now, there is someone I need for you to meet. Please come with me."

Cade and I followed Alejandro across the space, weaving between the small groups that were forming at each of the photographs. I kept my chin up and a smile on my face, willing myself not to blush as I heard men and women alike complimenting my body.

"Daniel Rickman." Alejandro stopped next to a short, stocky man with an expensively tailored suit and rings that were too ostentatious to be anything but real. The man turned towards us. "I'd like you to meet the artist, Cade Shepard, and his girlfriend, Aubree Gamble."

"Mr. Rickman," Cade said as he shook the other man's hand.

"Daniel, please." He smiled and then turned to me. "Miss Gamble."

"Bree," I said. His handshake was firm, not too clingy but also not too abrupt. This was a man who spent a lot of time shaking hands.

"Daniel is an art dealer," Alejandro explained. "Actually, he's the premiere art dealer for the entire east coast, and one of the most well-known dealers in the entire country."

I expected some sort of false modesty from Daniel, but he didn't say a word, just accepted the compliment like a fact and moved on.

"I've been looking for an exciting new piece to display," he said. "And I think this is it." He pointed to the picture in front of us.

Of all the ones Cade had submitted, this was probably the most risqué. The full series of shots had been of me on my hands and knees, coming while he pulled a string of small metal balls out of my ass. He'd managed to find one where my arm covered my nipple, though the curve of my breast was fully visible. He'd then cropped it so that it showed my face half-turned towards him, pleasure contorting my features, the side of my naked body back to my hip, stopping just before revealing what he'd been doing. What really had completed the shot, however, had been the metal balls lying across my hip, just visible enough that people could guess why I looked like I was enjoying myself. I still remembered how nervous he'd been asking me if he could use the picture in the show. It was the one I'd been the most anxious about too, though now I was glad I'd agreed.

"This is exquisite," Daniel said. "The way you captured the desire, the pleasure." He glanced at Cade. "I must ask. Your models, Alejandro said they aren't professionals?"

Cade shook his head. "No, they're not."

"Are they a couple?" Daniel took a step closer to the photograph, his eyes now fixed on the mask.

"Why do you ask?"

I tightened my arm around Cade. His voice sounded a bit sharper than was probably a good idea.

"Her face. Her eyes. I don't just see lust and desire there. I see love. Either they're a couple or she's an amazing actress who should consider modeling or acting as a profession." His gaze slid down my body and came to rest on the metal balls.

"They're a couple," Cade answered. "Who agreed to allow me to photograph them under the condition of anonymity."

Daniel nodded. "Understandable, though a pity. They are both quite beautiful."

"I thought so as well." Cade's voice had returned to its usual charming tone. "After all, it's the artist's job to find the beauty in life."

Daniel smiled as he turned back towards us. "I wish to purchase this piece. As I didn't see a listed price, I took the liberty of making an offer." He held out a folded piece of paper.

I was still trying to process the fact that a man was trying to purchase a picture of me having an orgasm when Cade opened the paper. I glanced down and my eyes widened. I wasn't stupid. I knew how expensive some art could be, and I had a true appreciation for what Cade could do, both with a brush and with a camera, but I'd never considered the photographs could be sellable art.

"I would also like to take the entire line on a tour of various galleries across the country," Daniel continued. "And I've no doubt that you'll receive many more offers like this one to purchase other pieces. For a modest fee, I would be happy to broker such deals and arrange for deliveries once the tour is completed."

"I..." Cade was speechless.

"How very generous and unexpected," I quickly said. "Cade will, of course, need to speak with the models and get their consent for further release of the photographs since he'd originally intended them to be local only."

"Of course," Daniel said. "Here's my card." He held out a business card. "I'd love to get an answer tonight, but if it takes some time, that's fine." He gave another wistful look to the photograph. "Now, if you'll excuse me, I do want to take a look at the other pieces."

"There's a particularly moving painting I think you might want to keep in mind for your clients," Alejandro said. "This way." He left Cade and I alone. Or at least relatively so.

Cade glanced around, making sure no one else was in earshot, and then spoke, "I'm not selling it."

"Why?" I'd seen the number of zeroes on that offer. We weren't hurting for money since Cade had been able to pay off his debts – including the loft – with money he'd had saved over the years, but in the six months since he'd moved into my apartment, we'd been living off of my salary. It was enough to pay the bills, but there wasn't much leeway. That sale would allow us some breathing room.

"Why?" He gave me an incredulous look. "I would've thought you'd be agreeing with me. I mean, it's one thing to have these pictures hanging up in a small gallery where I know the owner. Maybe a hundred, two hundred people will see them, but this would be national attention." He took a step towards me until our bodies were almost touching. "Men all over the country staring at your body. Lusting after you." His eyes blazed. "Wanting you."

A thrill went through me at the possessive note in his voice. I loved when he sounded like that. He wasn't the kind of man who kept me from my friends or told me what to do – well, not unless I wanted him to. No, this was pure alpha male sexuality at its hottest.

I reached up and ran my fingers through his hair. "It's okay. I love your work and this could do wonders for your career. Could you imagine the kind of exposure this could give you?"

"I'm thinking more about your exposure," he said darkly. "I don't care about my career. I'll go get a job working retail or something like that. I just care about you."

I put my hand on his chest, sliding just under his tux jacket so I could feel his heart beat. "I don't care who sees the photos. They don't know it's me. Besides." I flexed my fingers so that my nails dug in a little and he sucked in a breath. "Men can look all they want. Women too. But only you get to touch."

He put his hand on my hip and I could feel the desire radiating off of him. "Damn right."

A smile made my lips twitch. "If anything, I should protest the fact that just as many men and women will be checking out the sexy man in half of the photos."

He grinned and echoed my words. "They can look but they can't touch."

"No," I said. "They can't." I leaned forward, my heels making it so that I barely had to stretch to brush my lips across hers. "Now, why don't you go catch Daniel and tell him you made a call and your models are more than willing to let you decide what to do with the series." I glanced around. "I'm going to find Adelle and Mindy. You should mingle."

He took a reluctant step back. "All right," he agreed. "But I'm going to be thinking about how I want to ravish you later."

I chuckled as a bolt of arousal went through me. I may not have had panties to get wet, but that didn't stop anything. I had a feeling I was going to be walking around the rest of the night with the insides of my thighs slick. I needed to find a restroom.

The mischievous light in Cade's eyes told me that he'd known exactly what his statement would do to me. I glared at him as he walked away and then turned back around to find either my friends or a bathroom, whichever I happened to see first.

The rest of the night was a whirlwind of meeting new people and hearing everyone gush over how talented my boyfriend was. I could tell from the looks I received from some of the women that they'd been with Cade, but I wasn't jealous. The past was the past and I didn't care what they thought about me. I knew who I was and who he was. I knew who we were to each other and nothing else mattered.

Adelle and Mindy were great at fielding questions on how Cade and I met, sticking with the true, albeit sanitized, version where Cade had saved me from a bad date, then fate had brought us together again. Adelle and I had really made an effort over the last few months and it seemed that our friendship was back on track. It wasn't like nothing had happened, but rather that we'd both grown enough to move past it. For Mindy, it had been a bit harder for her to accept that I was in love with a former prostitute. I'd finally reminded her how well I'd reacted when she'd told me she was bisexual and that had been it. Things weren't the way they'd once been, but I was okay with that. I wasn't the same either.

As the hours slipped away, people began to leave until, finally, my friends said good-night as well and Alejandro told us to go ahead and lock up when we were done. The cleaning staff would come in first thing in the morning. We, he said, should take some time to appreciate the art without anyone else around. When Cade took my hand and we walked through the gallery, I thought that was exactly what we were going to do.

When we reached the back of the gallery where my photos were, he broke the silence.

"Alejandro said he had inquiries about two other photographs and four paintings. I referred them to Daniel."

"That's wonderful!" I exclaimed. I stopped and threw my arms around Cade. "I knew you could do it!"

"I know," he said as he put his hands on my waist. "I never would have had the guts to show anyone my work if it hadn't been for you." His expression was far more serious than I'd have thought possible for such a good night.

"Is something wrong?" I asked, immediately concerned.

"No." He shook his head as he cupped the side of my face. I leaned into the touch. "That's just it."

"I don't understand."

His thumb brushed against the corner of my mouth. "I love you so much, Aubree."

"And I love you." I was still confused.

He reached into his jacket pocket and went down on one knee.

My heart stopped. This couldn't be happened, could it?

"My Aubree." He took a deep breath. "From the first moment I saw you, I knew you were something special. I wasted so much time pretending I wasn't falling hopelessly in love with you. I don't want to waste anymore. I don't need years or even months more to know that you're the only one I want. The only one I'll ever want. Will you be mine? Forever?"

I didn't even look at the box as he opened it. I didn't care what the ring looked like. It could've been a prize from a cereal box. All I cared about was the question and the sincerity in Cade's eyes when he asked it.

"I already am." I pushed his hair back from his face. "I've been yours from the first moment I saw you. I love you, my Cade. And, yes, a million times yes. I'll marry you."

His face lit up as he slid the ring onto my finger. When he stood, he crushed me against him, his mouth covering mine. The kiss was fierce, possessive and filled with more joy than I'd ever felt coming from Cade. I pushed his jacket from his shoulders and yanked his shirt out of his pants. I needed to feel his skin. Now.

He sucked my bottom lip into his mouth as I slid my hands beneath his shirt, feeling the solid muscle there. When my nails raked over his nipples, he growled and picked me up. I wrapped my arms around his waist as he walked me back towards a wall. My arms went around his neck, helping hold my weight as he balanced me with one arm. The other hand moved between us and I heard one of my favorite sounds in the world. Cade's zipper going down.

I had a moment to be grateful that we'd gotten rid of the condoms months ago and then he was shoving inside me. I cried out, the sound echoing off of the walls. He buried his face in my neck as he thrust into me and I now realized how on edge he'd been all night. The knowledge that I'd wound him so tight was a heady aphrodisiac and I moaned.

He rotated his hips, the base of his cock hitting my clit just right, and I jerked. He repeated the motion and I cried out again. He found a new rhythm, adding that little rotation on every other stroke and, soon, I was writhing against the wall, desperate for release.

He raised his head, his eyes wild. He shoved down the strap of my dress, freeing one of my breasts. His hand went to it, squeezing and pinching at my nipple until I was gasping his name, begging to come. Finally, when I knew he was just as desperate as I was, he buried his cock deep inside me and nipped at my bottom lip. His fingers twisted my nipple with the right amount of pressure and I came. I raked my nails down his back and he shuddered, spilling himself inside me.

Even as we were still coming, he pulled away from the wall and wrapped me in his arms, lowering us both to the floor, me straddling his lap as he went to his knees.

"Forever, my Aubree." His lips moved against my neck as he spoke. "Forever."

I nodded in agreement, still too far gone to speak. I didn't have to though. He knew what I meant.

# Chapter 10

Everything was perfect.

I'd chosen a simple dress this time, something that complimented my body rather than traditional lace and beadwork. My friends told me it was even more beautiful than my previous dress. The one that had never made it up the aisle. I had only two bridesmaids, the two that mattered. This wasn't about what everyone else expected. It was about me finally getting to marry the man I loved.

I'd chosen something other than the wedding march, not wanting to jinx things, but when I heard the delicate strains of my song begin, it didn't stop the butterflies from taking flight in my stomach. As my dad and I stepped through the doors and began down the aisle, I looked towards the front of the church. Adelle was there, and Mindy. My brother stood on the groom's side. My sister-in-law had been too pregnant to fit into a bridesmaid's dress this time.

But none of that was on my mind. No, I was trying to figure out where the groom was. The space where he was supposed to be standing was empty. He wasn't there. He was gone. He'd left me too...

I woke with a start, my heart racing. I let out a breath and looked over at the stack of presents that were stacked in the corner of the room, the smaller ones covering my dresser. I ran my hand over my face, desperate to rid myself of the images still dancing in my brain. Automatically, I turned to the other side of the bed.

Empty.

Of course it was.

"Good morning, my Aubree."

I smiled as I sat up and watched my husband carry in a tray with enough food on it for both of us. The whole apartment smelled like pancakes and bacon. The nightmare had been just that. A nightmare. My wedding had been yesterday, and I had chosen a new wedding dress. My sister-in-law was pregnant with a baby due in two months so she hadn't been in the wedding. The rest of it, however, the part where Cade hadn't been there, that had been my mind merging the dim memories from almost two years ago.

He set the tray down on the bed and winked at me. He'd put on a pair of sweatpants, but his chest was bare and I enjoyed ogling it as he settled back in the space he'd been before. The cross tattoo was still there, but it had been joined by another tattoo. This one was up on his collarbone. A pair of linked wedding rings with our initials inside matched the tattoo I had on my hip.

"Like the view?" He wiggled his eyebrows at me and I laughed.

The movement made the blanket covering me fall to my waist, baring my breasts. The lingerie I'd worn on our wedding night was somewhere on the floor. Cade had loved it, but it hadn't lasted long before he'd stripped me naked and made me scream so loud I'd worried our neighbors would call the cops. If we'd been at my old place, they definitely would've, but our new apartment had slightly thicker walls.

"Damn, Aubree." Cade's eyes darkened as he stared at my breasts. "If you don't cover yourself up, we're never going to get to breakfast."

"I'm okay with that." I ran my fingers up over my breast and grazed my nipple. I sucked in a breath. It was swollen and sore from how hard Cade had sucked, twisted, pulled and bitten it, but I still felt a jolt of pleasure go straight through me.

His expression was regretful. "But then we'll miss our flight."

"What?" Because it was June, I wasn't in school and since Cade was self-employed, time off wasn't a problem, but finances were. We weren't doing badly, but we'd had to choose between a honeymoon and a deposit on an apartment in a better section of the city. Since we wanted to start a family in the next year or so, we'd decided the new apartment was more important. Our honeymoon was just going to be time to ourselves, in the apartment, maybe dinner or a movie.

He smiled at me.

"What are you grinning about?"

He held up something I hadn't seen when he'd first come in. They looked like airline tickets.

"Adelle and Mindy went in on a honeymoon present for us. We leave for Hawaii at one."

# Chapter 11

*Cade*

I looked down at Aubree as the plane began to descend. She'd fallen asleep after we changed planes and I was reluctant to wake her. Neither one of us had gotten much sleep last night, but I knew she hadn't slept well the night before the wedding either. I hated that what had happened to her before we'd met had made her so nervous, but I had to admit that when I saw her walking down the aisle towards me, I was actually grateful that her ex had been such an ass. I wasn't sure where I'd be if I hadn't met her.

Actually, I amended, I knew where I'd be. I'd be in some rich woman's bed, enjoying the physical act of fucking while still thinking that the idea of love was nothing but shit. I'd be alive, but not really living.

The pilot's voice cut through my thoughts, telling us that we would be landing soon and I knew I had to wake Aubree up. As much as I hated to disturb her, a flash of warmth went through me when I saw those gorgeous violet eyes looking up at me through her long lashes. When she smiled, my heart skipped a beat.

Damn, I loved this woman.

I barely registered the sunshine and warmth as we stepped out of the airport. All of my attention was on her face. Her eyes were wide, her expression one of pure joy. I made a mental note to buy something nice for Mindy and Adelle. Over the last year and a half, I'd gotten used to not being able to spend money like I used to, but I hated that I couldn't lavish Aubree with gifts. Worst had been when we'd realized we had to choose between a honeymoon and a new apartment. I'd wanted to give Aubree the wedding and honeymoon of her dreams. Thanks to her friends, she was getting what she deserved.

We rode to the hotel in silence with Aubree snuggled up against my side. It was peaceful, a state of being that I hadn't had any experience with until I'd fallen in love with Aubree. When we reached the room, I unlocked the door, then scooped Aubree up in my arms. She laughed and my heart soared as I carried her into the hotel room.

What had I done to deserve her? Over the course of our relationship, I'd found myself asking that question many times. When I saw her sleeping next to me. When our bodies were joined, moving together as we sought to reach that release. When she'd agreed to marry me. But never more than yesterday, when she'd taken my hands in hers and vowed to love, honor and cherish me until death parted us. I hadn't been able to stop the tears from forming, and there'd been no embarrassment when I'd wiped them away.

Now, as I carried her into the honeymoon suite, I made another vow. One to myself. I promised that I would spend the rest of my life making sure Aubree was happy. And the first step to doing that was to do what I did best, especially when I was with her.

I set her on her feet and she hurried towards the double doors that lead to the balcony. I followed. Of course I followed. I'd follow her anywhere. Everywhere.

When I reached the balcony, she was standing at the edge, looking out over a beautiful white, sandy beach and bright blue water. It was magnificent, but all I saw was her.

She'd worn a pale yellow sundress, simply cut, chosen more for comfort during travel than anything else. So fucking sexy.

I walked up behind her and slid my arms around her waist. She leaned back against me, relaxing against my body. I rested my cheek on her head and marveled at the way we fit together. It wasn't just during sex either. Our bodies just seemed to naturally come together like two puzzle pieces, whether we were standing like this or making love. I'd had sex with more women than I could count and I'd never experienced anything like it until Aubree. My Aubree.

"This is perfect," she sighed. She tilted her head up so that her lips could find mine. The kiss was gentle, almost chaste, or at least it started out that way. Then she turned in my arms and things got a bit more intense.

She wrapped her arms around my neck, pressing her body against mine until I started to harden against her hip. She moaned as her breasts pushed against my chest and I knew it was because her nipples were still sensitive. The memory of what I'd done to them last night made me squeeze her even tighter. My tongue thrust between her lips and hers met it with a ferocity that made me groan. Damn, she was amazing.

I wasn't even aware we'd made it to the bedroom until the back of my knees hit the bed. It didn't take long for us to lose our clothes and then we were falling back onto the bedspread. My hands ran over her, every familiar inch. It was odd, I thought, how I knew her body almost better than I did my own, but still never tired of touching her, tasting her.

I rolled us over so that she was on top of me and she grinned down at me. I didn't need to tell her what I wanted, but I did it anyway.

"Turn around."

She quickly situated herself so that her knees were on either side of my head, her pussy hovering just above my face. I felt her warm breath on my cock and it twitched. I reached up and took hold of her hips, using them to guide her down until I could put my mouth on her. As I ran my tongue along her slit, she dropped her head and took as much of my cock as she could. The wet heat of her mouth made me moan, but it didn't distract me from my task.

I'd never minded going down on women, but Aubree was the first I actually enjoyed doing it to. Not just the enjoyment of seeing her come, but the act itself. I loved the feel of her smooth skin, the way her walls quivered around my tongue. I loved her clit, sucking it into my mouth, flicking it with my tongue. I even loved the way she tasted. Every woman was different, and Aubree was intoxicating.

She came as I teased her clit and I flipped us over even as she was still climaxing. She cried out as I pushed inside her. She was stretched enough from last night that I didn't have to fight for every inch, but she was still tight. And she fit me like a glove. She called my name, nails raking down my back to join the marks she'd made before. I moved faster, pleasure coursing through me with every thrust. Pleasure and love.

When I'd first fallen in love with Aubree, I hadn't thought it'd be possible to love her more, but every day, I proved myself wrong. I leaned down and took her mouth, my lips parting hers. Her body rose to meet mine, driving me deeper even as my tongue thrust into her mouth. I heard her whimper as I thumbed her nipple and then I shifted so that I pressed against her clit with each thrust. Just two more strokes and she was coming again. Her pussy tightened around me and I tore my mouth away, swearing as I lost control, emptying myself deep inside her.

"My Aubree," I breathed as I slumped on top of her. I'd asked her once if I was too heavy and she'd told me that she liked feeling me laying on her after I came.

"My Cade." She ran her fingers through my hair and then kissed my forehead.

I rolled us over, staying inside her as I wrapped the blankets around us. It was still fairly early, but we were both tired. I kissed the spot beneath her ear. "I love you."

"I love you, too," she said. Despite having slept on the plane, she sounded sleepy.

"How did I get so lucky?" I murmured out loud. "A chance encounter? A weird coincidence?"

"Don't be silly," she said with a laugh. "It was fate."

"I don't believe in fate," I replied automatically.

She shook her head and laughed again. "Sure you do." She lifted my hand and pressed her lips against my palm. "You just don't know it yet."

"Oh really?" Now I was amused. "And you know me that well?"

"Of course I do," she said confidently. "You're mine."

I smiled as I held her closer. She was right. I was hers.

## - The End -

# Other book series from M. S. Parker

Sinful Desires Complete Box Set

Twisted Affair Complete Box Set

Forbidden Pleasures

Dark Pleasures – release April 7$^{th}$

Pure Pleasures – release May 12$^{th}$

French Connection (Club Prive) Vol. 1 to 3

Chasing Perfection Vol. 1 to 4

Club Prive Vol. 1 to 5

# Acknowledgement

First, I would like to thank all of my readers. Without you, my books would not exist. I truly appreciate each and every one of you.

A big "thanks" goes out to all my Facebook fans, street team, beta readers, and advanced reviewers. You are a HUGE part of the success of my series.

I have to thank my PA, Shannon Hunt. Without you my life would be a complete and utter mess. Also a big thank you goes out to my editor Lynette and my wonderful cover designer, Sinisa. You make my ideas and writing look so good.

# About The Author

M. S. Parker is a USA Today Bestselling author and the author of the Erotic Romance series, Club Privè and Chasing Perfection.

Living in Southern California, she enjoys sitting by the pool with her laptop writing on her next spicy romance.

Growing up all she wanted to be was a dancer, actor or author. So far only the latter has come true but M. S. Parker hasn't retired her dancing shoes just yet. She is still waiting for the call for her to appear on Dancing With The Stars.

When M. S. isn't writing, she can usually be found reading– oops, scratch that! She is always writing. ☺

Printed in Great Britain
by Amazon